REBELLION

THE CHRONICLES OF THE BLACK LION, BOOK ONE

RICHARD CULLEN

Boldwood

This edition first published in Great Britain in 2024 by Boldwood Books Ltd.

Copyright © Richard Cullen, 2024

Cover Design by Colin Thomas

Cover Images: Colin Thomas

Every effort has been made to obtain the necessary permissions with reference to copyright material, both illustrative and quoted. We apologise for any omissions in this respect and will be pleased to make the appropriate acknowledgements in any future edition.

A CIP catalogue record for this book is available from the British Library.

Paperback ISBN 978-1-83603-356-1

Large Print ISBN 978-1-83603-355-4

Hardback ISBN 978-1-83603-354-7

Ebook ISBN 978-1-83603-357-8

Kindle ISBN 978-1-83603-358-5

Audio CD ISBN 978-1-83603-349-3

MP3 CD ISBN 978-1-83603-350-9

Digital audio download ISBN 978-1-83603-353-0

Boldwood Books Ltd
23 Bowerdean Street
London SW6 3TN
www.boldwoodbooks.com

GLOSSARY OF TERMS

Acre – Capital of the Kingdom of Jerusalem, besieged by Christian forces during the Third Crusade (1189–1192 AD).

Alaunts – A breed of hunting hound, similar to the modern mastiff.

Almoner – One who gives alms to the poor.

Barbette – A piece of linen which passes under the chin and is pinned at the sides, usually worn in conjunction with additional head coverings.

Caparison – A decorated covering laid over the saddle or harness of a horse.

Cerecloth – Wax-impregnated cloth used to wrap dead bodies.

Coif – A hood, often made of mail.

Cill Chainnigh – Kilkenny.

Courser – A horse bred for speed and strength.

Damietta – City in Egypt, part of the Ayyubid Sultanate.

Demesne – Land possessed or occupied by the owner.

Destrier – A horse specifically bred for war. Also known as a 'charger'.

Gambeson – A padded jacket worn as armour. Often combined with mail for added protection.

Jennet – A small breed of horse used for riding.

Hauberk – A heavy coat of mail, consisting of interlinked metal rings.

Hibernia – Ireland.

Holy See – The office or position of Pope, the papacy.

Laigen – The ancient Kingdom of Leinster.

Outremer – Meaning 'overseas', is a term used for the four Crusader States established in the Middle East after the First Crusade (County of Edessa, County of Tripoli, Kingdom of Jerusalem, Principality of Antioch).

Mantlet – A portable wall used to shield attacker's during siege warfare.

Palfrey – A horse bred for speed and endurance.

Paternoster – The Lord's Prayer.

Pennon – A triangular or swallow-tailed flag, usually attached to the head of a lance.

Postern – A small door or gate to the side or rear of a fortification.

Rounsey – A horse used for a variety of purposes. An all-rounder.

Routiers – Mercenaries.

Sappers – Soldiers who specialise in siege warfare, particularly breaching fortifications by digging beneath their foundations.

Schynbalds – Plate armour that protected the shins, similar to greaves.

Spigurnel – A royal official appointed to seal writs.

Striguil – A Marcher lordship equivalent to modern Monmouthshire.

Surcoat – An outer garment worn over armour, usually marked with insignia to denote allegiance.

Trivium – The teachings of logic, rhetoric and grammar, all relayed in Latin.

Wesheil – A traditional word used as a toast, to which the polite response would be 'Drincheil', said before all present would drain their cups.

PREFACE

Upon his marriage to Eleanor of Aquitaine in 1154, King Henry II of England inherited vast territories in France and founded what would become known as the Angevin dynasty. These lands, combined with his existing holdings in England, bequeathed him an empire that stretched from the Scottish border to the Pyrenees. Naturally, such unfettered expansion of English power was a concern for the French monarchy.

The Capetian dynasty, which had ruled since 987, sought to assert its authority and centralise power in France. King Philip Augustus saw the Angevin dynasty as a threat to French sovereignty and worked tirelessly to undermine English influence. In 1183, he began hostilities against Henry of England, taking advantage of a dispute between the English king and his sons, and allying himself with the princes, Richard and John. But when Henry died in 1189, Richard inherited his father's title and Angevin territories, and he was of no mind to cede any of them to his former ally, King Philip.

The two fought a war of attrition for ten years, both Angevin and Capetian at one another's throats until finally, in 1199, they settled upon a truce. A treaty between the two seemed inevitable, the Angevin Empire finally secure under the watchful gaze of the powerful King Richard the Lionheart.

But no king lives forever...

PROLOGUE
FRANCE, 1199 AD

This was no execution. It was butchery at its most cruel.

He had listened to the boy screaming for hours. Sandre should have been numb to it by now, armoured against it, but as the midday sun shone brightly, it bathed the castle in a light that only intensified the misery.

Surrounding him, other routiers were gathered within the walls of Beaucaire. Men-at-arms who had fought in a dozen campaigns, from the mud-strewn battlefields of England to the baking rat pits of Acre. They had seen horrors, performed them, and at first most had watched the torture with solemn reverence. Some with relish. Now they all stood in silence as Mercadier acted out his vengeance, way beyond even their ability to stomach.

The boy Bertran screamed again. Cried for mercy. Begged for the hundredth time. There was no mercy here. He had been cursed by ill fortune, and this was the heavy price he had to pay for his bad luck.

'Piece by bloody piece,' growled Mercadier. He was a hulking brute if ever that description could be laid at any man's feet. A bush of beard covered his face. Thick muscle encased those bare arms. Eyes deep-set, like two pits of hate.

Young Bertran howled as the knife dug into flesh, flensing another strip from his back. Sandre flinched, gritting his teeth, tasting the bile that had gradually risen in his throat after too long watching this grim spectacle.

The boy was naked, bound at wrist and ankle, the ropes attached to four stout destriers. They had him splayed, stretching him beyond endurance. Were that not punishment enough, he had been all but flayed to the bone, but there was no quelling Mercadier's fury. As well as his patron, the late King Richard had been the mercenary's friend. They had fought together, bled together, and Mercadier felt Richard's loss more than most. Such a stroke of foul luck that it had been this stupid boy who'd killed him.

As they'd besieged the castle at Châlus, their king had taken it upon himself to examine the walls he was so keen to breach, but then Richard was nothing if not bold. Whether poor Bertran had mistaken him for a man of little import or had seen an opportunity to write his name in legend, no one could say. And it was too late to ask now. Either way, as he stood upon the wall of Châlus the boy had aimed his crossbow and hit his mark, striking the king in the shoulder.

At first, the wound seemed minor, but infection crawled inside the one they called Lionheart with swift claws, and within a tenday he was on his deathbed. Just like that, their lord and king was gone. The man they had followed for thousands of miles and served in countless battles, killed by a boy and a lucky shot. Or unlucky, depending on which way you looked at it.

Another scream of agony. Another strip of flesh in Mercadier's fingers.

Ironic then, that such cruel punishment had been against King

Richard's final wish. The Lionheart had gone so far as to pardon the boy on his deathbed, but Mercadier had other ideas. No sooner had the king breathed his last, and the castle surrendered, than Bertran had been spirited away. Stolen from Châlus and brought here to Beaucaire to meet this grisly fate. Not that Mercadier was the only conspirator.

Sandre glanced across from the horses, past the sullen crowd witnessing the scene, to the woman who stood at the edge of the courtyard. The Countess Joan watched proceedings with as little emotion as the rest. This was no place for a woman, but then she was no innocent maid. As King Richard's beloved sister, it had been as much her plan as Mercadier's to see his killer punished.

'Damn it!' Mercadier cursed, his voice rising above Bertran's screams.

Sandre looked back to see Mercadier's hands were so slick with blood he could find no more purchase on the boy's flesh. He threw down his knife in frustration.

With a bloody hand, he gestured to the grooms holding their destriers. 'Get on with it.'

They nodded in reply before tugging on their bridles. Sandre was struck by their casual regard, as though they were urging those horses to pull at a plough, but this was no pastoral scene.

Bertran's scream rose to a shrill crescendo as his limbs were stretched. The ropes binding his wrists and ankles creaked, those horses huffing at the effort.

Sandre should have looked away, but he felt compelled to watch, to not balk at the sight and sound of this boy's end.

Bertran's right arm was the first to be torn from its socket with a crack, one destrier clopping along the courtyard as it dragged the limb across the ground, leaving a crimson trail. Another scream of agony and crows roosting in a nearby tower were put to sudden flight.

One of the grooms slapped a hand to the flank of his stallion, urging it to greater effort, and there went a leg, smacking the ground like fallen meat. The boy was choking now, spitting up blood, retching on it. No longer did Sandre feel sorry for him. He only felt thankful that he was not the victim of such a wicked punishment.

When a second arm was torn free, Bertran fell silent, his body slapping to the cobbles to be dragged a yard or two until the groom stopped his horse.

Stillness settled over the courtyard. Relief that all this was over.

Mercadier glared at the gathered men, as though their silence was an insult. 'Well? Your king is avenged. What say you all?'

At first, no one dared speak until Renier, standing right beside Sandre, suddenly punched the air and cried, 'Death to the king killer!'

The mercenaries surrounding them took up the cry, cheering their approval, clapping their hands in appreciation, spitting at that dismembered carcass. Sandre did his best to bite back the vomit rising in his throat and tried not to look on the mutilated corpse of that unfortunate lad.

Mercadier made his way toward the countess, who still watched without emotion. Or did she? Was that a tear running down her pale cheek? Sandre's old eyes couldn't quite tell.

The crowd parted, opening a path to Joan, who was resting a hand on a belly ripe with child. Someone had already hacked Bertran's head from his corpse and handed it to Mercadier. He knelt before the countess, presenting it like a trophy. Joan said nothing before acknowledging him with a sharp nod of approval and turning back to her castle. The castellan of Beaucaire stepped forward, taking the head on her behalf before following her inside.

With the deed done, the grooms were already untying the ropes from their destriers, leading them away now their work was finished. The crowd began to disperse, but Sandre found himself rooted, wondering what all this had been for. What had it proven?

'Brutal,' Renier whispered, his left eye twitching as he looked on, the scar that crossed his eyelid and snaked down his cheek, stark white against his olive skin.

He too was looking down at the bloodstained ground, though he didn't seem shocked by what he had witnessed. In fact, if he did think it brutal he seemed wholly unaffected, even when a stable hand stepped forward with a sack, gingerly placing one of the severed arms inside.

'What do you think they'll do with the parts?' he asked.

Sandre shrugged. 'Perhaps feed them to the pigs.'

'You think? Not nail them to the gates? Use them as a warning?'

Sandre regarded Renier as he chewed on a clove of garlic as he was wont to do, not that it did his breath any favours. 'Warning against what? Killing kings? His shot was a lucky one. Richard's death was a mistake. One this boy has more than atoned for.'

'I suppose,' Renier replied, spitting what remained of the clove onto the cobbles.

Both men fell silent as Mercadier crossed the courtyard toward them. He was wiping the blood from his hands with a filthy rag, brow furrowed as he regarded them both. From past experience, both men knew it was best to shut their mouths and wait to be addressed when Mercadier had you in his sights.

'Renier. Sandre. I would speak with you.'

'With us?' Renier asked, with another twitch of his mangled eye.

Mercadier didn't feel the need to repeat himself, as he turned and made his way down the sloping ramp from the courtyard. Sandre and Renier offered one another a bemused glance before quickly following.

All Sandre could do was stare at Mercadier's broad back as

they trailed in his wake. The castle of Beaucaire seemed so calm now, so ordinary. Horrors had been enacted mere moments before, but now its inhabitants went about their business as though it were any other day. An almost serene calm hung in the air, but as they followed their leader, Renier couldn't help but ruin it with his loose tongue.

'It... it was good and just work you did today, Captain.'

Mercadier turned his head, one dark bushy eyebrow raised. 'You think?'

'Yes. Justice has been done. God's work—'

'God had nothing to do with it,' Mercadier answered gruffly. 'That boy killed the king, and with him any chance I had to earn a living. For that, he was punished.'

'But... wasn't it the Countess Joan who—'

'Requested the boy's death, yes.' Mercadier stopped at the castle's lower battlement and turned to the men. 'And to keep her happy and avenge the death of her brother he was executed accordingly. A punishment I was only too happy to stage if it keeps me in the good graces of her mother and brother. Now, to other business.'

Sandre could see out over the battlement to the river below. The fields of Toulouse County rolled away beyond it, portraying a beautiful scene, but he had an ever-tightening knot in his stomach. This would not be good.

'I need you both to complete an errand for me,' Mercadier continued. 'King Richard's body has been taken to the abbey at Fontevraud to await burial. But his heart is bound for a different resting place. It still resides at Limousin, where you will collect it, and carry it safely to the cathedral of Notre Dame at Rouen.'

Renier immediately nodded with his usual toadying obedience, but Sandre was not so quick to offer his service.

'Why us?' he asked.

Mercadier offered him a rare grin, displaying his brown teeth. 'Because you were loyal to the king. This matter requires discretion, and men I can trust.'

'It would be an honour,' Renier said, with a sycophantic bow.

'Good,' Mercadier replied. 'I would do the job myself, but I have to pay my respects to the new king, and try to secure his patronage.'

'I must decline,' Sandre said without thinking. When Mercadier's brow darkened, he felt compelled to explain. 'I have been away from my wife for almost two years. I promised her I would return—'

'Sandre Closier, are you refusing me? Are you refusing your king?'

A glance down at Mercadier's hands and he saw they were balled into fists. Despite the attentions of his filthy rag, they were still stained red.

'I... I mean...'

'Because it is important to me this job is done right. I need peace of mind, Sandre. That is why I chose you. There are rivals hidden in every shadow who wish me harm. That bastard Brandin threatens our entire company. If I do not meet with King John soon it will be Brandin's routiers who are given contracts, and not mine. I have to travel swiftly and watch my back. I cannot be distracted, and so I have picked men I can rely on for this very important task. Do you understand?'

'I do,' Sandre nodded. 'It's only my wife—'

'Good. Then that settles the matter. I am sure your wife won't care if you're gone for a few days longer. The bishop at Notre Dame expects your arrival soon. I suggest you don't keep him waiting.'

With a last glare that brooked no defiance, Mercadier left them at the battlement.

'That was unexpected,' Renier said, fishing in his pocket for more garlic. 'Mercadier thinks we are men to be trusted, eh. And I'm sure we'll be well-rewarded if we prove him right.'

The thought of a reward was the furthest thing from Sandre's mind. He had made a promise to Marion and was now forced to break it. Despite a fresh clove of garlic, he could still smell the stink of Renier's breath, but it paled next to the stink his wife would make when he eventually made his way home to Anjou.

PART ONE: THE LONG ROAD TO LAIGEN

IRELAND – 1213 AD

1

Estienne Wace was no stranger to a wagon ride, but he couldn't remember his arse being so sore before. The cart had bucked and juddered along the poorly laid road for half a day, as the old nag plodded ever westward. Beside him, Flann peered from beneath the brim of a leather cap, chewing on a piece of straw. It was almost down to the nub now, but the old man seemed determined to suck every last bit of goodness from it.

'Nearly there,' he muttered.

It wasn't the first time he'd said that, and Estienne was beginning to wonder if he even knew where they were going, despite his constant assurances.

At least he had fallen quiet now. When they'd first set off from the port to the south, Flann had done nothing but talk, telling Estienne about how he'd been making deliveries along this route for years, about the wine, ale and salted fish he carried in his wagon, about his wife and his seven daughters, about the unseasonal weather. Flann hadn't thought to ask Estienne any questions, which had been something of a blessing, and when he'd run out of things to say the old man had just chewed on that stalk and hummed tunelessly in his throat.

Estienne was happy to hold his peace. He wasn't much for talking at the best of times, prone to keeping silent and listening, where others would ramble on. Now though, he felt even less inclined to speak, but he supposed grief would do that. His uncle was only a few days in the grave, his aunt having passed two winters earlier. Now he was alone, travelling an unfamiliar road with no idea what was waiting for him.

Absently he reached inside his jerkin, feeling for the folded parchment before running his finger over the waxed seal. His uncle had given it to him before he died and told him not to read it. It should only be opened by one man, his safety depended on it. That letter would be his salvation. As he wondered what mystery it held, Estienne had to trust that his uncle was right.

'Here we go,' Flann said suddenly. 'I told you we were almost there.'

Estienne looked up, seeing they had crested the brow of a hill, and the road ahead was leading them down into a town. A river wound its way through the centre, and on the far side sat an ominous stone castle.

Flann raised a hand, as though praising the magnificence of the place. 'Cill Chainnigh. The jewel of Laigen.'

The closer they got, the more Estienne found that description confusing.

At the edge of town, a thin man in his filthy bedclothes was retching violently into a ditch. Two dogs appeared from nowhere, snarling and barking their welcome at the wagon's wheels, and trying their best to snap at the salted fish stowed away in the back. As they passed ramshackle houses topped with ragged thatch, a woman stood watching on a porch, hefting her naked baby in her arms, before hawking and spitting a huge gob of phlegm in their path.

If this was indeed the jewel of Laigen then it was hidden deep within a dog turd. Estienne suspected you would have to rummage pretty deep to try and recover that jewel, and most likely you'd only find more turd.

'What's wrong, lad?' Flann asked. 'Never been to a town this big before?'

Estienne shook his head, suddenly aware that he must have been staring in disgust at the deprivation. On occasion he'd accompanied his uncle to market at the local villages near their farm, but none of them had been so grim as this.

'I suppose you've never visited anywhere like that either.' Flann gestured ahead to the castle looming across the river.

Estienne was bewitched by it as the wagon clattered over the stone bridge. He had seen castles before, but only from a distance. Nothing that could have prepared him for this.

A vast wall of stone surrounded it, rising higher than the tallest tree. An arched entrance awaited, topped by the teeth of an iron portcullis. For all the world it seemed as though he was being driven ever closer to the gaping maw of a giant wyrm.

Flann appeared completely underwhelmed as he continued his tuneless humming, tipping his cap to a woman walking by with milk pail in hand. His easy manner did little to settle Estienne's nerves.

As they rumbled across the castle threshold, he couldn't look away from the iron gate above, expecting it to come crashing down at any moment to crush the wagon beneath its weight. Once inside, his attention was immediately drawn to the vibrancy of the place.

From the outside, the castle had appeared an imposing fortress, but within it was a hive of activity. The smell of bread wafted from a bakery to his left. A magnificent horse, glistening black and thickly muscled, snorted its derision in the stables to his right. At the far side stood a stone keep bigger than any tower he had ever seen, a banner hanging from it displaying a red lion rampant on a field of green and gold.

Flann drew up his cart in the centre of the yard, and a heavyset man with ruddy cheeks and very little hair immediately approached. He wore plain garb, but by the way Flann nodded to him, Estienne could tell he must have held some authority here.

'Goffrey,' the old man said.

'Flann, my friend,' Goffrey replied in a welcoming manner. 'What have you got for us today?'

The old man gestured to the back of his cart. 'Only the best of fare. Wine, ale and fish fit for a king. Oh, and this lad.' He tipped his head toward Estienne. 'Says he has business with Earl William. Paid me a fair sum to bring him from Port Láirge.'

'Did he indeed?' Goffrey looked Estienne up and down, as though he wasn't quite sure how to take him.

Estienne jumped down from the cart, ignoring the numbness in his backside. 'Yes, sire. My name is Estienne Wace. I have a letter for Earl William.' He reached into his jerkin and produced the paper with its plain wax seal.

Goffrey regarded it dubiously, then offered Estienne a wry smile. 'All right. Hand it over and I'll make sure he receives it.'

Estienne clutched the letter to his chest protectively. 'I was told it was for William Marshal's eyes only. I am to give it to him and no one else.'

Goffrey furrowed his brow. At first, Estienne thought he might argue his point but eventually he shrugged.

'Very well. Then I'd best go fetch him. But for your sake, I hope what's in that letter is worth disturbing a man as important as the Marshal.'

Goffrey turned and left him alone in the yard. Estienne turned to see Flann had already led his sorry-looking nag away and was talking with a steward, as two boys unloaded the crates and casks from the wagon.

A ringing sound caught his ear. Estienne turned to see that far across the yard was an area fenced off from the rest. Within it were two men, swords and shields in hand, swinging at one another with abandon. Estienne looked on with fascination as they fought under the watchful eye of their tutor, who wore a gambeson of bright yellow.

As one of them swung, the other ducked, retaliating with a swift strike with the cross-guard of his sword, driving the other to the ground. The victor did not stop, kicking his opponent in the chest before raising his weapon for a killing blow. Only the sharp yell of their instructor brought the fight to a bloodless end.

In the past, Estienne's uncle had shown him the rudiments of sword, knife and shield in the peaceful environs of their farm. It had never been like this. Never so violent. Never so merciless. But despite the brutality of it, Estienne found himself captivated by the spectacle. Envious that he was not the one on the other side of that fence, testing his mettle against an opponent who would offer no quarter.

Footsteps distracted him from the men training, and he saw Goffrey had returned. With him was a more imposing figure than Estienne had ever seen.

Earl William stood well over six feet, bearing the wide shoulders and slim waist of a man of much younger years. His hair was grey, forming a severe peak on his lined forehead, slim face tanned, moustache covering his lip to droop down past his mouth. He walked with a confident gait – some might have called it a swagger – but it was those eyes that were the most striking. Two grey pools that were focused on Estienne as though he were prey rather than a guest in his demesne.

'This is Estienne Wace, my lord,' Goffrey said, as though introducing a noble at court.

'Is it indeed,' William rumbled, looking Estienne up and down and seeing little to be impressed with. 'Where have you come from, boy?'

Estienne suddenly felt as though his tongue had been tied in a knot. 'From... from Anjou, sire.'

'And how did a waif like you get all the way to Hibernia with no guardian?'

'My uncle, lord. Before he passed, he made arrangements for our farm to be sold and instructed me where I was to come. My passage was bought with the proceeds.'

Earl William nodded his understanding. 'You have a letter for me?'

'Yes.' Estienne held out the letter, trying his best to stop his hand trembling.

William took it in his broad, meaty fist before breaking the seal. Estienne noted his response as he unfolded the parchment and began to read. At first, his expression of mild annoyance deepened, and Estienne felt himself begin to panic, wondering what words were causing this towering man such concern. Then that brow uncreased, and the more he read, the more confused he looked. Eventually that confusion waned, and only a mild look of sorrow remained.

When he was done, he held Estienne in a lingering gaze. 'Your uncle was Sandre Closier?'

'Yes, lord.'

'And you never knew your father?'

'I was told he died before I was born.'

William folded the letter and secured it away in his tunic. 'Do you know why your uncle wanted you to come here?'

Again, Estienne was none the wiser, and he shook his head.

'According to his message, he intended for you to become a squire in my service. To learn the sword and saddle. A hard road for any youngster, but especially so for one with little meat on his bones. Is that what you want? To become a knight?'

Estienne glanced across the courtyard, toward the fenced battleground where those swords were being swung once again. Then he fixed Earl William with as firm a stare as he could muster. 'Yes, lord.'

William nodded his approval. 'Good. Are you hungry? You look hungry.'

As though anticipating his answer, Estienne's stomach gave the faintest of rumbles. His short supply of food had run out on the sea crossing to Port Láirge, and none of his fellow passengers had seen fit to share their rations.

'I could eat.'

'Goffrey, take Estienne to the kitchens and see his belly filled. He'll need it if he's to prove himself worthy of service.'

'I will indeed,' Goffrey replied, placing a guiding hand on Estienne's shoulder and urging him toward the huge tower in front of him.

Estienne had no time to offer his gratitude before he was ushered toward the keep's entrance. Torches lit the stone interior, and Estienne marvelled at how impregnable this fortress was, even within its vast curtain wall. Before today, the sturdiest building he had set foot within was a wood-built chapel.

Goffrey led the way along a corridor and up a set of narrow stone stairs. At the top, Estienne could smell the welcome aroma of cooking meat, and feel the warmth of a distant fire wafting from up ahead. Goffrey stopped as someone approached them, before pushing Estienne against the wall.

An old monk shuffled by, leading a quartet of young ladies behind him. The first was likely the same age as Estienne, her

expression serene, head covered in a barbette, blue kirtle reaching
to her ankles. Likewise, the next two girls filed past adorned in
equal ambivalence and similar garb. The last though, a few years
younger than the rest, poked her tongue at Estienne before grinning mischievously and skipping after the others.

Goffrey led them on once more, and at the end of another
corridor they entered the fortress kitchen. A pig turned on a spit
within a huge hearth. Half a dozen scullions were chopping
vegetables, plucking foul, gutting fish. It looked as though they
were preparing a feast for the whole of Laigen.

'Mabil,' Goffrey said, and a severe-looking woman turned to
him, knife in hand. 'Earl William has an addition to his household.
This is Estienne, our new squire.'

The cook looked down her nose at him. 'Bit gangly for a squire,
isn't he? Never mind. We'll soon get some meat on those bones.'

Goffrey offered a reassuring pat on the shoulder, before leaving
him in Mabil's capable hands. As he took in the sight of more food
than he had ever seen in one place, Estienne began to think he
might like it here.

2

Ansel trotted ahead of her along the corridor, a horse made of sticks between his legs. He was only a boy, flush with innocence, but before she knew it he would be astride a real horse, training in the arts of war, just like her eldest sons. Isabel knew she would have to cherish these years with her youngest while she could.

Seeing him on that wooden charger conjured a familiar memory of the two eldest boys she had raised to manhood. Of how proud she had been to see them become so gallant, like their father. Of how she had lost them.

When she heard the droning tones of the monk from a chamber up ahead it came as welcome relief from the bitterness of her thoughts. Isabel stopped outside the open door, listening to him as he taught the rudiments of Latin to her youngest daughters. It had been her specific wish that all her children were educated in the trivium, a wish her husband had only reluctantly agreed to.

'*Salve pueri et puellae*, children,' the monk said in his monotone. 'Today, we will be learning about the declension of nouns. Nouns are the building blocks of language, and by learning their different forms we are able to express different meanings.'

Isabel peered through the opening. The four girls sat behind their tables, quill, ink and vellum in front of each. It had not been cheap to provide such materials for the purposes of study, but Isabel was sure it would be worth the cost. She was impressed that her daughters were showing particular attention, despite the monk's tedious approach. Well... almost all her daughters. As usual, Isabeau, Sybil and Joan sat upright and attentive, but the youngest, Eva, looked as though she would rather have been anywhere else.

'Let us begin with the first declension,' the monk continued, 'which includes feminine nouns like *puella*, meaning girl. The nominative form is *puella*, but when we wish to indicate possession, we use the genitive form, *puellae*. Now, who can give me an example of a sentence using the genitive form?'

Sybil was the first to raise her hand. The monk smiled, gesturing for her to answer, but before she could, little Eva teased Sybil's nose with the feather of her quill. Sybil slapped it away, and Eva giggled at her own mischief.

'Never mind,' the monk said, unsure of how to proceed in the face of such unruly behaviour. 'Let... let us move on to the second declension, which includes masculine nouns like *puer*, meaning boy. Can anyone tell me a sentence using the genitive form of *puer*?'

This time it was Joan's turn to raise a hand. Once more the monk smiled and gestured for her to continue. Before she could, Eva flicked the nib of her quill, sending black ink spattering onto Joan's kirtle.

Isabel moved away from the door as the flames were stoked. Joan yelped in fury, and Eva giggled louder than ever. The monk did his best to interject, as chairs were scraped along the floor and anger erupted, but his doleful demands for calm were ignored. Isabel should have interjected, but Eva had always had a wilful spirit. Perhaps one day it would be broken by the duties of a lady of her station, but for now, Isabel would allow her what freedom she could.

As she turned to escape along the corridor, Ansel was blocking her path. He looked up with those bright brown eyes Isabel found so difficult to refuse, his wooden horse now abandoned.

'Can I go and watch them sparring?' he asked hopefully.

No, it would not be long before he was riding and fighting, just like his brothers. As much as Isabel wanted to keep him a boy forever, she knew it was impossible.

'Of course,' she replied. 'Run along.'

He flashed a smile full of missing teeth, before racing past her and down the stairs to the courtyard. Isabel left the sound of her daughters' bickering behind and headed toward the kitchen.

A handmaid called Alis passed her in the corridor, stopping to curtsey. Isabel nodded her acknowledgement, taking some solace that she was still shown deference within her own castle, despite how far the Marshals had fallen from the king's grace in recent years. When she reached the kitchens she waited silently at the archway, watching proceedings with a sense of pride. Nothing else might be going right for her family, but at least the beating heart of this castle still thrived.

Mabil oversaw the place with an iron hand. The woman had been a good find – stern but fair, skilled at her craft, organised. But Isabel had always prided herself on being a good judge of character. As she took in the bustle of the kitchen, her eye fell on a boy sitting at a table close to the window. A stranger in their midst.

He was troughing from a wooden bowl as though he hadn't eaten for days. Despite the way he shovelled broth and bread in his mouth, he still held himself with an element of dignity. A handsome boy, for sure, but he was scruffy, his dark hair unkempt, his rangy legs swinging from the stool he sat on.

'My lady.'

Mabil had spotted her at the arch to the kitchen and curtsied. The rest of the scullions, seeing Isabel was present, stopped what they were doing and did likewise.

'Don't let me interrupt you,' Isabel said, before gesturing for Mabil to come closer.

'All is well, my lady,' Mabil said. 'Stores are full for now, though I'll need more salt before long.'

Isabel gestured to the boy by the window, who hadn't seemed to notice that the lady of the house was present. 'Who is that? I don't think I've seen him before.'

'Oh, him. Boy's name is Estienne. Just arrived this morning. Your lord husband's new squire, according to Goffrey.'

It was then the boy looked over. Still he offered no deference – just regarded her with eyes that looked so lost, and forced a sad smile onto his face.

Before Mabil could chide him for his lack of decorum, Isabel said, 'Very well. I see you have everything in hand as usual. Carry on.'

Another curtsey from Mabil before Isabel left, leaving the heat of the kitchen behind and making her way up to her chambers. She swung open the door on its well-oiled hinge and saw him waiting there. William was standing by the window, framed in golden light as he read from a scrap of parchment. Still tall and strong despite his years. Still handsome enough to take her breath away, as he had the first time she ever saw him.

Isabel had been his reward for loyal service to King Henry. He was a knight of no name, a second son who had fought his way up the bloody ladder to become a powerful lord in his own right. She was daughter to Earl Strongbow of Striguil and heiress to the House of Clare. It was a union she had not relished – naturally she had been terrified when she learned of her betrothal to an old man in his forties, but as soon as she saw him, tall and bold, that face so noble and kind, she knew that he should not be measured by his age. Now, even after she had borne him ten children, even though he fast approached his seventieth year, the sight of him always made her heart skip.

'Husband,' she said, as he continued to pore over that letter.

'Isabel,' he replied, still reading. There was a furrow to his brow, as though what he read was troubling.

'A message from the king?' she asked, hope and fear gnawing at her all at once.

William folded the parchment and finally looked at her. 'No. It's nothing.'

Clearly it was much more than nothing, but Isabel had long ago learned not to press her husband where politics was concerned. He bore a heavy burden, now more than ever, and it was not her place to add to his woes.

'We have a new squire. He seems a little skinny to be taken on as your shield bearer.'

'We do. And he is. But his uncle was one of King Richard's retainers. It was his dying wish that the boy come here and learn the code. Who am I to refuse a dying man's request?'

'I would expect nothing less from you, my love. But it is not your duty to take care of every orphan who comes to our gates. Especially now—'

William sighed, a rare show of discontent. 'What would you have me do, Isabel? Turn the boy out into the wilds?'

He moved to the bureau by the window, opening a drawer and placing the letter within. She watched as he locked that drawer with a key on its chain, then hung it around his neck. A key for which there was no copy. A secret hidden from her? As much as she hated the notion, Isabel would never make issue of it.

'No, I would never expect you to abandon a child to his fate,

William. But do not forget we are cast down from the king's favour because of your generosity. Remember what we have already lost because—'

He glared at her, quelling his anger, and she knew she had pushed him too far.

'I have not forgotten what we have lost, Isabel. And why.'

It did not need repeating. That deed of only a few years before, when the Lord of Briouze had fallen from the favour of the tyrant King John, and been forced to flee his estates. William had made the mistake of offering Briouze sanctuary within these very walls. Only when the king had landed on the shores of Hibernia with an army at his back had William been forced to compel his guest to leave.

Briouze had fled, but his wife and son had been forced to plead for the king's mercy. John had been deaf to it, imprisoning them both until they had starved. If rumour were true their rotting corpses had been found entwined, the Lady of Briouze having consumed part of her son's cheek.

It was an awful fate, but the king's wrath had not been quelled by those horrors he inflicted. To secure the Marshal's continued fealty, and ensure no further dissent, he had taken their eldest sons as hostages. Isabel had not seen Guillaume or Richard for almost three years and didn't know if she ever would again.

'I will get them back, Isabel,' William said, voice softening. 'I will do nothing more to provoke the king, I promise you.'

Could he sense her pain? Her loss? There was little doubt he shared it.

'I know,' she replied, forcing a smile. 'I am just being overly cautious. What trouble could one orphan boy bring us? He is just another child in our care.'

'He is,' William said, turning to the window and looking down on the courtyard below. 'Just one more child.'

Isabel saw that troubled look cast its shadow over his brow once more. What was he not telling her?

Despite the reassurance of his words, she could only hope that his kindness of spirit toward one orphan would not curse them once more.

3

Estienne's feet pounded the worn stone as he raced through the castle's corridors. His heart thudded in time with his footsteps, a frantic drumbeat urging him on.

He was late. And Earl William would not tolerate tardiness.

As he careened around a corner, a flash of dark hair caught his eye. The girl who had poked her tongue at him the day before leaned against the wall, picking at her nails with a small comb, her blue kirtle smudged with dirt at the hem.

She glanced up as he approached, mischief glinting in her eyes. 'Well, if it isn't the slugabed squire. Did you forget your way to the yard?'

Estienne gritted his teeth. The cook, Mabil, had informed him this was Earl William's youngest daughter, Eva. Clearly she had decided her one task was to ensure his life was nothing but misery. 'I have not the time to bandy jests with little girls. Some of us have duties to attend.'

'Little girl?' she scoffed. 'At least I can walk the castle corridors without getting lost. Best hurry now.'

Estienne carried on without another word as Eva's mocking

laughter dogged his heels. The clash and clatter of steel sang out as he rushed from the keep and headed across the yard.

Earl William traded blows with another squire. Despite the difference in age and vigour, the younger man met his lord stroke for stroke. His blade was a whir of flashing steel, battering at the older man's defences with brutal efficiency. No wasted movement, no hint of hesitation. Each strike was timed and angled for maximum impact, seeking to over-whelm through raw power and precision. In contrast, William looked to be holding back, deflecting the blows with an economy of motion that spoke of his decades wielding a sword.

Estienne couldn't help but marvel at the sheer mastery on display. The two combatants wove in and out, blades ringing and rasping. Dust puffed beneath their feet as they danced across the packed earth. The squire bore down with a vicious barrage, but William coolly turned each cut aside, giving ground steadily until, with a resounding clash of steel, he drove his opponent back to his knees.

As the contest ended, William caught sight of Estienne lingering at the edge of the yard. He lowered his blunted blade, mouth pressed into a thin line beneath his grey-streaked moustache.

'So, you decided to grace us with your presence after all,' he said. 'I trust you have a compelling reason for your tardiness?'

Every practised excuse withered to dust on Estienne's tongue. 'I... I was delayed, my lord. It won't happen again.'

'See that it doesn't. Crows feast on the eyes of men who cannot master themselves. Normally I would not tolerate such a lack of respect, but one of my squires has seen fit to leave my service quite suddenly.' William gestured to the other squire, who stood with his blade resting casually on one shoulder. 'Ilbert FitzDane will be

your peer in service. Ilbert, meet Estienne Wace, a new addition to
our flock.'

Ilbert regarded Estienne with a scornful look. 'This is the
whelp replacing Henri? Looks more like a stableboy than a squire.'

Estienne's face flushed, but he held his tongue. It wouldn't do
to snap at a warrior who so clearly outclassed him, but still he met
Ilbert's stare squarely. 'I'll do my best to fill his shoes. And to prove
myself worthy.'

'You'll have a chance to prove it now,' William said as he thrust
one of the blunted swords at Estienne, hilt-first.

Estienne took the weapon as though it might bite. 'Who will I
fight?'

'You'll start with the pell,' William announced. 'Show me your
forms. Cut, thrust, block, in sequence. Go on.'

The disappointment was sour as week-old milk, but Estienne
knew better than to argue. Shoulders slumped, he turned to face
the battered training post at the centre of the yard, sensing Ilbert's
disdainful eyes boring into his back.

No matter. He'd show them he had the makings, even if he had
to chop this pell to splinters to prove it.

Raising the sword, he took a deep breath and hurled himself at
the wooden post, hacking with more enthusiasm than skill. The
sword rebounded off the wood with a jarring thud, numbing his
fingers. He gritted his teeth and struck again, putting his back into
it this time.

Sweat gathered beneath his armpits as he rained blow after
blow. It felt good to let his frustration howl through his muscles, as
he tried to remember his uncle Sandre's advice – keep the blade
up, elbows loose, follow through with the hips. It wasn't pretty
sword-work by any stretch, but no one would be able to say he
lacked for effort.

The blade suddenly skipped off the pell, almost wrenching his shoulder from its socket. Estienne staggered back, breathing hard, sweat plastered to his brow. His hands ached from gripping the unfamiliar hilt, but he threw himself back into the drill, stubbornly ignoring the discomfort.

'Enough,' William barked.

Estienne lowered his sword, arms trembling from the strain.

William cast a critical eye over his newest squire. 'Decent strength, but you flail like a drowning cat. Elbows in, eyes on the target, balance cantered over the hips. Ten more strokes, and mind the form this time.'

From the sidelines, Ilbert snickered. 'God's teeth, it's like watching a pond rat dance on its hind legs. I'm not sure any amount of instruction will sharpen this dullard, my lord.'

Ilbert's mockery burned in his gut like coal, and Estienne whirled to face William. 'I can do more than wave steel about, my lord. Let me show him what I'm made of.'

Earl William's severe brow furrowed. 'You want to face Ilbert? That's rash, boy. You're nowhere near ready.'

'How will I ever be ready if I don't try, my lord?' Estienne demanded, anger making him bold, but he was past caring. 'Surely it will impart a greater lesson than beating at a wooden post.'

For a long moment, William studied him. Then, to Estienne's surprise, he nodded. 'Very well. Wooden swords, to three touches. Try to land a hit... if you can.'

Estienne took the practice sword his lord offered, as Ilbert stepped closer, mouth curved in a condescending smile.

'Begin!'

The thwack of wood split the air as Estienne barely got his sword up in time to block Ilbert's lightning-quick swing. The impact juddered up his arm, almost causing him to drop his weapon and he staggered back, trying to hold on to it with numbed fingers.

Ilbert was relentless, darting forward with a flurry of ruthless slashes. Each jarring parry drove Estienne further back. He could barely hear William shouting corrections to his stance and the position of his blade, as he fended off the rain of blows.

As Ilbert's sword scythed down once more, Estienne fell back on desperate instinct – dropping to one knee and rolling beneath the cut. He regained his feet behind his opponent and whipped his blade at the backs of Ilbert's knees.

Ilbert hissed in surprise as the wood cracked across his legs. He danced away, guard snapping back into place, but not before Estienne saw the flash of shock on his face.

'Touch to Estienne,' William said, a hint of approval warming his voice. 'Don't get overconfident. Again.'

Buoyed by his victory, Estienne flew at Ilbert with renewed enthusiasm. He battered at Ilbert's guard like a man possessed, and for a few wild moments, unhinged ferocity lent him the advantage. Ilbert fell back a step, assailed by the savagery of it as his parries came a fraction too slow, his ripostes a hair off balance.

But skill could only be overwhelmed by zeal for so long. As Estienne's burst of energy flagged, Ilbert seized his chance. He caught Estienne's descending blade on his cross-guard, their swords locked, bringing them chest to chest.

'You fight like a pig-fucker,' Ilbert snarled.

With a deft twist, he wrenched Estienne's sword from his grip. As the wood clattered away, he slammed his pommel into Estienne's face. White-hot pain exploded and Estienne reeled backwards, blood pouring from a flattened nose, as he crashed to the ground in a graceless sprawl.

Ilbert loomed over him, wooden sword levelled at his throat. 'Know your place, whelp. There, in the dirt.'

Humiliation seared, hotter than the blood smearing his face, but Estienne could only lie there, panting for air, head ringing as he choked on the taste of his own failure.

'Hold,' William snapped. 'The match is done. Ilbert, that blow was ill-struck. We train to control our strength, not unleash it on an inexperienced opponent.'

Ilbert straightened, though his sword remained pointed at Estienne's heaving chest. 'The little cock wanted to crow. I just taught him what happens when there's a bigger cock in the coop.'

His voice was belligerent, but he visibly shrank beneath William's glower. 'You've taught enough for one day. Go and clean the tack. All of it. I want the leather oiled until I can see my face.'

For a moment Estienne thought Ilbert might argue. A mulish look flashed across his face, but William's hard stare brooked no defiance. With a final contemptuous glance at Estienne, Ilbert stalked out of the yard.

Estienne lay still, trying to master the sickening churn of pain and humiliation. He could taste blood in his mouth, and every breath sent a fresh lance of agony through his nose.

William's weathered hand appeared in his blurry vision. 'On your feet, squire. You'll live. That's the main thing.'

Estienne accepted the hand, swaying groggily once he was pulled to his feet. He squinted at William through rapidly swelling eyes. 'I'm sorry, my lord. I thought I could—'

'You thought you could let your anger do your fighting for you. Raw ferocity is no replacement for control and skill. Lose your wits in battle and your head will soon follow.'

'I understand, my lord.'

William sighed, more weary than angry. 'You have heart, Estienne. And courage to spare. But heart alone is just bloody meat without the sense to temper it. You must learn to master yourself before you can hope to master the sword.'

Estienne nodded, the motion making his head swim queasily.

He'd been a hot-headed fool, letting Ilbert's gibes sting him to recklessness.

William clapped a hand on Estienne's shoulder, nearly buckling his knees. 'We'll remedy it, boy. Have no fear. For now, go get yourself cleaned up. Have the cooks bring you some meat for that nose.'

Estienne could only bob his aching head in acknowledgement. William gave his shoulder a final heavy pat and strode off, leaving Estienne swaying alone in the centre of the yard.

Gingerly, he prodded at his throbbing nose. It didn't feel broken, but the swelling was already puffing his left eye shut. But it was the wound to his pride that stung the sharpest. He'd been so eager to prove himself, but all he'd proven was how woefully outmatched he was.

As Estienne limped towards the keep, someone caught his eye and his heart plummeted. Eva stood by the wall, arms crossed, head cocked to the side as she watched him approach.

'Well fought, Ser Squire,' she called mockingly. 'A few more victories like that and you'll be ready to take your oath. If you can mumble it through a broken jaw, that is.'

He stumbled on, her snickers chasing him across the yard, stinging like hornets in his ears. Not a great first day. But no matter how hard he fell, no matter how often, he would always get back up.

4

The great hall thrummed with chatter as servants bustled to and fro. Estienne shifted on the rough wooden bench, acutely aware of his position at the far end, well away from the high table where Earl William and his family sat.

At the head of that table William himself presided, his weathered face stern. He made polite conversation with his guests, most of whom simply called him 'the Marshal' out of respect for his rank and reputation. Beside him was the Countess Isabel, her delicate features composed into a mask of regal serenity. To William's left, his daughters were arranged in a line, the eldest three – Isabeau, Sybil and Joan – sitting with perfect poise, hands folded on their laps. But it was the youngest, Eva, who drew Estienne's gaze. While her sisters were the very picture of courtly decorum, Eva fidgeted restlessly, picking at a loose thread on her kirtle, heedless of her mother's occasional sharp looks. As if sensing his scrutiny, her eyes flicked up to meet his, gleaming with barely suppressed mischief.

Estienne looked away. Bad enough to be relegated to the end of the table, without being caught staring by Earl William's trouble-some daughter.

Further down the table sat Ilbert, studiously ignoring him. The older squire hadn't so much as glanced in his direction since their fight in the training yard, his haughty features set in a permanent sneer of disdain. At least Goffrey was here, seated at Earl William's right hand. He caught Estienne's eye and offered an encouraging wink. A gesture of welcome, reminding Estienne that he was not entirely alone, but as the servers began to file in bearing the first course, he couldn't shake the sense that he was very much a cuckoo within the Marshal's nest.

The scent of saffron and cloves wafted through the hall as Mabil emerged from the kitchens, leading a procession of under-cooks bearing the meal. They set down platters of gleaming silver, each one piled high with delicacies.

'Pynnonade, my lord,' Mabil announced, as a server placed a dish of spiced nuts before Earl William. 'Followed by stewed pigeons in saffron and sour wine, and chrysanne – tench cooked in vinegar with figs.'

William inclined his head. 'My thanks, Mabil. Your skill never fails to impress.'

The cook flushed with pleasure at the praise, bobbing a curtsey before retreating back to the kitchens. As the servers laid trenchers of dense, crusty bread before each diner, William raised a hand.

'Let us give thanks,' he announced, his voice carrying through the hall. 'Bless us, O Lord, and these, thy gifts, which we are about to receive. Through Christ, our Lord. Amen.'

'Amen,' the assembled courtiers murmured, and Estienne echoed the word, a beat behind.

As the meal began in earnest, he couldn't help but marvel at the sheer abundance of it all. At home, a feast meant a bit of extra salt pork in the pottage, or perhaps a scrawny capon if times were good. But this... this was opulence beyond his wildest imagining.

He glanced along the table, watching as Isabeau, Sybil and Joan delicately speared morsels of pigeon on the points of their knives, conveying them to their mouths with effortless grace. Eva, by contrast, poked at her chrysanne with a sullen expression, mashing the tender fish into an unappetising pulp.

Further down the table, an array of unfamiliar faces chattered and laughed – men and women Estienne could only assume were local barons or wealthy landowners, invited to dine at the Marshal's expense. They paid him no mind, their attention focused solely on the delicacies before them.

Estienne focused on his own trencher, scooping up a portion of the savoury pigeon and trying not to wolf it down too quickly. It wouldn't do to betray his constant hunger, or his lowly origins, with poor table manners, but it was hard to maintain decorum when faced with food fit for a king.

'So, Estienne,' Goffrey said, his voice cutting through the chatter. 'How fares our newest squire? Are you settling in well?'

Estienne swallowed his mouthful of pigeon. 'I... I am, thank you. Earl William has been most generous.'

The Marshal leaned forward. 'The lad is raw as unworked iron, but he has potential. With time and tempering, he may yet make a passable knight.'

Down the table, Ilbert snorted. 'If he lives that long.'

The words were muttered under his breath, but Estienne heard them all the same. Heat rushed to his face, part anger, part shame, but he forced himself to stay silent. It would not do to rise to Ilbert's bait, not here in the hall under William's eye. Instead, he focused on his food, savouring the delicate flesh of the chrysanne, the sweet-sharp burst of vinegar and figs on his tongue. He had never tasted anything so fine, and he was determined to enjoy it, even if he had to force it down past the resentment lodged in his throat.

As the meal wore on, Estienne couldn't help but notice the subdued atmosphere at the high table. William ate with his brow furrowed as though his thoughts were far away. Isabel offered him concerned glances, but he seemed not to notice.

As the last crumbs were sopped up with hunks of bread, Goffrey pushed back his chair and stood.

'By your leave, my lord, my lady,' he said, bowing to the high table. 'I'll see the trenchers distributed to the poor outside the gates.'

William waved a hand in assent, still lost in thought. Estienne saw his chance and rose to his feet.

'I'll help,' he said, eager to escape the stifling atmosphere of the hall.

Isabel's eyes were on him, sharp as a hawk's. For a moment, Estienne feared she would refuse, deeming such a task beneath a squire of her house, but then she looked to Eva, still slouched sullenly over her trencher.

'Eva will go with you,' she said.

Eva's head snapped up. 'But Mother, I—'

'You will go,' Isabel repeated, steel beneath the silk of her voice. 'It is past time you learned some duty and charity.'

Eva's jaw clenched as if biting back a retort, but a stern look from her mother quelled any defiance, and she rose from the table with ill grace, stomping over to join Estienne and Goffrey.

As they gathered up stacks of gravy-sodden trenchers, Estienne caught the flash of a smirk on Ilbert's face. Of course the wretch would be amused by this, seeing Estienne reduced to little more than a servant. But Estienne knew there was no shame in helping those less fortunate, no matter what his fellow squire thought.

As they made their way down through the keep, trenchers stacked high in their arms, Estienne couldn't contain his curiosity any longer.

'Goffrey,' he said, keeping his voice low so Eva wouldn't over-hear. 'What happened to Earl William's eldest sons? I have only heard them spoken of in whispers.'

Goffrey's genial face darkened. 'They were taken hostage by King John, after Earl William defied him.'

'Defied him? How?'

'It's a long tale,' Goffrey sighed. 'Suffice it to say, William offered sanctuary to one of the king's enemies. A grave offence in John's book. As punishment, he demanded Guillaume and Richard be sent to his court to safeguard their father's loyalty.'

A chill ran down Estienne's spine. To be torn from one's family, held captive by a capricious king... he could scarcely imagine a worse fate.

'Are they safe?'

Goffrey's smile was grim. 'As safe as any man held at King John's whim. As long as Earl William does not defy him again, they will live. But if he were to provoke the king once more...' He trailed off, letting the implication hang heavy in the air.

Estienne felt his heart ache for the Marshal and his family. To live under such a shadow, always fearing for the lives of those you loved... it was a burden he could scarcely fathom.

The portcullis was raised as they approached the castle gates. Beyond, a small crowd was huddled in the shadow of the barbican, their ragged clothing fluttering in the chill breeze. At the sight of Goffrey and his trencher-laden entourage, a ripple of excitement ran through the gathered poor. Hands were thrust out, eyes bright with desperate hope in gaunt, pinched faces.

Eva wrinkled her nose as they drew closer, as if affronted by the sour stench of unwashed bodies. Without ceremony, she upended her stack of trenchers into the reaching hands, scattering them like chicken feed. The peasants fell upon them, snatching up the hunks of bread, stuffing them into their mouths as if they feared they might be snatched back at any moment.

Estienne approached more slowly, meeting the eyes of each man, woman and child as he carefully placed a trencher in their outstretched palms. He wished he had more to give them than just stale bread and cold gravy. He wished...

His thoughts were shattered by a wet slap, as one of Eva's few remaining trenchers smacked against the back of his head. Something slick and slimy ran down his neck, as Eva's mocking laughter rang out behind him.

'There you go, Ser Squire,' she called, dancing backwards as he wheeled to face her. 'Do you like your new hat?'

And with that, she turned tail and bolted, her giggles trailing behind her. Estienne stood frozen, gravy dripping from his hair, his face burning with humiliation. Slowly he dragged the sopping trencher from his head and handed it to another needy hand.

As they trudged back to the keep, Goffrey offered a conciliatory pat on the shoulder. 'Don't think too much on that, lad. Little girls will be little girls. It probably means she likes you.'

'Doesn't look like it from where I'm standing.'

'No matter. You'll have more important things to think on soon enough. Your training has only just begun. And if you're to be a knight, there's a code to follow.'

'A what?'

'The many tenets of knighthood. But the core of it, the heart of what it means to be a knight is about honour, lad. Honour and duty.' He ticked the points off on his fingers as he spoke. 'To be pious in all things, and serve God before all else. To be loyal to your liege lord, and defend his cause with valour and faith. To protect the weak and helpless, and fight for the welfare of all. To speak the truth, always, even when it pains you. To persevere in the face of adversity, and see every task through to its end. To respect the honour of women, as you would your own. And to never refuse a challenge from an equal, or turn your back on a foe.'

Estienne listened intently, trying to commit each precept to memory. They were daunting, these rules that would govern his life as a knight. A far cry from the rough-and-tumble code of the countryside, where might usually made right.

'It sounds almost impossible. How can anyone truly live by so many rules?'

'Many would say you can't, lad. Others would claim that the code is the cornerstone of knighthood, the sacred bond that separates the noble from the base.' He patted the flank of the warhammer hanging at his side, the head worn smooth by years of use. 'But those same men tend to be the first to forget their vows when the blood is up and the enemy is at the gates. Out there, on the field of battle, there's precious little room for honour when you're fighting for your life.'

Estienne frowned, trying to reconcile the harsh reality of Goffrey's words with the shining ideal of the code. 'So, it's all a lie, then? Just warm words?'

'Not a lie, no,' Goffrey said, shaking his head. 'An aspiration. Something to strive for, even if we know we'll never quite reach it.'

'So how do I know what's right? How do I know what to do if I have to break this code to stay alive?'

'That, lad, is something you'll have to discover for yourself. But if you ask me?' He leaned in close, his voice dropping to a whisper. 'When steel meets steel and the blood starts flowing, that's when you find out what kind of knight you truly are. And sometimes, the answer isn't pretty.'

He slapped Estienne on the back, his hand heavy as a boulder, before leading the way back to the keep. As Estienne followed, he had a feeling those words might come back to haunt him in the days and years to come. That they were a warning, of the bitter choices he would one day have to make.

5

The weeks had not been kind to Estienne. Though he had managed well enough with many of the adjustments of living in this foreign land – the dialect, the food, the cold and constant rain – it was his duties as a squire he had found most brutal. The days went by in a blur of cleaning and oiling mail, polishing weapons and helms, scrubbing down horses and mucking out stables alongside the castle's groom. And then there was the training.

His shoulders ached, his arms burned, his hands were rubbed raw and blistered. But he was growing, in both body and prowess. When he had first arrived at the Marshal household, a gangling boy, he had struggled to fight with anything approaching skill or even strength. Now his muscles strained against his tunic with every sure swing of the blade.

It was not just his swordplay that had improved under the relentless drilling of Earl William. He could loose an arrow, heft a lance, raise a shield. But it was the horse that gave him the most trouble. Learning to ride had not been so difficult in itself – he could sit a saddle well enough, and stay ahorse at a trot or canter.

Could mount by swinging a leg up and over the cantle, even in a mail hauberk.

No, it was controlling the beast with naught but pressure from his feet and knees that was the real challenge. His thighs burned with the effort of gripping the horse's flank, trying to guide it with subtle shifts of his body. All the while keeping his hands free to grip lance and shield. It was like trying to command the animal by thought alone, and Estienne had not yet learned to be of one mind with his troublesome destrier.

'Again!' William's voice cracked across the tiltyard.

Estienne gritted his teeth, gripping the blunted lance tighter, its dull point aimed at the cloudless sky. At the other end of the yard he could see Ilbert doing the same, the older squire's mouth twisted in a contemptuous smirk before he donned his helm.

They were both clad in thick, padded gambesons, the quilted fabric designed to cushion the impact of the lances, though not enough to prevent bruising and sore muscles. Estienne's body was a map of purpling welts and yellowing contusions.

He could feel Earl William watching him from where he stood with Domnall, the stableboy, at his shoulder. The grizzled knight's face unreadable beneath the crease of his brow.

Estienne dug his heels into the destrier's flanks, feeling the powerful muscles bunch and flex between his legs. The horse stamped and snorted, sensing his rider's unease.

'Steady,' he muttered, more to himself than the horse. He had to remember what William had taught him. Heels down, toes up, calves gripping the horse's barrel.

Ilbert spurred his own mount forward, lance lowering as he gathered speed. Estienne echoed him a heartbeat later, the destrier surging into a canter, then a gallop.

They met in a splintering crash of wood on wood. Estienne felt the shuddering impact almost tear the lance from his grip. He fought to keep his seat, thighs clamping desperately around the horse's flank, but it was no use as Ilbert's lance struck him high on the shield, the blow perfectly timed, and Estienne was wrenched backwards out of the saddle, limbs flailing as he tumbled through empty air.

The ground rose up to meet him with a bone-jarring thud. He lay there, winded, blinking up at the sky as the destrier cantered away riderless. Every inch of him throbbed with pain, head ringing like a struck bell.

'On your feet, lad,' he heard William say.

Someone gripped Estienne under the arms, hauling him upright. He blinked, finding himself face-to-face with Domnall. The stableboy's expression bore a glimmer of sympathy to it.

Ilbert's laughter rang loud in his ears as Estienne swayed unsteadily, fighting a wave of dizziness. 'Poor showing, Wace. You ride like a sack of wet shit. And fall much the same.'

Estienne's hands curled into fists. He opened his mouth to retort, but the words died on his tongue as Earl William strode across the churned earth towards him.

'Ilbert has the right of it. You're still fighting against your mount, Estienne. Riding as stiff as a plank.'

Estienne bristled at the humiliation. 'I'm doing my best, my lord.'

'Then your best needs to get better. Heels down, boy. Grip with your legs, move your hips to the stride of the horse.'

A fresh echo of laughter from Ilbert, quickly stifled as William shot him a stern glare. Estienne felt the shame and frustration churning in his gut. He knew he was better than this, knew he could master the horse if only given the time.

He met his lord's gaze squarely, his jaw clenched with determination. 'Again. Let me try again.'

For a long moment, William studied him, his expression

inscrutable. Then, to Estienne's surprise, he nodded. 'Mount up, then. And mind my words this time, or you'll be mucking stalls till Whitsun.'

Estienne didn't need to be told twice. Ignoring the protestations of his bruised body, he snatched the reins of his wayward destrier from Domnall and swung himself back into the saddle.

Before he could set heels, the clatter of hoofbeats echoed off the castle walls, drawing everyone's attention to the gate. A lone rider galloped through the archway, his horse's flanks lathered with sweat, its sides heaving. Estienne squinted against the glare of the sun, trying to make out the newcomer's features. He was tall and broad-shouldered with a shock of dark hair and a bearded face, clad in a travel-stained cloak, a sword at his hip.

'Richard!' The glad cry came from Earl William, who was already striding across the yard, his face split by a rare grin.

The rider swung down from his mount. 'Father.'

The two men embraced, pounding each other on the back. Their laughter rang out, warm and boisterous.

Estienne felt a pang of envy. He had never known his own father, had never felt that unshakeable certainty of blood and belonging, other than his aunt and uncle. Watching William and his son, he was sharply reminded of his own rootless state, adrift in a world where he was now the outsider.

'Is that the earl's son?' he asked, after dismounting the charger, the afternoon's tutelage clearly at an end.

Beside him, Ilbert snorted. 'Are you blind as well as thick? Of course it is.'

'But if the king has let him go it must mean he's not displeased with William any more. That's good, isn't it?'

The older squire shrugged. 'Who can say? The king's moods are as changeable as the tides. One day he's your friend, the next he's branding you a traitor.'

'Who's this, then?' Richard had broken his embrace with his father and was eyeing Estienne with curiosity.

William beckoned him forward. 'This is Estienne Wace. A new addition to our ranks. He shows promise.'

'Does he, now?' Richard looked him up and down.

Estienne had the uncanny feeling he was being evaluated for flaws and merits like a horse at market. 'It is good to meet you, my lord. Welcome home.'

'And good to meet you, Estienne Wace.' There was warmth in Richard's voice. A note of approval perhaps, gone all too quickly as his attention shifted past Estienne, focusing on Ilbert. The warmth bled from his face. 'Ilbert. I see you're still afflicting my father with your presence.'

'My lord.' Ilbert offered a bow, but the curl of his lip belied the respect in the gesture. 'A delight as ever.'

William grasped his son's shoulder. 'What news of Guillaume? Has he been released as well?'

Richard nodded. 'Aye, he is back in friendly hands. John of Earley has taken him into his household. He'll want for nothing there.'

'That is good news.' William blew out a breath. 'I feared the king might seek to keep one of you, even as he freed the other.'

'The winds are changing, Father. It seems John has need of you once again. There's trouble brewing in Flanders. Philip of France is eyeing English territories there, and with the Pope's blessing...'

'So while John is still excommunicate, King Philip seizes upon his chance.'

Richard nodded his head. 'But John must stand strong, now more than ever. He cannot show weakness, not with the French wolves circling.'

'And he needs his loyal Marshal at his side,' William finished grimly. 'Aye, I see it clear enough.'

Estienne felt a shiver run through him. War was coming, if Richard's words were true. This was what he had dreamed of, all those long days and nights of gruelling training. A chance to prove himself, to win glory on the field of battle.

Earl William turned abruptly toward Ilbert. 'Bring my messenger. I would have him send word to the barons of Hibernia. We will pledge our loyalty to King John once again.'

As Ilbert scurried to obey, Estienne stepped eagerly toward the Marshal.

'I stand ready to serve, my lord,' he said, his voice clear and unwavering. 'In whatever capacity I am needed.'

William studied him for a long moment, a faint smile playing about his lips. 'Be careful what you wish for, lad.'

Before Estienne could offer any further pledge, he saw Countess Isabel appear at the door to the keep.

'Richard! Oh, my boy!'

Her cry rang out across the courtyard, high and clear as a bell. She ran from the keep, her skirts hiked up around her ankles, all dignity forgotten in her haste.

William shot his son a warning look. 'Not a word of this to your mother. She has enough to worry her without borrowing tomorrow's troubles.'

Richard nodded, his smile a touch strained as he turned to greet Isabel. 'Mother. It's good to see you.'

'Oh, Richard.' Isabel flung her arms around her son, heedless of the grime of travel. Tears glistened on her cheeks as she held him close. 'I feared I would never set eyes on you again.'

'I'm here, Mother.' Richard's voice was rough with emotion as he returned her embrace. 'I'm home.'

Estienne watched the reunion, feeling the love between them, bright and fierce as a flame, but it only brought him sadness. War loomed over them all, a shadow that could not be ignored. Soon, the Marshal family might be sundered once more.

6

Hooves churned the muddy road as Estienne rode in the midst of William Marshal's train. The palfrey beneath him was a bad-tempered beast, its coat slick with sweat despite the chill that lingered in the air. Around them, the Kentish countryside rolled by in a patchwork of greens and browns that glistened from the morning's rain.

The crossing from Hibernia had been rough, the inclement weather plaguing them like an ill omen as they travelled to meet with King John. Now the elements had settled, but there was still a sense of foreboding as they made their way across the fields of England. To Estienne's left, Ilbert rode with his face screwed up beneath his hood, as if he'd bitten into something sour. Beyond him, Richard Marshal cut a striking figure on his pale destrier.

They crested a rise and the castle hove into view, its blue-grey ragstone walls stark against the bruised sky. Estienne felt a flicker of trepidation. Somewhere within those walls, the King of England awaited them. A man of uneven temper, who held all their lives in his grasping hands.

Their pace slowed as they approached the gatehouse, the hoofbeats of their horses ringing hollow on the drawbridge. A man with white hair wearing a tunic of red and green emerged from the shadow of the barbican.

Earl William raised a hand in greeting. 'Geoffrey FitzPeter, as I live and breathe. Well met, old friend.'

Geoffrey bowed, a smile breaking across his weathered face. 'William Marshal. His Grace will be pleased you made such good time. He is most eager to speak with you.'

William nodded grimly. 'And I with him. There is much to discuss.'

The inner ward was a hive of activity. Men-at-arms with surcoats bearing the three lions of the king's household stood vigil while grooms led lathered horses toward the stables and servants carried baskets of bread and barrels of wine toward the keep.

Estienne dismounted awkwardly, his legs stiff from hours in the saddle. He handed his reins to a waiting groom and fell in behind William, as Geoffrey FitzPeter led them across the courtyard toward the great hall.

A knot of men clustered before the open doors, their cloaks and tunics rich with embroidery. Among them stood a young man with the same steel-grey eyes as Earl William and Richard.

'Father.' The man stepped forward, a smile breaking across his face. 'You made good time.'

William clasped his firstborn son in a hard embrace. 'Guillaume. It's good to see you, lad.'

Richard strode forward to enfold his brother in a bear hug. The two laughed, slapping each other on the back. Estienne hung back, suddenly uncertain of his place, but Ilbert shouldered past to greet Guillaume. The two clasped forearms, grinning like old friends.

'My lords.' Geoffrey FitzPeter's voice cut through the babble of conversation. 'The king will see you now.'

A sudden hush fell over the assembled knights and Estienne

felt his stomach lurch. This was it. He was about to meet King John, the man who would decide all their fates.

They followed Geoffrey up through the vast keep until they reached the great hall. It was cavernous, the vaulted ceiling lost in shadow high above. Tapestries hung from the walls, their vivid colours faded with age, depicting scenes of hunt and battle. Rushes crunched beneath Estienne's feet, sweetening the air with their scent.

At the far end of the hall, a large group of knights in sumptuous velvets and furs stood clustered around a man seated in a throne-like chair. As William led his party down the centre, the knights fell silent, turning to watch their approach.

Then Estienne saw him. King John, Ruler of the Angevin dynasty, Lord of England, Hibernia, and half of France.

He was smaller than Estienne had imagined, almost slight of build, but he radiated an aura of coiled energy like a snake poised to strike. His eyes were a piercing blue, sharp and assessing as they pored over the approaching men. He wore a fur-lined cloak of rich crimson over a black velvet doublet, every finger adorned with jewelled rings that sparkled in the torchlight. When he smiled, his teeth gleamed white against the neat greying beard framing his mouth.

'Earl William Marshal.' John's voice broke the charged silence. 'Our faithful servant. We are most pleased to see you.'

Estienne's heart pounded as William sank to one knee before the dais, bowing his head. 'Your Grace. I am honoured to be in your presence once more.'

The king's smile widened, but Estienne could see the calculation in his eyes, the shrewd appraisal as he studied the Marshal. There was venom behind that genial grin, a serpent's guile.

'Rise, Earl William. You have been absent from our side for too long.'

The Marshal regained his feet, and Estienne felt the atmosphere lighten somewhat. 'Your Grace, I came as soon as I received your summons. How may I serve?'

William's voice was steady, respectful, but Estienne could sense steel beneath the velvet.

King John leaned back in his chair, steepling his fingers. 'You have come at a most opportune time, Earl William. We find ourselves beset by enemies on all sides. That howling dog Philip dares to paw at our gates, bolstered by the Pope's blessing.'

The Marshal inclined his head, his expression thoughtful. 'A grave situation, Your Grace. One that requires a delicate touch.'

'Delicate? The time for delicacy has passed. We must strike at Philip now, before he can mobilise his forces. Crush him like the meddlesome tick he is.'

'With respect, Your Grace, I believe there may be another path. One that strengthens your position in the eyes of God and man.'

The king's gaze sharpened, his fingers tightening on the arms of his chair. 'Speak your mind, Marshal.'

William spread his hands, his tone conciliatory. 'Your Grace, the Pope has already offered you terms by which England may become a papal fief. If you were to accept them, swear homage and fealty to him, surely His Holiness would have no choice but to withdraw his support from Philip.'

A deadly silence descended upon the hall. Estienne hardly dared breathe. To suggest the king should humble himself before the Pope was a bold move, one that could easily backfire.

For a long, tense moment, the king stared, his face unreadable. Then, slowly, he began to smile.

'Perhaps you have a point, old friend. Perhaps a touch of humility is exactly what we need.' The king's genial expression shifted, hardening into something more calculating. 'Of course, we must also show King Philip – and the world – the consequences of crossing the English Crown. Even now, our loyal servant and brother, Willem Longsword musters a fleet to strike at Philip's underbelly and put his ships to the torch.'

A murmur of approval rippled through the gathered knights. Estienne could feel their eagerness, their hunger for glory, but William held up a hand, his brow furrowed.

'Your Grace, I urge caution. Strike too soon and it might only strengthen Philip's cause.'

King John waved a dismissive hand. 'A risk I am willing to take. The fleet will sail.'

William bowed his head. 'As you see fit, Your Grace. But I must counsel restraint, at least until the Pope has been appeased.'

'Ever the voice of reason, Marshal. Very well. We shall play the penitent for now, and make our peace with the Holy See. But mark my words – Philip will pay. And when the time comes, we shall crush him like an insect beneath our boot.' He turned to the assembled knights, raising his voice. 'Rejoice. For soon, we shall feast in Flanders itself, with the blood of our enemies still warm upon our blades.'

A cheer went up from the men, a roar of bloodlust. Estienne had known that war was coming, had trained for it every waking moment, but faced with the terrible reality of it, he felt a cold knot of fear settle in his stomach.

'A toast.' King John's voice rang out, cutting through the cheers. 'To friendship reforged, and enemies laid low.'

He beckoned imperiously for wine. Estienne found himself shoved forward, a tray of goblets thrust into his hands. His heart leapt into his throat as he approached the king, the spiced scent of wine wafting up from the brimming cups. Marshal took them both, offering one to John.

'Wesheil!' The king raised his goblet high, the rubies on his fingers glinting like drops of blood.

'Drincheil,' Marshal replied, lifting his own cup in salute.

They drank deep, and Estienne held the tray steady, hardly daring to breathe as the king and Earl William drained their cups and placed them back on the polished silver.

He began to back away, his legs trembling with relief. Before he had taken a dozen steps, his foot caught on something and he stumbled, losing his balance, the tray slipping from his fingers. As the goblets tumbled through the air, Estienne hit the floor with a bone-jarring thud. Ilbert laughed close by, the sound cruel and mocking.

Estienne fumbled for the fallen tray, before a strong hand grasped his elbow, hauling him to his feet. He found himself staring up into a pair of keen blue eyes set in a bearded face. The man wore a surcoat emblazoned with red diamonds on a field of white.

'Th-thank you, my lord,' Estienne stammered, bobbing his head in appreciation.

The knight nodded his reply, before stepping back and melting into the crowd of knights.

'It seems your squire is as unsteady as a newborn foal, Marshal.' King John's voice was laced with amusement.

William looked almost as embarrassed as Estienne felt. 'For-give him, Your Grace. He is new to my household, and clearly over-whelmed by the honour of serving you.'

John's eyes lingered on Estienne. 'There's something familiar about that face. Have I seen you before, boy?'

Estienne could feel the scrutiny of every eye in the hall bearing down upon him. 'N-no, Your Grace.'

He risked a glance at Earl William, seeing a muscle twitch in the Marshal's jaw, but his expression remained calm.

'Where did you find this one, Marshal? Some stableboy you took pity on?'

'Pay him no mind, Your Grace. He meant no offence.'

For a moment, Estienne feared the king might press further, but then John waved a dismissive hand. 'No matter. More important is that we are back on terms, you and I. And it is past time you took up your duties in Pembroke again, to better serve your king.'

'As you wish, Your Grace.' William bowed low. 'Pembroke will be my home, and yours whenever you have need of it.'

'Good. Soon I will have further need of your sword and your counsel. The fate of this kingdom might rely on both.'

William made his final bows and began to usher his party from the hall. When they reached the courtyard it was startlingly bright after the shadowed confines of the keep.

'Estienne.' The Marshal's voice was stern. 'You must have a care, boy. The king's court is an adder's nest, and you came perilously close to being bitten.'

Estienne bowed his head. 'Forgive me, my lord. It won't happen again.'

William sighed, clapping a heavy hand on his shoulder. 'See that it doesn't. King John is not a man to cross. We walk a treacherous path, and the slightest misstep could spell imprisonment or death.'

'I understand, my lord.' Estienne's voice sounded small, even to his own ears. 'I will strive to do better.'

William's stern look softened. 'Don't be too hard on yourself, lad. These are perilous times, and we must all mind our footing.'

With that, he turned away, calling orders to his men as they prepared to depart. Estienne blew out a shaky breath, running a hand through his sweat-damp hair.

'Don't let it trouble you.' Richard Marshal appeared at his elbow, his voice low and reassuring. 'My father may seem harsh, but he only wants to protect you. The king's attention can be a dangerous thing.'

'I should have been more careful.'

'You should.' Richard patted his shoulder. 'And so should Ilbert.'

'He tripped me,' Estienne said, confirming what he had suspected.

'He did. Try not to think on it. He won't always be around to torment you. But there may always be someone there to pick you up, should you fall.'

Richard nodded to where a knight was mounting his destrier, the one who had helped Estienne to his feet.

'Who is he?' Estienne asked.

'Hubert of Burgh. One of John's most loyal servants.'

Estienne watched as Hubert reined his horse around and trotted from the courtyard. It was a rare kindness he had shown, and Estienne would be sure to return the favour one day, if the opportunity arose.

7

Estienne shifted in the saddle, the mail chafing at his shoulders. He'd thought he was growing used to life at Pembroke, to the relentless pace of his training, but donning a full harness was a fresh hell, the weight of it bearing down and unbalancing him so much he feared he might topple right off his horse.

Sweat trickled into his eyes as he squinted across the yard at Richard. The Marshal's son sat tall in the saddle, lance couched with the easy grace of a born horseman. A far cry from how Estienne felt – awkward as a duck trying to dance – but still he would see this through if it killed him.

At least it wasn't Ilbert he faced. His fellow squire had been scarce these past days, off sporting with Guillaume Marshal. Instead, Richard had stepped into Ilbert's place, drilling him mercilessly in lance and sword. A kinder foe than FitzDane, but no less exacting.

Estienne shifted his grip on the lance, making it more comfortable in the pit of his arm. Across the yard, Richard raised his own weapon in salute. A heartbeat's pause, the world narrowing to a single moment. Then Richard spurred his mount forward, hooves churning up clods of earth.

Estienne took a steadying breath. Nudging his knees into his horse's flanks he raised the lance, point wavering as his arm trembled with the strain, but he clenched his teeth as his own horse bolted. The speed at which they advanced was terrifying, but he bit back any fear, every muscle braced, ready for the impact.

They met with a splintering crash. Estienne felt the lance connect, a solid blow to the centre of Richard's shield. Felt himself rock back in the saddle, barely keeping his seat.

Richard cantered past him, lance intact, while Estienne's lay in shards on the churned ground. He'd struck a good blow, dead centre of his opponent's shield. Perhaps there was hope for him yet.

'Well ridden,' Richard called as he reined up. 'Your aim is improving.'

'My aim, maybe,' Estienne replied as he trotted closer. 'But not my horsemanship. I still feel like a sack of turnips up here.'

Richard laughed. 'It will come, with time and practice. But I think that's enough for one day.'

They dismounted, handing off their huffing horses to Domnall. As they did so, Estienne heard a slow hand clap from the edge of the tilt-yard. Goffrey watched with a wry grin, sun glistening off his bald pate.

'You're coming along well, lad. That was a good effort. Soon you'll be solid as a rock in the saddle.'

Estienne was pleased by the praise but unable to fully accept it. 'Still not good enough. Ilbert would laugh himself sick if he saw that sorry display.'

'Let him laugh. You've got time yet to improve. Richard here was just as rough at your age. Couldn't stay in his saddle even when we strapped him to it.'

'It's true,' Richard said with a rueful grin. 'Father and Goffrey despaired of me. It was only after years of their tender tutelage that I managed to topple either one of them.'

Estienne huffed a laugh, but it sounded forced even to his own ears. 'Be that as it may, not everyone has such faith in my progress. To hear Ilbert talk, I'm naught but a lost dog, doomed to failure.'

Richard and Goffrey exchanged a glance, before Goffrey said, 'He wasn't so steady himself when first he came into Earl William's service.'

'Then why does he hate me so?' The question burst from Estienne, more plaintive than he'd intended. 'What have I done to earn such scorn?'

Another glance passed between the two men. Finally Goffrey sighed, scratching at his hairless head. 'It's not you, lad. Not really. It's more what you represent.'

Estienne frowned. 'I don't take your meaning.'

'Ilbert...' Richard began, then hesitated, as if choosing his words with care. 'Ilbert is not so different from you, in many ways. He is a fourth son, with little to his name. His father is a minor landholder, and if rumour is to be believed, Ilbert may not even be trueborn. More than a few wagging tongues name him a royal bastard, sired after our beloved king paid a visit to his father's estate.'

'A royal...?' Estienne could barely believe what he was hearing. 'You mean to say King John is his father?'

Richard shrugged. 'So the talk goes. Not that it did Ilbert much good. Lord FitzDane foisted him off on my father the first chance he got.'

'Poor fortune to be a bastard,' Goffrey said. 'Even a king's. Ilbert's brothers will inherit what little lands and titles there are. He must make his own way in the world. Forge his own path and make his own name.'

'And having me here threatens that. He thinks I've stolen his place as Earl William's favoured.'

Richard clapped him on the shoulder. 'Aye. So you see, it's got naught to do with you and everything to do with his own shame. Don't let his bile trouble you.'

Estienne shook his head. 'Perhaps I should never have come here. I have caused such trouble for him.'

'Nonsense,' Goffrey replied. 'We are all exactly where we should be. Never let anyone tell you that you don't belong. God has his plans, and sends us where we are most needed.'

'So why did he send you here?' Estienne asked, suddenly curious. 'How did a man such as yourself come to be in Earl William's service?'

Goffrey looked suddenly wistful. 'I was a Templar once, if you can believe it. Fought alongside Earl William in Outremer, years ago now. He saved my life, during a skirmish near Jerusalem. When he returned to England, I came with him. Seemed the least I could do, to serve as his almoner.'

'And now you're stuck training the likes of me,' Estienne said with a crooked grin. 'A step down, some might say.'

'Nay, lad. An honour and a privilege is what it is.'

'So is Earl William a Templar as well?' Estienne asked, curiosity piqued.

'Not as such,' Richard replied. 'Though he's vowed to take the cross one day, and join Goffrey's brotherhood.'

Goffrey nodded, something close to pride kindling in his eyes. 'Aye, and a finer brother I couldn't ask for. Though at the rate he's going, he'll be too old to even lift a blade, let alone ride on crusade.'

Richard laughed. 'Perhaps Estienne and I will have to go in his stead, eh? Win glory for the Marshal name in the Kingdom of Jerusalem.'

A thrill chased down Estienne's spine at the thought. To ride on crusade, like the heroes of old. To pledge his sword to God and king, and carve his name into the annals of history...

No. Such dreams were beyond him, at least for now. He was still a squire, unblooded and untested. His spurs were a distant glimmer, and Jerusalem further still.

But one day, perhaps...

8

The funeral mass droned on, the priest's Latin a dull buzz in Estienne's ears. He stood in the cold stone nave of Shouldham Priory, wreathed in incense and the beeswax stench of burning tapers. All around, the faces of the assembled lords were masks of pious solemnity, but he could see the undercurrents of politicking beneath the surface. Geoffrey FitzPeter's death had created space at the king's side. The position of justiciar was now vacant, and there were many here eager to fill it.

Beside Estienne, William Marshal stood tall and stern. Geoffrey had been his friend and ally, a steadfast supporter through the turbulent years of King John's reign. It was obvious to those who could see that he felt his friend's loss keenly, and they had travelled the flat expanse of Norfolk in mournful solemnity to pay their last respects.

As the priest completed the final blessing, William turned abruptly and strode from the nave, his footsteps ringing on the flagstones. Estienne watched him go, understanding his need for a moment alone with his grief.

He followed the rest of the mourners out into the priory courtyard. Most sidling towards the promise of wine and sweetmeats that were arrayed on tables across the yard, but Estienne hung back, uncertain of his place among this highborn gathering.

As he stood, he spotted Richard Marshal in animated conversation with Ilbert. They stood close together, heads bent in conspiratorial whispers. His curiosity piqued, Estienne began to drift closer, wondering what could have sparked such intense discussion on this solemn day.

Seeing Estienne's approach, Richard broke off his hushed conference with Ilbert and adopted a smile that seemed almost out of place amid the sombre atmosphere. 'Estienne. Just the man I wanted to see.'

'My lord?' Estienne replied, puzzled by Richard's good cheer. 'Is all well?'

'Things couldn't be better.' Richard's grin widened. 'Trouble is brewing.'

'Trouble?' Estienne frowned, wondering if he'd misheard. 'Forgive me, my lord, but I fail to see how that would be a cause for celebration.'

Richard leaned in close. 'War is coming, Estienne. A chance for glory. For honour. For men like us to prove our worth.'

'War? With whom?'

Ilbert scoffed, shaking his head. 'God's bones, Wace. Do you pay no attention to the world around you? With the French, of course.'

'King Philip has moved against John's territories in France,' Richard explained more patiently. 'And there are some closer to home who would see John overthrown entirely. But never fear. His Grace intends to take the fight right to Philip's door.'

'You mean...?'

Richard's smile was fierce. 'The king will take his army to France. And we, dear Estienne, shall ride at his side.'

Estienne's head spun with the implications. A chance to see real battle, to win renown on the field of honour. It was all he had dreamed of since first taking up a sword.

'But why now? What has driven the king to this course? I thought King John had made peace with the Pope and driven off the French threat.'

'Despite Willem Longsword's victory over his fleet at Damme, Philip remains undeterred. Even now he masses his forces, bent on seizing all the king's fiefs held in vassalage from the French Crown.'

'But surely the Pope—'

'The Pope will do nothing. Even though he and King John have put aside their differences, His Holiness turns a blind eye to Philip's ambition.'

Estienne frowned. 'Then why has this not come to open war already if King Philip is so brazen in his intent?'

'The destruction of his fleet cost him dearly. It bought us some respite, but Philip has used that time to gather new strength. He has already marched on Flanders, Estienne. He will not stop there.'

'And the king means to stop him before his conquests can begin in earnest?'

Richard nodded grimly. 'John cannot allow such naked aggression to stand unanswered. To do so would be to invite further challenge, both from France and England. He must respond with decisive strength. He must show the world the English lion still has claws.'

A tingle raced down Estienne's spine at the prospect of what might be. 'Perhaps, then, I might be given the chance to stand at your side, as you lead the charge.'

Ilbert barked a harsh laugh. 'Stand at his side? What good is a squire on the field other than to fetch new lances?'

'Ilbert.' Richard's voice was low and serious, reminding Estienne of his father Earl William. 'There will be glory enough for all of us. But our enemy may not be only the French. There are some closer to home who would see John deposed.'

'Men in England?' Estienne asked.

'Aye.' Ilbert's face was grim, all trace of mockery fled. 'There are barons who whisper that John is unfit to rule. That England would fare better with a different head beneath the crown.'

'Who are they?' Estienne asked. 'Surely the king knows of their treachery?'

'Oh, he knows. But the rot runs deep. Some carry great influence, and the king must tread carefully.'

'The ringleader is there,' Richard said, nodding toward the far side of the courtyard. 'Robert FitzWalter. A pious man, or so he'd have the world believe. In truth, he's a viper, ever whispering poisonous words to his fellow barons.'

Across the courtyard stood a tall, hawkish man in a surcoat of yellow, cut across with a red line, chevrons above and below. He made for an imposing figure, even among this esteemed gathering. All lean strength and coiled power, like a wolf among dogs.

'Then why does the king not act against him?' Estienne frowned. 'Surely such treachery warrants the dungeon or the block?'

'Were it so simple,' Ilbert said. 'FitzWalter has powerful friends. Lands, coin, men sworn to his banner. To move against him risks open rebellion.'

'And there are others who share his views,' Richard added grimly. 'To crush him now would be to risk martyring him to his cause. Perhaps even drive the waverers firmly into his arms.'

'Then no wonder the king is so eager to prove his strength.' Understanding dawned cold in Estienne's gut. 'He must deter those who would seize his crown.'

'Just so.' Richard replied. 'And we shall be the instruments of that deterrent, God willing. I tell you, Estienne, I am half mad with impatience to cross the sea and come to grips with the French. To feel the press of the enemy, the thunder of hooves.'

A shiver chased down Estienne's spine. Real battle was still a stranger to him, but he knew, with certainty, that he wanted it. Wanted to prove himself, alongside Richard and Ilbert and the other knights, and strike back against the king's foes.

'I would be there too,' he heard himself say. 'If Earl William would allow it.'

Richard studied Estienne with an appraising eye. For a long moment he said nothing, and Estienne felt his cheeks heating at his own folly, to invite himself to the king's war. Who was he, to fight alongside men like Richard Marshal? He was no noble, no knight. Only a farm boy aping the manners of his betters.

He dropped his gaze, mumbling, 'That is... I mean, I know it's not my place...'

Richard reached out to nudge up his chin. 'It is a good thought and shows great heart. Come, let us put it to my lord father. I would be glad to have you at my side.'

Hope blossomed fiercely as Richard steered him across the courtyard. He tried to squash it, tried to stifle the wild surge of need. The Marshal was a fair and generous master, but even he would surely balk at sending his rawest squire to war.

They found Earl William in quiet conference with two other knights. At his son's approach he broke off, turning to cast an enquiring look over them.

'Richard. Estienne. What would you have of me?'

Richard bowed. 'Father, I would beg a boon of you. I wish Estienne to accompany me as my squire on the king's campaign to France.'

'Estienne? He is green as spring grass, and you would take him to battle?'

'He is ready, Father,' Richard insisted. 'He has strength, skill and courage. And he will have me to watch over him. As you know, there is no finer teacher than experience.'

The frown deepened as William wrestled with his doubts. Eventually, he heaved a sigh.

'Very well. I entrust him to you, Richard. See that he learns, and comes to no harm.'

It was all Estienne had dreamed of, and yet now that it was upon him he felt the first stirrings of fear. Nevertheless, he bowed to his master. 'Thank you, my lord. I swear I shall not disappoint.'

The Marshal gave him a long, searching look. 'See that you don't, lad. And make sure you come back in one piece.'

They left him then, Richard clapping Estienne heartily on the back as he steered him away.

'You'll do well, I know it. We'll make a knight of you yet.'

Estienne could only nod, his throat tight with emotion. Knight or squire, it mattered not to him. All he wanted was the chance to prove himself, to be forged and tempered in the heat of battle. To finally earn his place among these men.

PART TWO: A LION IN SHEEP'S CLOTH

FRANCE, 1214 AD

9

Estienne slumped in his saddle, swaying with the motion of his palfrey's plodding gait. Beside him, Richard rode with bowed shoulders, his face drawn and pale beneath the shadow of his hood. Concern gnawed at him as Estienne studied his friend. Richard had been flagging for days now, a wracking cough rattling his lungs, his brow slick with fevered sweat. But there was no respite to be had, no time to tend to sickness. Not with the French hounds baying at their heels.

If only Earl William was here, or even Guillaume, but both had been tasked by King John to defend the Marches from the trouble-some Welsh. Estienne could only hope his lord fared better against King Llywelyn than John did against the French.

Their campaign had begun with such promise. A congregation of dukes and barons flocking to the king's cause. They had landed at La Rochelle in February, spirits high, flush with visions of glorious conquest. Allies had joined them as they marched inland – Hugh of Lusignan, Herve of Nevers, bringing armies of their own, swelling their ranks and lending steel to their cause. The road to Anjou had lain open before them, ripe for the taking.

If only it had been that simple.

Months of hard campaigning had stripped the gilt from Estienne's dreams of chivalrous combat, leaving only the brutal truth beneath. What he had seen would forever be seared into his mind. Villages put to the torch, peasants raped and butchered, babes impaled on the points of lances. War in all its savage horror, unmatched by tales or tourneys.

The wounded haunted him most. Men with shattered bones jutting through skin, limbs hewn away, entrails spilling into the mud. Each night their howls raked the air, the rotting stink of them thick in his nostrils. This was the grim reality the troubadours never sang of. The part of warfare that was drenched in piss, shit and bile-inducing agony.

Estienne knew he would carry those images to his grave. There was no honour here, no matter how his betters tried to paint it. Only an endless mire of misery and death.

It had become a deadly dance between their army and Philip's. Lunging and feinting, seeking an opening to strike a mortal blow. When King John moved to besiege La Roche-aux-Moine, Estienne had thought it would be their chance to dig in, to make a stalwart stand. But King Philip's whelp, Prince Louis, had other ideas. Marching to relieve the garrison, his forces fell upon John's army like a hammer on an anvil.

And now they ran, tails tucked like whipped curs, while the French bayed for their blood. Estienne could almost feel their breath on his neck, hot and hungry, ready to tear out his throat. Overhead, carrion crows wheeled against a dull sky, drawn by the prospect of new flesh.

No, this was not the glorious crusade Richard had promised. It was a scrambling flight, a slaughter waiting to happen. And the wolves were at their heels, gaining ground with every passing day.

Ahead, Ilbert rode with squared shoulders beneath his surcoat, the red wyvern of his house emblazoned upon his pennon as it billowed in the wind. Marshal's favour had seen him knighted before they set out, though Estienne thought it an honour ill-deserved. Knowing Ilbert, he likely revelled in the brutality around them and the licence to vent his cruel urges without consequence. He had the bearing of a knight now, to be sure. The trappings and airs, puffed up like a preening cockerel. But stripped of pageantry, Estienne suspected his heart was that of a carrion-eater – black and bloated, glutted on the suffering of the fallen.

A wet, rattling cough drew his eye to Richard. Estienne's heart sank at the sight of him, wan and glassy-eyed atop his destrier. How long had that fever ravaged him? Days? A week? In the chaos of their flight, Estienne had lost track. And still Richard pushed on, never slowing, never complaining. If only they could rest and tend to him properly, but such luxury was denied them. All Estienne could do was watch his friend wither as they continued their flight from the French.

Beside him, Richard suddenly wavered like a puppet with cut strings. His head lolled forward, chin nudging his chest.

'Richard?' Estienne urged his palfrey closer. 'Are you all right?'

'Fine. I'm... fine.' Richard sounded anything but, and the lie rang hollow even as it left his lips.

Estienne opened his mouth to argue, but Ilbert beat him to it.

'For God's sake, Wace, stop clucking over him like an old maid.'

'His welfare is my charge, FitzDane. So I'll cluck as I see fit.'

Richard lifted his head. 'Enough... the both of you...'

The rest was lost as he convulsed, retching bile over his saddle. His face went slack, eyes rolling back to white, as he slid from his mount and hit the ground, sprawling like a broken doll.

Estienne flung himself from the saddle and scrambled to Richard's side. There he fell to hands and knees.

'Richard, look at me. Look at me.'

He loosened the cloak about Richard's neck, then placed a hand to his cheek. Beneath his palm, Richard's skin blazed like a forge and was sheened with sweat.

'Help me.' Estienne cast about wildly. 'I need a surgeon.'

Eventually a figure stumbled through the milling soldiers, satchel bumping at his hip. He dropped to his knees at Richard's side, reaching to pry back an eyelid and press practised fingers to his sodden brow.

'His fever's peaked,' the surgeon muttered. 'He cannot ride like this.'

'We can't just leave him.'

Ilbert's face was marred by worry, most likely for himself. 'We have to. The French are too close. If we linger...' He let the implication hang.

Estienne clenched his fists. Ilbert would leave his own sworn brother to die. Abandon him like so much baggage to save his own misbegotten hide.

'No. We will not leave him here.' He surged to his feet, rounding on Ilbert with bared teeth. 'Get a cart. Now.'

'Watch your tone, squire. You don't command me.'

Estienne stepped closer, forcing Ilbert to look right at him. 'How do you think Earl William would greet the news that you left his son to the French? That you fled like a craven while Richard lay helpless?'

For a long moment, Ilbert looked as if he might argue, but he soon saw the futility in it. With a last venomous glare, he marched away, barking orders to the milling men-at-arms.

Estienne sank to his knees at Richard's side, reaching to clasp his limp hand. Regret choked him, thick and cloying as marsh-fog.

'I'm sorry. I'm sorry, Richard. I failed. I should have seen how ill you were. I should have...'

He trailed off as Richard's eyes fluttered open. They were glassy and fever-bright, but there was recognition there.

'No.' The word was a thin rasp, barely audible. 'No, Estienne. I'm the one who's sorry. I brought you here... to this hell. Not what I promised. You deserve... better...'

'Hush.' Estienne tightened his grip on Richard's hand. 'Save your strength. I'll get you home, you hear me? I'll get you back safe. I swear it.'

A clatter of wheels made him look up. Ilbert had returned, pulling a rough-hewn cart trundling in his wake. He halted it by Richard's prone form.

'Well?' he snapped. 'Are you going to help me get him in, or not?'

Estienne bit back his retort as he stood. They heaved Richard into the cart as carefully as they could, as he lolled like a rag doll. Once they'd hitched Estienne's horse to the yoke, he clambered up to kneel at Richard's side, one hand braced on his chest, feeling its stuttering rise and fall.

'Just rest now. I'll take care of everything. I swear it.'

The words rang hollow, but he had to believe them. Had to cling to that slender thread of hope, even as the French hounds bayed at their back. One way or another, he would see Richard safe.

10

The road stretched out behind them in an endless trail. Estienne's arse ached from days of sitting in the cart, riding along road after wearying road. Richard lay in the back, his face sheened with sweat, lips cracked and pale. The fever had broken, thank God, but he was still weak as a lamb, drifting in and out of fitful sleep.

Estienne glanced over his shoulder for the hundredth time, half-expecting to see French banners cresting the rise, sunlight glinting off a thousand blades as they howled for English blood, but there was only the empty road.

Up ahead, Ilbert rode with his shoulders hunched. He'd hardly said a word since they'd veered off the main road. When they had fallen behind the bulk of King John's army it had seemed a sensible thing to do. They had managed to avoid the pursuing French all right, but now they were hopelessly lost in the middle of the countryside with no friends and the potential for ambush all around.

Richard shifted in the cart, mumbling something unintelligible. Estienne leaned over to adjust the cloak covering him.

'Just rest,' he murmured. 'I'll get you to safety, I swear it. Just hold on a little longer.'

Richard made no reply, lost to the depths of his dreams and Estienne fought down the panic clawing at him. They had to find help, and soon. He didn't know how much longer Richard could endure this bone-shaking journey.

As if in answer to his desperate prayers, Ilbert reined up sharply at the top of a rise, twisting in his saddle. 'Wace, look.'

Estienne squinted through the sun's glare in the direction Ilbert was pointing, and his heart leapt at the sight before him.

There, nestled in the lee of a green valley, was a village. Thin plumes of woodsmoke drifted from crooked chimneys, and in the distance he could hear the faint clang of a blacksmith's hammer and the lowing of cattle, but it was the banners snapping in the breeze that he noticed.

'Whose colours are those?'

Ilbert leaned forward in his saddle. 'Otto of Brunswick. Ferrand of Flanders too, if I'm not mistaken. And that, there... Renaud of Boulogne. King John's allies.'

Estienne felt hope blossom in his chest. Surely they would find aid and shelter there, a chance to rest and let Richard heal.

He urged the weary horse forward. 'Come on then. Let's not keep them waiting.'

The hamlet was alive with activity as they made their way through. Men-at-arms bustled about the place, as smiths hammered at dented helms and notched swords, the ringing of their anvils near-deafening. Squires brushed mud from their masters' hauberks, while stable hands led destriers to water.

Everywhere Estienne looked, he saw the grim industry of war. It clung to the village like a feverish sweat. These men were preparing for battle, and soon.

A hard-faced soldier in a stained gambeson intercepted them

before they'd gone a dozen paces, his hand resting on the hilt of his sword.

'Hold there, and state your business.'

Ilbert looked down his nose at the man-at-arms. 'I am Ilbert FitzDane, knight in the service of—'

'I don't give a tinker's balls if you're the Virgin Mary herself,' the man growled. 'This is encampment to the Holy Roman Emperor, not a wayside inn. Now state your business or piss off.'

Ilbert's face darkened, but before he could unleash his churlish tongue, Estienne stepped forward. 'Please, we are in desperate need of aid. My companion, Richard Marshal, is gravely ill. He is the son of Earl William Marshal, the king's own man. We only seek a place to rest and heal.'

At the mention of William Marshal's name, the soldier's gruff demeanour wavered. He leaned forward, peering into the cart where Richard lay pale and shivering beneath his cloak.

He let out a low whistle. 'Poor bastard looks half a corpse.'

Estienne swallowed down his sudden annoyance at the man's disregard. 'We've ridden hard and long to escape the French. Will you grant us shelter?'

The man-at-arms scratched his stubbled jaw, looking between Estienne's pleading face and Richard's gaunt visage. Finally, he gave a curt nod.

'Willem Longsword holds command here. The Earl of Salisbury will want to know of Ser Richard's condition.'

Relief bloomed in Estienne's gut. 'God bless you. If you could show us to—'

'There's a tent at the end of the row should serve.' The man jerked his chin toward a line of shabby canvas structures. 'Get your lordling settled. I'll inform the earl you're here.'

With that, he strode off, shouting for a camp boy to attend him.

'Charming fellow,' Ilbert drawled.

Estienne paid him no mind as he focused on the small, shabby tent that promised rest. Clicking his tongue, he urged the horse onward, Richard's shallow breaths rasping loud in his ears.

Inside, the tent was thick with the scent of unwashed men. Estienne wrinkled his nose as he and Ilbert carried Richard to the crude pallet in the corner. It was little more than a pile of musty straw stuffed into a moth-eaten sack, but it would have to serve. In short order they had unloaded the cart of their scant belongings lest they be pilfered by camp followers, and piled them in one corner.

Richard groaned as Estienne knelt by his side. 'Easy. You're safe now.'

'Where...?' Richard's voice was a thin whisper.

'A village in the middle of nowhere. The king's allies are mustered here. We've found sanctuary, of a sort.'

Richard huffed a laugh that turned into a wince. 'Some sanctuary. Smells like a privy.'

'Don't worry, my lord. Once you're well, we'll have you back in a down-stuffed bed quick enough.'

'Your confidence is heartening,' Richard said, a smile plucking at his chapped lips.

'Rest now,' Estienne said, pulling the moth-eaten blanket up to Richard's chin. 'Regain your strength. The worst is surely behind us.'

Estienne heard a scoffing grunt and looked up to see Ilbert silhouetted against the pale sunlight.

'You're a half-wit if you truly believe that,' he said.

Estienne felt his hackles rising, and not for the first time. 'What do you mean?'

Ilbert gestured sharply toward the ordered chaos of the camp. 'Are you dumb? Use the piss-puddle between your ears. They're mustering for war.'

Estienne's heart sank as the implication settled in. 'You think the French are close?'

'Of course they bloody are. We've been running for days, only to arrive right on their doorstep.'

Estienne looked down at Richard's pale, slack face, and felt his blood run cold. They couldn't move him again, not in this state. If battle found them here...

The heavy tread of mailed feet jolted Estienne from his grim reflection. A shadow fell across the tent flap before someone ducked inside. The man who faced them was tall and broad-shouldered, his sorrel hair streaked with grey, his bearded face creased in a grim greeting.

Estienne hastily ducked his head in a bow as he recognised Willem Longsword. 'My Lord, we—'

The Earl of Salisbury ignored him, moving to Richard's pallet. 'Damn, boy. You've gotten yourself in the shit, haven't you?'

Richard cracked a sorry smile. 'Just a... summer cold, I fear.'

Willem looked at Estienne. 'What ails him?'

'Fever, my lord. It's been raging for days now. This is the most lucid he's been.'

Willem grunted, one meaty hand brushing Richard's sweat-slick brow. 'He needs a surgeon and a proper bed. I'll have a word with Otto's camp master, get you settled.'

'Your lordship is too kind, but you shouldn't trouble yourself. We can manage here.'

'Manage? In this shithouse? Not bloody likely. If word gets back to William Marshal that I let his sick son wallow in a dung-pit, I'll never hear the end of it.'

Estienne opened his mouth to stammer his thanks, but Willem was already turning to Ilbert.

'And you are?'

Ilbert's chest puffed up as he tried to stand like an equal next to the Longsword, but he failed miserably. 'Ser Ilbert FitzDane, milord.'

'Knight, eh? Well, I hope you're not sick too. The French are close. Philip Augustus marches right at us. We'll not be avoiding a fight this time.'

Ilbert leaned forward. 'When do we engage them?'

'Soon. Otto wants Philip's head on a spike, the arrogant prick. Thinks he can piss in the Pope's eye and get away with it. We'll show him what it means to fuck with King John.' Then he turned to Estienne. 'You. Stay with Richard. See him well.'

Estienne bowed again. 'As you command, Earl Willem.'

'Good lad. Now I must see to marshalling the men. I'll have someone find Richard better lodgings.' Then he turned to Ilbert. 'And I'll see you on the field.'

With a last appraising look at Richard's fever-bright face, he ducked out of the tent. No sooner had Willem's shadow vanished from the tent flap than Ilbert rounded on Estienne, grin stretching wide and vicious.

'Glory awaits.' he crowed. 'To hear Willem speak, Philip himself leads this rabble. And the Holy Roman Emperor rides to meet him. Songs will be sung of this day.'

Estienne glanced down at Richard's lax face, feeling a sudden wild recklessness seize him. 'Let me fight in Richard's stead. We have his arms and armour. His destrier, too. Were I to don his trappings no one would know the difference.'

For a single heartbeat, the idea hung between them. Then Ilbert's face twisted into laughter. 'You? A squire, riding to war in a knight's trappings? Don't make me laugh.'

Estienne felt anger and humiliation swelling in equal measure. 'I've trained for this. I can hold my own.'

'As a page, maybe. Mucking stalls and fetching wine. What do you know of true battle, boy? You'd shame yourself and your betters. Maybe get some good men killed into the bargain.'

Estienne trembled with a fury that threatened to tear its way out of him and make a ragged ruin of Ilbert's sneering face. Sensing he'd struck a nerve, Ilbert pressed his advantage, baring his teeth in a wolfish grin.

'Know your place and tend Richard, like the little wetnurse you are. Maybe try teasing a bit of milk from your tit while you're at it.'

It was all Estienne could do not to fly at Ilbert and crack his head against the tent pole. But the ugly truth was, Ilbert was right. He was a squire. A nobody. And no one would allow him to stand in a knight's place, no matter how dire the need.

Drawing in a shuddering breath, he glared his defiance into Ilbert's smirking face. 'Go then. Do your duty. And I will do mine.'

Ilbert offered a long, measuring look, then he was gone. In the suffocating stillness of the tent, Estienne stood trembling, his fury raking his innards like talons.

He could fight. He *would* fight. And damn what Ilbert FitzDane or anyone else had to say about it.

A low moan broke him from his black thoughts, and he turned to see Richard tossing on the pallet, sweat beading his ashen brow. Estienne was at his side in a heartbeat, hands smoothing that tangled mane back from fever-hot skin.

'Rest easy. I am here.'

If his friend heard him, he gave no sign, lost once more to delirium.

Richard's gear was piled haphazardly in the corner, hauberk glinting dully, surcoat bearing the Marshal's lion, snarling its defiance.

No, Estienne would not ask permission. He was done being the dutiful squire, content with scraps. This was his chance to show the world and Ilbert both what he was made of. What kind of knight he could be, given half a chance.

11

Richard lay on a pallet in the corner, his face pale and sheened with sweat, but his breathing was deep and even. Estienne knelt at his friend's side, reaching out to brush lank hair back from his brow. Still too warm, but no longer blazing like a forge.

'I'll be back soon,' Estienne murmured.

Richard made no reply, lost to the depths of sleep. Estienne rose to his feet and crossed to the door of the tiny cottage secured for them by the Earl of Salisbury. Ilbert had already left just before dawn, without a word. Estienne should have said a prayer for the fledgling knight, but couldn't bring himself. Better he say prayers for himself since he was about to fling himself into the same crucible.

With some trouble, he had bedecked himself in gambeson and mail hauberk, securing schynbalds at his lower legs. He also wore the surcoat of the Marshal household, bold with the red lion rampant. Though younger, Estienne was already of a height with Richard, and all had fitted him well, if a little loosely. Richard's sword was buckled at his side, comfortable on his hip, but his hands were clammy as he reached for the helm.

This was madness, and he knew it. If anyone discovered him, surely he'd be punished for daring to don the arms of the Marshal's son. But he had to do this. He'd come too far to turn back now. To prove to himself more than just a farmer's boy.

With a deep breath, he set the helm over his head, feeling the world contract around him, narrowing his vision to a thin slot. His breath was loud in the confines, tasting of steel and leather and his own fear-sour sweat, but when he opened the door, his spine was iron. He was as ready as he'd ever be.

The path outside the cottage was deserted, the village emptied of life with no one remaining to witness his misdeed, and yet still his heart hammered against his ribs as he made his way to the stable. The destrier whickered a greeting as he approached, tossing its proud head. It was a fierce beast trained for war and the finest horse he'd ever seen, all rippling muscle and gleaming coat. It pawed the ground as he grasped the saddle, eager to be away. Eager for blood.

'Easy,' Estienne murmured, gathering the reins. 'Easy now.'

The horse blew out a breath as he swung astride, feeling the power of it beneath him. A final breath to steady himself, and he touched heels to its flanks. The destrier bolted, and Estienne let out a yell as they thundered out of the stable in a spray of straw. He crouched low over the horse's neck, feeling the bunch and surge of muscle between his thighs. His blood sang with a fierce, wild joy. All he had trained for, all he had dreamed of, and now it was upon him.

Swiftly his mount ate up the league or so he had to travel, before he found them. The land fell away into a broad basin, and there they lay, spread across the plain like a great, glittering serpent – thousands strong, the hosts of England and France drawn up against one another in battle array.

The sun flashed off the panoply of war, banners fluttering in the wind. At the centre of the English ranks, he saw footmen massed in a bristling briar, their spearpoints gleaming. Before them, a great wagon loomed, draped in gold. Atop it, a carved dragon twined about a pole, wings half-spread, serpentine head thrust forward. Above the dragon, an eagle with wings of beaten gold. The imperial standard of Otto, Holy Roman Emperor.

To the left and right, the mounted knights, all aglitter in their heraldic splendour, lances raised, pennons asnap. Estienne squinted, picking out sigils and blazons, spotting the six lions rampant of the Earl of Salisbury among the throng.

And beyond them, across that trampled plain... the French. Their numbers consumed the horizon. A steel-fanged tide, bright with their own banners.

Estienne reined in at the fringes of the right flank, letting the destrier find its place in the line. He could feel the tension in the other knights around him, the creak of leather, the champ of steel bits. Scanning the ranks he looked for that familiar blazon with the red wyvern rampant. Ilbert was here somewhere, spoiling for blood, and Estienne had no wish to cross his path now. Best to avoid his scrutiny and blend with the faceless host.

As he sat, a flag was raised at the front of the French host. It was such a simple thing – a length of scarlet silk, rippling like blood on the wind.

'What is that?' asked one of the knights nearby.

'The Oriflamme,' replied another. 'The French king's battle-banner.'

'It looks a paltry thing.'

'It's not what it looks like,' the knight replied grimly. 'It's what it means. No quarter. No prisoners.'

Estienne's hands tightened on reins and lance.

A figure was riding before the French lines, garbed in a surcoat of azure, blazoned with golden fleurs-de-lys. The crown he wore spoke that this must be King Philip himself, tall and fierce atop a pale destrier.

The French ranks rippled as he passed, men brandishing their arms as he bellowed at them, stirring them into a battle ardour. Estienne strained to make out his words, but the wind whipped them to shreds. The cadence was enough. Strident, exhorting. A warlord, rousing his troops for the slaughter.

Estienne realised he was trembling, a cold sweat prickling his skin. He dragged in a shuddering breath, trying to master himself as Philip cantered to take his place beneath the Oriflamme. The French lances made a steel thicket, bright in the sun. Waiting. Watching.

Then a trumpet blast shattered the silence, wild and brazen.

A wedge of horsemen broke from the French vanguard and thundered across the space between the armies, manes and tails streaming, hooves churning the earth. They were not armed as knights, but as men-at-arms. Most likely mercenaries come to claim their stake.

Estienne gripped the reins as he stared at the oncoming horde. A hundred fifty, two hundred, screaming their war cries, brandishing their swords and maces with wild abandon.

He braced for the clash, expecting the English knights on the left to wheel and meet the charge, but the flank held its ground. They couched their lances, locked their shields. The mercenaries swept down on them in a black tide and the lines met with a crash. The snap of lances, the crunch of impact. Splinters flew. Horses reared and screamed.

The mercenaries battered against the shield wall like hail on a keep roof. Mad, savage. Estienne wanted to look away but couldn't as the English battered their attackers, driving them back. Blades hacked down, crunching through mail and bone. Horses fell thrashing, spilling their riders.

In heartbeats, it was over. The last few mercenaries wheeled away in ragged retreat, harried by laughter and jeers. They left their dead and dying heaped before the shield wall, leaking their lifeblood into the muck.

Bile stung Estienne's gullet. This was nothing like the tales. Nothing like the sweet songs spun to gentle lutes. This was a reeking charnel house... and it was just beginning.

The French were already reforming. Grim men on tall destriers, couching their lances. Pennons and banners flying with pride. Dozens of proud sigils, borne by killers ahorse.

'Here they come,' someone said, as the enemy knights began their advance.

A clarion call from down the line, clear and piercing, shattering the hush. Estienne saw a detachment of knights spur forward from the centre of the English ranks. As one they advanced, from trot to canter to gallop until they thundered across the plain, closing the distance to the French in a clatter of hooves and ringing of harness.

The lines smashed together with a crash like thunder. Estienne flinched at the impact as lances splintered, spraying shards. Shields cracked. Horses reared, lashing out with iron-shod hooves. The bellowing of men and beasts rent the air in an unholy din. Riderless horses bolted through the crush, mad with terror. The lines heaved like a sea in storm, roiling and seething. Blades hacked and thrust, ringing from helms and shields.

It was a melee now. The savage, swirling dance of cavalry in close quarters. Bludgeoning with sword hilts when their blades snapped. Grappling, hacking, locked in that intimate brutality.

Estienne watched, transfixed. He felt sick down to his bones, shaken by the sheer murderous clamour of it. So much hate and fury, unleashed in reckless abandon. Men united in only one desire... to kill.

And yet, beneath the horror, something stirred in him. A yearning to be out there, amidst the slaughter. To add his blade to that heaving chaos.

As if in answer to that need, a horn blared, wild and fierce, rising above the din. Estienne twisted in his saddle as the Earl of Salisbury cantered along their line.

'Make ready!' roared the Longsword. 'Prepare to charge! For God and England!'

'For God and England!' The bellow rose from every throat, shrill with bloodlust.

Estienne joined his voice to the chorus, fear and exhilaration twisting in his gut like serpents. He gripped his lance, the weight of it suddenly alien and unwieldy, his focus fixed on the heaving carnage ahead.

'Charge!'

The order cracked across the line like a whip. Estienne tensed, teeth gritted. The destrier sensed his agitation, prancing sideways, coat slick.

'Charge! For England!'

A roar from a hundred throats. The knights to Estienne's flank surged forward in a rattle of harness, destriers leaping into a gallop. He was swept along, caught in the tide as the ground shook with the rumble of hooves.

The plain flashed by in a blur. Enemy knights milled ahead. Fifty paces. Thirty. Twenty. He could see their faces, contorted and snarling. His own face ached with tension, a rictus grin of mingled dread and exultation. He felt drunk with it. Mad with it.

He couched his lance. Braced in the stirrups, angling for a blood-smeared shield, a crosshatch of gouges ruining the gilt paintwork.

Estienne screamed a wordless challenge...

Impact.

The lance struck like a hammer, punching the air from his lungs. Splinters exploded, his shoulder wrenched with the force. The French knight reeled back, nearly torn from the saddle. Estienne had one glimpse of bulging eyes and flying spittle before he galloped past and into the fray.

All was turmoil, a seething morass of steel and struggling bodies. The screams of men and horses melded into one unholy clamour. Lances shattered, spraying needles of wood. Swords rang on helms and mail. The stench of blood and piss and shit clogged the air.

Estienne dropped his ruined lance. Drew his sword with a hiss of steel. Hacked at a jostling press of men, aiming at eyes, at exposed flesh, the shock of impact numbing his arm.

A French knight loomed, blade swinging. Estienne caught the downstroke on his shield, the oak shuddering, pain lancing up his arm. He bellowed, hacking back, baring his teeth and snarling at the knight's contorted face.

Then his horse bolted, rearing and bucking as a spear stabbed at its haunch. Estienne clung on desperately as he was wrenched away, losing sight of his foe. He burst free of the press into a pocket of clear ground, the warhorse galloping wildly, half-maddened with pain and terror. Estienne wrestled it around, fighting to regain control. His sword felt heavy, arm numb from elbow to fingertips. His shield hung on broken straps, the proud lion rampant of the Marshal all but obliterated.

He blinked stinging sweat and tried to steady the bucking, heaving beast. All around, the battle raged. A hellscape of blood and brutality. Overhead, carrion birds wheeled and screamed, waiting for their glut of flesh.

This was madness. This was hell. How could men be so steeped in senseless savagery? So eager to butcher their fellow man?

'Death!' A shout rose above the din. 'Death to the French!'

Estienne turned towards the voice, seeing a knight, unhorsed and brandishing a notched sword. He waved it with abandon, caught up in his own battle lust, but it did not stop the enemy. They came from nowhere, falling upon the hapless knight like wolves. As one wrenched the helm from his head, another plunged in a dagger to his throat. Then more came, hacking the man till his cries fell silent, frenzied in their labours.

Estienne stared in horror, the world skewing around him. He fought the urge to retch inside his helm, no wish to drown in his own vomit.

A trumpet blast shocked him back to grim reality. He whipped around to see a French knight bearing down on him, lance couched for a lethal strike. Estienne had a fleeting impression of a snarling wolf's-head crest, a surcoat of red on black. Then the lance tip filled his vision, steel hungering for his heart.

He wrenched his shield up and the lance struck with a sickening crunch. The force of it sent him reeling back in the saddle, his already-battered shield exploding. The destrier reared wildly, forelegs pawing at the air. Estienne lost his balance, tumbling backwards over the cantle, and slammed to the ground.

For a moment he could only lie there, stunned. The world was a muffled haze as if he were sunk in deep water. He stared up at the wheeling sky, tasting blood.

Instinct forced him aside a scant heartbeat ahead of thudding hooves. A knight leapt his destrier over Estienne's prone form, whooping a war cry. Then he was past and gone, consumed among the melee.

Estienne dragged himself to his knees and spat blood inside his helm. He groped for his sword, numb fingers fumbling at the quillons, just as a shadow fell over him. A man-at-arms loomed, clad in mail with an open-faced helm, axe clenched in one meaty fist.

'Yield, dog.' A thick French accent, voice harsh. 'Or I'll rip out your bowels and strangle you with them.'

Estienne staggered to his feet. His head swam, but he would not yield. Could not. Instead, he raised his blade in mute challenge, and the man-at-arms laughed, an ugly bark.

He came on in a rush, axe whirling. Estienne caught the heavy blow on his sword and staggered, barely bringing the blade back to guard before the axe fell again.

Clang. Clang. Overhand chops, brutal and strong as a woodsman hewing logs. Estienne gave ground, teeth gritted as each thunderous stroke drove him backwards. He couldn't last long like this. Already his arm ached, his shoulder screaming with each desperate parry.

The man-at-arms was relentless, lips peeled back in a rictus snarl. Estienne concentrated on that whirling axe-head, doing all he could to avoid its bite. He dodged aside on pure instinct, the axe slamming down where he'd stood a scant heartbeat before.

Estienne lurched forward, throwing everything into a desperate lunge. His sword punched into the man's throat, just above the mail, parting flesh like butter, grating on bone. Hot blood sprayed, drenching Estienne's mailed fist as the man's eyes bulged in their sockets, his mouth gaping, spilling scarlet. That axe tumbled from nerveless fingers, thudding to the churned earth, and his hands clutched at the steel sprouting from his throat. Then he slumped to his knees before toppling sideways.

Estienne's blade tore free with a gristly sound, and he could only gape at the corpse sprawled before him, leaking its lifeblood into the mud. He had done that. Killed a man. Snuffed the life from him, quick as blowing out a candle-flame.

His head swam and he was suddenly on his knees, bracing himself on his sword, the point sinking into the muck. He retched helplessly, struggling to breathe.

'Fall back! Fall back to the standard!'

The cry jolted Estienne from his stupor. He raised his head, blinking through the narrow slit of his visor. All around, English knights milled, their ranks ragged, lances splintered and shields cracked as they were harried from all sides by whooping French.

He staggered to his feet, gulping air, struggling to make sense of the madness. They were being pushed back. Herded like cattle and scattering before the French advance. Through the seething press, he caught a glimpse of blue and gold – the Earl of Salisbury's standard, with its six lions rampant. It dipped and swayed as Willem Longsword battled beneath it and French knights swarmed him like dogs on a bear.

Estienne lurched forward, numb feet stumbling. He tried to raise his sword, intending to fight his way to Longsword's side, but it was no use. The press was too thick, the French tide too strong. He could only watch helplessly as Willem Longsword was dragged from his saddle, and hauled off through the melee.

Estienne felt something break inside him. They were lost. Scattered and leaderless...

'Wace? Is that you?'

A gauntleted hand grasped his shoulder, wrenching him around. He found himself staring into a pair of wild blue eyes, set in a narrow, blood-smeared face. Ilbert, panting, his helm gone, mail coif askew.

'Have you lost your mind?' Ilbert roared over the din. 'What are you doing in Richard's arms? I ordered you to stay with him.'

Estienne blinked, still reeling. 'I... I had to... had to fight...'

'You disobeyed me.' Ilbert's snarl was pure venom.

Anger surged, blotting out the horror as Estienne twisted free of Ilbert's grip. 'We don't have time for this. The French—'

'Damn the French,' Ilbert snarled. 'I should cut you down myself for this insult.'

A horn-blast split the air, long and mournful, rising above the fray. The signal for retreat. Ilbert's head whipped around as he recognised the sound. Then he pushed Estienne away, turning, seizing the reins of a wayward destrier, its flanks lathered with sweat and blood. He swung astride in a clatter of armour, wrenching the horse's head around.

'Ilbert.' Estienne stumbled after him, reaching out. 'Wait.'

FitzDane ignored him, digging in his spurs, the destrier leaping into a gallop. He vanished into the milling chaos, leaving Estienne alone amidst the carnage.

The French surged around him, baying like predators scenting blood, drunk on imminent victory. Estienne raised his sword in a pitiful attempt at guard. Knowing it was futile, but still he stood his ground. He would not turn craven now. He was Estienne Wace. Squire to William Marshal himself. He would die with courage, even as the wolves tore out his throat.

The French men-at-arms closed in, blades thirsting. Estienne braced his own to meet them, a defiant snarl on his lips.

'Look here.' One jabbed at him with a sword-tip. 'A lost lamb, crying for his mother.'

Rough laughter, the press of bodies tightening. Estienne hissed through clenched teeth, slashing out with his blade. A pitiful defiance that only made them cackle all the harder.

'Oh, he's got some spit,' shouted another. 'Let's stick him like the pig he is.'

'Aye, cut his gizzard!' Another, this one clutching a notched axe. 'Spill his guts for the dogs to fight over!'

They lunged as one, blades flashing. Estienne caught the first on his sword, staggering back. More hacked at him and he parried desperately, steel clanging, each brutal impact nearly wrenching the sword from his grip. He flailed. Hacked blindly. His arms ached and the breath sawed in his throat, but he would not yield. He would die as a—

'Hold!'

The bellow cracked across the clamour. The men-at-arms froze, blades raised. Estienne sagged, gulping air, as a figure strode through the press, clad in a surcoat of red and white.

'This one is mine,' the knight pronounced from behind his helm.

Estienne took another gulp of air, before raising the sword that now felt heavy as a log. Nevertheless, he faced the approaching knight as the men-at-arms watched on, and when he had advanced close enough, threw himself into the attack, heedless of his screaming muscles.

His blade hissed and sang. Steel crashed on steel, and he snarled, slashed, cut. The knight weathered the storm with contemptuous ease. His own blade dancing and darting, batting Estienne's aside. He seemed to be everywhere. Effortless. Relentless.

A strike he didn't even see coming, and Estienne's helm went spinning into the mud. He reeled back, gasping, raising his sword in a futile guard.

The knight surged forward and smashed the flat of his blade across Estienne's temple, an explosion of light and pain. Estienne hit the ground hard, the world reeling drunkenly. He scrabbled for his sword, blinking back stars...

Cold steel kissed his throat, and he froze. The knight loomed over him, the tip of his sword pressing Estienne's flesh.

'Yield,' the knight said softly.

Estienne tasted copper, despair weighing heavy in his gut. Then he went limp and let his head fall back into the filth, the fight draining out of him.

'I yield,' he whispered.

The sword-tip lifted. Hands seized him and wrenched him to his feet.

'Do we kill him now?' one of the men-at-arms asked.

'No,' the knight replied, his voice still muffled behind his helm. 'He is my prisoner. Take him.'

Estienne sagged in his captors' grip. The last tatters of defiance left him as he was dragged away. This was not the glorious day he had envisioned, but at least he was alive.

For now.

12

Night crept over the field as Estienne huddled with the other prisoners, a sorry bunch of battered men in torn and bloodied rags. The stink of them mingled, a sour reek of sweat and piss. Many had taken grievous wounds in the battle – gashed faces, shattered limbs, bellies pierced by sword and spear – and they moaned piteously, slumped against each other in abject defeat.

The French had bound him tight, and Estienne's wrists chafed where the ropes bit into his flesh. Some distance away, the strains of victory songs drifted on the evening breeze, the French revelling in their triumph. Each mirthful note twisted like a knife, shame and fear in Estienne's gut, a potent brew that curdled in his stomach.

He could feel the eyes of their captors upon them. The French men-at-arms paced about the edge of the huddle, a restless menace. Every instinct screamed at him to flee, but the ropes held fast and there would be no escape. He was well and truly snared, trussed up like a lamb for the slaughter.

A rattle of mail jolted Estienne from his misery. He looked up to see a figure striding towards them, hand resting on the pommel of his sword. When he drew close enough, Estienne recognised the red and white surcoat of the knight who had bested him upon the field, only now he had removed his helm.

He was older than expected, his hair more grey than brown, face grim beneath a close-cropped beard. The knight came to a halt before the prisoners, eyes roving over the pitiful assembly. When they fixed on Estienne, he felt a shiver run down his spine, like a mouse pinned by a hawk's stare.

'You.' The knight's voice was gruff. 'Stand.'

Estienne struggled to his feet, hampered by his bonds, chin lifted in defiance he did not feel.

'Bring him,' the knight commanded, and Estienne found himself being cajoled by two of the French men-at-arms.

He was led away from the rest of the prisoners, away from the warmth of the fires and the noise of the camp. When they had gone far enough the knight stopped, turning to regard him.

'I am Guillaume of Roches. I rode with William Marshal in service to the Lionheart, years ago now. He is known to me of old. You wear the raiments of his house, but you are not one of his sons.'

Estienne's mouth was dry as bone and he struggled to find his voice. 'I... I am Marshal's squire, my lord.'

'A squire?' Roches barked a laugh. 'Truly, King John grows desperate, to send beardless boys into the fray.'

Shame flushed Estienne's cheeks and he was unable to bear the weight of Roches' scorn.

'Look at me, lad.' The command was so stern and unyielding that Estienne could do nothing but obey. 'How many summers have you seen? Fifteen? Sixteen at most?'

Estienne wanted to throw out his chest and proclaim himself a seasoned youth, blooded and battle-hardened, but beneath that piercing stare the lie shrivelled on his tongue.

'Fourteen, my lord. Or near enough, as I can reckon.'

Roches' mouth twisted wryly. 'Barely weaned, and already playing at war. God grant you never set foot upon another battle-field, boy. Else you'll not live long enough to see your stones drop.'

One of Roches' men shouldered forward, face twisted in disgust beneath his steel cap. 'Dumb pup. Shall I take his tongue, my lord? Teach him proper respect?'

The man-at-arms seized Estienne's jaw in a bruising grip, fingers digging into his cheeks. Estienne tried to jerk free, but the man's hold was iron.

'Enough.' Roches growled. 'Turn him loose.'

For a moment, the man's grip only tightened, then, with a last contemptuous squeeze, he released him. Estienne staggered back, heart hammering against his ribs. The man glared at him with malice, hand hovering near the hilt of his sword.

'The boy's impertinence demands answer,' he growled. 'Let me cut it from him, my lord. A few stripes will mend his manners.'

'Are you deaf?' Roches said, leaning closer. In response, the man-at-arms looked to shrink bodily. 'He is just a witless child. Strip him of that pilfered armour. It will serve as recompense enough.'

Rough hands seized Estienne, pawing at the straps of his mail. He tried to twist away, but a cuff to the side of his head left him reeling. They cut the bonds at his wrist and stripped away his armour until he stood in only a rough-spun shirt and drawers, then they dragged him to where firelight gave way to shadow, away from Roches and his pile of borrowed armour.

'Get you gone,' one of the French said, giving him a rough shove. 'And pray we don't meet again.'

Estienne stumbled, nearly pitching face-first into the trampled mud. With a final, barking laugh, the men turned and strode back towards the firelight, leaving him kneeling in the dirt.

Slowly, he pushed himself to his feet and began the long, trudging march into the night. Weariness dragged at him, but it was nothing to the heaviness in his heart, the yawning maw of failure that threatened to swallow him whole.

Memories of the battle flashed. The crash of lances, the screams of the dying. His own wild, terrified charge, desperate and doomed. He had ridden to war, to cover himself in glory, but it had all been a mummer's farce.

Eventually, as the sky began to lighten with the promise of dawn, he crested a hill and saw the village he had departed the day before. No sounds drifted up to greet him. No clank of armour, no whinny of horses. Only an eerie silence, as if the place had been abandoned in haste.

Estienne stumbled along the path, each jarring step sending a fresh ache through his battered body. His vision swam, but even through the haze, he could make out a figure standing before the cottage where he had left Richard...

Ilbert.

The young knight stood beside a pair of horses, their saddlebags bulging, ready for a hasty departure. At the sound of Estienne's approach, he turned, those haughty features twisting in a sneer as he took in Estienne's bedraggled clothes and the hollow defeat in his face.

'So,' Ilbert drawled. 'The conquering hero returns.'

Estienne drew to a halt before Ilbert. Shame burned in him, a scalding tide that seared from within.

'Nothing to say?' Ilbert pressed. 'No tales of valour and victory? I see the French have divested you of your stolen finery. A fitting reward for your fool's errand.'

Estienne's hands knotted into fists. The urge to lash out, to smash that sneering face to pulp, was almost overwhelming. But he held himself in check, jaw clenched so tight his teeth ached.

'You abandoned me,' he said quietly. 'Left me for dead on the field, while you tucked tail and ran.'

For a moment Ilbert gaped, mouth working soundlessly. Then his face contorted, a rictus of rage.

'You dare? You dare to name me craven, you fucking whelp?' One hand fell to the hilt of his sword. 'I should gut you where you stand.'

Estienne felt a reckless laugh bubbling up his throat as he flung his arms wide. 'Then do it. Cut me down, if you've the ballocks. Finish what the French couldn't.'

For a taut moment they stood, inches apart, air crackling on the cusp of violence.

The cottage door banged open, cutting through the tension like a knife. Richard stood there, one hand braced on the doorframe. He looked haggard, his face grey and sheened with sweat, but his eyes were bright. They swept over the pair, taking in Estienne's dishevelled state, Ilbert's hand on steel.

'Enough.' That single word was stern and unyielding, as Richard stepped forward, legs trembling. 'Put up your sword, Ilbert. Now.'

For a moment, Estienne thought Ilbert might refuse as his knuckles whitened on the hilt, but something in Richard's expression brooked no defiance. With a last, venomous glare at Estienne, Ilbert moved his hand away from the blade.

'I was only—'

'I know what you were doing.' Richard looked at Estienne. 'Go inside. You look ready to drop.'

Estienne wanted to protest, to stand his ground and give voice to the fury still churning in his gut, but instead he turned and stumbled for the cottage. Once inside, the cottage door swung shut with a thud, muffling the voices beyond. Estienne sagged onto a rickety stool, head falling into his hands.

When they had finished their arguing, the door opened once more, and Richard entered. He limped over to join Estienne, steps heavy with exhaustion, but a wry smile plucked at the corners of his mouth.

'You look like something even a dog wouldn't drag home,' he said, easing himself down onto a stool with a wince.

Estienne huffed a laugh. 'I certainly feel it. Richard, I... I'm sorry. I lost your mail, your horse, your sword... I failed you.'

Richard reached out to clasp Estienne's knee, his grip weak but steady. 'You did no such thing. Ilbert told me what you did. How you rode out in my stead, bore my raiment into battle. You fought for my house when I could not. That's a debt I can never repay.'

'I dreamed of glory. Of proving myself worthy. But the reality...'

'War is an ugly thing,' Richard finished for him. 'There's little glory in it, only blood and shit and screaming. But you survived. You endured. And now, we can leave this blasted place behind us.'

Estienne looked up at that, hope kindling in his breast. 'We can go home?'

'Aye.' Richard pushed to his feet, swaying slightly. 'God willing, we'll be sighting English shores before the month is out.'

Something eased in Estienne. A lightness unfurling in his chest with the promise of home. Of leaving the stench of blood and despair far behind them. Of going home to a peaceful land.

And by the grace of God, things would stay that way.

13

He had expected no hero's welcome when they returned to Pembroke and had not been disappointed. Countess Isabel had seen to the care of her son, Richard still held in the grip of whatever malady he had contracted in France. For Estienne, things had returned to normal. His training continued under the Marshal's watchful eye. Ilbert still treated him with all the contempt he could muster. It was as though Bouvines had never happened. As though it was a shame that had to be forgotten. But some things were not so easily achieved, and he often found himself waking just before dawn with the face of the man he had killed startlingly vivid in his mind's eye.

So this morning, as most mornings, Estienne walked the torch-lit halls of Pembroke, the keep quiet at such an early hour, household still abed. He paused at a window, looking out over the inner bailey. The keep here was smaller than the great fortress at Laigen, the ceilings lower, the passages narrower. And yet, it didn't feel as oppressive.

Perhaps it was the sea air that seeped in through the arrow slits, carrying with it the cry of gulls and the distant sighing of waves. Or maybe it was the faces, both familiar and new, that he passed in the halls.

Mabil still ruled the kitchens with an iron ladle, her sharp tongue lashing any scullion who dared to slouch. Goffrey continued to dole out alms to the poor who gathered at the gates each night. Even the new folk, those who had not come with Earl William from Hibernia, lacked the hard eyes and tight faces Estienne had grown accustomed to.

It was almost as if the very stones here were infused with their master's nature. Solid and unforgiving, yes, but upright and just in equal measure. Estienne should have felt comfort in that, but a part of him couldn't help but wonder how he might earn Earl William's favour. He wanted to believe he had proven himself by returning Earl William's son safely from France, had shown him the measure of his courage and loyalty, but the Marshal's stony silence offered nothing.

Estienne shrugged off the morose thoughts, letting his feet carry him outside. The dawn air was cool as he emerged into the inner ward, torches burning low in their sconces. He breathed deep, letting the chill settle into his lungs as he turned towards the training yard, and the wooden pells standing sentinel. It would be good to lose himself in the familiar rhythms of sword-work, to quiet his churning thoughts with the burn of exertion. He was halfway across the ward when a clatter broke the pre-dawn hush.

It came from the stables, a thudding crash followed by a yelp of pain. Estienne frowned, altering his course, heading for the half-open doors. Within, the stables were dim, lit only by the guttering flame of a single lantern. The horses shifted in their stalls, whickering softly. And there, illuminated in the weak light, were two figures. Estienne recognised them both – Ilbert and Domnall the stableboy.

Ilbert had the boy pushed against the wall, one fist grasping his rough-spun tunic. Domnall was wide-eyed, face pinched with fear.

'Dumb Irish clod,' Ilbert snarled, punctuating each word with a sharp shake. 'I told you to have my horse ready at first light. But here we are, and no horse.'

'Please, lord,' Domnall stammered. 'I was just... I had to... the other horses—'

He was cut off as Ilbert shook him again, slamming him back against the wall. 'I don't want your excuses. You'll do as you're bid, or I'll have the hide flayed from your back.'

Estienne stepped forward. 'Leave him be, FitzDane.'

Ilbert turned, lip curling in a sneer of contempt. 'Well, if it isn't the Marshal's pet. Come to stick your nose where it isn't wanted?'

Estienne forced his fists to unclench, keeping his voice level. 'I said, leave him be.'

Ilbert barked a laugh, shoving Domnall aside. 'Giving orders now, Wace? A baseborn dog like you? What would you know of the way a man disciplines his servants?'

Estienne stepped closer. 'I know knights are meant to protect the weak, not abuse them. To act with honour.'

Ilbert's face twisted in an ugly sneer. 'Honour? What would a landless peasant know of honour? You're nothing, Wace. An orphan boy of no blood. The Marshal may have taken you in out of pity, but you'll never be one of us. You're a black sheep in the fold, tolerated for now, but you'll never belong.'

The words struck like a fist. Estienne moved without thinking, snarl twisting his lips as he launched himself at Ilbert. He drove his head forward, smashing it into Ilbert's face with all his strength. Felt the crunch of cartilage, heard the howl of pain and outrage.

Ilbert staggered back, hands flying to his nose as blood poured between his fingers. 'You little bastard. I'll kill you for that.'

He lunged, hands hooked into claws. Estienne slipped aside at the last moment, driving his fist hard into Ilbert's stomach. The knight doubled over, and Estienne clouted him hard across the ear, sending him reeling.

Ilbert recovered quickly, shaking his head, spittle and blood flecking his lips. 'You're going to bleed, Wace.'

Estienne bared his teeth. 'Then make me.'

Ilbert charged, head down like a bull. They crashed through the half-open door and out into the pre-dawn chill of the ward. Estienne staggered, feet slipping on dew-damp cobbles and Ilbert pressed his advantage, raining blows. Estienne ducked and weaved, throwing punches of his own, and for long moments they traded strikes, a graceless brawl with nothing held back. Ilbert fought with a taunting sneer, precise and confident in his skill. Estienne had only raw ferocity, a berserk determination to make Ilbert regret his words.

His fist smashed into Ilbert's ribs, once, twice. Ilbert folded slightly, and Estienne lunged, going for the throat. Too slow; Ilbert caught him with an uppercut that snapped his head back, pain exploding through his jaw. He stumbled, off balance, and Ilbert kicked out, sweeping his feet from under him.

Estienne hit the cobbles hard. He had one glimpse of Ilbert's snarling face before the first kick slammed into his ribs. Estienne curled instinctively, covering his head, but Ilbert showed no mercy. His feet thudded into Estienne's back, his ribs, relentless and brutal. Each impact forced the air from Estienne's lungs, leaving him writhing and breathless.

'Not such a fierce cub now, are you?' Ilbert's voice was thick with savagery. 'Just the same mewling milksop you've always been.'

Estienne saw Ilbert draw back his foot again, poised to deliver a kick to his face. He braced himself, unwilling to beg, unwilling to yield...

'Stop! Leave him alone.'

Ilbert staggered back at the words. Eva Marshal stood at the edge of the ward, still in her nightgown, dark hair unbound around her shoulders. Her eyes flashed with fury as she advanced on Ilbert, heedless of her bare feet on the chilly cobbles.

'Eva,' he began, holding up his hands in placation. 'I was only—'

'Only what?' She drew herself up to her full height, chin thrust forward imperiously. 'Only about to commit murder?'

Ilbert's face darkened, his fists clenching at his sides. 'I was only trying to teach him a lesson, my lady. The whelp doesn't know his place.'

Eva crossed her arms, unimpressed. 'The only one who needs a lesson is you, FitzDane. You're a coward.'

Ilbert looked at Estienne, still on the ground. 'At least I'm not the one who needs a lady's skirts to hide behind. She won't always be around to shield you, so best watch your back, milksop. One day you might find a—'

'Enough,' Eva snapped. 'You forget yourself, FitzDane. My father shall hear of this, and—'

'Eva.' A new voice, deep and commanding. The Marshal stood framed in the doorway of the great keep, face like stone. 'Come away now.'

For an instant, Eva looked as though she might protest, but with a last scathing glance at Ilbert, she gathered her nightgown and hurried inside.

Ilbert bowed hastily. 'My Lord, I was just—'

'We'll speak of this later, FitzDane. For now, see to your business… elsewhere.'

Ilbert shot Estienne a last poisonous look, then stalked away. Estienne pushed himself to his knees, then to his feet, every movement a fresh agony. He spat a wad of blood onto the ground and tried to muster some semblance of composure.

The Marshal regarded him for a long, fraught moment. Estienne had the unsettling sense of being judged against whatever exacting standard William held in his head.

'See to those cuts,' was all he said, and with that, turned and strode back into the keep, his footsteps echoing with dread finality.

Motion caught Estienne's eye and he turned to see Domnall watching from the stable doorway. The boy dipped his head, a tentative smile tugging at his mouth, and then he ducked back out of sight.

Estienne stood for a long moment alone. The morning sun was just beginning to touch the battlements, its warmth lost to him. He felt hollowed out, bruised in more than flesh, but that flicker of acceptance from Domnall was enough to tell him he had done the right thing.

Winning acceptance from the Marshal might be an altogether more bruising prospect.

14

Steel rang against steel, the clangour reverberating off the high walls of Pembroke's yard. Estienne barely raised his shield up in time to catch the whistling cut aimed at his head, the impact setting his teeth on edge.

'Shield, Estienne.' The Marshal's voice, harsh and grating. 'It's as much a weapon as your sword. Use it.'

Estienne grunted acknowledgement as he circled. They had been at this for what felt like an age. The bruises from his fight with Ilbert had faded to mottled yellow, but the ache of them lingered, a dull throb that flared with every movement.

Ilbert had made himself scarce in the intervening days, no doubt nursing his grudge. Richard was also gone, sent to his father's castle in Laigen to recover from his illness, and Estienne tried not to dwell on his friend's absence. He needed to focus, to pour himself into the training. To be better. Stronger. Worthy.

He lunged, blade probing for an opening, but the Marshal batted it away with ease, moving with fluid grace belied by his advanced years.

'Mind your footwork,' William said, punctuating the words

with a hissing riposte that Estienne barely managed to deflect. 'A knight is only as good as his foundation. Lose that and you're dead, no matter how quick your blade.'

The next flurry of blows came hammering down like the wrath of God. Estienne weathered them, teeth bared in a snarl as each impact slammed into his battered shield. His arm had long since gone numb, exhaustion dragging at his limbs, but he refused to yield.

Something sparked through the fog of pain and fatigue. He was more than this. More than the baseborn brat Ilbert named him. More than just some landless peasant, struggling to rise above his mud-stained roots.

With a raw yell, he surged forward, lips peeled back from his teeth as he drove into the Marshal's guard, steel ringing. When the Marshal's sword hammered down again, Estienne was ready and he caught the blow on his cross-guard, snarling into his master's startled face.

'Hold!'

The barked command seared through the red of Estienne's vision. He staggered back a step, letting his sword fall to his side. For a long moment, the Marshal studied him.

'Better,' he said eventually, the word curt but threaded with something that might almost have been approval. 'You're learning to use your anger. To let it sharpen your focus rather than master you.'

The simple praise hit him unexpectedly. 'Thank you, my lord. I—'

A thud of approaching hoofbeats. Estienne turned to see two figures ride through the castle gates, clad in the muted tones of travel, their horses' flanks streaked with lather. The lead rider reined up close by and swung down from the saddle.

'Father.' Guillaume Marshal approached and clasped wrists with Earl William. 'It's good to see you.'

William frowned. 'And you, lad. Though I confess, this is unexpected.'

Guillaume's smile faltered. 'I am sorry for arriving unannounced, but there are matters we must discuss. Urgently.'

As he spoke, the second rider dismounted. Estienne's stomach knotted on seeing Ilbert FitzDane. The young knight looked much as he had when they'd parted on such brutal terms, only that hawkish nose was now flattened.

'What's troubling you, son?' William asked, ignoring Ilbert's presence altogether. 'Come. We'll discuss it inside.'

Guillaume scanned the yard, taking in the looming walls and grim-faced men-at-arms. 'No. It's best we speak out here. Who knows what ears might be listening in the halls?'

William's frown deepened. 'Speak plainly, Guillaume. What is this about?'

'Rebellion, Father. It's more than just whispers now. There are those who would see the king deposed.'

William's face looked carved from granite. 'The king is the king. Ordained by God to rule.'

'The king is a fool,' Guillaume snapped. 'A cruel, capricious tyrant with no right to the throne he clings to.'

'And you would judge him so? You would speak treason?'

'It's not treason to name the truth. After his failure in France, John is a laughing stock. They call him John Softsword in the streets, while King Philip's son Louis has earned himself the title of the Lion. Is it treason to want a stout oak on the throne in place of a rotten stump?'

'Careful, son.' William's tone dropped to a growl. 'Those are words that could see you shortened by a head.'

'You think I'm alone in this? The barons are ready to rise, Father. The kingdom teeters on a knife's edge.'

'If what you say is true,' William said slowly, 'then we must be ready. The king will expect my sword in his defence.'

'You cannot mean to stand with him? To prop up a king all of Christendom reviles?'

'I mean to honour my oaths, boy. As should any true servant of the crown.'

'Even when those oaths were sworn to a devil? A man who would grind the kingdom to dust beneath his heel? He is a murderer, Father. He would make a charnel house of England to preserve his regency.'

'Whatever his faults, he is our liege. I have bent the knee and sworn him my sword.'

'And what good is a sword in service to a sinner?' Guillaume met his father glare for glare. 'You wish to speak of oaths? What of the oaths meant to bind king to kingdom? Care and honour, shield and succour that should stretch between a sovereign and his subjects? John has made a mockery of his duties.'

'He is still your king.'

'One that murdered his nephew and imprisoned his sister.'

William stepped in close. 'Have a care, Guillaume. Never speak those words again, and certainly not beyond the walls of this castle.'

In the thunderous silence that followed, Guillaume was unable to look the Marshal in the eye. 'Please, Father, I beg you, think of your honour.'

'Honour? You who would seduce me to break faith with my king, and yet you dare speak to me of honour?'

'Father, I only wanted—'

'No.' William dragged in a steadying breath, reasserting his iron control. 'I'll hear no more of this. You dishonour yourself with this talk, Guillaume. Dishonour our house with talk of such treachery.'

Guillaume stared, pain and determination warring in his face. 'You would name me traitor? Your own son, who seeks only to steer you from a course of folly?'

'It is no folly to honour my vows. I understand your anger – King John held you hostage for a long time – but I was the one who broke faith with him. It was my punishment, not yours. There is no need for you to—'

'You think I would revolt against the king because of some petty grievance? You think I would risk open warfare, Englishman against Englishman, because my pride was hurt? Risk having to face my own father on the field of battle? King John is a tyrant. The barons rail against his rule and would be free of his cruel yoke. That is why we must rise.'

William held that stare, unyielding as stone. 'Must I say it again? The king is the king. Appointed by God's will. I'll hold to my oaths, come what may. As must you.'

Estienne watched as Guillaume's features twisted, anguish and outrage replaced by something colder. For a moment, father and son stood mirrored in their resolve, and Estienne knew with bleak certainty that neither would bend.

'Guillaume,' William said finally. 'Follow this course and it will be your neck in the noose.'

'What care I for my neck, when the kingdom rots? The barons cry for change, and you would have me hold my tongue? Pretend all is well, while John drags us closer to the abyss?'

'The abyss you speak of is war. Would you have our people bleed? Tear each other apart in a mad scramble for the throne?'

'The decision is made, Father. A new king must—'

'A new king? John's son is but a boy. Would you thrust the crown onto a child's brow?'

'Not Henry. Another. The barons have settled their choice. When John is cast down, it will be Prince Louis of France who takes his place.'

'Louis,' William breathed at last. 'You would hand him the keys to the kingdom? A French boot stamping on an English neck?'

'Better a strong hand from across the sea, than a tyrant's yoke choking us here.'

'Can't you see?' William growled. 'You are setting the great houses of England against one another to seat a French king on the English throne.'

Guillaume's eyes burned with fervour. 'Can't *you* see, Father? Change will come, whether we welcome it, or break against its tide. What matter if it is a Capetian or Angevin king upon the throne? We must look to our future, not cling to a crumbling past.'

'Our future? You speak of your own interests, boy. Your own advancement. Not the good of the kingdom you would so blithely barter away. Have I taught you nothing?'

Guillaume flinched as if slapped, but his voice remained hard. 'I speak of survival. The barons will have their due, and woe betide any man who stands in their path. The question is, would you be such a fool?'

'I am the king's man, Guillaume. His leal servant, sworn to his defence. My oath is ironclad. Sacrosanct. I will not break it. Not for you. Not for any man.'

Guillaume's mouth twisted into something between fury and despair. 'Then you're ten times the fool I feared.'

He spun away, cloak billowing, long strides carrying him to his horse. Ilbert handed him the reins before they both mounted and rode from the castle grounds as swiftly as they had come. The Marshal stared fixedly at the path his son had taken, jaw working as if chewing on the bitter words of their exchange.

'We're done for today,' he said at last.

Estienne opened his mouth, desperate to offer some word of support, but the lead weight of his tongue defied him. In the end, he could only duck his head, mumbling some half-formed assent, as William turned and made his way back to the keep.

He was left in silence, scarcely daring to breathe. All the dark spectres Estienne had thought safely consigned to the past now loomed on the horizon.

Rebellion.

War.

And his master would be thrust into this crucible... with Estienne by his side.

PART THREE: THUNDERHEAD

ENGLAND, 1215 AD

15

The stench of London mingled with the salt tang of its river. It was the fetor of teeming humanity – sweat and ordure, woodsmoke and boiling offal. As their party clattered through the streets, that stink only intensified, underscored by the uneasy muttering of the crowds that lined their path.

King John rode at the head of the column, his mount's banneret of red and gold fluttering on the breeze. He sat stiff in the saddle, jaw clenched, as if he could barely stomach the miasma of his own capital. To his right rode William Marshal, grim-faced as ever. On the king's left was Stephen Langton, Archbishop of Canterbury, his vestments standing out brightly against the dolour.

Estienne kept his head down, trying to avoid the curious stares of the city folk as they passed. He felt out of place here, a country boy thrust into the heart of England's greatest city. The clamour of it assailed him – the cries of hawkers, the clatter of hooves and wheels on cobbles, the incessant yammering of gulls. Everywhere he looked there was the motion and din of street pedlars plying their trade on corners, wagons laden with produce trundling by, packs of snarling dogs squabbling over scraps. This place had a restless energy to it, a sense of barely leashed turmoil. Shutters clattered closed as they rode by, and more than one passerby spat in their wake. The common folk, it seemed, had little love for their king.

'Misbegotten rabble,' John muttered, just loud enough for those closest to hear. 'They breed like rats in a granary.'

'They are your subjects, Your Grace,' the archbishop said, his voice leavened with gentle reproach. 'The flock you were born to shepherd.'

John's lip curled. 'A shepherd often needs to cull his flock, lest the rot spread. Perhaps it is time I unleashed some wolves amid their pens.'

Marshal stirred in his saddle, a frown marring his stern features, but he held his tongue. Estienne didn't miss the uneasy looks that darted between the king's knights. Even they could sense the brittleness beneath John's bluster, the fear gnawing at his bowels.

At last, the Temple Church loomed before them, its pale stone standing starkly against the drabness of its surroundings. As they drew closer, Estienne saw knight-monks gathered beneath the Temple's vast archway in full regalia, their mail and surcoats pristine.

The Master of the Temple stepped forward to greet them. King John clambered down from his destrier, but there was no warmth in the nod he directed to the Templars, just stony acknowledgement. The archbishop murmured a blessing after he too dismounted, clutching the crucifix that swung from his neck.

Only William Marshal took a moment to greet the Templar master, clasping his hand before nodding. 'Brother Aimery.'

The Templar inclined his head, respect flickering in those pale eyes. 'Marshal.'

Their party was led into the depths of the Temple, footsteps echoing. The nave opened out around them, its sheer immensity enough to take Estienne's breath away. Shafts of light speared down from the high windows, motes of dust dancing in the beams. Candles guttered in iron sconces, their meagre flames doing little to alleviate the gloom.

And there, at the far end of the hall, a sea of steel-clad men waited.

The rebel barons.

A wary hush fell as Estienne and the others proceeded down the aisle, the march of their feet against the flagstones loud as drumbeats. Even from a distance, Estienne recognised Robert Fitz-Walter, his arms crossed, a sword belted over his surcoat. There was a score more besides, grim and bristling, surcoats aglitter with the sigils of England's greatest houses. But none made Estienne's gut clench like the two figures flanking FitzWalter. A pair he knew all too well.

Guillaume Marshal strode to the front, every inch the young lord. At his side, Ilbert FitzDane, a wolf in mail, looking as fearsome as the wyvern emblazoned on his chest.

The barons waited as King John approached, and Estienne felt the hairs prickle on his nape as he marked their scowling faces. This was no gathering of courtiers, no council of the realm; these were men on a war footing, armed and armoured. King John seemed to sense it too, for he stopped a bare dozen paces from the assembled throng. When he spoke, his voice echoed in the silence, dripping with injured pride and spite.

'I am not accustomed to being summoned within my own kingdom, least of all by those who style themselves my leal vassals. It should be I demanding your presence, not the other way around.'

For a long, fraught moment, the barons said nothing. Then Robert FitzWalter took a step forward. He was taller than the king and leaner in the face. When he spoke, his voice was deep and measured.

'Your Grace, forgive our presumption, but the current discord has forced our hand. We come to you not in defiance, but in the hope of redressing the grievances that plague this kingdom.'

'Grievances? You speak of grievances, FitzWalter, when it is I who should voice complaint. I, who have been forced to bear the brunt of your obstinance and treachery.'

A low, angry mutter rippled through the barons' ranks, and FitzWalter held up a hand for silence. 'There is fault enough on all sides, Your Grace. But we are not here to bandy accusations.'

The king drew himself up. 'Then why exactly are you here, my lord? From where I stand, it looks ominously like an armed rebellion against your anointed sovereign.'

'No rebellion, Your Grace.' A shout came from the depths of the barons' ranks, thick with barely restrained wrath. 'Only honest men, driven to desperation.'

The cry seemed to galvanise the rest of the barons, and suddenly the Temple was ringing with a dozen clamouring voices, each trying to shout over the other.

FitzWalter raised both hands. 'Peace. All of you.'

Slowly the noise subsided, but the air was still thick with their fury. King John's face was set, and Estienne could almost hear his teeth grinding.

'Your Grace,' FitzWalter began again, 'we have indeed been driven to desperate measures, but it is not without just cause. For too long now, you have ruled this kingdom with scant regard for the rights and dignities of your barons. You have levied punitive taxes, seized lands and titles on a whim, and subverted the very laws meant to govern this realm.'

John's eye twitched. 'You overstep, FitzWalter.'

The baron ploughed on, heedless. 'The barons of England

will suffer these abuses no longer. Nor will the Church, whose coffers you have plundered, and whose ancient rights you have defiled.'

The archbishop stirred at that, spreading his hands in a placating gesture. 'My lord, let us not—'

'What would you have of me, then?' John cut across him, his voice dripping scorn. 'What must I do to appease this nest of disloyalty?'

Robert FitzWalter met the king's glare levelly. 'We ask only that you uphold the Charter of Liberties once sworn by your grandfather, King Henry. That you affirm the ancient rights, laws and customs of this kingdom. Rule by the law, not above it.'

'I am to sign a proclamation binding me to laws written a hundred years ago?'

'Of course not,' FitzWalter replied calmly. 'There will be a new charter. With new statutes.'

'You dare dictate terms to me?' King John's face flushed. 'As if I were some serf, dancing to your command?'

'No man is above the law, Your Grace. Not even a king. Swear to us that you will abide by the charter and uphold justice for all, and there need be no more strife between us.'

For a long moment, John glared at the baron, hands clenching and unclenching at his sides.

'And if I refuse?'

FitzWalter's eyes were hard as iron. 'Then, Your Grace, there may be violent consequences.'

Silence met FitzWalter's words, and for an instant, Estienne was certain the king would fly at him in a rage. But then John drew in a shuddering breath, visibly mastering himself.

'If I bend the knee to your demands, what guarantee do I have that you and your fellow barons will not simply use this... charter... as a pretext to cede further power and privilege? Do not think

I am deaf to the whispers in my kingdom. The poison dripping from your lips as you spin your webs.'

The archbishop made to speak again, but it was William Marshal who stepped forward.

'I think,' he said, each word freighted with care, 'that what His Grace desires is an assurance of your own faith, my lords. A promise that you will cleave to him as your liege and put aside any thought of... other pretenders.'

Estienne saw more than one baron shift uneasily. Marshal's meaning was plain enough, that King John feared the shadow of the French prince looming beyond his shores and he would have their allegiance over a potential usurper.

Robert FitzWalter was the first to speak. 'We seek only to have our traditional rights and liberties upheld, to be ruled with justice and honour, as is our due. We do not speak of false kings.'

John snorted. 'You do not? Then why do I hear rumours of you sounding Louis the Lion on his prospects? Because if it is true, it will be a black day for any who would support his claim.'

Murmurs of discontent ran through the barons again, and Estienne caught more than one black look cast the king's way.

'Your Grace,' the Marshal cut in again, his voice ringing with authority. 'This accomplishes nothing. The purpose here is to find accord, not cast aspersions.'

King John rounded on him. 'Aspersions? These snakes come to me with threats and demands, and yet you would have me—'

'I would have you consider their petition, sire. For the good of the kingdom.' Marshal looked at the barons again. 'I am sure my lords here would be willing to affirm their allegiance to you once more, should you swear to uphold the charter they propose.'

Mutterings arose at that, but Robert FitzWalter swept his gaze over the malcontents, quelling them with the force of his stare alone.

'Earl William is right, Your Grace. If you would show good faith to us, we would do the same to you. Let the terms of the charter be written, that you may judge them fairly. If you find them just, my lords here will have no qualms affirming their oaths to you once more.'

'And if I find I cannot submit to your terms?' John replied. 'What then, my lord? Will you and your fellow barons rise in revolt, as you so clearly yearn to do?'

FitzWalter's face hardened. 'It is not revolt we seek, Your Grace. Only a just accord between king and vassals.'

John barked a laugh. 'An accord? One where I play the serf, it seems, while you and yours play lord over me. What king rolls over for his subjects like a spaniel, with his belly bared and his tail between his legs?'

'We only wish to see a lasting peace won for this kingdom.'

'A peace won with swords bared and threats on your lips? You have a strange notion of accord, FitzWalter.'

It was the archbishop's turn to interject, moving between the two men with his hands raised. 'Your Grace, please. In the eyes of God, we are here to seek common ground, not—'

'I will not be dictated to in my own kingdom,' John snarled. 'Not by you, not by them, not by any man living.'

The barons erupted then, pent-up fury spilling out in a torrent. Estienne's heart slammed against his ribs as he readied himself for the first of them to seek violence...

'Enough!'

William Marshal's bellow thundered across the clamour. In a blink he was between King John and the barons, one hand raised, the other resting on the hilt of his sword. The very force of his presence was enough to halt the barons in their tracks, and an uneasy hush fell over them.

Marshal regarded the face of every baron. 'There will be no

bloodshed in this holy place. You dishonour yourselves with this display.'

For a long, taut moment, it seemed the barons might defy him, but slowly, they began to settle back, hands moving from sword hilts.

Marshal turned to King John. 'Your Grace, I beseech you. For the sake of the realm, let us have peace here. Allow the barons to set down their grievances. Read their charter and judge it with a fair hand. Only then may we hope to see this discord resolved.'

John glared at him, nostrils flared. Estienne feared he would let his temper master him, but instead he nodded. 'Very well. Have your damned charter drawn up. I will read it, though I promise nothing more.'

Robert FitzWalter offered a bow. 'We thank you, Your Grace. The charter will be delivered to you with all haste. We trust you will weigh it with care, and see the justice in our cause.'

Without another glance at the assembled barons, King John stormed from the Temple, his knights scrambling to follow with the archbishop hurrying in their wake. Only William Marshal lingered, casting one last look at the barons. Estienne saw his eyes land on Guillaume, but his son offered no acknowledgement, and after a moment, Marshal turned away.

Estienne fell into step beside him as they emerged into daylight. Marshal's face was bleak as weathered stone.

'This will not hold,' he muttered, more to himself than Estienne. 'John may bend for now, but this is no true peace. Only a drawing of breath before the next clash.'

Estienne said nothing, but the knot of dread in his belly grew larger with every heartbeat. He could not help but think that steel would soon sing. And God help them all when it did.

16

The tournament field of Stamford stretched before them, a sea of green beneath an azure sky. On any other day, the thunder of hooves and the crash of lances would have filled the air, as knights tested their mettle in the joust and the melee. But today the field played host to a very different kind of assembly.

Ilbert reined in his destrier at the edge of the mustering ground, the warhorse tossing its head and stamping at the turf, eager for action. Beside him, Guillaume Marshal sat tall in the saddle, his handsome features grim.

'God's nails, what a sight,' Ilbert breathed, unable to keep the relish from his voice.

The field was aswarm with mounted men, England's nobility out in force. Everywhere he looked, knights in full harness sat upon their champing destriers, the wind snapping at their pennons in a storm of colour. The greatest lords of the realm were gathered here, their esquires clustered close, a chequerboard of surcoats emblazoned with lions, griffins and dragons.

'Have you ever seen such a host assembled?' He glanced sidelong at Guillaume, expecting to see his own eagerness mirrored, but the young Marshal's countenance remained bleak.

'There is nothing magnificent in this, Ilbert,' he replied. 'Only necessity.'

Ilbert frowned. 'The king has brought us to this. He will not see reason. Will not sign the charter. This is the only recourse left to us.'

'Aye. Instead of yielding to our just demands, he sets about reinforcing his castles for war. Bolstering his strongholds with men and supplies, as if that will save him.'

It was true – John's response to their entreaties had been typical of the capricious bastard. Rather than parley or even consider their grievances, he had hardened his heart, retreating behind his walls like vermin to its lair. Rebellion was now their only recourse.

A sudden hush rippled through the host, and Ilbert saw Robert FitzWalter riding to the centre of the field. The baron made for an imposing figure, seated on a huge black destrier in a surcoat of gold slashed with red. At his approach, the assembled knights fell silent.

'My lords,' FitzWalter's voice rang out. 'We are gathered here in common purpose. In shared outrage at the crimes and oppressions of the tyrant who styles himself our king.' A rumble of assent rolled through the ranks, and FitzWalter raised a hand for silence. 'Too long have we laboured beneath John's yoke. Too long have we suffered his avarice, his cruelty, his disdain for the ancient rights of this realm. He would grind us to dust beneath his heel, strip us of the dignities gifted us by his forebears.'

Ilbert found himself nodding, caught up in the passion of Fitz-Walter's rhetoric. The baron's words echoed his own smouldering resentments. John was a blight upon the land, a king unworthy of the name. What choice did true Englishmen have but to rise against him?

'Hear me now.' From within his surcoat, FitzWalter drew a folded sheaf of parchment. 'This is a letter I have received from His Holiness, the Pope himself. In it, he commands us to abandon our pursuit of justice. To bend the knee to King John and submit to his tyrannies, as is the duty of faithful subjects.'

A storm of outrage greeted his pronouncement, voices raised in furious dissent. The Pope's betrayal cut deep, and FitzWalter let the uproar continue for a long moment, then raised his letter in the air.

'I know the anger you feel, my brothers. The betrayal. That we should be so abandoned by those charged with defending our right. But if we cannot look to Rome for justice, then we must seek it for ourselves.' With a sudden, violent motion, he rent the letter in two and cast the pieces to the ground. 'I say the Pope has no authority over us. No right to command free Englishmen to suffer beneath a tyrant's lash. We are the masters of our own fates, and we will have the liberties that are our birthright, or we will water the fields of England with blood.'

The gathered host roared its approval, a primal sound that set the ravens scattering from the treeline. Ilbert felt his own blood stir, swept up in the swell of righteous wrath. The barons stood alone now, their cause excommunicate in the eyes of the Holy Mother Church. But what of it? They had each other, bound by ties of blood and honour and a shared thirst for justice. And that would be enough.

'If John will not bow to the will of his barons, there can be no accord with such a creature. No peace while he yet wears the crown. Only one course remains to us now. The course of defiance. Of rebellion. Of war. We are the Army of God. The defenders of the Holy Church and the ancient liberties of this kingdom. By taking up arms against the tyrant John, we do the Lord's work.'

All around Ilbert, a roar went up – a hurricane of assent that set the very heavens ringing. Men brandished swords and lances, bannerets of every hue rippling in the wind. The thunder of their acclaim rolled across the tourney field, fierce and exultant.

'As God is my witness,' FitzWalter bellowed, 'I swear to you that our cause is righteous. That the Almighty stands with us, in all our works. Will you ride with me, proud men of England? Will you rid this benighted kingdom of the curse that sits upon its throne?'

Again that great shout shattered the air, and Ilbert found his own voice rising to join the tumult. Beside him, Guillaume sat stiffly in the saddle, knuckles white on the reins. Ilbert sought his eye, but the young Marshal's face was stony. For all the baron's fine words, it seemed Guillaume yet harboured some kernel of doubt.

FitzWalter spurred his horse forward, wheeling to face the host. 'I will be your Marshal. And by Christ, I swear that together, we shall scour the traitor John from this fair land. That we shall not rest until England is free of his venom.'

For the third time, a concussive bellow rose from the army of rebel barons. The host was already moving, barding jangling, hooves pounding on the turf. Ilbert felt a thrill swell in his breast – the promise of glory and renown, the joy of riding to war with a just cause. This was what he had trained for, all those long years as William Marshal's squire. And now, at last, it was upon him.

He glanced at Guillaume as they fell into the column, the young knight's profile sharp and austere.

'This is how it must be,' Ilbert said aloud, the words almost lost beneath the drum of hooves. 'We cannot falter now. The king has forced our hand. Made rebellion our only recourse.'

For a long moment, Guillaume said nothing, staring straight ahead between his destrier's ears. 'Perhaps you are right, Ilbert.

Perhaps there is no other way. But I fear for what is to come. For the blood that must now be shed. But our course is set. And may God defend us on it.'

'Just so, my friend. And He will. How can He not? We are His true servants, riding beneath His banner.' He raised his voice suddenly, caught up in a tangle of exultation. 'For God and England!'

All along the column, that cry was taken up. It swelled to a ragged cheer, fierce with bloodlust. Ahead, rank upon rank of knights thundered across the greensward, hooves churning up great clods of earth.

At the end of their path lay the ancient seat of Brackley, where Eustace of Vesci waited with another host ready to join this one. This was the first charge in a campaign that would shake the very foundations of the kingdom.

And Ilbert could hardly wait to be in the midst of it.

17

The sun struggled through wisps of cloud, casting a pale glow over the walls of Pembroke. In the shadow of the keep, Estienne pored over a book, lips moving silently as he traced a finger beneath the Latin text. His brow furrowed as he wrestled with a particularly knotty passage. The concepts seemed to twist away from his comprehension, dancing just out of reach, until with a sigh, he leaned back against the sun-warmed stone, letting the book fall closed in his lap.

It was a perfect day for riding, or trading blows in the yard. Anything but having his head crammed with dusty philosophies, but the yard stood empty, the whole castle seeming to hold its breath. And Estienne knew why.

Earl William had been absent for days now, riding between the king and his barons, acting as peacemaker. Estienne had heard snatches of gossip from the servants – whispers of the barons' mounting discontent, their fury at King John's callous rule. Of the storm brewing on England's horizon.

Still, there was nothing he could do but apply himself to his studies. Reaching for the book again, Estienne flipped it open to the offending page, steeling himself to untangle those Latin knots once more.

A feather-light touch ghosted along the rim of his ear, raising gooseflesh on his nape. He twitched, swatting at the damned fly that plagued him, but the touch came again, delicate as silk, and this time Estienne slapped at it hard.

A peal of laughter sounded behind, and he turned to see Eva grinning down at him, a long stalk of grass between finger and thumb, which she'd used to tease his ear.

'Lost in your books again?' She dangled the stalk of grass from her mouth.

'Some of us have studying to do,' he replied. 'I'm sure you can find something else to occupy your time rather than tormenting me. Needlepoint, perhaps? Or prayer?'

Eva screwed up her nose. 'Prayer? I'd sooner watch grass grow.' She leaned over him, peering at his book. 'What's this one about then? More dull history?'

'It's... Latin. Theology and the like.'

'Sounds thrilling.' She plucked a flower and set about shredding it, showering Estienne's book with yellow petals.

He snapped the volume shut. 'Did you want something, Eva?'

A sly smile curved her lips. 'I wanted to know when you were going to take me riding. You promised, remember?'

Estienne cast his mind back. He had promised her a trot through the fields, in a moment of weakness, but she had a way of needling him until he gave in, just to shut her up.

'I don't recall saying today.'

'Well, it's not like you're doing anything important.'

'I'm studying. You know, that activity you avoid like a plague.'

Eva's grin only widened. 'The book will still be here when you get back.'

There was a certain pull to that impish smile he found increas-

ingly difficult to resist. 'I can't. Your father charged me to be dili-
gent in my studies. I won't abandon that duty.'

Eva rolled her eyes. 'Fine then. Read your mouldy book. I'll
just waste away from boredom, shall I?'

'Do whatever you think is best, Eva. Just do it away from here.'

Eva stuck her nose in the air. 'When I'm a shrivelled crone, old
before my time, you'll regret those words, Estienne Wace.' She
turned to flounce away, but paused, pointing right at him. 'Oh, and
you've got petals in your hair.'

Her laughter pealed out, bright as church bells. Estienne
couldn't hide his own rueful smile as he brushed the petals away.

The clatter of hooves on flagstones shattered the relative peace
of the courtyard. Estienne saw a familiar figure riding through the
barbican, surrounded by a small train of men-at-arms.

'Father!'

Eva went tearing across the bailey, skirts hiked up around her
knees, propriety forgotten. William Marshal swung down from his
destrier, moving stiffly from the long ride. When Eva barrelled into
him, he caught her up in a strong embrace, a weary smile breaking
across his face.

'Hello, little hellion.' His voice was gruff, but warmth threaded
the words. He set Eva back to look at her, large hands engulfing her
shoulders. 'Keeping the devil busy in my absence?'

Eva looked back at him with concern. 'You're back so soon this
time. Is everything all right?'

The lightness faded from William's expression and for a
moment he looked every one of his years. 'That's nothing for you
to worry on.' Eva's face set into defiant lines, but before she could
open her mouth to argue, William forestalled her with a raised
hand. 'I mean it, Eva. These matters are not for a child's ears.'

'I'm not a child,' Eva muttered.

'I'm weary to the bone, and I'll not have you pestering me with questions. Now off you go and plague your maids or the scullions.'

Eva looked set to protest, but something in William's expression stopped her. With ill grace, she turned and stomped back toward the keep.

The Marshal watched her go, a shadow passing over his features. Estienne knew that he was only taking care to preserve his daughter's innocence, shielding her from the kingdom's woes.

He shut his book and scrambled to his feet as Earl William approached. 'My lord. Is all well? You look as though you've had a hard road.'

William smiled, but it was a thin, strained thing. 'That I have, lad. That I have.'

'What happened with the barons, my lord? Did you not reach an accord?'

William blew out a heavy breath. 'Accord. Would that it were so simple. The archbishop and I rode to Brackley to entreat with the barons. To hear their grievances and seek some path to peace. Instead, we were handed a list of demands as long as my arm. Clauses and conditions, each one more galling than the last.'

'What manner of demands?' Estienne asked.

'The kind that would strip the king of his power. Hobble him like a gelded stallion. They call it a charter. I call it a blatant bid for power.'

'I take it the king did not receive these demands kindly.'

William barked a laugh devoid of humour. 'That's putting it mildly. When I laid the demands before him, he was enraged. Called the barons traitors and outlaws, the lot of them. Swore he'd see them all hanged before he bent to their yoke.'

A sick dread settled in Estienne's stomach. 'What will happen now?'

William looked suddenly very old, the lines of care deepening. 'John has commanded his sheriffs to seize all the rebel barons' lands and holdings. To bring them to heel through force of arms.'

'But that will only enrage them further.'

'Aye,' William agreed grimly. 'They will not bend to such actions. Not proud men like FitzWalter and Vesci. They have too much to lose. And now, with John branding them traitors, declaring their lives and lands forfeit, they'll fight like cornered rats. I thought I could make King John see reason. Appeal to some shred of wisdom in that overgrown boy's head, but there is no reasoning with him. No yield in his marrow. And now we'll all pay the price for his spite.'

Estienne stared out over the inner ward, watching as William's men-at-arms led their horses to the stable, weary to the bone. Their grim faces and terse movements only underscored the air of urgency, the sense that time was swiftly dwindling.

'You'll be leaving again soon, won't you?'

William nodded. 'I must. Everyone is jumping for each other's throats like half-starved dogs. If I don't get between them, force some measure of restraint, this land will be drenched in blood before the season's out.'

'Let me come with you.' The words were out before he could call them back.

William blinked, refocusing on Estienne as if seeing him anew. 'I don't doubt your courage, lad, but this is no tourney. If it comes to battle, it will be a grim and bloody business.'

'All the more reason to have loyal men at your side.'

'Aye, I'll need loyal men in the days ahead. Men I can trust, when all around is cast in shadow.'

'I will not fail you. I swear it.'

William's smile was grim. 'I hope you won't.'

The earl walked on, disappearing into the keep. In that moment, Estienne felt the weight of his oath settling over him. He had pledged himself to Marshal's cause, and his life to the service of a doomed peace. And now, come what may, he would have to see it through.

18

The road had been churned by hundreds of passing horses. Ilbert glanced around at the men riding alongside him, their faces drawn and weary, the failed siege of Northampton still hanging over them like a pall, souring the air with the stink of defeat.

It should have been a simple thing – the castle was ill-provisioned, undermanned. By all rights, it should have fallen easily, but the defenders had fought like cornered wolves, raining arrows and bolts down upon their attackers with merciless aim. Ilbert's gut still clenched at the memory of FitzWalter's standard-bearer struck down, a crossbow bolt jutting obscenely from his skull.

In the end, they'd had no choice but to abandon the assault, leaving their dead for the carrion crows. A bitter draught, and one that left a sour taste in Ilbert's mouth. But as they drew closer to London, a sound began to swell upon the morning air to sweep away those dark memories – the pealing of church bells, ringing out in joyous welcome.

He glanced to his left, to where Guillaume rode in brooding silence. The eldest Marshal son had spoken little since Northampton, his brow perpetually furrowed as if wrestling with some great doubt. It irked Ilbert to see such hesitance in his sworn brother.

As if sensing his regard, Guillaume lifted his head, and Ilbert flashed him a confident grin. 'Listen to those bells, Guillaume. London already knows her rightful lords. She opens her gates like a whore lifting her skirts, eager for our coming.'

Guillaume's frown only deepened. 'And what of her people? The common folk, who must weather this storm we bring down upon them? Do you think they cheer our coming?'

Ilbert scoffed. 'They don't concern me. They'll bend to whoever holds power, as they always have. We are the ones who matter. The men of influence, and the swords we command.'

Guillaume said nothing, only urged his mount forward to catch up to FitzWalter at the head of the column as Ilbert watched him go. No matter. Guillaume would come around, once he saw how the city welcomed them. Once he understood this was their destiny. The future was theirs for the taking, and Ilbert meant to seize it with both hands.

The city rose before them, sprawling and smoke-wreathed, the stink of its teeming masses carried on the wind. As they clattered through the gates, Ilbert drank in the press of the crowd, the cries of the whores and beggars. Overhead, crows wheeled against a clear sky, dark as the habits of the monks who lined the road, their hands folded and heads bowed in deference. Or was it simply resignation Ilbert saw etched upon those wan faces? He spat to clear the taste of doubt from his mouth. It mattered not. They held the city now, and the hearts of its people would surely follow.

All around him, the rebels were fanning out, seizing control with ruthless efficiency. Men-at-arms cantered down side streets, spearheads glinting in the sunlight. Knights galloped to secure the roads inward – Aldersgate, Newgate, Ludgate, Cripplegate, Bishopsgate. London Bridge itself, the great stone span arcing over the dark ribbon of the Thames.

Among those knights, Ilbert marked the younger sons of great houses. To a man they were of an age with Ilbert – fierce and hungry, spoiling for a fight. For the chance to prove themselves and carve out a legacy. This was their time. Their moment to make a mark, to etch their names into the pages of history, and Ilbert was damn sure he would be among them.

Ahead he saw Guillaume pulling away from the main host, FitzWalter close at his side. The pair made for the squat, crenellated bulk of a high tower – Baynard's Castle. FitzWalter's stronghold, and the key to London's heart. Its curtain walls were thick though part of it was still being rebuilt after the king saw fit to teach FitzWalter a lesson not so long ago and raze it. From there, they could control all travel in and out of the city, by road or by river. The perfect stronghold from which to oversee their uprising.

Ilbert spurred his steed after Guillaume, managing to rein up alongside him, just as FitzWalter cantered out before the assembled host. The great baron made for an impressive sight – tall and imperious astride his warhorse.

'Behold, London lies prostrate at our feet,' FitzWalter cried. 'Her gates stand open, her people cheer our arrival. Truly I say to you now – with the city in our grasp, so too is this kingdom.'

A great roar went up from the gathered knights and men-at-arms, the clatter of sword against shield. Ilbert added his voice to the din, the hot swell of triumph burning in his breast.

'Even now John cowers, pissing himself with fear. He knows his reckoning is at hand. He knows the true strength of England is arrayed against him.'

Another rapturous cry. Ilbert glanced at Guillaume, seeing he was far from caught up by the fervour. He leaned close, pitching his voice for Guillaume's ears alone. 'Why so glum? We've done it, Guillaume. London is ours.'

Guillaume blinked as though dismissing some dark thought. 'Aye. And now we must hold her.'

Before Ilbert could press further, FitzWalter's voice cracked out once more.

'The next time we treat with John, it will be on our terms. We are the masters now.'

As the roar of the host rose to a deafening crescendo, Guillaume grasped his reins and nudged his horse away from the crowd. Ilbert considered following, but best he leave the Marshal alone. There would be time enough for reassurances later.

* * *

The sun was sinking low over the rooftops by the time Ilbert found a moment to pull Guillaume aside. They stood atop the barbican of Baynard's Castle, looking out over the teeming streets. In the courtyard below, squires and farriers bustled back and forth, leading horses to the stables, fetching bags of oats and bundles of hay. The business of war, carrying on as it always had.

Ilbert leaned his forearms against the battlement, drinking in the sights and smells of the city before he glanced sidelong at Guillaume, taking in the hard set of his friend's jaw, the furrow between his brows. Guillaume had been distant since FitzWalter's speech, pulling away to oversee the garrisoning of the castle as if he couldn't beat a retreat fast enough. It sat ill with Ilbert, that distance. That unspoken thing, coiled in the air between them.

'You're brooding again,' he said lightly, aiming for jovial and missing by a mile. 'Like you've turned up at a brothel and forgotten to bring your cock.'

Guillaume huffed, a mirthless sound. 'There is much to brood on. Holding London is one thing, but the kingdom... That's a prize that will cost us dear.'

'Cost? Think of what we stand to gain.' Ilbert turned to face him fully. 'New lands, new titles. A chance to reshape the realm as we see fit. Is that not a prize worth fighting for?'

Ilbert glimpsed the struggle raging behind his friend's eyes – the clash of duty and ambition, of loyalty and desire. 'And all I have to do is sacrifice the love I hold for my father.'

'We're on the brink of something glorious, Guillaume.' Ilbert gripped his friend's shoulder. 'A new age, with us at its vanguard. Your father is a great man, but his time is passing. This time is ours.' He saw Guillaume waver, that iron certainty buckling. 'The old order crumbles. John's kingdom is ripe for the taking, and by God, I mean to take it. And I want you at my side when I do.'

Something flickered in Guillaume's eyes – a spark, quickly smothered. 'You always were an ambitious bastard, Ilbert.'

Ilbert grinned. 'And you love me for it.'

Guillaume snorted, some of the tension easing from his shoulders. 'You'll be the death of me.'

Ilbert laughed, slinging an arm around his friend's neck. 'Not if I can help it. We'll go far, you and I.'

As they stood there, shoulder to shoulder, Ilbert felt the swell of possibility. The future was theirs. And God help any fool who stood in their way.

19

The day dawned grey and sullen; the sky pressed low with clouds that threatened rain. It was unseasonably miserable for June but seemed a fitting herald for the business to come.

Estienne settled into his saddle, as around him the king's entourage made ready to depart – squires checking girths and straightening caparisons emblazoned with the royal arms of England's three lions passant guardant. King John sat rigidly atop his white destrier, mouth pressed into a thin, uncompromising line. He wore a tunic of rich crimson, and a fur-lined cloak was draped carelessly across his shoulders as if donned in haste. His grey hair peeked out from beneath a simple circlet – a deliberate choice, Estienne was sure. Today of all days, John had no patience for the trappings of his office.

In stark contrast to the king, those riding closest to him were all stately in their composure. Three resplendent archbishops – Canterbury, Dublin and London – their vestments of rich silk and gold braid. There too rode veteran warriors, grim of face – Willem Longsword, Earl of Salisbury, so recently ransomed from French captivity; and Hubert of Burgh, the king's justiciar, his hand never far from his sword hilt. And of course, Earl William, stern and upright in his saddle, armour gleaming beneath his red lion rampant. A talisman of enduring loyalty, staunch amid a sea of discontent.

As Estienne guided his mount into place at Marshal's right hand, John gave the curt signal to ride out. Their party clattered from the courtyard of Windsor Castle, hooves loud on the cobbles. Down from the promontory they trotted, the road wending south to their destination. John's face remained stony as they travelled that short distance before cresting a gentle rise, and it came into view...

Runnymede.

A broad meadow of sighing summer grasses, bounded by ancient oaks and ghostly wisps of mist off the river. Today this stretch of quiet greenery would play host to the highest powers in the land, and Estienne could appreciate the choice – here was a place that spoke silently of old rights, old ways. Of a deeper, truer authority than passing crowns. The symbolism, he was sure, would not be lost on either side.

As their party drew closer, Estienne saw the barons were already present in force. Tents crowded the far end of the field, bright silk pennons blowing in the quickening breeze. The press of mounted knights seethed beneath a thicket of fluttering banners, their steel winking in the listless sun.

Estienne found himself taking inventory of the sigils proudly displayed. Shields and surcoats were emblazoned with arms he had committed to memory during long hours of study under Goffrey's tutelage. The chequy of Mandeville, Vesci's cross patonce, the cross gules of Bigod, Quincy's seven mascles. Robert FitzWalter, of course, was at the centre of that martial storm, his red chevrons a stark promise of blood to come if accord could not be reached.

The barons had eschewed their great helms, their faces bare to the morning air. Stripped of that armour, they seemed somehow more defiant, these men who would bring their king to heel. Saer of Quincy's brow was furrowed with resolve, prominent jaw set and uncompromising. Richard of Clare's ageing features were bereft of all levity. And there, at FitzWalter's right hand, Guillaume Marshal stood proudly, mail coif thrown back, fair hair stark against the grey sky.

Looking at those determined faces, Estienne felt a slow, sinking dread. These were not men in a mood to bend. Not malleable lords who would scrape and submit with bared throats. They had been pushed beyond the brink, and their presence here, armed and armoured, sent a clear message.

At the centre of the field, a broad oaken table had been set up, its surface draped with a pristine white cloth. Upon it, weighted against the breeze, lay parchment – many sheaves of it, covered in close-written Latin, dense with articles and clauses.

Estienne slid from the saddle, as the king and his entourage likewise dismounted. He took up his place at William's shoulder as the barons approached from the other side. King and vassals faced each other across that cloth-draped table, the pages of the charter between them.

There was little of introduction or preamble. No jovial greetings or honeyed entreaties, not on this day. The time for negotiation had passed. All that remained was to fix seals to deed, and pray it would be enough to stem the tide of rebellion.

Estienne was close enough to see the vein pulse at John's temple as he stepped forward, those beringed hands twitching at his sides, as if yearning to rend that charter to shreds. In a voice leached of all emotion, King John swore his oath. The words seemed to grind from his throat, each one tainted with ill grace.

'Firstly, we have granted to God and confirmed by this, our

present charter, for us and our heirs in perpetuity, that the English Church shall be free, and shall have its rights in full, and its liberties intact...'

Estienne stood in taut stillness, barely daring to draw breath as John spoke the words that would forever alter the balance between crown and subject. Mere paces away, he could see Earl William's face set with relief and trepidation in equal measure.

FitzWalter and the barons spoke their own oaths in turn, their voices fervent with the weight of this moment. Vows of loyalty and service, conditional as they were, carried upon the wind. Estienne wondered if John heard the subtle absence of unquestioning fealty. A declaration not of blind obedience, but of allegiance with reservations.

At last, John beckoned his spigurnel with an ill-tempered flick of his wrist. The official scuttled forward, clutching a leather satchel from which he produced the king's wax seal. With a silken cord, the spigurnel attached the king's seal to the charter, before stepping back.

When at last it was done, John turned away without another word, his shoulders rigid beneath his cloak as he stalked back to his steed. Estienne caught the triumphant looks traded among the barons before they suppressed their satisfaction beneath impassive brows. Only FitzWalter allowed himself the indulgence of a smile as he gestured to a clerk of the chancery to gather up the charter for safekeeping.

As he made to follow William back to the horses, Estienne's eye fell upon Guillaume. The young Marshal stood apart as he watched the proceedings. For an instant, Estienne thought he might step forward, breach the void yawning between himself and his father. But the moment shattered as John's cold voice cracked across the clearing.

'We're done here. Let us hope, my lords, that your words are proved more constant than your loyalties.'

FitzWalter stepped forward, chin thrust high, one hand resting deliberately on the hilt of his sword. 'Let this be an end to it then, Your Grace. We have each sworn solemn oaths this day. Let us pray to Our Heavenly Lord that we have the strength to hold to them.'

'Indeed,' John bit out. 'Let us pray.'

And with that he hauled brutally on the reins, his destrier shying and half-rearing at the sudden savagery. John brought the beast under control with a curse then, with a last poisonous look toward the barons, he dug in his spurs and set off at pace.

Estienne scrambled into the saddle, riled snorts and the stamping of horses all around, and he saw Earl William's jaw was set as they fled that field. A glance behind, and the barons stood unmoving beneath their wind-teased banners. Among them, Estienne saw Guillaume watching his father ride away.

As they reached the road north, Estienne couldn't help but shudder, despite the warm summer wind. The charter was sealed, the oaths spoken, but he could still taste the sourness of unfinished business.

No, this was not the end of it. Not by far.

20

Despite the winter chill, Estienne's gambeson was sodden with sweat. He squinted into the sun's glare, hands locked around the battered hilt of his tourney sword as he faced Goffrey across the churned earth.

Around them, the snow-capped hills of Pembrokeshire stretched away, the sparkling span of the Cleddau Ddu glinting in the near distance. The castle at their backs thrust proud from the rock, the red lion of Marshal blowing in the breeze. But Estienne spared little thought for the view. His whole world was focused on the man before him. The wily veteran in his worn harness, his blunt blade weaving patterns in the air.

They had been at it for what felt like days. Estienne's arms burned, his lungs fit to burst. And still Goffrey came on, that old wolf's smile on his lips, feet quick beneath him despite the years and the extra weight he carried.

'Come on, lad.' Goffrey beckoned with his shield, the oak already splintered and cracked. 'Put your back into it. My grandsire hits harder.'

Estienne surged forward, sword battering at Goffrey's shield with all the strength he could muster. The splintered wood buck-led, a jagged crack spiderwebbing through the grain.

A pounding of hooves tore through Estienne's focus. William Marshal reined in his destrier nearby, stopping to observe them. Behind him, poised side-saddle on a fine-boned jennet, Eva looked on from beneath a hood of white fur.

Estienne faltered, sword lowering a fraction. Goffrey lunged, snake-quick and caught the cross-guard of his hilt in the rent in his shield. A brutal twist sent Estienne's sword spinning into the snow.

'Focus on your enemy, boy,' Goffrey growled. 'Distractions will see you dead.'

Estienne dove for his blade, but Goffrey was faster. The old knight stamped down hard, pinning the sword beneath his foot. Then, dropping his battered shield, he drew something with a blur of steel, chains clinking. The hammer he always kept at his side.

Estienne threw himself back. Not fast enough. The hammer hissed toward his face and a cold gust chased down Estienne's spine. Goffrey halted the hammer a hairsbreadth from his skull. Then the old knight leaned close, something playful in his grin.

'You're dead, boy.'

Estienne stifled a curse, just as Goffrey stifled a laugh. He was conscious of William and Eva still watching, but Goffrey seemed unconcerned by their audience.

'Here. Give it a try.' He held out the hammer, and Estienne took it in his empty hand.

It was lighter than he expected as he wrapped his palm around the haft, feeling the chill of the steel against his calluses. It lacked a blade's elegance but there was a brutal efficiency to it as he gave it a practice swing.

'She's not a pretty lass twirling at a dance,' Goffrey said gruffly. 'Let the hammer do the work. Get it moving and aim for the weak spots, but skulls are the best. It'll punch a hole in a helm sure as cracking a walnut. Here, try it against the pell.'

Estienne approached the wooden pole they used for practice and hefted the hammer again, trying to find the balance of it. He was clumsy, and each swing felt awkward as he hammered at the wood.

'Plant your feet,' Goffrey barked. 'Root yourself. And put your hips into it.'

Estienne gritted his teeth and widened his stance. The next swing was better, the hammer's momentum lending force to the blow. He swung again. Again. Falling into a rhythm, each impact a jolt of savage satisfaction. What the hammer lacked in finesse it made up for in sheer, crushing power. Splinters flew, and a fierce grin pulled at Estienne's mouth. There was a raw, primal thrill to this. The unleashing of something dark and wild that slept coiled within his chest. He could get used to the hammer's song.

A bright peal of laughter rang out. He turned to see Eva watching him, eyes sparkling with something that might have been mirth. Or mockery. He was never sure with her.

'Keep your head in the fight, lad,' Goffrey growled.

Estienne raised the hammer, ready for another swing, when hoofbeats broke the morning calm. He turned to see another rider galloping up the hill toward them. The horseman reined up in a spray of snow, his mount's flanks lathered with sweat – Hubert of Burgh, riding with mail beneath his surcoat of red and white. His arrival armed and armoured could mean nothing good.

Hubert dismounted and William Marshal swung down from his destrier, striding forward to clasp Hubert's wrist. The men looked almost alike, two war dogs in service to their king, but where William was lean and sharp-featured, Hubert was broad of shoulder and solid, a mastiff to Marshal's wolfhound.

'Hubert.' William's voice was warm, but there was a note of

concern. 'It's rare to see you this far west. What brings you to Pembroke?'

Hubert's answering smile was grim. 'Would that it were pleasure that drew me here, William. But I fear I come as the bearer of black tidings. The king has appealed to Pope Innocent for aid. His Holiness has declared the Charter of Runnymede invalid. All those who stand against John are to be excommunicated. Cast out from the grace of God.'

For a long, brittle moment, William said nothing. When he spoke, his voice was sullen. 'And the barons? How have they answered this news?'

'With defiance. Already the rebels have struck out from London and seized Rochester Castle. Robert FitzWalter and his allies have also reached out to France. They mean to invite Prince Louis to challenge John for the throne.'

A shudder chased down Estienne's spine at those words. To defy the Pope was one thing, but to lure a foreign prince into their rebellion was treason of the blackest sort.

'Prince Louis.' William spat the name like a curse. 'And John knows of this?'

Hubert nodded. 'Aye. The king has already set siege to Rochester. He means to quell this rebellion with fire and sword. To grind FitzWalter and his ilk beneath his boot heel before Louis has even set foot on these shores.'

'Then we must act. The king will have need of every loyal man in the days to come.' He clasped Hubert's shoulder. 'You've done well to bring this to me. To ride so far with such haste.'

A ghost of a smile touched Hubert's lips. 'We've weathered worse storms than this, William. And we'll weather this one, God willing.'

'Aye. Sup with me tonight, Hubert. Take some rest. At dawn, we ride.'

Hubert offered a shallow bow. 'You have my thanks. A bed and a hot meal would be most welcome.'

As the two men mounted their horses, Estienne stood rooted, the hammer suddenly heavy in his hand. His mind reeled as he tried to comprehend the enormity of what was unfolding.

He watched as the three riders made their way back toward the castle walls. As if sensing his gaze, Eva glanced over her shoulder. There was something in her face, a flicker of emotion quickly shuttered. Then she turned away.

Beside him, Goffrey heaved a sigh. 'This time it's war, lad. No running from it now.'

'What do we do, Goffrey?' Estienne asked. 'How do we fight fellow Englishmen?'

The old knight's smile was grim as a slash of steel. 'We sharpen our swords. We oil our mail and say our prayers. We do what must be done.'

Estienne nodded, looking to the horizon where dark clouds lurked, heavy with the promise of yet more snow. A portent of the storm to come.

21

Fat flakes drifted down, blanketing the land in snow. Estienne hunched deeper into his cloak, breath steaming in the frigid air as he rode at the Marshal's side. Their destriers stamped and snorted, hooves crunching through the fresh powder. Ahead, the monastery at Saint Albans rose from the frozen earth like a great stone sentinel. Its high walls and square towers stood stark against the colourless sky, a looming promise of shelter from the bitter cold. But as they drew closer, Estienne felt a chill that had little to do with the winter wind. Somewhere within those walls, King John waited, and it was doubtful he would be in a sunny mood.

William reined in before the heavy oak gates, a score of men-at-arms at his back. Their surcoats were crusted with snow, the red lion of Marshal rendered in frost. At a word from William, the gates creaked open and they rode into the monastery's yard, the sudden absence of wind almost jarring.

Estienne dismounted, handing his reins to a nearby groom. He stamped feeling back into his feet, taking in the soaring arches and intricate stone carvings with a sense of awe. He had never seen such grandeur, even in Earl William's keeps, but there was little time to marvel. With a curt gesture to a waiting monk, William strode towards a small door set into the wall. Estienne hurried to follow, unease settling in his gut. Whatever awaited them beyond that door, he knew it would not be pleasant.

The cloister was huge, the air thick with the stench of tallow and goose fat. In the centre of the vast chamber, King John sprawled in a high-backed chair, attended by a pair of nervous-looking monks who were rubbing unguent into his bare feet, their hands glistening with grease.

At John's right hand stood a brutal slab of a man, his arms crossed over a barrel chest. He wore a red surcoat, a white griffin embroidered upon the breast, marking him as Falkes of Bréauté. The king's most feared enforcer, and a man with a reputation for slaughter.

Beside him, Hubert of Burgh cut a statelier figure, though his features were no less hard. And there, resplendent in a blue surcoat blazoned with six rearing lions, stood Willem Longsword, the Earl of Salisbury. But it was the last man who held Estienne's attention. Tall and lean, with a face like a blade, he wore a surcoat of red, a lion rampant picked out in thread of gold. Savari of Mauléon, one of the king's most lethal servants, brutal and cunning in equal measure.

William bowed to the king, a gesture Estienne hastened to mirror. 'Your Grace. We came as soon as we received your summons.'

John waved a hand, a garnet flashing on one beringed finger. 'So you did, Marshal. So you did. And not a moment too soon.' He smiled, a sharp, unpleasant thing. 'But we've had some sport of late, haven't we, my lords? Rochester has proven most diverting. Who knew swine could serve so well as sappers?'

The king laughed at that as though it were the funniest thing he had ever heard. Estienne already knew of the victory at

Rochester. How they had dug under one of the castle's towers and burned pigs by the score beneath. The heat from their fat had caused the foundations to crumble and offered the king's besieging forces a way inside.

William's face remained impassive. 'A cunning stratagem, Your Grace. The capture of Rochester has struck a great blow against our foes.'

John waved a dismissive hand. 'Yes, yes, very good. But one defeat will hardly cow these traitors. They're like rats, Marshal. Scurrying to hide in their hovels when the cat comes calling. But never fear. We'll burn them out, every last one.'

William inclined his head. 'A worthy aim, sire. But if I may, we must also look to the wider threat. The army gathering beyond our shores.'

'Ah, yes. The French cur. I wonder when he will come?'

'I think he's already on his way, Your Grace. Prince Louis has made no secret of his ambitions. With the rebel barons offering him a foothold, he'll seize this chance to claim England's crown with all haste.'

John surged to his feet, wincing as his inflamed joints complained. 'Then we'll have to disabuse him of that ambition, won't we?' The king began to pace, his bare feet slapping against the rushes. 'Falkes, Willem and Savari will take command in the south. Muster what men you can and fortify the ports. If the French make landfall, I want them greeted.' He flashed a savage grin. 'Given a proper English welcome.'

Falkes bared his teeth in an answering smile. 'It will be our pleasure, sire.'

'Good man.' John turned to the rest of his knights. 'As for me, we ride north. I will raze every rebel stronghold, put their lands to the torch. Starve them out, grind them down until they've naught left to offer their French master.'

William's already troubled brow furrowed yet deeper. 'And the common folk, sire? The peasants who work those lands?'

John shrugged irritably. 'What of them? Let them burn with the rest. I'll not have traitors in my kingdom, high or low.' He grinned, teeth flashing like fangs. 'Besides, I've a host of mercenaries champing at the bit. Godless brutes, but they know their work. They'll put the fear of God into those northern rats. By the time that French pup sets foot on our shores, he'll find only ashes and bones.'

William stepped forward, his jaw tight. 'Your Grace, I must counsel caution. The use of mercenaries on English soil, men who fight not for loyalty or honour, but only for coin, it's a dangerous path.'

'Dangerous? No, Marshal, what's dangerous is allowing rebellion to fester unchecked. Those sell-swords are a means to an end. A tool, nothing more.'

'A tool with no master,' William countered. 'Mercenaries have no loyalty, no code. They'll rape and pillage at will, and it's the innocents who will suffer.'

'Then let them suffer,' John snarled. 'If it brings these rebels to heel, I call it a fair price.'

'The smallfolk are not our enemy, sire. They're not soldiers or rebels, only people trying to eke out a living.'

John's face twisted, his fists clenching at his sides. 'You seem very concerned with the plight of these mud-grubbing peasants, William. One might question where your true loyalties lie.'

Estienne felt the hairs on his nape prickle at the king's tone, the undercurrent of menace there.

William stood very still, his voice carefully measured. 'My loyalties have always been to the crown, Your Grace. You know this.'

'Do I?' John's smile never reached his eyes. 'What of your son,

Marshal? That cur Guillaume who's thrown in his lot with the barons? I don't see you dragging him before me in chains.'

'Guillaume has made his choices. They're not mine.'

'No?' John stepped closer. 'A pity, then. A loyal father should have better control of his brood. Perhaps, if he can't bring his own blood to heel, he has no place leading armies in his king's name...'

William drew himself up, towering over the king. In that moment, Estienne saw not an ageing knight, but a pillar of iron, unbent and unbreaking.

'I am the king's man,' William said, each word ringing with conviction. 'I have always served with honour and will continue to do so. But my fealty does not make me blind. Nor does it rob me of my reason, or the right to speak it.'

John offered no reply. For a long, taut moment, Estienne feared his master had gone too far. The king was not a man to suffer defiance, even couched in courtesy.

But then John exhaled a sharp hiss through his clenched teeth. 'You'll do as I command, Marshal. As is your sworn duty. It seems King Llywelyn has been emboldened by the actions of the barons. He smells blood. So you'll secure the Welsh borders and leave the rebels to me. Are we clear?'

'We are, Your Grace.' William's voice was cold as ice. 'I will do as my king commands. But the fate of this realm is the concern of every man who calls it home. And I'll not stay silent while it burns.'

Without waiting for a reply, he turned and strode from the chamber. Estienne stood frozen for a heartbeat, transfixed by the look of naked fury on John's face. Then he hastened after his lord, his chest tight with dread.

Outside he was greeted by the cold once again. Climbing upon his horse beside Earl William, he considered it much preferable to the warmth they might share with King John.

PART FOUR: STORM OF FIRE

WALES, 1216 AD

22

The camp sprawled across the trampled field, a sea of mud-spattered tents shivering in the bitter wind. Estienne picked his way between them, careful not to trip over guy ropes or slumbering bodies. The stench of blood and sweat hung thick, underlaid by the sour reek of infection.

Men-at-arms huddled around winnowing fires. Their helms and shields were dented, gambesons crusted with filth. Squires scurried here and there, bearing steaming kettles and blood-stained bandages. The moans of the injured haunted the air, piteous and unrelenting.

King Llywelyn the Great had attacked with vigour, his Welsh spearmen swarming down from the hills like wolves upon the fold. Earl William had rallied his men, marshalling charge after desperate charge. Estienne had been at his side through it all, witnessing the grim consequences of this war. Now the campaign languished, both sides bled to a stalemate. They were dug in, licking their wounds, circling like wary dogs.

Estienne skirted a gaggle of men dicing over an upturned

shield. Their movements were listless as they waited for the next
mad charge, the next battle that might end it all. He turned his
back on their hopeless faces, striding on towards the command
tent, Marshal's banner hanging limp above the entrance. Estienne
ducked inside, squinting in the gloom. Candles guttered on the
table, casting shifting shadows across the maps and markers
strewn there. And bent over it all, William Marshal stood unmoving, a missive crumpled in one fist.

He looked old and weary, bowed beneath the weight of his
years. The stalemated campaign had taken its toll on them all,
but none more so than the earl. His mouth was drawn into a grim
line as he stared down at the parchment as though it offended
him.

Estienne stepped forward, reaching for the jug of wine on the
table's edge. He poured a generous cup, the rich scent temporarily
drowning the pervasive stink of the camp.

'My lord,' he said softly, pressing the cup into William's hand.

The earl blinked, seeming to come back to himself. He took the
cup with a grunt that might have been thanks, and drained half of
it in one long swallow.

'The news from the rest of the country,' Estienne ventured. 'Is it
good?'

'Good?' William whispered. 'The opposite, boy. The king has
ravaged the north. Plundered his own people's lands like a
common brigand. Those foreign mercenaries of his... they've left a
trail of corpses from York to Carlisle.'

Estienne had heard the rumours, of course. The whispers of
horror carried from one camp to another. But to hear those atrocities confirmed tasted bitter indeed.

'And in the south, Falkes of Bréauté has done his share of
murder,' William continued, each word dripping bitterness.
'Sacked Ely without pity, put half the town to the torch. They say

the screams could be heard for leagues, the gutters running red with blood.'

'Is nowhere safe, then? Does the whole country burn?'

William drained his cup, thumping it back to the table. 'It may soon come to that. Cruelty begets only cruelty. I fear we've sown a bitter crop, and the reaping will be long and red. But that is not all. I've had word of a planned attack on Worcester Castle. Ranulph of Blondeville seeks to claim it for the king once more.'

Estienne frowned. 'I do not understand why—'

'My son is there. Guillaume. If the castle is besieged, he'll be caught up in it. Trapped. And I cannot warn him with this damned incursion blighting the Marches.'

The anguish in those last words cut Estienne deep. William was stuck here while his son was in peril. The earl lived and breathed loyalty, to crown and kin alike, and to be unable to ride to Guillaume's aid would be a torment beyond bearing.

'Send me.' The words left Estienne's lips before he'd fully formed the thought. 'I can warn him. Get him free of the castle before the siege closes in.'

William looked up. 'You? Alone? It would be dangerous. The roads are thick with rebels and cutthroats.'

'There is danger everywhere,' Estienne countered. 'What's a little more? I ask for this honour, my lord. Let me serve as your hand in this.'

For a long moment, William stared at him. Estienne half-expected a curt dismissal, a reminder of his place. But then the earl sighed, his face softening into something almost like pride.

'You've grown bold, lad.' A ghost of a smile touched his lips. 'Very well. You will carry my message to Worcester. See Guillaume safe but heed me well – I'll have your hide for a saddle blanket if you get yourself killed. Understood?'

Estienne bowed his head. 'Understood, my lord.'

He paused at the threshold of the tent, looking back at William's bowed head. In that moment, he seemed diminished, as though the weight of the world rested on his shoulders, crushing him inch by inch.

Estienne would not fail in this. For his lord's sake, and for Guillaume's, he would see it done. No matter the cost.

23

The chestnut palfrey's flanks were slick with sweat as Estienne crested the final rise. A hundred miles lay behind them, a gruelling journey of forest paths and game trails, anything to avoid the main roads. His limbs felt heavy, but he dared not rest. Not with Worcester Castle looming ahead.

He reined in, listening to the wind sigh through the bare branches. Distantly, a crow cawed, the sound carrying in the stillness. No hint of marching feet or jangling of tack, but still Estienne's nerves thrummed. He urged the palfrey on, keeping off the road where an overgrown hedgerow offered some scant cover. Ahead, the castle walls thrust from the earth, and he could make out tiny figures scurrying along the battlements.

His jaw clenched. Guillaume was still inside those walls, unaware of the noose tightening around his neck. Estienne touched heels to the palfrey's sides, urging the weary beast onward. There would be no rest, no respite. Not until he reached Guillaume and saw Earl William's warning delivered.

He dismounted in a coppice of trees, far enough from the gates to avoid being seen, and tied the palfrey's reins to a low branch, murmuring an apology to the tired beast. Shouts drifted from the castle as he edged closer, keeping low. A train of carts trundled up the road towards the barbican, piled high with barrels and sacks. Men-at-arms swarmed about them, unloading the cargo and making their way through the yawning gate.

Estienne chewed his lip, mind racing. To walk up bold as brass and demand entry would be madness. They'd clap him in irons sooner than let him cross the threshold, Earl's squire or not. But as they took in their supplies, a man might slip through unremarked. If he were quick.

Breath held, he waited for the guards' backs to turn, then darted from cover. A hogshead of ale teetered on the edge of the nearest cart, and Estienne slung his arm around it, bracing it on one shoulder as though he'd been tasked to shift it.

'Ho there!' A shout from the walls. 'You lot, get that all stowed. Hop to, unless you want to be eating rats come a fortnight.'

Estienne kept his face down as he carried the awkward load. Feet churned around him, men grunting beneath barrels and sacks of grain. He was jostled, but he gritted his teeth as he passed beneath the iron teeth of the portcullis. The bailey opened up before him, teeming with urgent industry. Estienne dumped his hogshead among the rest and carried on walking, hugging the shadow of the wall.

He was inside, but his task was only half done. Guillaume waited somewhere in this hive, unaware of the danger encircling him with every passing moment. The bailey seethed with activity, an ant's nest of men hauling timber and stone to shore up the walls. Hammers rang and horses stamped as Estienne wove between the outbuildings, trying to get his bearings. The keep rose at the far end, a solid mass of weathered stone. If Guillaume was anywhere, it would be there, overseeing the defence.

Estienne set off across the muddy expanse, shoulders

hunched, trying to affect the purposeful stride of a man with a task. All around him, the castle hummed with urgent work. Carpenters and smiths laboured as men-at-arms drilled with pikes and crossbows in the shadow of the wall. There was an air of grim anticipation, a sense that all this frenzied effort might soon be put to the test.

A shout cut through the clamour nearby and Estienne flinched, but it was only a jongleur trying to whip up morale with a bawdy song. He drew a deep breath, trying to slow the thunder of his heart as the weathered stone of the keep loomed before him.

'You there. Halt.'

Ice trickled down Estienne's spine. He froze, fighting the urge to bolt like a startled hare as a man-at-arms appeared to block his path. The guard was burly and wary-eyed, one hand resting on the hilt of the sword at his hip as he closed the distance between them.

'State your business,' he growled. 'I've not seen you before.'

Estienne's tongue cleaved to the roof of his suddenly dry mouth. Excuses and half-truths bubbled up, but under that iron stare, they all withered to dust.

'I'm here to see Ser Guillaume,' he managed at last. 'I have an urgent message for him. From his father, Earl William.'

Suspicion darkened the man's stern features. 'That so? And I'm to just take your word, am I?' His sword rasped an inch from its scabbard. 'In times like these, a man can't be too careful about who he lets near his lord.'

Cold sweat prickled Estienne's nape. He was keenly aware that all he carried was a knife. If this came to blows, it would be short and bloody. He opened his mouth, fumbling for some way to convince the guard of his sincerity. Then a shadow fell over them both, and a hand clamped down hard on Estienne's shoulder from behind.

'Well, well.' Ilbert FitzDane's voice was a dark purr, his fingers digging into Estienne's shoulder like talons. 'What have we here? A spy? Caught in the act?'

'No, I—'

The blow came out of nowhere, an explosion of pain that snapped Estienne's head back. He reeled, but Ilbert's fist was knotted in Estienne's jerkin, wrenching him around.

'Bind him,' Ilbert snarled.

Rough hands seized Estienne, the man-at-arms cinching his arms behind his back with ruthless efficiency. He thrashed, tasting blood, but it was useless as they dragged him away, his feet scrabbling on the flagstones.

The outbuilding they hauled him to was little more than a stone box reeking of old straw. Estienne hit the floor hard, grunting as the air whooshed from his lungs. Before he could roll to his feet, a boot cracked into his ribs, driving him back down.

'Did you think you'd just waltz in here unchallenged?' Ilbert's face swam above him, lips peeled back from his teeth. 'Worm your way in, undermine us from within?'

'Ilbert, listen—'

Another blow, this time to the belly. Estienne curled up in pain, gasping.

'I'll not hear your lies, traitor.' Ilbert grasped Estienne's hair, wrenching his head back. 'Did King John send you? Is he so craven now, to use his lapdogs as spies?'

Estienne coughed, spitting blood. 'I'm not a spy. I swear it.'

'No? Then why skulk in here like a thief? Why spin falsehoods to get close to Guillaume?'

Ilbert dragged Estienne to a chair and lashed him to it with a length of rough hemp. The ropes bit into his flesh, his shoulders screaming at the awkward angle.

'I have a message,' Estienne panted. 'From Earl William.'

That earned him a backhanded slap, hard enough to snap his

head to the side. 'More lies. Did you truly think I'd allow a base-born churl like you to spread his poison here?' Ilbert drew his knife and it glinted in the half-light before he placed the tip beneath Estienne's chin. 'I'll cut the truth from you if I must. Strip the skin from your bones. You were sent to kill him, weren't you? Admit it, cur.'

Estienne swallowed, feeling the knife-tip bob against his vulnerable throat. Fear soured the back of his tongue, an acrid taste of bile and blood, but he clenched his jaw hard.

'I wasn't, I swear it,' he said thickly. 'I'm telling the truth.'

Ilbert's blade carved a line of fire across Estienne's collarbone, his shirt blossoming red. He clenched his teeth hard on a scream as Ilbert leaned close, breath hot against his cheek.

'This is only the beginning,' the knight hissed. 'I'll flay you by inches, peel the skin from your lying mouth.'

The knife twisted, worrying at the wound. Estienne squeezed his eyes shut, tears leaking from beneath the lids.

'Tell me why you're here.' Ilbert punctuated each word with a fresh jolt of agony, the knife-tip digging and slicing. 'Who sent you? What mischief were you to sow among us?'

Estienne ground his jaw tight, determined not to utter a word.

'Speak, curse you.' Ilbert seized Estienne's jaw in a crushing grip, wrenching his face up.

Estienne blinked, the knight's snarling visage swimming in and out of focus. 'No. My words are for Guillaume alone.'

With a wordless snarl, Ilbert kicked him in the chest. The chair tipped backwards, crashing to the ground, and Estienne's head cracked on the floorboards in an explosion of bright pain.

'I'll spill your life here, dog,' Ilbert panted. 'Paint the floor with your traitor's blood.'

Estienne heard the grind of iron hinges. A voice, raised in sharp question. Ilbert snarled something, an animal sound of fury and frustration. Then hands were on Estienne, his chair suddenly righted, as he drifted in a red sea of pain.

'Speak plainly, man. What is the meaning of this?' Guillaume's voice, sharp with anger.

Estienne fought to raise his head, his neck a column of agony. The heir to Pembroke stood over him, his face set in a grim mask.

Ilbert faced him, bloodied knife still clenched in one fist. 'I caught this dog sneaking into the castle. He claims to carry a message from your father, but it's clear he's naught but an assassin for the king.'

Guillaume's gaze flicked to Estienne. 'Is this so? You come bearing word from Earl William?'

Estienne struggled to order his scattered wits. 'Yes, my lord. I was sent to warn you. Your father has learned of a plan to besiege this castle.'

'Lies,' Ilbert snarled. 'The craven seeks only to lead us astray. To feed us false counsel and weaken our resolve.'

'The attack will come within days.' The room swayed drunkenly as Estienne forced the words out past his split lips. 'The earl bids you flee, my lord. Get to safety while you still can.'

Guillaume's face was unreadable, a mask carved in stone. For an endless moment he was silent, glancing from Estienne's battered face to Ilbert's seething fury.

'Guillaume, surely you cannot credit the word of John's lick-spittle,' Ilbert pressed. 'He is a deceiver, sent to whisper poison in your ear.'

'Please,' Estienne gasped. 'I speak only truth. If you stay, you'll be trapped here.'

'You cannot seriously entertain this base deceit. I beg you, let me put this dog out of his misery.'

Guillaume turned to Estienne. 'You claim to speak with my father's voice? Swear to me now, on your honour as his man, that you have told me true. That this is no ruse, no ploy born of King John's spite.'

Estienne met Guillaume's stare squarely. 'I swear it. On my life and my loyalty to the earl. I am no spy, only a faithful servant tasked with seeing you safe.'

The young Marshal was silent, then, slowly, he nodded. 'I believe you. You took a great risk coming here as you did. I will not see that loyalty repaid with doubt and suspicion.'

Ilbert made to speak, but Guillaume raised a hand for him to be silent. 'Go, saddle our horses and meet us beyond the gatehouse.'

For a moment, Estienne feared Ilbert might defy Guillaume outright, but with a muttered curse, the knight stalked from the room.

Guillaume stepped close, drawing a small knife from his belt. Estienne tensed, but Guillaume merely reached for the ropes still binding him to the chair. A few deft strokes and they fell away, the blood rushing back into Estienne's numb hands.

'Come,' Guillaume said, helping Estienne stand. 'If what you say is true, we must move swiftly.'

Together, they stumbled from that dark room. Estienne leaned heavily on Guillaume, each step an effort. The bailey was a scene of ordered chaos as they emerged, and they were barely noticed as Guillaume helped him back across the bailey to the gatehouse. Men-at-arms standing guard at the gate looked on in confusion but made no move to stop Guillaume Marshal as he crossed the castle threshold.

When they were far enough from the walls, Guillaume drew them to a stop. Estienne managed to stand on his own, as the eldest son of his lord looked down at him.

'You risked much to see me safe. I'll not forget that.'

'I did only as my lord commanded. As any true squire would.'

Hoofbeats shattered the moment as Ilbert cantered toward them with a destrier in tow. He drew up short at the sight of them, jaw tight with barely leashed anger.

'Your horse,' he bit out. 'As you commanded.'

Guillaume offered Estienne a nod before he swung into the saddle. Before they could ride away, Estienne took hold of Guillaume's rein.

'Do you have a message for your father?'

A shadow passed over Guillaume's face. 'No. My path lies apart from his now. Let it stay that way.'

All Estienne could do was release the rein and step back, watching as he rode away, with Ilbert close at his back. The sting of the knife wound seemed to sharpen as they disappeared. Estienne had succeeded in his task, but it still left a bitterness on his tongue. Some part of him knew it would not be the last time he would taste it.

24

The stink of blood and sweat clung to the encampment like a funeral shroud. Moans of the wounded threaded between the tattered tents, piteous and unrelenting as Estienne picked his way through the churned mud, leading the palfrey behind him.

He passed a knot of men hunched over a spitting cookfire, and a sound rose above the camp's dour rhythm – a snatch of laughter, jeering and bright. Estienne frowned. Surely the campaign couldn't have turned so quickly in his absence. Last he'd seen, Earl William had been locked in a grim stalemate with the Welsh king, each side circling the other, hackles raised.

'Oi. You there.'

Estienne turned to find a pair of men-at-arms striding toward him. He stood his ground as they closed in.

'State your business,' the taller of the two growled.

'I'm Estienne Wace. Squire to William Marshal.'

The men exchanged a glance, doubt writ plain on their wind-chapped faces.

'The Marshal's squire, eh? Sent off on some errand, were you?'

Estienne straightened. 'I was. And now I've returned. So, if you'd be so kind as to let me pass...'

He made to step around them, but the shorter one moved to block his path. 'Not so fast. You could be anyone. How do we know—'

'Estienne.' William Marshal's voice was gravel.

The men-at-arms turned to see the earl approaching through the gloom.

'My lord, we were just—'

'Yes, you were,' the Marshal replied dismissively. 'See to the lad's horse.' One of them took hold of the palfrey's reins, and they led the steed away. Alone with his squire, William took in the bruises mottling Estienne's face, the blood crusted to his jerkin. 'You look like hell, lad.'

Estienne bowed, trying not to grimace as his wound pulled. 'It's been a long road, my lord.'

'I'll wager it has.' Marshal jerked his chin at Estienne's collarbone where the blood had seeped through. 'Let's see to that before it's infected.'

He turned and Estienne stumbled after. The surgeon's tent was close and fetid, thick with the cloying stench of blood and herbed unguents. Estienne perched on a stool, jaw clenched as the surgeon peeled away the torn material with care.

'This is nasty.' The man's breath puffed sour against Estienne's cheek as he bent close to examine the wound. 'And deep. Right down to the bone.'

Estienne hissed through his teeth as the surgeon pressed around the edges of the gash. Marshal stood watching, arms folded over his broad chest.

'How did this happen?' There was no censure in Marshal's voice, but the question hung heavy nonetheless.

'There was some... trouble. When I reached Worcester.'

'Trouble?'

Estienne gripped tight to his knees as the surgeon began to clean the wound with stinging spirits. 'I was taken for an enemy.'

'By whom?'

A lance of pain shot through him as the surgeon pressed a pad of linen against the gash, and Estienne sucked in a steadying breath. 'Ilbert.'

Marshal was still for a long moment. When he spoke, his voice was dangerously soft. 'FitzDane did this?'

'Yes, my lord. He took me for a spy. Thought he'd cut the truth out of me.'

A muscle ticked in Marshal's jaw. The surgeon began to stitch and Estienne felt suddenly nauseous.

'I curse the day I took that runt into my household,' Marshal growled. 'I knew he was poison from the start. Should have drowned him like a rat in a rain barrel.'

Estienne focused on the bite of the surgeon's needle, the sharp tug of catgut through flesh. When the last stitch was tied off, Marshal stepped closer to Estienne. 'The message. You delivered it? Guillaume is safe?'

'He is, my lord. I reached him in time. He quit the castle before the siege closed in.'

'That's something, at least. You did well, lad. Acted with true courage and loyalty.'

The praise sat uneasily in Estienne's gut. He thought of Guillaume's stony face. The absence of any message for his father.

The surgeon tied off his bandage and stepped back. 'He'll need rest to heal. To keep the wound from festering. I suggest you send him back to Pembroke.'

'No.' Estienne's voice rang loud in the close confines. He stood, ignoring the startled look of the surgeon. 'I'll not be left behind. Not now.'

Marshal frowned. 'Estienne, you heard the man. That gash needs time to knit.'

Estienne met his lord's gaze squarely. He'd crawled through blood and muck to reach Worcester, all to deliver Marshal's message. It would take more than a stitched cut to stop him now.

'I can ride, my lord. I can fight.'

Marshal studied him for a long moment, assessing him from head to heel. 'You've a spine of steel in you, lad. Stubbornness, too, by the wagonload.' A flicker at the corner of his mouth, there and gone. 'You'll need it for what's to come.'

'My lord,' he began, half-dreading the answer. 'What happens now?'

'Now we finish this. Llywelyn thinks to catch us at a weak moment, wear us thin while the kingdom frays at the edges. I mean to disabuse him of that notion.'

Estienne straightened, suddenly eager as a hound on a scent. 'I'm fit to ride, my lord. Give me a fresh horse and I'll be at your side when—'

'No.' Marshal fixed him with a stare that brooked no argument. 'I have another task for you. One of vital importance.'

He drew a folded letter from his surcoat, sealed with a blob of dark wax. Estienne took it, a prickle of unease chasing down his nape at the seriousness on Marshal's face.

'I need this carried to Hubert of Burgh. With all haste.'

'Lord Hubert? At Dover?'

Marshal nodded. 'My spies send word from France. Louis means to land on our shores, and soon. You must reach Hubert. Warn him of what's coming. A lot depends on this, lad.'

'I won't fail you, my lord. I swear it, on my life and honour.' The words sounded braver than he felt, and he hoped Marshal couldn't hear the waver in them.

'Then go. Ride hard and fast, and pray you reach Hubert before the French do.'

Estienne bowed his head, feeling the weight of the letter in his hand. He ducked out into the light, blinking at the sudden brightness. Exhaustion dragged at him like an anchor, but beneath it, a thrum of fierce elation. He would ride for the coast, carrying his lord's word, and deliver his dire warning before calamity fell.

25

The hooves of their destriers clopped through the mud as Ilbert and Guillaume rode through the squalid streets of London. Ilbert wrinkled his nose at the stench that rose to greet them – a heady mix of smoke, effluent and rot that clung to the back of his throat. He would never get used to the reek of this city, teeming with the unwashed. And yet, something was different this time. An undercurrent that ran through the filthy lanes, a sense of excitement. Ilbert saw it in the faces of the rag-clad beggars and soot-stained smiths, a glimmer of anticipation in their eyes as they went about their wretched business.

'Do you feel it?' he asked Guillaume. 'Something's happened while we were gone.'

Guillaume nodded. 'Aye. The whole place hums with it.'

Ilbert glanced down, marking how the mud of the streets had been churned to a froth, rutted with the passing of countless feet. 'Looks like we missed quite the parade.'

A ghost of a smile touched Guillaume's lips. 'Then we'd best find FitzWalter and see what all the fuss is about.'

They spurred their mounts onward, eating up the remaining

distance to Baynard's Castle. With every stride, the sense of restless anticipation grew, until Ilbert could almost taste it in the air.

The walls of the castle loomed before them, surrounded by scaffolding, although the work to rebuild it was almost done. But it was the sight of the banners snapping above the battlements that drew Ilbert's eye and held it. Azure flags, emblazoned with the golden fleur-de-lys of France. The arms of Prince Louis.

'God's eyes,' Ilbert breathed. 'He's here. The prince actually came.'

Guillaume said nothing, but the tightening of his jaw spoke volumes. They spurred their destriers through the barbican, the portcullis yawning open. Beyond, the castle bailey seethed with activity. Knights and men-at-arms crowded every inch of the yard, more than Ilbert had ever seen gathered in one place. The great lords of the realm, all flocked to the French banner.

And at the heart of that storm stood Robert FitzWalter, his hauteur palpable even at a distance. The great baron stepped forward as they dismounted, a lupine smile on his lips.

'Guillaume, Ilbert. You're late to the festivities.'

'Our apologies, my lord,' Guillaume replied. 'The ride from Worcester was not a gentle one.'

FitzWalter waved a dismissive hand. 'You're here now, that's what matters. Come, there's someone you should meet.'

He led them up the keep steps, to where a slim figure waited, clad in a surcoat of rich blue worked with gold. Prince Louis was surrounded by grim-looking men, some dressed almost as regally as he, others clad in the hard leather of mercenaries. He was more handsome than Ilbert had expected, clean-shaven with dark hair oiled back across his scalp. The prince held himself with the easy arrogance of a man born to rule, a lazy smile playing about his lips as FitzWalter presented them.

'My lord, may I introduce Guillaume Marshal and Ilbert Fitz-

Dane. Two of our most stalwart companions in this noble endeavour.'

Louis raked them with eyes the colour of the summer sky before he focused on Guillaume. 'Your reputation precedes you, Lord Guillaume.' His voice was smooth and cultured, holding none of the grating petulance that so often soured King John's speech.

As both men bowed, Ilbert couldn't help but appreciate how easily their fealty came. How this young prince was truly their rightful king. A lion, come to claim his place at the head of the pride.

'If we may,' Robert said. 'There are some things we should discuss.'

He looked at Ilbert with a gracious smile, though it was obvious he wanted privacy. Guillaume shot an apologetic glance as he allowed himself to be led to the far side of the bastion, where he, Robert and the prince put heads together in urgent conference.

Ilbert was left to watch from afar, his place in all this made clear. But there could be no complaint. He had always been the lowly fourth son of an insignificant lord. To have already risen so high was no small achievement and a testament to his ambition. And he had only just begun the climb...

'FitzDane, is it?' The rasping voice made him start. He turned to find a gaunt figure at his elbow.

Ilbert inclined his head, taking in the man's threadbare robes. 'You have the advantage over me.'

The man's smile was as thin as a knife. 'Eustace Busket. Although you may know me by another name. The Black Monk?'

Indeed Ilbert did. 'The common pirate?'

'There is nothing common about me, boy.' Eustace grinned, silver tooth glittering at the back of his mouth. 'I am God's instrument, sent to scourge the wicked from the earth.'

'And plunder every galley in the Channel into the bargain.'

'If I grow rich in the doing, what of it? Even crusaders must fill their purses.'

Ilbert frowned, unease prickling his nape. He had known men like this before – mercenaries who cloaked their avarice in piety, who spoke of honour while pillaging like common brigands.

'And is that why you've thrown in your lot with Prince Louis? For the glory of God and the weight of his coin?'

Eustace leaned close, his breath sour as a whorehouse at dawn. 'I fight for the true king, against the forces of tyranny and sin. The fact that Louis pays well for my loyalty is incidental.'

'How very noble of you.' Ilbert couldn't keep the acid from his tone.

The monk's eyes narrowed, twin chips of ice. 'You doubt my conviction, FitzDane?'

Ilbert refused to look away. 'If your conviction is so easily bought, perhaps it is not as ironclad as you think.'

For a taut moment, they stood locked in silent contest. Then Eustace threw back his head and laughed, a saw-blade rasp of sound.

'Oh, I like you, FitzDane. A rare sort of shark, swimming in these muddy waters.' His grin was a slash of yellowed teeth. 'Stick close to me when the killing starts. I'll show you what true conviction looks like.'

Ilbert's gorge rose but he tamped it down. He would not give this carrion crow the satisfaction of seeing him flinch. 'I'll manage well enough on my own, monk. My loyalty is to our new king, not your bloated purse.'

'Loyalty? A shifting pile of sand to build a kingdom on. Only steel and terror can make men bend the knee.' Eustace gestured to where Louis and FitzWalter still held Guillaume in conversation. 'Take your fine, young lord there. How long will his loyalty to you last, when the prince fills his head with promises of titles and wealth? When he sits at the right hand of a king?'

Ilbert bristled at the notion he would be forgotten, but he shoved it down, fixing Eustace with a stare. 'Guillaume is my brother, more than blood. He'll stand with me, as I stand with him. Until our last day.'

The monk seemed amused. 'Pretty words, FitzDane. Let us hope you do not choke on them one day.'

He offered a mocking bow and melted back into the crowd, leaving Ilbert alone with the dry taste of foreboding. Before he could quell his growing ire, Guillaume returned to his side and guided him from the keep.

'God above, that monk is a lunatic,' Ilbert hissed as they strode down the stairs to the courtyard. 'What the hell kept you so long?'

Guillaume didn't answer until they had reached a private part of the castle yard. Only then did he turn to face Ilbert, his expression grave.

'Louis has the support of the barons, that much is clear. They're ready to crown him in a heartbeat.'

'So why don't they get on with it?' Ilbert demanded. 'Christ knows we've all had enough of that bastard John.'

'The Pope's excommunication of the barons complicates matters. London is under interdict; no holy rites can be performed. Louis cannot claim the crown without the Church's blessing. Not until we deal with John first.'

'Easier said than done. The fucker has more lives than a tomcat.'

To his surprise, Guillaume smiled. 'Ah, but the tide is turning, my friend. Louis doesn't just have rebellious lords flocking to his banner. It seems some of John's own faithful have seen the light.'

Ilbert frowned. 'What are you saying?'

'I'm saying that we may have some unexpected allies in this

fight. Men who once broke lances for the king, now ready to bend the knee to his rival.'

'Who?' Ilbert felt his pulse quickening.

'The earls of Arundel, of Albemarle, of Warenne.' Guillaume grinned, triumph kindling in his eyes. 'And Salisbury too.'

'Longsword? The king's own kin?'

Guillaume nodded, satisfaction writ plain on his face. 'It seems even John's war hound has a sense of justice.'

Ilbert whistled softly. 'Well, damn. Never let it be said old Longsword lacks backbone.'

'Aye, Salisbury's defection is a boon, but let's not get ahead of ourselves. John may be a rancid shit, but he's still a cunning one. Already he has fled upon seeing the might of Prince Louis' army, and now he has gone to ground. Putting him down will be no easy task.'

'True enough. The slippery bastard has more tricks than a two-penny bawd. So what's our play? Where do we strike first?'

'Louis has brought with him two hundred knights, and they have their eyes set on Dover. The key to England's door. If he can take the castle, deprive John of his greatest southern stronghold, we'll have him by the balls.'

'I've seen Dover's walls. Thick as ten men and twice as high. We'll need more than French knights and a few defecting earls to crack that nut.'

'My thoughts exactly, but it's Burgh that worries me most. The man's loyal as a hound and ten times as vicious. He won't yield Dover without a fight.'

'Well, I wish Louis luck. Dover will be a tough needle to thread.'

Guillaume's hand landed on his shoulder. 'And we will have needles of our own to thread, brother. Mark me on that.'

Ilbert smiled. 'Oh, I will. To the bloody end.'

26

Estienne slumped low over his palfrey's lathered neck. Four days' hard riding had left them both spent, man and beast pushed beyond the brink of endurance. The road unreeled before him, rutted and treacherous in the guttering light of dusk, trees framed beneath a darkening sky, their branches creaking in the rising wind. The promise of rain hung heavy, another hardship heaped upon the rest.

He gritted his teeth, swaying a little in the saddle, but he dared not stop. Not when he was so close he could almost smell the salt tang in the air. He would deliver Marshal's warning, even if he had to crawl the last leagues on his belly. Too much depended on it.

Estienne dug his heels into the palfrey's heaving flanks and the beast lurched into a shambling trot, head hanging low. They crested a rise, and for a moment Estienne glimpsed the distant glimmer of the sea, obscured by a snarl of naked branches.

'Nearly there,' he whispered into the palfrey's twitching ear. 'Nearly there, boy. Hold on a little longer.'

The palfrey snorted its reply. How far had they come, since Marshal pressed that parchment into his hand? A hundred leagues? Two? Distance lost all meaning, with exhaustion plaguing his every stride. All he knew was the need to keep moving, to outrace the urgency dogging his heels.

Brine-tainted wind bit at his cheeks as Estienne emerged from the trees. In the gathering darkness, he had only the palfrey's heaving stride to guide him, the road little more than a scant trail snaking through the gloom. Somewhere ahead lay Dover. His joints ached at the thought, his emptied belly cramping. So close now. So close to journey's end...

'Halt! Who goes there?'

The challenge rang out, harsh and sudden. Estienne wrenched on the reins, hauling the palfrey to a stop. He blinked into the darkness, trying to make out the source of that voice.

Shadows detached from the gloom. Three of them, closing in with a wary tread. Moonlight gleamed dully from helms and hauberks, and glinted along bared steel. Not the king's men. Their speech carried the unmistakable lilt of Gallic tongues.

French mercenaries.

He had come too late.

'State your business.' The lead man held up a hand, his companions fanning out to flank Estienne.

His mind raced. The first instinct was to spur the palfrey on, to outdistance them with speed and surprise, but the horse was near-broken, and these men looked uncommonly keen.

'I... I am a traveller,' he managed, hating the tremor in his voice. 'Headed for Canterbury, to pray at the shrine of Saint Thomas.'

'Canterbury?' The mercenary's mouth curled in disbelief. 'You're a long way off course for Canterbury, boy.'

Estienne licked at his dry lips. 'I was set upon by bandits some miles back. Driven off the road. I must have gotten lost in the dark.'

'A likely story.' One of the other men whispered in the leader's ear, and he nodded slowly. 'My friend thinks you're not being entirely honest with us. He thinks you might be one of the English king's spies, sent to sniff around our camp.'

'No, I swear it.' Estienne spread his hands, all too aware of the letter concealed inside his jerkin. 'As I said, I'm a simple pilgrim—'

'Shut your lying mouth.' The mercenary stepped forward, one hand falling to the hilt of his sword. 'Dismount. Now.'

Estienne darted a glance at the other two men, saw their hands tighten on their own weapons. No way out. No clever words to sway them.

Estienne sucked in a tattered breath...

Then dug his heels into the palfrey's sides. The horse leapt forward with a startled squeal, more life in its battered frame than Estienne could have hoped. He crouched low over its neck as they plunged past the startled mercenaries. Shouts bellowed in his wake, confused and furious.

A crossbow bolt whipped past Estienne's cheek, so close he felt its kiss of displaced air. He hunched lower, heart slamming against his ribs as the palfrey's hooves thundered on the muddy ground. More shouts behind him, the crash of foliage as his pursuers gave chase. He didn't dare look back, every ounce of will focused on keeping his seat, urging more speed from his flagging mount.

A camp sprawled up ahead. Shouts of alarm dogged Estienne's heels as he clung to the reins with numb fingers and the beast ploughed a path through milling mercenaries and guttering fires.

'Stop! Stop the spy!'

Cries rose in a meaningless babble, French and English mingled. Estienne rode through it, all thought consumed by the need to escape. Tents loomed out of the darkness, and he wrenched the palfrey's head around, veering into the narrow aisles between the fluttering canvas walls.

Another bolt whipped past his cheek. Estienne snarled, the
reins cutting into his hands as he fought to control the palfrey's
panicked swerve. His thighs burned with the strain of keeping his
saddle, the horse near-maddened with terror.

'Don't let him reach the castle!'

Castle. The word penetrated the darkness, bright as a beacon.
Estienne lifted his head, searching. There. Pale walls up ahead,
proud banners whipping in the wind that carried the salt stink of
the sea.

Dover.

His heart leapt, even as another quarrel screamed past his ear.
He fixed his attention on those walls, the promise of sanctuary. If
he could just reach them. Just a little further...

'Take him down! Cut the bastard off at the—'

The twang of an arbalest, all too close. Estienne braced for the
punch of steel in his spine, but it was the palfrey that screamed.
The horse plunged forward, front legs buckling, and it crashed to
the ground in a tangle of thrashing limbs.

Estienne hit the earth hard, the air blasted from his lungs. He
rolled desperately, trying to pull free of the dying horse as it kicked
and flailed. A hoof caught him a glancing blow, bright pain
blooming in his temple. He staggered, ears ringing, the taste of
blood thick on his tongue.

Shouts. The pounding of feet on hard-packed earth.

They were coming for him.

Estienne lurched to his feet, reeling. The walls of Dover
loomed ahead, so close. Sucking air into battered lungs, he began
to run, shambling, graceless, vision swimming. But still he ran.
Weaving like a drunkard, each stride an agony through muscles
that screamed for respite, Estienne focused on the dark bulk of the
castle and drove himself onwards.

Jeers and curses dogged him, the sing of crossbow bolts ripping the air, but he was a moving target, insubstantial in the guttering light. He could hear them at his back, closer now, the heavy thud of their feet, the rasp of their breath.

A wooden palisade reared up ahead, weathered and pitted by the teeth of wind and sea. Estienne flung himself against the timbers, the rough grain biting into his palms as he scrabbled for purchase. The French voices rose behind him, a pack baying for blood.

'Help me!' The words were raw and desperate. 'For the love of Christ, let me in!'

Faces appeared atop the barbican, pale in the gloom. Hard faces, deep lined and wary. Estienne saw the glint of arrowheads trained on him and he waved his hands wildly.

'Please! I'm not one of them. I'm here on behalf of Earl William Marshal. I must see Hubert of Burgh.'

More shouts from behind, horribly close now. Estienne stared up at those grim faces, at the sharp points that could spell his salvation or his doom.

One of the defenders leaned out over the barbican, a heavyset man with an unkempt beard. 'And why should we believe you, boy? For all we know, you're just some French whoreson looking to worm your way inside, slit our throats while we sleep.'

With trembling hands Estienne reached into his jerkin and withdrew the letter, Marshal's seal dark and damning in the torchlight. 'Here.' He thrust the parchment toward the man. 'I carry this from the Marshal himself. Please, you must let me deliver it to Lord Hubert. I swear on my life, I am no spy.'

The grizzled man squinted at the proffered letter, suspicion writ on his craggy face. Estienne held his breath, ears straining for the whisper of a loosed bowstring, the thunk of steel in flesh. A heartbeat. Two.

Then a crossbow bolt slammed into the timber a hairsbreadth from his cheek. He flinched, a cry knotting behind his teeth as wooden shards peppered his face like stinging nettles.

Estienne whirled, pressing his spine against the palisade. Dark shapes charged toward him, moonlight rippling along bared steel. He looked upward, hardly daring to hope. The bearded defender glared down at him, his expression unreadable.

A groaning of hinges and clatter of chains. The gates of the barbican juddered open, a sliver of darkness yawning between the timbers. Estienne hurled himself at that gap, as another crossbow bolt buried itself in the palisade a foot from his head. Shouts of fury and frustration rose behind him, but he paid them no heed as he stumbled across the threshold, legs threatening to fold beneath him as he blinked into the sudden flare of torchlight. Hands seized him, hauling him deeper within as the gates slammed shut at his back with a crash.

Safe. He was safe. Estienne sagged in the grip of his rescuers, hardly registering their rough handling as they hustled him away from the gate.

'Move, you sluggard.'

A hard shove between the shoulder blades sent Estienne staggering. His vision swam, exhaustion pressing like a lead weight.

'I must...' His voice emerged as a croak, his tongue a dry, swollen thing behind his teeth. 'I must see Hubert of Burgh. The message—'

'Shut yer trap.' A hard-faced man in a sweat-stained gambeson cut him off. 'His lordship will hear your piece when he's good and ready.'

Estienne looked about him, meeting nothing but cold stares boring into him from all sides. The air rang with the noise of men arguing, but in his exhausted state he could discern no words.

'What is this? Were we expecting visitors?'

The voice cracked through the clamour like a lash. Estienne turned with the rest to see a bear of a man striding across the bailey, his powerful form clad in a gambeson that strained across a barrel chest. His face was broad and grim, a salt and pepper beard bracketing a mouth set in a humourless line.

Estienne hardly dared to breathe as he recognised the castellan of Dover, King John's war wolf.

Hubert of Burgh.

'My lord.' One of the men-at-arms stepped forward. 'We've caught an intruder. Claims to have a message from the Marshal.'

Hubert's keen gaze focused on Estienne, who met that stare squarely, though his knees threatened to buckle.

Slowly, comprehension dawned on Hubert's face. 'I know you. You're Marshal's clumsy squire.'

'Yes, my lord,' he replied, though the assessment seemed a little harsh. 'Estienne Wace. I bring grave tidings from Earl William.' He thrust his letter toward Hubert, the parchment trembling between his fingers.

Hubert squinted at the missive, then waved it away. 'Save the reading for daylight, eh lad?'

Estienne blinked, thrown by the sudden dismissal. 'As you wish, my lord. But I must tell you—'

'Let me guess.' Hubert cocked a brow. 'The French are coming? Aye, we'd worked that bit out for ourselves.'

Estienne felt his face flush. 'Forgive me, my lord.'

'Ah, don't look so crestfallen, lad.' Hubert reached out to clap him on the shoulder, the blow damn near staggering him. 'You've ridden hard and taken great risk to bring your lord's word, and that's no small thing. Your loyalty does you credit. And welcome to Dover. Best make yourself comfortable... you might be here a while.'

He offered Estienne a parting blow on the arm. Then he was striding away, barking orders as he went.

Estienne stood rooted amidst the bustle, Marshal's letter clutched in his fist. He felt a bone-deep weariness he thought that no amount of rest might ease. But rest he would, for he would need his strength in the coming days...

Prince Louis had come to claim his first victory.

27

Estienne leaned against the crenellated stone, the weathered edges rough against his palms. To the north, the town of Dover spread out before him, thatched roofs huddling in the shadow of the castle's bulk. South, the sea stretched to a pewter horizon, water stippled with white-capped waves. But it was the activity beyond the palisade that drew Estienne's focus. Like bustling ants, the French forces swarmed over the landscape. The distant figures of men and horses moved between the skeletal frames of siege towers and trebuchets, their instruments of war growing larger by the day.

For near a week now he had watched the enemy constructing their siege engines, the sense of impending doom pressing close, like a knife to the jugular. Dover's defences were strong, her walls thick and her stores well-stocked, but no fortress was impregnable. Not when faced with the might of France itself.

The wind picked up, sending a scatter of grit into Estienne's face. He blinked hard, surveying the outer palisade of wooden stakes bristling to the north. Thus far, that wall of timber had repelled the French attacks, a bulwark against their initial probing assaults, but Estienne knew it was only a matter of time before they brought their full strength to bear.

He glanced down into the bailey, seeing men hurrying about, faces grim. The atmosphere within the castle had grown increasingly taut, like a drumskin stretched close to breaking. Hubert of Burgh drove his men hard, overseeing the shoring up of defences, the stockpiling of arms and foodstuffs, but no amount of industry could mask the spectre of fear that clung to every stone.

Estienne pushed away from the wall, rolling stiff shoulders. The wound above his collarbone pulled, not yet fully knitted. A lingering ache, but far from his chief concern. No, that dubious honour belonged to the French.

'Wace!' Estienne turned at the hail to see Peter of Créon striding towards him. 'Lord Hubert wants us. He has summoned a war council.'

Estienne fell into step beside the grizzled knight who had first admitted him to the castle. In the short time since, he had come to know Créon as a doughty fighter and a man of few words. The fact that he'd deigned to fetch Estienne himself spoke volumes, and Estienne felt it an honour.

They made their way to the keep, the bustle of the bailey giving way to the relative hush of the great hall. Hubert stood at the far end, surrounded by a cluster of knights. Their faces were stark in the guttering torchlight, all hard angles and tense jaws. Estienne and Peter joined the throng, the murmur of low conversation fading as Hubert raised a hand.

'Sers, I'll keep this brief. The French grow bolder with each passing day. It's only a matter of time before they finish their engines and bring them to bear against our walls.'

A ripple of unease passed through the assembled men. Estienne saw more than one hand tighten on a sword hilt.

'Now, we could cower behind our stone and wait for them to

come to us. Wait for them to grind us to rubble. But I say we take the fight to them first. Disrupt their plans. Throw their damned siege into disarray.'

'You intend a sortie,' a knight said from the front rank.

Hubert's smile was wolfish. 'Aye. A swift strike, before they can react. We'll ride out and burn those bloody machines to cinders before they can breach our walls.'

A rumble of approval rolled through the knights, and Estienne saw fierce grins flash in the torchlight.

'So let's make ready,' Hubert barked over the rising chatter. 'Check your arms. Marshal your squires and see to your steeds. We ride at nightfall.'

As the knights dispersed in a clatter of mail, their voices raised in eagerness, Estienne made to follow, but Hubert's voice stopped him. 'A moment, lad.'

He turned to see the castellan regarding him curiously. 'My lord?'

'I trust you're finding your way among all these ruffians?'

Estienne mustered a smile. 'I manage, my lord. It's a struggle to remember the names, but I find if I call a man "Will" there's a chance I'll be right.'

Hubert snorted. 'Aye, this country has a glut of unimaginative sires. I suppose you're keen to join them in battle. Show them what the Marshal's boy is made of?'

Estienne shifted uncomfortably on his feet. 'I... I only wish to serve, my lord.'

'Oh, you'll serve.' Hubert stepped closer, lowering his voice. 'Seems to me this is your chance to make a name for yourself. Wet your blade in earnest.'

'I've fought before.' The words came out more defensive than he'd intended. 'At Bouvines. But... I was taken prisoner.'

'Trussed up like a goose for the spit? There's no shame in that.

You stood your ground and lived to fight another day. Not every novice boy can say the same.'

Estienne cringed at the memory of that blood-soaked field, the crush of bodies, the screams of the dying. And his own final stand, cut short by Guillaume of Roches.

'Tell me true, lad.' Hubert's voice cut through that memory. 'You ready to try your hand again? Shed blood for your rightful king?'

Estienne met the old knight's gaze, his jaw tightening. 'I'm ready. I won't let you down.'

Hubert clapped him on the shoulder. 'See that you don't. Else your head will likely be decorating a French lance.'

With that cheerful notion, Hubert turned and strode away.

Estienne stood within the hall, the air humming with anticipation. Hubert had offered him a chance to redeem his failure at Bouvines. A valuable gift indeed.

God willing, he would prove himself worthy of it.

28

Estienne waited in the northern bailey, surrounded by the ominous bulk of the wooden palisade. Around him, knights sat atop their steeds like sentinels, moonlight glinting off mail. Not a word passed between them, the hush heavy with grim anticipation.

Horses stamped and snorted, harness jangling with each toss of their heads, as they sensed the rising tension. Estienne's own mount shifted beneath him, eager for action. He reached down to pat its neck, murmuring soothing words, more to reassure himself than to calm the destrier.

It was a sturdy beast and more than a substitute for his lost palfrey. Along with it, he had been given gambeson, mail, helm, sword and shield from the stores, bequeathed by its previous owner, now dead at the hands of the French. Estienne would be sure to repay him for those gifts with vengeance, were he able.

Up ahead, closest to the towering gates, Hubert of Burgh sat rigid atop his black charger. The castellan was clad in full mail, a grim spectre against the pale stone. His gaze raked the gathered ranks and with a hiss of steel, he drew his sword. The blade flashed silver in the torchlight as he raised it high. At the signal, the gates groaned open, timbers shuddering as Peter of Créon and other men-at-arms heaved against them. The knights surged forward as one, a steel-clad tide funnelling through the gates. Estienne was swept along with them, the pounding of hooves drowning out the hammer of his heart. His torch sputtered in the wind of their passage, smoke stinging his eyes.

Around him, the night was rent by battle cries, raw and fierce. Voices raised in bloodlust, the glee of warriors unleashed. Estienne gripped his reins one-handed, his sword a dead weight at his hip.

Ahead, the French camp sprawled in the darkness, oblivious to what was coming. Then shouts of alarm knifed the air, fear and confusion rising as the knights descended on them like falcons on easy prey. The element of surprise was theirs, but it would not last. The chaos of their charge could only mask their intent for so long before the French rallied to meet them.

Estienne scanned the looming shapes rising from the camp, seeking a target. The great siege engines hunched in the gloom like slumbering giants – towers and trebuchets, mantlets and rams. The array of destruction waiting to be visited upon Dover's walls. And their one hope was to send them up in flames before that could happen.

'Burn them all!' Hubert's bellow rose above the cacophony, loud and exultant.

Their vanguard smashed into the French like a tide of steel. Lances splintered, men screaming as they were impaled, horses screeching and rearing. In a heartbeat, the night dissolved into utter chaos, a writhing mass of struggling bodies and flashing blades.

Estienne veered to the left, following a knight named Will as they drove towards one of the looming siege towers. The crude structure rose from the earth like a skeletal hand, timbers lashed together with ropes and iron brackets. The stink of pitch was heavy on the air, oppressive in Estienne's nostrils.

They reached the base of the tower, Will already swinging down from the saddle with fluid grace. Estienne followed, torch gripped tight, heart a rampant drum in his chest. Will unstoppered a barrel lashed to his saddle and upended it over the timbers, the reek of oil drowning out the stench of distant campfires. Estienne moved to thrust his torch into the pool of oil, to send this instrument of war up in cleansing flame...

A figure lunged from the shadows, sword flashing.

Estienne glimpsed a snarling face, a surcoat stained with filth. Then the blade struck, shearing through Will's throat in a spray of black blood. He crumpled without a sound, life pouring from his rent neck, and the French mercenary stood over him, grin spreading across a gore-flecked face, as he readied to strike again.

The torch fell from Estienne's fingers and he grasped his sword, steel rasping from leather in a flash. He brought the blade up as the mercenary's sword scythed down, the impact jolting up his arm and nearly tearing the hilt from his grip.

Estienne moved without thought, the days, weeks and months of hard training guiding his muscles like a puppet master's strings. He stepped inside the mercenary's guard, jamming his shoulder into the man's sternum. The Frenchman stumbled, thrown off balance, and Estienne's blade flashed, shearing through the gambeson where shoulder met neck.

Hot blood jetted, drenching Estienne's fist. The mercenary made a choked sound, sword falling from a hand suddenly nerveless. Estienne wrenched his blade free in a spray of crimson and the man crumpled.

No time to think, to process what he'd done, as another figure charged from the shadows, roaring a challenge. Estienne pivoted, body moving faster than thought. His blade bit out, striking the charging mercenary in the centre of his chest. The man's momentum carried him forward, onto the length of Estienne's sword. He had an instant to see the shock bloom on the man's face, before he sagged to the ground, blade sliding free with a wet sound.

Two men. Two lives snuffed out between one heartbeat and the next by Estienne's own hand. He stared at the crumpled bodies, bile scorching his throat. It had been so easy. So horribly, damnably easy. As if his years of training had been for this very purpose – to make him an instrument of slaughter, as thoughtless and brutal as the sword in his fist.

'Wace!' The shout woke him from his stupor. Estienne looked up to see Hubert atop his warhorse, sword by his side, blood slicking the fuller. 'Stop tarrying, boy. Light that bastard fire.'

Fingers still trembling, Estienne snatched up the torch from where it smouldered in the mud. Its flame sputtered, a heartbeat from drowning, and Estienne thrust it into the pool of oil, willing the spark to catch.

For an instant, nothing. Then the flames leapt, a great whoosh of blistering heat and orange light. The fire raced up the siege tower's timbers, hungry and vicious, scouring the wood with tongues of leaping flame.

Will still lay there, lifeblood congealing in the mud. Estienne caught one last glimpse of sightless eyes before he climbed shakily back into his saddle. He dug his heels into his horse's ribs, pointing the beast back toward the castle, all thought fleeing as instinct took over once more.

He galloped into the whirling mess of retreating knights, following their trail back toward the safety of the castle walls. Behind them, the French camp was a field of flame, men shouting in anger and terror as their siege machines went up in great pillars of fire.

The knights poured back into the bailey, horses tramping the earth as the gates boomed shut behind them. Torches sputtered in the sudden hush, beasts blowing and stamping. Men clung to reins and saddles, blood-splattered and breathing heavy in the wake of their victory.

A cheer went up, starting low and building to a roar. Men thrust swords aloft, clanging them against shields in exultation. They had struck a blow this night. Struck it hard and true, and the French would be reeling. But Estienne could not share in the revelry. He sat numbly in the saddle, the image of Will's dead face seared into his mind's eye.

And the other two... the mercenaries he had cut down. The ease with which he had dispatched them playing over and over, a vicious cycle he could not escape.

What was he becoming? These days of war, of blood and desperation, were they forging him into something he no longer recognised? A killer, merciless and cold? He had thought himself an aspiring knight. A protector of the weak. But the men he had slain this night, they had not fallen to some noble paladin. They had been cut down by a butcher. An instrument of death.

Estienne closed his eyes but the images remained. And God help him, but a part of him revelled in it. A part of him he had not even known existed until it was unleashed in the madness of battle.

In that moment, as the cheers of those knights battered at his ears and the stink of mud and blood clogged his nostrils, he felt he had lost something precious...

A purest shard of his innocent soul, never to be regained.

29

Estienne's feet skidded on the wooden planks as another volley slammed into the wall, showering him with splinters. He barely flinched, numb to it all. How many days had it been? How many weeks? The siege had blurred into a hellish barrage and all that mattered now was survival.

He reached the cluster of archers hunched behind the wooden parapet and dumped a sheaf of quarrels at their feet.

'That's almost the last of them,' he panted.

The closest man, whose leathery face was slashed by a livid scar, spat a stream of brownish spittle over the battlements. 'Bloody frogs don't know when to give in, do they?'

He snatched up a bolt, slotting it into the groove of his crossbow with practised ease. The defenders of Dover were haggard and hungry, pushed to the brink by Prince Louis' tireless assault. Estienne's own body felt like a sack of bruises, every muscle aching, stomach rumbling from hunger, but he pushed himself onward, ducking as a boulder sailed overhead to smash down amid the bailey.

He risked a glance over the wall. The French had arrayed their rebuilt siege engines to the north, trebuchets that hurled boulders the size of hay bales, ballistae flinging deadly spears. And behind it all, a sea of colourful tents and flapping pennons stretching as far as he could see. It was enough to fill him with dread, but he could not let despair take hold. There was a job to do.

Estienne forced himself onward, carrying the last sheaf of quarrels. He skidded around the corner of the gatehouse, breath rasping in his lungs. Another group of crossbowmen hunkered up ahead, and if he—

A shout of warning. Estienne caught sight of a looming shadow before he heard the crack of timbers. Then the parapet ahead of him exploded in a maelstrom of splinters.

The world tilted. Estienne felt himself lifted, flung, tumbling through the air. The breath whooshed from his lungs as he slammed into the earth, teeth clacking together like dice in a cup.

For a long moment he lay stunned, blinking up at the smoke-smudged sky. Shapes moved at the edges of his vision. Someone was screaming, shrill and feral. It took Estienne a long, dazed minute to realise it wasn't him.

He struggled to sit up and agony lanced through his shoulder. Christ have mercy, was it broken? Gingerly, he prodded at the joint, hissing through gritted teeth. No, not broken. One bit of luck, at least.

'On your feet, Wace.' Estienne squinted up to see Lord Hubert glaring down at him, the castellan's face lacking any sympathy. 'The king is not done with you yet.'

Estienne struggled to rise, his legs trembling. Hubert seized him by the elbow, hauling him unceremoniously to his feet. His shoulder shrieked in protest, but he locked his knees, willing himself to stay standing.

Hubert was already turning away. 'With me,' he barked.

Estienne stumbled after as Hubert outpaced him effortlessly.

He was halfway up the steps to the barbican when he realised the world had gone blissfully silent. The bone-juddering smash of missiles, the howl of torn air, all of it had ceased.

Hubert reached the summit, staring out over the field.

'What is it?' Estienne asked. 'Why have they stopped?'

By way of answer, Hubert pointed. Estienne followed the line of that blunt finger, out beyond the killing field. The French siege lines seethed like a kicked anthill, men boiling out of tents and swarming to assembly points. Their shouts drifted on the wind, a babble of distant voices. But rippling above it all, proud and defiant, he glimpsed an ocean of snapping pennons. And on each one – a rampant lion, picked out in scarlet thread on a yellow field.

'Mother of God,' someone murmured. 'Is that...?'

'Aye.' Hubert's voice was a low rasp. 'Alexander.'

As if conjured by mention of his name, a figure on horseback detached itself from the milling throng. Even at a distance, the shock of the man's hair was a beacon, copper-bright beneath a circlet that winked with the glint of gold.

King Alexander, the Lion of Scotland.

Knights flanked him as he rode to greet another ornate figure. Royal blue plumes nodded from the second man's helm, and his mount was caparisoned in fleur-de-lys.

Prince Louis himself, come to greet his guest.

Estienne watched as the two men clasped arms, their laughter carrying faintly. Brothers in arms, united against a common foe. Against England herself.

'Well now, would you look at that?' The man-at-arms next to Estienne leaned over the parapet. 'The Lion of the Scots and the Lion of France, staring longingly into each other's eyes. Think they're gonna fuck?'

A bark of laughter, harsh and jagged. It rippled down the line of defenders, gathering strength as it went.

'Nah,' someone else chortled. 'With all that armour on? Would chafe bloody awful, that's for sure!'

Another peal of mirth.

'You've got it wrong, lads.' Another pitched his voice high in a mincing imitation of a French accent: 'Milord Alexander, s'il vous plaît introduce mon royal sceptre to votre tender fundament.'

That sent up a fresh gale of laughter, several men weak-kneed with it.

Estienne felt his own lips quiver despite his better judgement. It was mad, this desperate, gallows humour. But what else could they do? Weep and wail at the doom poised to engulf them?

As the strained laughter continued, Estienne risked a glance at Lord Hubert. The castellan stood apart, his craggy face set in stone, and not even a flicker of mirth touched those eyes as he stared out over the massed ranks of French and Scots.

Estienne edged closer, unease coiling in his gut. 'My lord? You sense our situation worsens?'

'Aye, it does.' He jerked his chin toward the glittering host spread across the field. 'Alexander and his Scots didn't just happen to stumble across the French out on a stroll. And they sure as hell didn't cut a path through half of England on a whim.'

Estienne frowned, trying to grasp the implications. 'You mean...?'

'I mean the Scottish king wouldn't have dared set foot in the south, not without knowing he had allies waiting. And not without a clear path to march along. English lords, ones who are supposed to protect the kingdom from incursion, have granted him passage all the way to the south coast.'

'Then... does that mean we should surrender? If the kingdom has already fallen then—'

'Surrender?' The word was spat through tight lips. 'We do not yield, lad. We took an oath to hold this castle, to defend it with our last breath. And by God, that is exactly what we will do. If the kings of France and Scotland want Dover, then let them come and take it. We'll drown the bastards in their own blood before they ever set foot across this threshold.'

The words rang in the sudden silence, hard as iron. A vow and a challenge all at once. And in that moment, staring at the fierce set of Hubert's shoulders, the unyielding slate of his profile, Estienne felt something kindling in his own breast. A spark, fanned to sudden flame by his lord's implacable resolve.

Aye. Let them come.

30

Steel sang against steel, a discordant choir belting out its battle dirge. Estienne's sword arm ached, each impact shuddering up his shoulder as he hacked and slashed with a strength born of desperation. The French surged through the breach in the palisade, a tide of mailed bodies and bared blades. The wall had fallen as the sun was setting. Now, in the black of night, they still fought to defend the gap.

'Hold the line!' someone bellowed. 'For God and King John, hold!'

Estienne snarled, ramming his shield into the face of a French knight who came at him with a spear. The man reeled back, blood spattering from a crushed nose, and Estienne lunged, sword taking him under the arm and slicing through mail.

No time to see if the blow was mortal. More came on, trampling their fallen comrade, hungry for English blood. Estienne fell back a step, bracing his shield as a sword hammered into the oak. The world had shrunk to a single breached wall, time passing in swift beats, each gasping breath, each parry, riposte and slash. Blood ran down his sword, spattered his surcoat, and he could taste it in his mouth. The press of bodies, screams of the dying. He had no thought but to keep fighting, to hold this narrow stretch of ground for one more heartbeat, and then another.

At his side, Peter of Créon roared his defiance, laying about him with an axe already blunted by shattered helms and splintered shafts. The old knight was a bull, shouldering foes aside, unstoppable in his fury... until the spear took him, punching through his hauberk to lodge in his guts with an obscene sound. Peter folded, a froth of blood on his lips.

A cry tore from Estienne's throat, and he surged forward to slash at the spearman who loomed over Peter's crumpled form. The blade rebounded from a hastily raised shield, splinters flying across Estienne's vision, but it was enough to drive the spearman back.

He planted himself astride Peter's body as the French pressed in, hacking and lunging. A blade scythed toward his head and he caught it on his cross-guard, teeth bared in a snarl as he shoved the swordsman back. The Frenchman's eyes widened in shock as Estienne bulled into him shield-first, staggering him. Then his sword lanced out in a vicious thrust that hacked through mail and into the soft flesh beneath.

No time to savour the kill. Hands seized Estienne's shoulders, trying to drag him down. He twisted like an eel, sword lashing out, howling in rage as blood spattered across helms and bared teeth. A space opened around him, French knights desperately reeling back from this maddened creature who fought with the strength of ten.

Estienne seized his chance. Dropping his shield and sheathing his blade before scooping Peter's limp body up in his arms. The old knight was a dead weight as Estienne heaved him over one shoulder.

'Fall back!' The cry rang out over the clash of steel and screams of the dying. 'Back to the keep!'

Estienne ran with the rest, staggering under his burden. He caught a glimpse of the barbican gate, men streaming through it in a fighting retreat. Gritting his teeth he raced for the safety of the castle as arrows hissed past his head, French howls dogging his heels.

No sooner had he stumbled across the threshold than the gate crashed shut behind him, timbers shuddering. Estienne collapsed to his knees, breath sawing in his lungs as he lowered Peter to the blood-slick cobbles with trembling arms. Around them, men sagged against the walls, some sliding to the ground, chests heaving. Moans rose from the wounded, prayers and curses mingling in a piteous chorus.

Estienne knelt over Peter, removing his helm as gently as he could. Blood bubbled on his lips, a last breath rattling in his chest.

'Peter.' Estienne's voice cracked on the word. He reached out to touch the man's arm, feeling the slackness of death settling into his limbs. A wordless snarl rose in his throat, half-grief and half-fury.

A hand landed on his shoulder. Estienne looked up to find Hubert looming over him, the castellan's face grim.

'On your feet, lad. It's not over yet.'

As if to punctuate his words, a great boom shuddered through the keep, sending grit sifting down from the high arches. The French trebuchets, still hurling their spite. Estienne clambered upright, joints screaming, and followed Hubert up the steps to the parapet.

The world beyond the walls was a scene from his nightmares. The French seethed across the ruined outer defences, steel bristling. Their war engines squatted like obscene toads, vomiting boulders and ballista bolts that crashed into the stone walls. A trail of corpses laid a path from the castle gates to the breach in the outer barbican. But it was the figures scuttling below that snatched Estienne's eye and held it.

Sappers. Already driving forward their wheeled mantlets, shielding them from missiles as they began their deadly work. Even as he watched, picks rose and fell, chipping relentlessly at the ground.

'They mean to undermine us,' Hubert growled. 'Bring down our walls from below like a rotten tooth.'

Estienne had heard how effective such tactics were – King John had used them well enough at Rochester. 'Can we stop them?'

'We'll make them bleed for every inch,' Hubert said. 'But without relief, without some miracle...' He trailed off, letting the implication hang.

Estienne's gut tightened. They were alone, a single bastion standing against the French tide. But soon their walls would crack and crumble, and the foe would pour through like a ravening flood, offering no mercy.

And no mercy would be given in return.

31

Estienne stood shoulder to shoulder with the knights within the inner bailey, an island of grim-faced men adrift in a sea of silence. Before them loomed the gatehouse tower, proud stone seeming to shiver with each muffled scrape and thud rising from its bowels – those enemy sappers, worming deeper with every passing moment, a canker devouring the castle's roots. The very foundations were being dug away, to be replaced by wooden fascines that would keep the structure aloft... until the time came for it to fall.

His hand tightened on the hilt of his sword, the leather binding burning against his palm like a brand. His chest was tight, every breath straining against the tension winding him like a windlass. A sidelong glance and he saw Lord Hubert standing mighty as a watchtower, only the twitch of his eye betraying the coiled energy coursing through that powerful frame. To Estienne's left, a grey-beard knight muttered soundlessly, lips working in a constant loop of prayer as he recited the Paternoster over and over. Directly ahead, a younger man, barely more than a stripling, trembled visibly, the head of his spear glinting in the evening light.

Then the digging fell silent.

Time stretched out in that dreadful quiet. Each heartbeat an aeon, each breath a tortured gasp. Sweat beaded Estienne's brow and trickled down his spine, though the evening held no hint of warmth. His focus was on the wall of stone before him, and the gatehouse that would inevitably fall.

It began with a curl of smoke, grey tendrils creeping through the cracks between the great foundation stones. Estienne saw it in the same instant he smelled the acrid stench. A heartbeat later, the first flames licked out, orange tongues setting light to timbers beneath.

'Make ready, lads.' Hubert's voice was a low growl. 'The bastards have lit their fires. It won't be long.'

The grating sound of steel on leather, a score of blades hissing free in unison. The weight of Estienne's own blade was a cold comfort, as the smoke thickened, acrid and blinding.

A deep rumble shook the earth, the stones beneath his feet heaving like the deck of a galley on a roiling sea. Cracks split the base of the gatehouse, the proud edifice shuddering on its moorings.

'Steady, men,' Hubert's bellow rose above the tumult. 'Here it comes.'

Thunder swelled to a deafening roar, the death scream of the gatehouse tower before it collapsed, slumping sideways as its bones turned to rubble. A great plume of dust and pulverised mortar exploded outwards, choking debris that swept across the inner bailey. Estienne threw up an arm to shield his face. His mail and helm protected him from the worst, but he choked on the dust that coated his tongue and throat.

The world was lost to a sea of swirling grey, shapes moving as indistinct blurs in the twilight. Dimly, he could hear voices raised in consternation. The thud of falling masonry. But all was muffled as if he'd been plunged into a lake of mist.

'Ready yourselves.'

Hubert's words cut through the murk. And from beyond the thick cloud rising from the tumbled ruins where the gatehouse had stood only moments before, a sound was building. A roar. A bloodthirsty howl torn from a hundred throats, cresting like a wave fit to drown the world.

The roar of the French, surging forward to storm the breach.

It built to a crescendo, a cacophony of bloodlust and glee. Forms moved in the dissipating cloud of debris, resolving into mailed men with raised swords and contorted faces, as they scrambled over the tumbled ruins of the gatehouse. The French surged forward, a seething mass of straining bodies and bared teeth. They were a pack of wolves scenting wounded prey, drunk on the promise of slaughter.

'For God and King John, stand fast!'

Hubert's bellow rose to meet the French, his sword thrust skyward, a beacon amid the swirling murk, and the men took up the cry.

'*For God and King John!*'

Estienne found himself screaming with the rest, the words a fierce exultation as they tore from his throat. Fear burned away on a surge of berserk fury as his blood sang to the savage sound of war. He was moving before he could even think, racing forward with the rest, borne along on that red tide of defiance. The sword in his fist, the shield braced before him, a leash leading him into the teeth of the foe.

The lines met with a crash, a collision of meat and mail that slammed the breath from Estienne's lungs. He hit the French in a storm of flailing limbs and lashing steel, battering at them with both sword and shield.

A snarling face lunged at him, curses spilling from a frothing mouth. Estienne slammed his shield rim into that gaping mouth, the crunch of teeth shattering, the hot splatter of blood. The Frenchman reeled back, shrieking, and Estienne bulled forward, knocking him sprawling. He stamped down hard on the man's face, feeling bone crunch beneath his foot.

No time for thought, for pity. The crimson madness was on him, the hammer of his pulse, the heft of his sword as it thirsted, taking a life of its own as he stabbed at another charging body, feeling the satisfaction as his blade slid through armour and into flesh. Estienne wrenched his blade free of the screaming man's gut and cast about, seeking a new foe to rend.

They seethed around him, a sea of surcoats emblazoned with the fleur-de-lys, a rapacious horde hurling themselves upon the crumbling walls. A never-ending flood, steel and screaming faces cresting over the ruined gatehouse like a human tide. Where one fell, cut down by desperate English blades, two more clambered over that twitching corpse, hungering for their share of glory. It was a vision from a nightmare – a churning sea of ravening foes, spreading out to engulf the bailey beneath their weight.

'Push them back!' Hubert's voice rose above the roar of battle. 'By the lance of God, push them back!'

He was a giant amid the carnage, a blood-drenched titan set upon by swarming ants. His great blade sheared and smote, reaping Frenchmen like wheat. Where he advanced, the enemy fell away, but they were too many, a horde spilling between the fallen stones, clambering over their dead to crash upon the English shields in waves.

'For Louis!' A cry in mangled French, thick with hate. 'For the Lion!'

Estienne snarled his defiance as he smashed aside a lunging French blade, kicked its wielder in the chest with a mailed foot. The man went down and Estienne stabbed him where he lay.

Hubert's cries echoed in his ears, stoking the fire in his blood.

He threw himself at the French, hacking and hammering, denting helms and smashing aside blades with sheer ferocity. His sword ran red, his lips curled back from his teeth in a feral snarl. Estienne moved as if divorced from thought, a lethal instrument acting on pure instinct.

A French knight came at him, sword in one hand, hammer in the other, hurling himself at Estienne like a beast unhinged. Their swords met in a shivering clang, blades binding at the hilts. Estienne heaved against the clinch, teeth bared, muscles burning as he strained to break the deadlock.

The French knight grinned, a death's-head leer in a ravaged face, and smashed down with the hammer in a sudden, savage motion. Estienne was at pains to catch it on his shield, feeling the thud and hearing the wood crack. The knight's blade slid free, steel rasping on steel, and Estienne stepped back, off balance. His foe's sword lanced in, punching toward his unprotected face—

A hammer blow of pure force, and the Frenchman lurched, mouth slackening in shock. His sword arm dropped, blade clanking to the stones, as he swayed drunkenly. Estienne blinked in a daze as the knight's knees folded, ichor sheeting from the dent in his shattered helm.

'Head in the fight, boy.'

Hubert's voice.

He loomed over the fallen Frenchman, blood dripping from the heavy blade clutched in his fist. His surcoat was rent, smeared with filth and gore, but the fire in his eyes was undimmed. Beyond him, more defenders poured into the gap, forcing the French back with hammer and blade.

'Forward!' the castellan roared, raising his sword like a banner 'For God and England, forward!'

They surged into the press, Estienne in their midst. He launched himself at the enemy, smashing aside spears with his

cracked shield, his blade ripping and tearing with ruthless efficiency. Another French knight rose before him, sword clutched in
mailed fists. Estienne met the charge head-on, planting his feet
wide. He caught the downward sweep of the sword on his upraised
shield, grunting at the effort. The Frenchman bore down with all
his weight, trying to use his height to lever Estienne to his knees.

With a twist of his shoulders, Estienne deflected the brunt of
the Frenchman's weight to the side. As the knight stumbled past
him, Estienne rammed an elbow into the small of his back,
sending him sprawling face-first into the muck.

No time for chivalry. His sword lanced down, finding the gap
between helm and hauberk, shearing through the neck beneath.
The French knight shuddered as the blade bit deep, paring
through flesh and spine. Then he was still, leaking his lifeblood
into the churned earth.

All around, the tide was turning, driven by Hubert's
indomitable will, by the ferocity of men with their backs to the
wall. Defenders clogged the breach, the stones slick with blood.
And Estienne could see, with relief dawning, that the French were
falling back. Bloody step by bloody step, they withdrew, melting
away to leave the fallen gatehouse choked with their dead.

Estienne stood panting amidst the carnage, leaning on his
sword as the strength bled from his limbs. The fury that had
sustained him, armoured him against fear and fatigue, guttered
like a wood-starved fire. In its absence, he felt an exhaustion that
left him swaying on his feet.

'Shore up that breach, lads.' Hubert's voice, edged with grim
determination. 'Bring timbers. Oak fascines. Whatever you can
find.'

Estienne straightened, dragging himself forward, body
screaming in protest with every step. His gambeson hung heavy
with the weight of blood and sweat. The taste of it coated his

tongue. All around, men staggered through the devastation, pale and hollow-eyed. Numbly, they bent to their grim work, wrenching timbers from the fallen gates, hauling the battered corpses of their comrades and foemen alike to one side.

'Stack those barrels,' Hubert bellowed. 'And get some planking across that gap. Move, damn you, or the French will be back to send us all to our graves.'

Estienne stumbled to the nearest timber, a length of solid oak as thick around as a man's thigh. His hands closed around the rough grain and he heaved. Beside him, another knight grabbed the other end, fingers bone-white on the blood-smeared wood. Together, they manhandled their burden toward the shattered gatehouse, each lurching step an effort.

Other men took up the task, rolling barrels and dragging beams, plugging the wound in Dover's flank with splintered wood and staved-in casks. Estienne added his timber to the pile, watching as it settled into place. He stumbled back a step, and nearly toppled as his treacherous legs threatened to give way beneath him.

A hand grabbed his elbow, steadying him. Estienne raised his head to find Hubert at his side.

'That will have to do,' Hubert said, his gaze picking over their crude barricade. 'It may not hold for long, but any respite is better than none.'

Estienne followed his stare out beyond the barricade, to where the French were falling back to their siege lines in ragged disarray. 'We hurt them today.'

'Aye.' Hubert spat a gobbet of phlegm. 'Let's hope we hurt them enough.'

32

Estienne squinted into the glare. Ahead, the killing field stretched away, a muddy waste churned to ruin. Broken bodies littered the ground, the stink of them mingling with the ever-present reek of smoke, sweat and shit.

Time had lost all meaning, measured now only in the throb of hunger in his belly, the ache of exhaustion dragging at his limbs. The attackers had not had the strength to press home their assault, and so they remained locked in a listless stalemate. Waiting. But now it seemed that wait might be over.

A stir along the French line drew his eye and Estienne straightened, fatigue forgotten as he saw a lone rider picking his way across the corpse-strewn field. A herald, white pennon draped from his lance tip. Estienne leaned out over the battlements, hardly daring to breathe.

Was this the end, finally? Or just some fresh torment the French had devised?

The herald reined up before the barricaded gatehouse. His stallion stamped, tossing its head, the only sound in the sudden hush.

'I come bearing word from Prince Louis.' The herald's voice rang out, French accent thick. 'Who among you has the authority to treat?'

A figure detached itself from the cluster of mail-clad defenders. 'I am Hubert of Burgh, castellan of Dover. Speak.'

The herald bowed his head. 'My prince sends word that he would have a truce.'

A ripple ran through the gathered defenders. Estienne gripped the edge of the merlon, pulse thudding in his ears.

'A truce.' Hubert's voice was flat as hammered steel. 'Your prince sings a different song than he did when first he darkened our door. What's brought about this change of heart? Grown weary of hurling himself upon our walls?'

The herald shifted in his saddle, the simple motion betraying his fatigue, the toll these gruelling weeks had taken on besieger and besieged alike. 'Prince Louis is prepared to withdraw. To quit the field and return to London, provided you vouchsafe for your men to abide by the truce. To make no attempt to disrupt our departure.'

'And why should he think I'll agree to any such terms? After he's spent the last month and more battering at my gates?'

'Because there's nothing more to be gained here.' The words from the herald were tinged with desperation. 'This siege has bled us all, and to no good end. You know it as well as I. What glory is there in slaughter for slaughter's sake?'

Hubert was silent for a long moment as he took in the French encampment, the great engines of war now sitting quiet, the pennons hanging limp in the dead air. Estienne held his breath, half-convinced the castellan would give the order to loose what remaining quarrels they had, to send the herald back to his master bristling with bolts.

'Very well.' His voice carried to the farthest reaches of the bailey. 'Tell your prince I accept his terms. My men will keep within the walls, provided he keeps to the road. Let this be an end to it.'

A ragged cheer went up from the defenders, men pounding sword hilts against shields. Estienne slumped against the merlon, knees suddenly weak, as the herald wheeled his horse about and cantered back to the French lines. Already they were preparing to leave, hitching horses to wagons, forming up in ragged columns, suddenly eager to be away from this blasted field. And at their head, Prince Louis himself, sitting atop his destrier like a king. No backward glance for the scores of his men rotting in the summer sun. No spare thought for the hundreds he'd thrown against Dover's walls, as if lives were chaff to be winnowed in the pursuit of his ambition. Estienne stared at that straight, arrogant back as the French column wound away, until the last of their bright pennons vanished into the heat haze.

Then the celebrations started. A discordant chant, hoarse voices lifting in delirious relief. It was over. After all the blood and desperation, the screams in the night and the cries of the wounded, it was finally done.

Estienne made his way down from the parapet. In the bailey, men were laughing, weeping, clasping each other like long-lost brothers. The sheer riotous joy of men granted their reprieve.

A hand grasped Estienne's shoulder, and he turned to find himself face-to-face with a knight he vaguely recognised – one of Hubert's household men.

'We did it, lad.' The knight's grin was all the more startling for the deep lines of strain carved about his eyes. 'God preserve us, but we did it.'

Estienne could only nod, feeling curiously divorced from the men surrounding him, as if he were watching their celebration from a great distance.

Hubert's bellow cut through the din. 'All right, you dogs. Don't go celebrating your victory just yet. This war's not won.' The castellan stood atop the rubble of the gatehouse, his surcoat more patches than whole cloth, but he dominated the bailey nonetheless. 'The French may be running back to London with their tails between their legs, but I'd wager it's not just wounded pride weighing them down. Louis has left for a reason, and until we know what that is we need to remain on our guard.' Estienne felt unease trickling through the surrounding survivors. 'But that's a worry for the morrow. Tonight, we revel in our victory. And you miserable whoresons have more than earned a drink.'

Another raucous cheer went up as a cask of ale was muscled out into the bailey. Estienne couldn't recall the last time he'd had anything but brackish water and weevil-riddled biscuits. The thought of a proper drink, of the pleasant burn of it down his gullet, made him light-headed.

He took a proffered cup and drank deeply. The ale was warm and slightly stale, the lip of the cup sticky, but Estienne gulped it down like a man dying of thirst. Around him, his fellows were doing the same, faces tilting skyward as they quaffed.

When he came up for air, a flicker of movement caught Estienne's eye. He turned to see a rider galloping across the field toward the castle, cloak billowing in the wind.

The messenger reined up hard before the gatehouse, his horse lathered in sweat. He vaulted from the saddle, staggering a little as his feet hit the ground. Up close, Estienne could see the concern on his face.

Hubert pushed through the gathered defenders, one hand resting on his sword hilt. 'You've ridden hard,' he said to the man. 'I trust you bring news of import?'

'My lord. I come bearing grave tidings.' He drew a deep breath as if steeling himself. 'The king is dead.'

Estienne nearly dropped his ale as he gaped at the messenger, convinced he must have misheard. Around him, the defenders had fallen silent. Even the gulls wheeling overhead seemed to still their raucous cries.

'Dead,' Hubert repeated as if tasting the word. 'How?'

'It was a flux of the bowels, my lord,' the messenger replied. 'Came on sudden, as he travelled the coast. He weakened quickly, and...' He trailed off, grief choking the words.

'Where?' Hubert asked. 'Where did he die?'

'The castle at Newark, my lord. They laid him out in the chapel there, in the sight of God.'

Estienne took a step forward. 'And William Marshal, was he with the king?'

A nod. 'He was, aye. Rode at the king's side those last days. Held his hand as he breathed his last.'

'And where is he now? William? Where did he go after?'

'Last I knew he was taking the Gloucester road westward,' said the messenger. 'To see the young Prince Henry to safety.'

Of course. Even in a world upended, the Marshal would cleave to his duty. His master following the straight road, no matter where it led.

Estienne turned to Hubert, desperation rising in his throat. 'I must go to him.'

Hubert regarded him solemnly. 'Aye, lad. I expected nothing less.' The castellan turned, looking to a nearby squire. 'You there, bring up a fresh horse, and food for two days' travel.'

The boy scampered to obey.

Hubert stepped close, a hand resting on Estienne's shoulder. 'You did well here, lad. Fought hard and true. Marshal should be proud to call you his.'

Estienne nodded his head, feeling suddenly awkward at the

compliment. 'I only did as my lord would expect. As any loyal man would.'

Hubert's grip tightened. 'You stood fast in the teeth of hell itself, and you never wavered. That's a rare thing, Wace. Rare and worthy.'

The squire returned, leading a rangy palfrey. As Estienne gripped the rein, murmuring soothing nonsense, the horse sidled and snorted, tossing his head against the unfamiliar hand on his halter. He swung up into the saddle, the palfrey dancing beneath him, eager to be away.

Hubert stepped forward, grasping the harness and leading them toward the open gate. 'You'll give William my regards. And tell him, if he has need of me, I'll come.'

Estienne nodded, holding Hubert's gaze for a long moment. So much passed unspoken in that moment. Acknowledgement of what they'd endured together. Respect, hard-won and true as forged steel.

Then Estienne put heels to flanks, hooves scattering grit across the battle-scarred flagstones. The French were already a distant plume of dust on the horizon, their proud banners faded to faint smudges of colour, and Estienne spared them hardly a glance as he pointed his mount toward the Gloucester road.

His master was waiting for him. The last man standing between a child-king and a ravening pack who would rend the realm asunder.

33

All he had heard for miles was the steady thrum of the palfrey's hoofbeats mimicking the pounding of his heart. Every sinew ached, every joint groaned in protest, but he dared not slow. His place was at Earl William's side, and he would not rest until he had reached it.

The road ran on endlessly before him, rutted and pitted by the recent rains. To either side, naked trees clawed at the sky, and in the distance, tendrils of woodsmoke rose from unseen hearths – home fires, welcoming travellers in from the cold, but Estienne had no time for such comforts.

He passed another sign on the road, nailed to a weathered post, and it bore a single word – *Malmsbury*. No sooner had he left it in his wake than the landscape opened out, revealing a wide plain of rolling fields. And in the midst of one, he saw a gathering in the distance.

The field was a sea of milling horses and men, bright with banners. Knights in mail and rich cloaks, their surcoats bold with heraldry. As Estienne approached at a trot, he scanned the crowd, hardly daring to think he had found his master.

There. Sitting tall above the swell, William Marshal atop his charger with the poise of a king. His great helm was cradled in the crook of his arm, red lion on his chest. Though his hair shone silver and care scored deep lines across his brow, the Marshal was still as mighty a sight as ever.

Estienne spurred his mount forward, heart in his throat, and as he drew close he saw the reason for the gathered host. On the field's edge, a second party waited. Amid a knot of retainers and men-at-arms, a boy shared the saddle of a grey destrier with his brooding escort. He was dressed in a smart tunic of royal blue, a fur-lined cloak draped across his narrow shoulders. Sandy hair fell to his chin, brow pinched with concern beyond his tender years.

Prince Henry. England's king-in-waiting.

A thrill chased down Estienne's spine. He'd known, in some distant way, what the news of John's death meant. But to see that boy, little more than nine summers, surrounded by the pomp and peril of kingship stole the breath from his lungs. What desperate times when the fate of the realm rested upon such fragile shoulders.

Estienne dragged his gaze away, fixing once more on the solid bulk of his master. Marshal had yet to note his arrival, his gaze fixed on the royal party. Estienne guided his palfrey to the edge of Marshal's entourage, and slid from the saddle. He took a steadying breath, then moved to greet his lord. Before he could reach him, the Marshal turned to the gathered knights.

'Attend. We'll greet England's heir with every honour.'

As one the knights formed up, Marshal at their head, all arrayed to pay solemn homage.

'Forward.'

The order was soft as snow as Marshal spurred his warhorse. Estienne tried to catch his eye as he passed, but no words of acknowledgement came, no nod or instruction. All he could do was watch as his master rode out to greet the princeling who would be king.

At the knights' approach, young Henry shifted atop his charger, a child adrift amid a sea of hard men and grasping ambition. The man behind the prince raised his chin proudly but said nothing as Earl William, reined up, and the boy seemed to shrink within that warlord's shadow.

'My prince.' Marshal's voice rang out. 'We come to offer our swords in your service. To pledge our lives and lands to your cause, as each of us swore to your father before you.'

Henry wet his lips, and when he spoke, his reedy child's voice fought for steadiness. 'I give myself over to God and to you, so that in the Lord's name you may take charge of me.'

Estienne felt for the prince upon hearing the tremble in those words, the ill-concealed fear. What a burden to lay upon one so young. To entrust the fate of the kingdom to a child. He found himself willing the boy to be strong, and show no sign of weakness before these men whose lives he would command.

The Marshal dismounted, the thud of his feet lost to the squelch of damp earth. Then, with a stately grace belying his years, he sank to one knee, head bowed.

'I will be yours in good faith. There is nothing I will not do to serve you while I have the strength.'

Around him, the assembled knights followed his lead and dismounted. One by one they knelt as Estienne watched, hardly daring to breathe. Then they gave their oath, each mailed fist clenched to an armoured breast to affirm that Henry, third of his name, was England's one true king.

Earl William stood, and the prince nodded in solemn acknowledgement, the barest tremor in that boyish jaw. Then, with no further word or ceremony, the royal party turned their horses and began to ride. Marshal and the other knights mounted up, turning back to where their retainers awaited. Estienne stood obediently, waiting to attend his master. Only when he reached his side did the Marshal look down, as though seeing him for the first time.

Estienne bowed his head. 'My lord.'

'You took your time, lad.'

Estienne glanced up, to see one of Marshal's eyebrows raised severely.

'Forgive me, I—'

A mailed hand waved away his apology. 'I trust Lord Hubert made good use of you?'

'He... Yes, lord. Dover was...' He trailed off, struggling to encompass the desperation of it. 'It was a trial hard-weathered. But we held fast, Lord Hubert and his men. To the last.'

Marshal slowly nodded. 'You did well.'

Three small words, but they seared through Estienne like a bolt loosed from the heavens. Praise from William Marshal was more precious to him than any jewel.

'So, tell me this,' Marshal continued. 'After Dover, do you still yearn for a knight's life? To pledge your sword to king and cause, come what may?'

Estienne met that weighing stare, fatigue seeming to bleed away, the aches and pains fading to inconsequence. 'I do, my lord. More than ever, I do.'

The twist of Marshal's mouth became an unmistakable smile, fierce as a wolf baring its fangs. 'Good. We have a prince to crown and a rebellion to quell. I'll have more work for you.'

He wheeled away in a spray of earth, his destrier's hooves pounding the soft earth. Estienne scrambled into the saddle of his own lean steed, hastening to spur up behind.

As he followed Marshal's banner, in turn following the boy they would soon crown, he felt a fierce grin pulling at his lips.

Let the trials come. He was ready.

34

The courtyard outside the cathedral at Gloucester was a sea of undulating banners, flying the royal colours, lions raging in the sun. All eyes were focused on two figures amidst the crowd, and Estienne squinted against the glare as he watched the scene unfolding.

In the middle of the throng stood his lord, William Marshal, resplendent in his armour and surcoat. Before him knelt a small figure, fair-haired and slight – Prince Henry, clad in a tunic of rich crimson tailored for his child's frame, a fur-lined cloak pooling on the flagstones behind him.

The flat of William's sword touched the prince's shoulders, left then right. Henry lifted his head, a solemn expression on his boyish face. In that moment, Estienne felt a sharp pang somewhere behind his ribs. Jealousy, hot and bitter. This child, barely past his ninth year, was being raised to the lofty ranks of knighthood, while Estienne, squired and blooded, still coveted spurs that remained elusive. The thought curdled like sour wine in his gut and he fought to dismiss it, unbecoming as it was.

'Be thou a knight, in the name of God.' Marshal's voice rang out, clear and commanding. 'Arise, Ser Henry.'

As Henry rose to his feet, the gathered crowd erupted into cheers of, '*Long live Ser Henry.*'

Estienne joined his voice to the chorus, the words bitter on his tongue. He watched as Marshal beamed, clapping a hand on the prince's narrow shoulder. Pride and affection radiated from that noble face, and Estienne felt that spike of envy twist deeper.

As the prince was conveyed within the cathedral, Estienne did his best to dismiss those unwelcome feelings. There was no need for them. He would do his duty, and when his time came he would receive the reward he so craved.

The vaulted ceilings of Gloucester Cathedral soared above their heads. Shafts of coloured light spilled through the stained glass, painting the stone in shades of ruby, sapphire and emerald. The air was thick with incense, the beeswax stench of a hundred guttering candles.

Estienne followed the prince's procession down the long nave, footsteps echoing on the ancient flagstones. Ahead, Henry walked alone, his small form dwarfed by the solemnity of his surroundings. The fur-lined cloak had been replaced by a long robe of cloth-of-gold, the hem whispering over the worn stones, and behind him, Marshal and the other great lords of the realm kept a stately pace.

At the altar waited Peter des Roches, Bishop of Winchester, clad in resplendent vestments of white and gold. His watery eyes skimmed the assembly as the prince climbed the steps to kneel at his feet. Des Roches raised his arms.

'Bless you, my child. Are you willing to take the oath?'

Henry's reply was high and clear, his child's voice steady. 'I am willing.'

The bishop nodded solemnly. 'Will you swear that you will

enjoin and, as far as in your power lies as king take care, that a true peace shall be maintained for the Church of God and all Christian people at all times?'

'I solemnly swear so to do.'

Estienne listened with half an ear as Henry pledged to uphold the laws of the land and to show justice and mercy in his dealings. The words washed over him like the droning of flies, and instead he watched the faces of the lords gathered. They watched in grim silence as this child swore to treat them justly and abandon any unfair laws and customs. It became clear that they were vows made to benefit them, rather than the king, and Estienne could only wonder if this boy would become a puppet, where his father had been a tyrant. Who would really rule this land, once the ravenous French dogs had been expelled from its shores?

At the altar, Henry recited the last of his oaths beneath a cloak of ermine and samite. The trappings of rule, already weighing heavy upon him. Estienne pitied him, even as he had envied him. So much power, and so very much to lose. Even as the bishop raised the crown, he could think of no worse fate than to be burdened by it.

The crown settled on Henry's brow, gold glittering in the light. The great helm of state, bequeathed by kings past, to carry their memory and might into an uncertain future. Estienne held his breath as the boy-king rose, and in that moment he seemed to stand taller, chin lifted, a flicker of something like steel in his gaze.

'Behold!' The bishop's voice rang to the vaulted ceiling. 'Henry, your undoubted king.'

The cathedral erupted in cheers, a thunder of voices rising to shake the foundations beneath them. *'Long live the king! God save King Henry!'*

The rafters rang with it, a swelling tide of sound that buffeted Estienne like a physical force. He added his own voice to the clamour, as around him the great nobles jostled to be the first to bend the knee and swear their fealty to this child who was now their ruler. Marshal stood at the king's right hand, face solemn as he beckoned the lords forward one by one to make their oaths.

As he watched every man make his pledge, Estienne couldn't shake the sense of unease. For each magnate who knelt in faith, there were others whose smiles did not reach their eyes. Men unhappy with a boy-king, perhaps? Men who saw only discord in their future?

Once the last lord bowed his head and muttered his oath, the choir swelled in a great hymn of praise. Estienne watched the new king carried down the nave, head high beneath the weight of the crown. Marshal followed in his wake, a looming shadow at his shoulder.

Outside the sun still shone, but Estienne couldn't shake the feeling that the shadows were already lengthening, straining toward a dark and uncertain horizon. The courtyard was abuzz with activity as squires rushed back and forth, seeing to their masters' horses and gear. Lords clustered in knots, voices lowered in urgent conversation. The air hummed with a restless energy, a sense that there was little time for celebration. Their battles were far from over.

'Wace!' The bellow made him start, and he turned to see Lord Hubert striding toward him, a rare smile creasing his bearded face. 'A good day's work, lad. The king is crowned and anointed. Let's see that French dog Louis try and claim the throne now.'

Estienne nodded, mustering a smile of his own. 'Aye, my lord. A good day. But I fear there are still storms ahead.'

Hubert's smile faded. 'Indeed. The Lion still snarls. And there are those among the barons who'd happily toss Prince Louis scraps beneath the table.'

'But with a new king crowned, how can he hope to still stake his claim?'

Hubert grimaced, one meaty hand scrubbing over his jaw. 'Louis won't give up so easily. And the rebels still lurk – not all have returned to the fold and pledged their fealty to the new king. But we'll face them. And we'll win.'

The tramp of heavy footfalls made both men turn. William Marshal strode toward them, and Estienne bowed hastily.

'Hubert. Estienne,' the Marshal said.

'Earl William,' Hubert replied. 'A day to rejoice, now England has crowned its rightful king.'

Marshal nodded. 'The boy is king in name. Now we must make him one in truth.'

'What's our plan?'

Marshal was silent for a long moment, gaze distant. 'We start with the Charter of Runnymede. The barons want their precious document enshrined in law? Then they shall have it. Henry will put his seal to it before the week is out.'

Hubert's dark brow rose. 'You think that will satisfy FitzWalter and his ilk?'

'It will cut the ground from under their feet,' Marshal said grimly. 'Take away their reason for rebellion. We will give them just what they asked for. If they still defy their king after that, they declare themselves traitors for all to see.'

'And what of Louis?' Hubert ventured. 'What if he still covets the crown, and persuades his supporters he is a better option than the boy we just placed upon the throne?'

'The French will be dealt with. One way or another. But first, we secure Henry's crown. Offer the barons what they want, send them letters offering pardons and restitution of lands if they return to the royal fold. And you, my friend, I will need back at Dover.

Who knows how Louis may react to this. We must shore up our defences and prepare for the worst.'

Hubert nodded. 'Aye, then I'd best get back. It was good to see you, Wace.'

Estienne bowed his head curtly. 'And you, my lord.'

As Hubert hurried away, Estienne could sense Earl William's unease. He had made his plans, and thought of all contingencies, but still there were no guarantees. Now they would have to see if they had done enough to bring the barons back onside, or if they would still hearken to the roar of the French Lion.

PART FIVE: THE LINCOLN FAIR

ENGLAND, 1217 AD

35

Ilbert stood at the narrow window, knuckles whitening on the sill as he glared down at the teeming streets below. London sprawled before him, a festering sore upon the arse of England. Beggars and cutpurses, whores and wastrels, all crammed cheek by jowl in a seething mass of ramshackle hovels. The air was thick with the stink of them, a miasma of piss and filth that coated the back of his tongue. One he could not rid himself of no matter how much he spat it out.

'Fucking cesspool,' he muttered. 'Wallowing in its own dung.'

Behind him, Guillaume was silent. That alone was enough to set Ilbert's teeth on edge. Guillaume had been uncharacteristically grim these last days, his ready wit and easy charm replaced by a pensiveness that cloaked him like cerecloth.

Ilbert shot him a sharp look over one shoulder. 'It's all turning to shit. Louis tucking tail back to France, mewling for more men and coin. Half the northern barons have thrown in with that brat Henry like dogs returning to their vomit. All those noble lords who flocked to Louis' banner, now scurrying back to lick the boots of a nine-year-old. And now we've this outlaw Willikin roaming the

Weald, picking off Louis' scouts and leaving their heads on fucking pikes.'

Still Guillaume said nothing.

Ilbert threw up his hands, rounding on him fully. 'Christ's balls, man, are you even listening? The rebellion is crumbling around our ears. Everything we've bled for, fought for, slipping through our fingers like sand.' He stalked closer, teeth bared. 'Falkes of Bréauté still runs roughshod over half the country, and Hubert of Burgh roams the south coast like a watchdog, snarling at anyone who dares piss in his yard. We're beset on all bloody sides.'

Ilbert snatched up his wine cup, downing the dregs in one long quaff, before slamming the cup back on the table. The sour vintage burned his gullet, a welcome distraction from the turmoil churning in his gut.

Finally, Guillaume stirred, a sigh gusting from his lungs, heavy with some unspoken weight. In the candlelight, Ilbert saw the deep creases of care marring that noble brow.

'Guillaume?' Sudden unease coiled in Ilbert's chest. 'What is it? What ails you?'

Guillaume said nothing. With one hand he drew something from the breast of his tunic – a folded square of parchment, crumpled and smoothed as if it had been read and re-read a hundred times or more.

Ilbert frowned. 'A letter? From who?'

'My father.' Guillaume's voice was bereft of emotion. 'He writes to tell me the king... that is, the boy Henry... has pledged to uphold the Charter of Runnymede. To rule by law, not by whim.'

Ilbert scoffed. 'That infant king grants an edict? So what? It doesn't mean—'

'My father wants me to return to the royalist side, Ilbert. To bend the knee to Henry and acknowledge him as England's rightful king.'

The words fell like an axe on wood in the sudden silence. 'You can't be serious. Louis is our king, Guillaume. Or he will be, once we sit the crown upon his brow.'

'John is dead. Without him to rail against, the heart has gone out of the rebellion. Louis is not the answer. And I don't know if he ever was.'

'Not the answer? He's the only bloody answer. England needs a strong hand to rule her, not some mewling infant and a charter full of hollow promises.' Ilbert crossed the distance between them in two quick strides, seizing Guillaume by the shoulders, fingers digging into the fine wool of his tunic. 'Henry is a child. A puppet. And do you honestly believe he'll honour his father's pledges once he comes of age? Once he has the crown firmly on his head?'

'I have to believe it. Too much blood has been spilled already, Ilbert. If there is a chance for peace, for an end to this strife, I must take it.'

Ilbert released him, staggering back a step. 'Christ's wounds, listen to yourself. Where is this craven bleating coming from? The Guillaume I know would never turn tail at the first sign of trouble. Would never abandon the cause he swore to uphold.'

'Our cause was just. It always was. But the methods... The slaughter and burning. The rebels we called friends and brothers, acting no better than brigands. It's not why I took up arms, Ilbert.'

'And you think running back to lick the boy-king's arse will change that? That your father will welcome you with open arms after you stood against him? Grow up, Guillaume. In this game we're playing you're either the boot or the ant. There's no middle ground.'

'The game is over.' Guillaume's voice was iron. 'John is beneath the earth. It's time to put old hatreds aside. To forge a lasting peace, for the good of the kingdom.'

'I'll tell you what you can do with your lasting peace.' Ilbert spat to the side as if the very words were poison on his tongue.

Guillaume looked at him, something perilously close to pity moving across his face. Ilbert felt his gorge rise, black hatred coiling in his guts. He welcomed it, stoked it to a savage flame. Anything was better than the cold dread knotting beneath his ribs.

'It's all well and good for you, isn't it?' The words were thick and bitter on his tongue. 'Precious little Guillaume, with his lands and titles. His dear old father, hand up the new king's arse, working him like a side-street puppet. Must be nice, knowing you'll come up smelling of lavender no matter who sits on the fucking throne.' Guilt chased across Guillaume's face, there and gone, but still Ilbert pounced on that flicker of weakness, baring his teeth in a vicious grin. 'But where does that leave me, eh? The landless knight, with no family to wrap around me like a shield. What do I get, Guillaume, when you scamper off with your tail between your legs? A traitor's noose? A short road to the fucking block?'

'It won't be like that.' A desperate edge to Guillaume's voice. 'I'll speak to my father. To the king. There will be pardons, I'm sure of it. For any man who bends the knee and swears his loyalty to Henry—'

'I swore my loyalty to you!' Ilbert roared. 'We took a vow, you bastard. Bound our fates together. Does that mean nothing to you now?'

'Of course it does.' Guillaume stepped closer, hands raised in a placating gesture. 'Ilbert, if you would just listen—'

Ilbert moved without thought, fist cracking across Guillaume's jaw, snapping the taller man's head to the side. Pain lanced through Ilbert's knuckles, bright and vicious and good, chasing away the doubt churning in his gut.

For a moment Guillaume just stood there, a thread of blood

leaking from the corner of his mouth. Then, slowly, he reached up to touch his split lip, staring at the smear of crimson on his fingertips as if he couldn't quite comprehend it.

'Enough,' he said softly. 'This gains us nothing. I'm leaving on the morrow, Ilbert. Don't try to stop me.'

Ilbert bared his teeth, rage boiling through him in a scalding tide. He raised his fist again, but Guillaume moved faster than he could have believed for a man his size. He caught Ilbert's hand in an iron grip, twisting savagely. Ilbert grunted in pain as Guillaume torqued his wrist, the bones grinding. His legs folded and he crashed to his knees, arm wrenched up behind him at an excruciating angle.

'Enough.' Guillaume's voice was low and cold as frosted steel.

He shoved Ilbert away and he sprawled, cradling his wrist, all his savage fury drained away. In its place was only yawning emptiness. Guillaume looked down at him, something like regret moving across those harsh features. Then he turned away and strode to the door.

'This isn't over.' Ilbert's voice was thick with pain and humiliation. 'You hear me, Guillaume? You walk away now, you turn your back on me, and I swear by Christ's bones the next time I see you I'll have your fucking head.'

Guillaume paused on the threshold. For a moment Ilbert thought he might turn, might speak. Apologise, perhaps. Beg forgiveness and come up with some way to salvage the scraps of their tattered loyalties. But he simply walked out, the heavy oak door thudding shut with a terrible finality.

The sound echoed in the sudden stillness, tolling through Ilbert's head like a bell.

Gone. His dreams of wealth and power, of carving his name with fire and steel were naught but ashes. And Guillaume with them, the brother of his heart, walking away without so much as a backward glance.

Ilbert squeezed his eyes shut, despair rising to devour him in its black tide.

Fool. Fucking fool.

Slowly, he dragged himself to his feet, cradling his throbbing wrist. He stumbled to the window and braced himself against the sill. Below, London writhed like a nest of maggots.

Staring into that abyss, he felt something harden inside him to cold, implacable purpose. Guillaume had made his choice. Let him rot in the boy-king's shadow, just another dog begging for scraps. Ilbert would not go so quietly. He would not bend the knee, not to Henry. He would fight to the last drop of blood. Let the streets run red with it. Let the strongholds of his enemies burn. He would tear this kingdom apart if he had to, set it ablaze and dance in the cinders for one reason... Hate.

Let it be a fire in his belly, a forge upon which to temper his killing edge. He had nothing left to lose. Nothing but vengeance, red and raw.

And by God, he would have it.

36

Estienne stood at the window of Newark's keep, gazing down at the sea of banners rippling across the fields below. The armies of England had converged here at the Marshal's behest, a tide of steel and flesh ready to crash down upon their enemy.

Never had Estienne seen a host of such size. Knights had flocked to the call, bringing their bannerets and retainers. He counted near four hundred before losing track, their numbers swelling with each new arrival. Crossbowmen added to their bristling ranks, perhaps two hundred and fifty carrying sheaves of quarrels, faces grim beneath steel helms. As for the common soldiery, the men-at-arms and sundry auxiliaries, they were beyond counting, a shabby sea of kettle hats and gambesons, armed with pikes and polearms, bills and bows.

Behind him, the highest chamber of the keep hummed with the great and the good still loyal to their fledgling king, drawn from every corner of England. Estienne saw the imperious figure of Willem Longsword, the Earl of Salisbury, his tabard bearing the six rampant lions of his coat of arms. There was Robert of Vieuxpont, the Earl of Derby, fingers drumming on the hilt of his sword with ill-concealed impatience. Ranulf, Earl of Chester, grey brows drawn in a perpetual scowl. Brian of Lisle stood beside Robert of Gaugi, both doughty veterans of a dozen campaigns. The kinsmen Philip and William d'Albini stood close, their whispered exchange heated. But it was the brutal visage of Falkes of Bréauté that drew Estienne's eye and held it – King John's infamous enforcer, a bull of a man whose mere presence struck fear in Estienne's guts. He was little reassured by the presence of the clergy. Half-dozen bishops conversing like gaggling geese, their rich robes and jewelled crosses at odds with the stark brutality of their martial companions.

The Marshal stood before them all, a lion surveying his pride. When he spoke, his voice carried to every corner of the chamber.

'We thought this war might be over. That with the crowning of our new king, and his confirmation of the Charter of Runnymede, that those barons who stood against King John and would have seated a French pretender on the throne would be satisfied. It seems we were mistaken.' William's eyes narrowed as he regarded the gathering, the import of his words hanging heavy above them all. 'In case any man here needs reminding, we face a battle that will decide the fate of England. At Lincoln, rebel forces have joined with foreign usurpers to besiege the castle and wrest it from the king's appointed castellan, Lady Nicola de la Haye.' A rumble of anger went through the assembled nobility. Marshal raised a hand for silence. 'Count Thomas of Perche, Saer of Quincy, Robert FitzWalter – all have brought their armies to aid the traitors Gilbert of Gant and Hugh d'Arras in their treachery.'

'Then let us ride out and destroy the bastards.' Falkes of Bréauté stepped forward, one meaty hand resting on the hilt of his sword. 'Lure the French curs out of the city and into the open where we can cut them down.'

Mutters of agreement rippled through the lords, but Marshal silenced them with a sharp glance.

'You'll have your chance for slaughter, Falkes. Do not doubt, the stakes for which we play could not be higher. Lose the great city of Lincoln, and we may well lose England. The castle still stands resolute, Lady Nicola holds it for the king, but the rest of the city has fallen. It must be liberated, along with its fortress. This is the crucible, and we must emerge from it victorious, or our lands will be in ruin. But we will not lure out the French. We will enter their hive and destroy them where they nest.'

The Earl of Salisbury stirred, his weathered features set into a scowl. 'An inspiring notion, Marshal, but words alone will not secure our victory. That will take men, steel, and a strong leader. Who is to have the honour of leading our vanguard into the fray?'

Marshal met the earl's gaze squarely. 'I will. The king's enemies will feel the sting of my blade before any other.'

A hush fell and Estienne saw exchanged glances. Marshal was no longer a young man, his mailed fist not as strong or sure as it once had been, but no man dared give voice to those doubts. Not to William Marshal's face. His will was iron, his conviction absolute. If he intended to be the first into the breach, then so it would be.

'You all know your parts in this,' Marshal's voice echoed once more. 'See to your men. Marshal your retainers. Make peace with God. We march at dawn.'

Estienne lingered as the great hall began to empty, lords and bishops departing in a clatter of spurs and low, urgent conversation. Marshal beckoned him closer, and Estienne obeyed. Up close, his master looked tired, the lines of care cut deep.

'You have your task?' There was a heavy weight to the words.

'In... in truth, my lord, I don't. What would you have me do?'

The barest hint of a smile touched Marshal's lips, gone as swiftly as it appeared. 'I'd have you show the courage and loyalty I know lives in your breast. It will be up to you to infiltrate Lincoln ahead of our attack. Lord Falkes of Bréauté will lead a force inside the walls unseen. You will go with him.'

Estienne tried to hide his concern. He had hoped to ride at his master's side, to be knighted on the field by the man he revered above all others. To be entrusted with such a vital task was an honour, but still, a selfish part of him wished that it was otherwise.

The Marshal's eyes were keen as he read Estienne's doubt. 'You wish to speak your mind?'

'It's... nothing, my lord. I am ready to serve, however you see fit.'

The Marshal reached out to clasp Estienne's shoulder. 'I know you hunger to prove yourself worthy of your spurs. But trust me in this, your role will be crucial. The fate of England may well rest upon it. I would wish you at my side, but I must place my men where they will do the most good. You understand?'

Estienne nodded. 'I do, my lord. And I will not fail you. I swear it.'

A heavy tread cut through the sudden stillness. Estienne turned to see a figure ducking into the hall, a face he knew all too well. Guillaume Marshal, shame and contrition writ stark on those noble features.

William straightened, his face a blank mask as his eldest son approached. Guillaume stopped a few paces away, as though uncertain of his welcome. When he spoke, his voice was rough with apprehension.

'Father, I... I hardly know where to begin.'

'Then find a way, boy.' William's voice was winter frost.

'I have no excuses. Only regrets. I allowed myself to be swayed by misplaced ideals. By ill-chosen loyalties. My actions... my lack of judgement... they shame me to my core.'

Father and son stood in silence, the air heavy with the weight of unspoken pains. The Marshal's jaw worked as he ground his teeth, and Estienne half-expected him to hurl recriminations before banishing his wayward heir from his sight.

'We've all made choices we regret, Guillaume,' he said instead. 'Done things that left scars. What matters is that you're here now.'

'I want to make amends, father.' Guillaume stepped forward. 'Let me ride with you. Fight at your side. Let me wash clean the stain of my dishonour with the blood of England's enemies.'

For a moment, the Marshal stood unmoving. Then he closed the distance between them in a single stride and pulled Guillaume into a fierce embrace. His son returned it, hands grasping his father's cloak, face buried against his shoulder.

'There is nothing I could wish for more,' William said. 'To have you with me again. You've been sorely missed, son.'

Estienne looked away, feeling like an intruder in this private moment. Beneath it though, was a pang of envy, hot and sharp. To have a father who cherished you, who would welcome you with open arms despite your sins. To ride to war at his side, united in purpose and blood alike...

No. Such thoughts served no one.

He had a task before him.

An oath to uphold.

And by God, he would see it done.

37

Ilbert rode south through the streets of Lincoln, the hooves of his destrier echoing along the abandoned thoroughfare. At his side, Thomas of Perche sat tall in the saddle, his youthful features set in a mask of grim determination. Ilbert studied the young knight from the corner of his eye, marking the effortless way he held himself, the casual arrogance of a man secure in his authority. Thomas was close to Prince Louis, high in the Lion's favour, and that alone was enough to command Ilbert's respect.

As if sensing his regard, Thomas turned to face him. 'I'm glad you chose to stay true to our cause, FitzDane. It demonstrates wisdom, siding against the boy-king and his simpering lords.'

Ilbert inclined his head, allowing himself a smile. 'Aye, well, there's no sense in flocking to a doomed banner. Louis will make a strong king. A true one.'

'That he will,' Thomas agreed. 'And those who stood with him from the first will be well-rewarded when he takes the crown.'

A screech of tortured wood and the dull boom shattered the moment. Ilbert glanced up to see a boulder arc over the rooftops, before slamming into the upper reaches of the central keep. A shower of shattered stone sprayed outward, pelting the roofs below.

'How many days has Gant assaulted those walls, and still they hold?' Ilbert asked.

Thomas shrugged. 'Too many. But let them hide behind their stone. It only delays the inevitable.'

They rode on, passing beneath the shadow of the keep, its once-proud walls pocked and scarred, the surrounding buildings reduced to rubble. But still it stood defiant, a sullen fist of stone jutting against the pallid sky.

'Lady Nicola is a stubborn bitch, I'll grant her that,' Ilbert murmured.

'She'll bend.' Thomas's voice held a certainty to it that inspired confidence. 'Or she'll break.'

They left the keep behind, passing the siege engines that squatted in its lee. Hugh d'Arras and Gilbert of Gant stalked among them, shouting orders, faces ruddy with exertion and rage. Ilbert thought them fools, wasting effort on such fruitless endeavour, but he held his tongue. The city was theirs, whether the central keep fell today or a month hence.

The streets of Lincoln stretched out before them, empty as a fresh-dug grave. What little populace remained were hidden in their hovels, huddled like rats while their city crumbled around them. Ilbert felt a stab of satisfaction at their misery. Let them cower. Let them tremble, while their betters decided their fate.

'We're close now, FitzDane,' Thomas said. 'The crown is within our grasp. All that remains is to close our fist around it.'

Ilbert grinned at the thought. 'And squeeze until the life bleeds out of the old order.'

'How very poetic,' Thomas laughed. 'I knew I liked you for a reason.'

They rode on in companionable silence through the shell of

Lincoln. A clatter of hooves on cobbles drew their attention, and Ilbert turned to see two figures riding hard toward them, the Fitz-Walter and Quincy coats-of-arms bright atop dull mail.

Thomas reined up as Robert FitzWalter and Saer of Quincy drew alongside, their destriers stamping and snorting.

'My lords.' Thomas inclined his head. 'You have news?'

FitzWalter urged his horse forward. 'The king's company approaches from the south. The Marshal rides at their head.'

Ilbert felt a twist of unease at the mention of his former master. 'How many?' Thomas asked.

'Enough.' Saer of Quincy spat. 'We outnumber them, but not convincingly.'

'Still, it would be better if we took the fight to them, beyond the narrow streets of Lincoln.' FitzWalter said. 'Crush them in open battle before they can threaten the city.'

Thomas held up a hand. 'We hold the walls. That's no small advantage. Ride out to meet them, and we throw it away.'

FitzWalter shook his head. 'Our knights will be penned in within the boundary of the city. We cannot manoeuvre, as we would on an open field, to take advantage of our numbers.'

'This city's defences have vexed the likes of Gant and d'Arras for weeks now,' Thomas retorted. 'Use your head. The loyalists want us to leave the protection of the city. That's their best chance and they know it.'

FitzWalter looked set to argue further, but Quincy laid a hand on his arm. 'Peace, Robert. The boy talks sense. Let him ride out and get the measure of them.' He looked to Thomas. 'That's your intent, is it not?'

Thomas gave a curt nod. 'Aye. And then I'll decide on our course.'

Grudgingly, FitzWalter sat back in his saddle. 'As you will.'

Thomas gathered his reins, the discussion clearly at an end.

'Get the men ready. Spread the word our enemy approaches. I'll return as soon as I'm able.'

He set heels to his destrier's flanks. Ilbert spurred his own mount and he cantered after Thomas. He caught up to him at the city gates, the narrow passage yawning open to the south. Beyond, the land swept away, as Ilbert drew alongside Thomas.

'Idiots,' Thomas growled. 'Riding out to face the Marshal in the open would be purest folly.'

'FitzWalter hungers for a swift end to this,' Ilbert replied. 'As do we all.'

Thomas shot him a scathing look. 'A swift end is all well and good, but only if we are victorious. Charging to meet the enemy as though we were on the tourney field is naught but madness. This is war.'

With that, he spurred his horse forward. The road stretched out, rutted and well-used. Ilbert kept his destrier close on the tail of Thomas's mount as they crested the first swell of high ground, and he scoured the horizon, dreading what he might eventually see.

'Do you think the king rides with them?' Ilbert asked as they continued along the quiet road. 'Henry, I mean. Not that the boy is fit to command, but as a figurehead?'

Thomas shook his head. 'I doubt it. The Marshal may be many things, but he's no fool. He wouldn't risk the boy in open battle.'

'Would that Prince Louis were here. To fight alongside us. To be at hand when his final victory is sealed.'

'When he is crowned he'll remember who stood for him.' Thomas's voice rang with conviction. 'Lordships, land, coin... all will flow to those who bled for his cause.'

Before they could talk further they crested the final rise, and the words died on Ilbert's lips.

An army stretched before them, a forest of steel beneath an

ocean of writhing banners. Rank upon rank of knights and men-at-arms, their helms glinting in the sunlight. And more distant still, black specks massing on the horizon, resolving into purposeful lines of infantry and horse.

Ilbert swallowed against the sudden constriction of his throat, as the full extent of the threat sank in. The loyalist host was vast, far larger than any rebel force he had seen mustered. So many pennons it defied their counting. How could they hope to stand against such a tide?

Thomas drew up short, his face drained of colour. 'Mother of God. There's so many.' He turned to Ilbert. 'Get back to the city. Tell FitzWalter to shore up the defences. Man the walls, muster the knights. Now, FitzDane.'

Ilbert nodded, wheeling his destrier around. As he pounded back along the track, the thunder of hooves loud in his ears, he couldn't quell the dread uncoiling in his stomach. But even as the fear rose to choke him, a darker thought reared its head... would Guillaume be among the host, avid for rebel blood?

He knew he should dread such a reunion. Should fear to meet the man he had called brother across a killing field. But some part of him thrilled at the prospect. Yearned to see Guillaume's face grow pallid as Ilbert's sword carved a path through his innards. To repay betrayal with retribution.

The gates of Lincoln loomed, and Ilbert thundered beneath the portcullis, already shouting for FitzWalter. Preparations would need to be made, and with all haste. War had come to Lincoln.

38

Estienne crouched in the shadows as, around him, Falkes and the other crossbowmen waited, still as stone, barely daring to breathe. The air was thick with anticipation, undercut by the reek of smoke that clung to the city.

Ahead, the western postern gate stood, small and insignificant, but it might well be their way to turn this siege in their favour. Guarding it was one lone figure – a young man, barely more than a boy, his face pale beneath the rim of his steel cap. He clutched a spear in white-knuckled hands, gaze darting northward, a rabbit scenting the wind for foxes.

In the distance, the din raged. The relentless clash of ram against wood carried on the air, Earl Ranulf of Chester hurling his might at the northern gate in a bid to draw the enemy's eye. All so Estienne and the others could slip in unseen, a blade between the ribs of their unsuspecting foe.

Beside him, Falkes shifted, the big knight a shadow given form. Estienne watched as he slid forward, uncoiling from the under-growth. The young guard never even had time to cry out. One moment he was standing, the next he was in the grip of the knife-wielding Falkes, hands scrabbling at the ruin of his throat, his life spraying out in a hot gush. The knight let the body slump to the ground and turned to the others, teeth flashing in a wolf's grin, as he jerked his head toward the postern. Estienne's hands tightened on his crossbow as he moved to the entrance.

Falkes hammered on the door, the boom of his mailed fist echoing. For a moment, nothing. Then a rattle of iron, the groan of hinges, and the postern yawned open. Estienne readied himself as Falkes ducked inside.

They moved like ghosts across the worn stone. Estienne followed close on Falkes's heels, heart lodged in his throat as they wound their way up, up, toward the battlements. A flicker of movement in a side passage made Estienne start, but it was no threat that greeted them. An old woman stood flanked by a pair of men-at-arms, her face lined and stern, silver hair caught back in a braid. She watched them pass, and Estienne had the uncanny sense she was taking their measure, weighing their worth in a glance. Nicola de la Haye. The lady of Lincoln, unbroken by the siege that had assailed her for so long now.

Then they were past, taking those last few steps to the battlement. The wind gusted, cold and cutting, as Estienne reached the top. He moved to the parapet, peering out, and below the enemy teemed. Armoured knights milled, horses stamping and snorting. They looked almost like ants from this vantage. Ants with swords and lances, hungering for blood.

All along the wall, the crossbowmen took up positions. As one, they hooked bowstrings to spanning belts, stood in the stirrups and pulled back to notch their bowstrings. Then they slotted quarrels into grooves. Estienne unslung his own bow, hands moving in a deft long-practised manoeuvre. He could feel the thrum of anticipation building, the indrawn breath before the hammer stroke.

Falkes raised a hand, as he watched those knights. Estienne

sighted down the stock, the wood cool against his cheek. Below, a mass of men and horses, unaware of what was to rain down. Estienne lined up the shot, time stretching out between one heartbeat and the next.

Falkes's hand dropped.

As one, the crossbows thrummed. A deadly volley, punching down into the massed ranks below. Horses screamed, lashing out with iron-shod hooves. Men tumbled, shafts standing out from mail. Confusion rippled through the besiegers, but Estienne was already working his crossbow, slotting another bolt, sighting on another rampant horse and rider...

* * *

Ilbert cursed, wrenching brutally on the reins as his destrier shied and grunted. All around him, horses reared and bucked, eyes rolling in terror as crossbow bolts rained down like a torrent. They punched through mail, driving men from their saddles to sprawl in the muck.

A knight just to Ilbert's left took a bolt to the eye, his shriek abruptly silenced as he toppled, blood gushing down his face. His horse bolted, and Ilbert barely wrenched his mount aside in time.

'Get to cover,' a voice bellowed. 'Shields up.'

But the cry was lost in the tumult as the crack of bolts skipped off stone, the raging of horses, the screams of the wounded. The massed ranks began to buckle, knights circling in confusion, cursing, shouting, all discipline fled. It was bedlam, a seething cauldron of terror and rage.

And then, rising above the din, the groan of tortured timbers. The boom of a great gate crashing open. Ilbert twisted in his saddle in time to see the northern gate yawn wide, vomiting forth a tide of steel. They poured through the gap, streaming into the city in a flood – rats swarming from a stirred nest. The king's loyal knights.

The French line buckled, thrown back on its heels by the sudden fury of the attack, horses colliding, men tangling. Ilbert glimpsed Thomas of Perche trying to rally his men, his raised shield bearing red chevrons on white, a beacon in the heart of the confusion.

Ilbert gritted his teeth, grasping his reins. No more dancing. No more twitching helplessly under sniping bolts. With a roar, he couched his lance and spurred forward into the fray, hooves clacking on cobbles. He smashed into the royalist press, the crack of his lance a sweet song, the crunch of bones and screaming of men the only music he could ever wish to hear.

Dropping the broken weapon, he wrenched his blade free, teeth bared in a snarl, in the thick of it now. An enemy knight loomed before him, sword hacking. Ilbert bellowed his challenge, surging to meet him in a clash of steel on steel.

He lashed out, feeling the impact of sword on helm, hearing the metallic thrum and the knight before him swayed, leaning back in his saddle, as his horse lurched by.

Fighting for breath, Ilbert cast about, seeking a new foe to challenge. All around, battle raged – the clash of swords, the screams of the dying – but there was a savage joy singing in Ilbert's blood now, drowning out all caution, all fear.

'To me!' The cry rang out over the clamour, raw-throated and fierce. 'Rally, for Prince Louis. Rally for the Lion of France!'

Ilbert twisted to see Thomas of Perche, still mounted, sword thrust to the sky. Men were already streaming to him, steel bright in their fists, prepared to follow their lord into hell's embrace. Ilbert spurred towards him, a fierce grin stretching his face. This would be a charge for the ages. A death ride to make the bards sing his name for generations. He opened his mouth, a cry building in his throat, a roar to bring these royalist scum to their knees...

Ilbert watched in horror as a sword lanced through the eye slit of Thomas's helm and his white surcoat was drowned in the red wash of his blood. The sword wrenched free, and Thomas folded in his saddle before falling to crumple beneath the stamping hooves.

No. This wasn't how it was supposed to be.

The line fractured, men fighting now in knots and clumps, robbed of leadership, of direction. But there, in the thick of them, the man whose presence made Ilbert's gorge rise, red and bloody.

Guillaume Marshal, helm lost, teeth bared. His sword rose and fell with a butcher's efficiency, no artistry, no glory, just cold-blooded slaughter. Ilbert watched as he slammed his battered shield into a mercenary's face, the man falling with a scream. More animal than man in his savagery. So unlike the loyal fool Ilbert had once thought he'd known.

Red rage seared across his vision as he watched the man he had called brother. A traitor. A turncoat who would spit on his own if he thought he would reap benefit.

Ilbert gathered himself, heedless of the screams, the clash of battle, his focus on naught but the man before him. Then he charged, a roar of pure hate tearing from his throat, sword drawn back for the killing blow...

* * *

'With me, you dogs of war,' Falkes bellowed as he led them from the castle.

Estienne stumbled after him, through the open gate, and into hell.

Screams rent the air, the clash of metal, the roar. Men grappled and cursed, writhing like animals in the mud of the street. Blood ran slick, howls echoed, and rising over it all, the pale facade of the cathedral. It loomed above the slaughter, its spires clawing at the clouds, such beauty and horror that should never have been allowed to meet.

But he had no time for such musings as the enemy surged towards him, and he fell into the melee, knife rising, a wordless snarl tearing from his throat as he cut and thrust. Estienne lost himself to it, to the savage drumbeat of battle. Dimly he was aware of Falkes at his side, the big knight laughing like a fiend as he swung his sword in great, cleaving arcs. Of the other crossbowmen, they were a pack of lean and hungry hounds harrying the French-men's flanks. The enemy was already falling back, stumbling over their own dead in their haste to disengage and retreat downhill, to the south.

A flicker of movement in the corner of Estienne's eye. He turned, expecting a fresh wave of enemies, but instead saw two knights, circling one another on horseback, trading blows with a savage grace that belied the crude brutality surrounding them. One wore a surcoat bearing the wyvern of FitzDane; the other was proud in the livery of Marshal.

Ilbert and Guillaume. Tooth and claw, striving for the kill.

Even as Estienne watched, Ilbert drove forward. His destrier crashed into Guillaume's with bone-shaking force. Guillaume was knocked from the saddle and flung to the cobbles in a clatter of mail. His horse screamed and bolted, an arrow protruding from its haunch. Riderless, it ploughed into the ranks of the fleeing merce-naries, kicking and biting.

Guillaume foundered on his back, reaching for a sword too far from his grasp. Ilbert leapt from his saddle, striding forward to stand above him, his own blade reflecting sickly light through the blood-spatter that obscured its sheen.

Ready to thrust down. To end Guillaume Marshal as he lay helpless.

Estienne started forward, a surge of desperation lending wings to his heels as he threw himself towards the two men – Ilbert, towering over Guillaume's prone form, sword poised for the killing blow. Guillaume, scrabbling for a blade that wasn't there, fingers churning the muck.

Estienne snatched up a fallen sword and closed that last, yawning gap in a heartbeat.

Ilbert's weapon flashed down.

Estienne's rose to meet it.

The blades met with a shriek, the killing blow halted.

'Fucking whoreson!' Ilbert spat.

Then he was on Estienne in a whirlwind of steel. A storm of hacks and cuts, of parries and counters. Estienne met him blow for blow, the song of sword on sword rising to a deafening tumult.

He moved on instinct, all Ilbert's focused hate and savagery against Estienne's desperate, frenzied defiance.

'I'll cut you to bloody rags.' Ilbert's voice was thick with hate, the words snarled between the crash and ring of steel.

Estienne saved his breath for the fight, each blow more desperate, every one of Ilbert's strikes threatening to breach his defence.

And then, distant but distinct, the blare of a trumpet. The call to retreat, high and piercing. A moment of distraction and Estienne seized his chance, stepping into Ilbert's guard and smashing his sword pommel hard into the side of his helm.

Ilbert reeled back, spitting curses. Estienne raised his blade, ready to end it, but before he could land the killing stroke, Ilbert was turning, fleeing with the rest of the French rabble.

'This isn't over, Wace,' he shouted over his shoulder, voice thick with malice. 'Next time, I will tear out your guts!'

And then he was swept up in the tide of bodies flooding

towards the southern gate. Estienne watched him go, sword suddenly boulder-heavy in his grip...

* * *

Ilbert ran, the taste of blood filling his mouth.

All around him, men fled like rats from a flooded nest, throwing down arms and shields, all thoughts of valour and glory left trampled as they scrambled to save their own skins. The French, so proud and peerless, stripped of dignity and driven before the royalists like curs.

Disgust welled thick and oily in Ilbert's throat. At them, at himself. He should be standing fast, blade in hand, spitting defiance to his last breath, but the tide of bodies was inexorable, carrying him toward the southern gate. And there, the final indignity. The square was packed tight as a barrel of fish, men crammed shoulder to shoulder, the reek of sweat and fear rising.

Horses screamed, lashing out in the confined space, and men cried out as iron-shod hooves found flesh. The gate loomed, dark and narrow, and bodies pressed through it in a writhing mass. Too small. It was too damned small to pass so many so swiftly.

Ilbert snarled, elbowing his way forward through the crush. Men piled up at the gate, clawing and trampling in their desperation to squeeze through that too-narrow gap.

An unholy din filled the air – curses, moans, desperate cries. Panic hung thick enough to choke on, like smoke from burning pitch, but still Ilbert muscled forward, heedless of who he trod underfoot, seeing only open road and escape.

The wind hit him like a slap when he finally broke free. The stink of battle and cowardice clung to him, a foul perfume, and his fingers cramped white-knuckled on the haft of his sullied sword. He staggered, gagging for breath.

Behind, Lincoln burned. The flames of ambition and rebellion, doused in royalist piss. The taste of failure rose up to coat his tongue. How had it come to this? How had it all turned to ash?

But beneath the humiliation, hope glowed forge-hot behind his ribs. The rebellion was not done yet. This was just a battle lost. He would return to Prince Louis' side and make everyone, loyal to the child-king, pay in blood... starting with Estienne Wace.

'You're a dead man, whoreson.'

The vow tasted like iron, and Ilbert relished it. He'd put the fucking mongrel down. Like he should have done the first time Wace darkened William Marshal's door...

* * *

The world seemed oddly muted after the din of battle. A great, ringing silence broken only by the crackle of flames and the low groans of the wounded. Estienne stood amidst the ruins of slaughter, the mud and cobbles churned to a red slurry.

A grunt, the scrape of metal on stone, and he turned to see Guillaume struggling to rise. His surcoat was torn and bloodied, but he was alive. Estienne slipped an arm about his shoulders.

'Easy,' he murmured, as Guillaume leaned into him with a hiss. 'I have you.'

Guillaume's face was sheened with sweat, but his eyes were bright as they met Estienne's, something perilously close to gratitude lurking in their grey depths.

'You saved my life, squire,' he said simply.

Estienne found it difficult to acknowledge the fact, modesty or fatigue staying his answer. Instead he helped Guillaume north, through streets strewn with the dead and dying. Past the looming edifice of the cathedral, its pale stone smeared with soot. The keep rose proud opposite, the three-lion banner of King Henry fluttering in the wind from its highest tower. And in between both, the man who had won this victory.

William Marshal sat upon his destrier like a graven idol, hewn from granite. He watched as Estienne and Guillaume approached.

'You are both well?' His voice was roughened from a day of shouted commands.

'We are, Father.' Guillaume bowed his head as best he could manage.

'Good.'

No warmth, not even for his son saved from the brink of death. Estienne shifted, chafing under that measuring gaze, but Marshal had already turned away, wheeling his destrier to survey the captured city.

Around them, the rats began to appear from their hidey-holes, the people of Lincoln creeping into the sun now the French dogs had been driven out. But Estienne could see that already looting had begun. Men loyal to the king, driven on by zeal if not loyalty, were now making ready to claim their just rewards.

For liberated Lincoln, the coming night would be a long one.

39

Estienne stood atop the battlements of Lincoln castle, barely feeling the chill of the wind as he surveyed the carnage below. Men swarmed through the narrow streets, drunk on their victory, their shouts of glee and the screams of their victims rising into the night sky.

A woman's piercing shriek knifed the air, abruptly silenced. Estienne flinched but did not look away. He made himself watch as a pair of men-at-arms dragged a slight figure from a doorway, her kirtle ripped, her struggles feeble in their iron grip. They hauled her into an alley, and Estienne could imagine well enough what would come next.

Elsewhere, a knot of soldiers kicked in the door of a chandler's shop, whooping as they spilled inside to plunder its wares. Glass shattered, shelves collapsing under the assault of grasping hands. Estienne tracked their progress, watching them emerge again with arms laden, bounty to be trampled into the muck of the streets or lost in a drunken night of dicing.

The stink of smoke hung heavy as fire took hold in the poorer quarters. The flames leapt from thatch to thatch, the hungry crackle almost drowned by the rising wails. Estienne rested his hands on the cold stone. The battle had been well fought, and hard won. He'd acquitted himself with honour, taken bold risks for his liege and land. He should be flush with the thrill of victory and yet, as he watched the sack of Lincoln unfold, he felt only a yawning emptiness.

From behind the heavy oak door leading into the keep, he heard the raucous sounds of revelry – the clink of goblets, the boisterous laughter, the off-key bellow of some victory song. No doubt the great lords were in their cups already, toasting the day's work, vying to outdo each other with tales of their glorious deeds. Estienne had no wish to join them. He could not bring himself to smile and laugh as if all were well. Not with the city spread out before him, splayed and bleeding. Let the mighty feast on the fruits of conquest. He'd take his solace in solitude.

'You fought well today.'

The words startled Estienne, and he turned to see William Marshal himself emerging from the tower door. Estienne dipped into a hasty bow.

'My lord, I did not hear you. Forgive me, I was—'

Marshal waved away Estienne's apology as he joined him at the parapet and gazed out over the city. 'At ease, lad. We're past standing on ceremony. I saw how you acquitted yourself today. With bravery. With honour.'

Estienne struggled with the compliment. 'I did as I was bidden, my lord. As any loyal man would.'

'Loyal man, aye. Though I fear there are fewer of those than there should be, in times such as these.' He nodded toward the great hall behind, where the victory feast continued. 'Hark at them. Clamouring over the tally of the slain as if they had fought at a tourney, and not for the survival of a kingdom.'

Estienne could hear them – Falkes of Bréauté's booming

guffaws, Willem Longsword's strident baritone, each trying to outdo the other as to who was the greater braggart. He could only think of the corpses still littering the streets below, the slow spread of blood over the cobbles. The images sat ill in his gut.

'The real heroes of this day are not the loudest at the table,' Marshal said softly, looking to where a banner flew bearing the three escallops argent of de la Haye. Though smoke-stained and ash-flaked, it flew unbroken, the arms of Lady Nicola proud in the dying light. 'If any soul deserves praise this day, it is she. Holding firm against siege and assault, with no surety of relief. That is valour.'

'It is over now though, is it not?' Estienne asked. 'We struck a mighty blow against the rebels today. Surely now they'll see the futility of opposing the king's will?'

William turned to him. 'Over? No, lad. Not while Prince Louis still covets the crown. We are not done yet.'

Estienne's jaw clenched as he looked out over the city. He saw only misery and brutality. Dogs fought over scraps, snarling and snapping. A boy, scarcely older than five summers, sat hunched in the mouth of an alley, tears striping the soot on his pinched face as he cradled a bloodied rag doll. The crash of timber and a belch of smoke drew his eye as another hovel was put to the torch.

'Does it trouble you, lad?' Marshal's voice was soft with understanding. 'This wanton ruin visited on the smallfolk?'

'It feels... wrong, my lord. These people, they did not choose this war. They are not soldiers or rebels. Only folk trying to live their lives. And yet they suffer, while those who stood in revolt, committed treason, escape the worst of the reckoning.'

He knew the truth of it, had heard the whispers already. Men like FitzWalter, Gant and Quincy would bend the knee and be pardoned. They would lose some lands, some coin, but their lives would be spared, the price of their rebellion measured in acres and silver, not blood.

When Earl William had no answer but silence, it began to stir something new in Estienne's chest. Something bold, something he had suppressed but could keep silent no longer.

'When I first came into your service, those years ago, I thought my path was clear. To be a knight, bold and true. To fight for what was right. But now... I am not so sure. What is the worth of a code, of honour, when it is so quick to crumble? When vows fall to dust as soon as they become inconvenient to those who swear them?'

He heard the hurt in his own voice but could not call back the words. The ache of it had been building in him for months. Festering like a wound that would not heal.

William sighed and Estienne half-expected a sharp rebuke for his honesty. 'There are no easy answers, lad. Not for the likes of us. You must find a way to make peace with the demands of duty and what you believe to be right, even when those two things seem on opposite sides. It is a battle every knight must fight, within himself.'

'And what if I lose that battle, my lord? What if I cannot reconcile the blood on my hands with the code I swore to uphold?'

'Then you are not the first good man to stumble on that hard road. Nor will you be the last. The vows we take, the code we swear to uphold – they are a heavy burden to bear. A weight that can break the back of even the most steadfast man.'

'But how does one bear it? How do you carry that weight and still keep standing?'

Marshal laid a heavy hand on his shoulder. 'You find a way to make the burden a part of you. To let it shape you, strengthen you. Then you do what must be done, even when it cuts against the grain of your soul.'

Estienne shook his head. 'What if I am not strong enough to walk that line? What if I fall?'

'Then you pick yourself up and you try again,' William said simply. 'You push on. Serve your lord, defend the weak, hold to your oaths as best you can.'

There was something in his voice, a raw edge that spoke of old wounds, scars that still ached under the weight of years.

'Forgive me,' Estienne replied. 'You have burdens enough without me adding to them. It was selfish of me to—'

'No.' The single word cut through his mumbled apology. 'Never think that, lad. These doubts, these questions... they are not weakness. They are the sign of a good heart. Never be afraid to look at what we do, and ask if it is right.'

Estienne had to look away, fixing his stare on the smoke-stained pennants. 'I will try, my lord.'

'See that you do. I have faith in you, Estienne. Faith that you will find your way through this mire.' The words kindled a tiny ember of warmth amidst the ashes of Estienne's doubt. 'But come. We have tarried here long enough. There is still work to be done. Louis is a tenacious whelp. He will not give up his claim to the throne. Not when he believes God and might are on his side.'

'What would you have me do, my lord?'

Marshal regarded him steadily. 'For now, you rest. And you prepare yourself for the battle to come. For I fear this war is not done yet.'

With that, he turned and strode away, his footfalls heavy on the stone. Estienne watched him go, feeling the weight of his words settle like a mantle across his shoulders. The burden of duty, of service, of all the things he had sworn to uphold.

He cast one last look out over Lincoln, taking in the smoke and the sorrow, the ruin and the weeping. Letting it sear into his mind, a reminder of the cost of his calling. Then he turned his back on the bleak scene and followed his master inside.

40

Hubert stepped onto the quay, the salt-scoured wood creaking beneath his boots. He breathed deep, letting the brine-sharp air fill his lungs, purging the phantom reek of smoke and blood that still clung to him.

Two sieges he'd now weathered behind the walls of Dover. Two storms of fire and steel, as the French hurled themselves upon him like the ocean dashing against a cliff. And like those cliffs, he'd held fast.

He rolled his shoulders, feeling the weariness that had settled into his bones, but he had no time to rest. Not now, with the shadow of the French fleet looming once more.

Hubert strode down the quay, drinking in the sights and sounds of Sandwich. The creak of ropes and timbers, the snap of wind-taut sails, the cries of sailors as they loaded arms. The harbour was abustle, every able-bodied man preparing for the battle to come as they readied their ropes, and made seaworthy their bowlines, guide-ropes and guys.

He made his way up from the dock, seeing the narrow streets of the town proper. And there the preparations took on a different cast. Everywhere he looked, he saw the proud colours of England's greatest lords, come to answer the Marshal's call to arms. Banners flapped of Earls Warenne, Salisbury, Hertford and Albemarle; the twin lions of Richard FitzRoy and the four fusils in fess argent of Philip d'Albini. And above them all, waving proudly, the royal arms of England's boy-king, Henry.

As he looked, a familiar figure detached itself from the milling crowds. Tall and rangy, with a shock of dark hair and keen eyes, more grey than blue.

'My Lord Hubert.' Estienne Wace's grin was fierce as he moved forward. They embraced, thumping each other on the back like two bears testing their strength. 'God's teeth, it's good to see you.'

'And you, lad.' Hubert held him at arm's length, studying the planes and angles of a face that had hardened into manhood since he'd last seen it. 'You're well?'

Estienne shrugged. 'Well as any man can be, with the French wolf still scratching at our door.'

Hubert barked a laugh. 'Aye, there is that. And the Marshal? How fares he?'

'As well as can be expected. Lincoln took its toll on him.'

Hubert felt a sudden sorrow at that. William Marshal was a titan, and to think of him laid low, even by age and long labours, sat ill in his gullet. 'Take me to him.'

Estienne nodded, turning to lead the way. They wound through the streets, leaving behind the bustle of the town and striking out along the headland. To their left, the sea sighed against shingle, grey and choppy beneath a cloudy sky. Ahead, a lone figure sat upon a sturdy wooden chair, a silhouette of bowed shoulders and silvered hair. At his sides, two men-at-arms, one holding aloft the red lion banner of Marshal.

Estienne hung back as Hubert approached, and when he drew closer, he could see Marshal looked worn as a sword honed past its fighting edge. The long years hung heavy on him, and there was a new frailty to that solid frame that set a chill in Hubert's blood. But when William turned to greet him, some of the old fire still kindled behind those slate-grey eyes.

'Hubert.' William Marshal's voice was still the sound of millstones grinding.

'William.' Hubert nodded. 'You look like shit.'

A wry twist of the lips. 'Ever the blunt one, Hubert. Though I cannot imagine I look much rougher than you.'

Hubert stifled a grin. 'Few men can make siege-craft look pretty. Though God knows we gave those French dogs as good as they gave us.'

Marshal's smile turned grim. 'But they're not done yet. Prince Louis licks his wounds, but his pet admiral is a determined bastard. You've heard the Black Monk threatens us with his fleet?'

Hubert spat to the side. 'Eustace, aye.'

'He's at Calais. The weather threw him off last time, but he'll come straight back to our shores once he's resupplied. If he lands with more men and horses for the prince, there's no telling how long this conflict will last.'

'How soon do you expect him?'

'Within the week is my guess. Maybe less.'

Hubert blew out a breath. 'Christ. That's precious little time.'

'It will have to be enough. Starve Louis of reinforcements and we have all but won this bloody war. This is our chance, Hubert. To cut the head from this French serpent, once and for all. But I need a strong hand to wield the blade. I would have you lead our fleet. Meet Eustace and crush him, before he can sow more strife upon our shores.'

Hubert huffed a laugh, but there was no mirth in it. 'And here I thought you were just pining for my company.'

'I always pine for your company,' Marshal retorted dryly. 'The fact that you happen to be the fiercest war dog in Christendom is merely a perk.'

The jest hung between them for a long moment, the silence heavy with all the words that need not be said. A friendship forged across decades, tempered in a shared crucible of strife.

'I'll do it,' Hubert said at last. 'Of course I will. Though it grieves me that you won't be at my side for this one.'

'Would that I could, old friend. But this old warhorse isn't fit for the saddle any longer. Best I can do is choose my champion well.' He glanced at Estienne, still standing at a respectful distance. 'You'll take the lad? Put him to good use?'

Hubert took in the set of Estienne's shoulders, the quiet intensity of him. 'Aye. I'd be a fool not to.' He turned back to Marshal. 'About the boy. Don't you think it's time you gave him his spurs? God knows he's earned them.'

Marshal's gaze flitted toward the sea. 'Estienne has done... admirably. Shown courage beyond his years.'

'Admirably?' Hubert barked a laugh. 'He fights like a man possessed. Like a lion. Reminds me of someone we used to know.'

That earned him a sharp glance. 'He has proven himself, aye. But there are things you don't know.'

'The lad's worth any two knights I could name. You know it, I know it. If you won't knight him, I bloody will. The boy deserves—'

'You will not.'

Marshal's voice struck hard as a hammer. For an instant, Hubert saw a flash of the old warrior – that unbending will, the steel that had broken men and armies alike.

He held up his hands. 'Peace, William. I meant no offence. But you cannot deny the boy has the heart of a true knight beating in that chest.'

Marshal took a long, steadying breath. 'That is why you must watch over him, Hubert. Why I must think carefully before raising him to such a noble position. There are those who might... who might use him ill if they knew...'

He trailed off, gaze distant, and Hubert felt a trickle of unease down his spine. Knew what? What secret lay in Estienne's blood? Hubert almost pressed the issue and demanded Marshal speak plain, but something in the set of the old warlord's jaw, the iron behind his eyes, stilled the words on Hubert's tongue.

'Keep him close,' Marshal said finally. 'Let him fight at your side. I will consider what is best for the lad before you leave.'

It was not enough, not with that unease still writhing in Hubert's gut, but he knew the tenor of a battle lost. Once William Marshal set his mind to a thing, easier to turn the tides than sway his course.

'As you will it, old friend.'

'Go, then. Ready your fleet. I'll not keep you any longer than I must.'

Hubert hesitated a moment, wrestling with the urge to clasp Marshal's shoulder, to offer some gesture of friendship, of thanks for all that lay unspoken. In the end, he merely nodded and turned away.

As he strode back along the headland toward Estienne, the boy straightened, looking over Hubert's shoulder to where Marshal sat, alone and still against the grey horizon. 'My lord grants you the honour of command?'

'Aye.' Hubert came to stand beside him, his own gaze drawn inexorably back to Marshal's distant form. 'I'm to take our fleet to meet the French. The Black Monk is on his way with fresh ships and men. It'll be up to us to send them to the bottom of the sea.'

'What would you have of me?' Estienne said without hesitation.

There it was – keenness, stubbornness, bravery all at once.

Each one crying for a single reward. Knighthood. The one honour Hubert had been forbidden to grant.

'I would have you at my side,' he said simply.

For a long moment Estienne just stared at him, then slowly a grin spread across his face.

'And I will be there.'

41

The stink of Calais harbour clung to the back of Ilbert's throat, thick enough to choke on. Everywhere he looked, men swarmed like rats. Horses stamped and whickered as they were goaded up the ramps and into the dark bellies of ships that bobbed at anchor. Shouts in a mishmash of tongues – Lemosi, Proensal, Flemish, Occitan, the occasional smattering of English – rose to an incessant din.

Ilbert stood at the edge of the quay, watching the chaos of the muster swirl around him. Eighty ships of varying sizes crowded the harbour, their decks teeming with men-at-arms and sailors alike. Of the vessels, ten loomed largest – cogs with a capacity for scores of fighting men and their horses. The rest were smaller craft, their holds crammed with barrels of salt beef and sacks to supply the rebellion across the Channel.

He craned his neck, eyes narrowed against the glare of the sun on the water. In the near distance rose a large pavilion, above which flew the triple torteaux flag of Robert of Courtenay, Lord of Champignelles, Prince Louis' commander in this endeavour and cousin to King Philip himself. Beside the tent, a bevy of high-ranking barons milled, conversing with all the self-important bellowing Ilbert had come to expect.

A horse shrieked, high and panicked, hooves clacking against the gangplank as it was shoved and prodded up into the hold. Soldiers hauled on guy ropes, cursing as the destrier fought them every step. Its terror was a palpable thing, as if the beast could scent the trials that awaited it on the other side of the narrow sea.

Ilbert's lip curled in disgust, as much at himself as the whole wretched scene. Here they all were, jostling for position on the eve of sailing to war, and yet he felt more akin to the panicked destrier than any of these preening, self-assured lords.

He pushed the thought aside as soon as it surfaced. He'd cast his lot, and by God, he would see it through. His course was set, even if it meant chaining himself to the prow of Louis' flagship and riding the coming storm as its figurehead. Still, even with conviction firming his spine, he couldn't shake the gnawing unease. The sense that the tide had already begun to turn. That perhaps he'd lashed himself to a sinking ship.

A figure walked from the milling crowds, moving toward him with a peculiar grace, at odds with the frenetic energy all around. Recognition dawned as the man drew close, and Ilbert fought not to recoil at that gaunt face.

'Eustace,' Ilbert said in greeting.

The Black Monk inclined his head in a mock bow. Up close, he looked more cadaverous than ever, the stark black of his robes throwing the hollows of cheeks and eyes into starker relief. A silver tooth flashed as he smiled, bright against the rotten stumps surrounding it.

'FitzDane. How pleasant to find you here.'

Ilbert kept his face carefully blank. 'Where else would I be? We're all bound for the same destination.'

'Some more reluctantly than others, I think.' That silver tooth winked again, sharp as a blade. 'Though I confess, I'm surprised to see you still cleaving to Louis' banner. Given the way the wind is blowing.'

Ilbert's jaw clenched. 'The wind is ever changeable, but a man's convictions should be constant as the northern star.'

Eustace barked a laugh, the sound grating like a rusty hinge. 'Convictions? Is that what you call it?' He leaned in, close enough that Ilbert caught a whiff of stale incense and something more organic beneath, faintly rotten. 'Do you still believe yourself one of Louis' leal men? A knight riding to his king's salvation? Even after fortune has abandoned him and the armies of the child-king press him on all sides?'

Ilbert met that probing stare unflinchingly. 'What I believe is no concern of yours, monk. You'd do better to see to your own soul. If you still have one.'

When Eustace smiled, it was a death's head rictus. 'As you say. Let your conviction be your armour then and pray it's sufficient to turn an English blade.'

His words lingered like a niggling worm. 'I have more than my conviction. I was taught to fight by the greatest knight in Christendom.'

Eustace nodded knowingly. 'And now you fight against him.'

'For a rightful king against the son of a tyrant. A boy. At least I have a cause, monk. What do you fight for?'

Eustace's eyes glinted as they roamed across the teeming docks. 'Look at that, FitzDane. A fleet to cow the world, poised to set England to flame. If there were ever a time to find your fortune, this is it. So much potential for profit in chaos.'

'Is that all you think about then? Coin. Plunder. What you can line your coffers with, like a common thief.'

'And why not?' Eustace turned that unsettling visage back on Ilbert. 'What use is a war if not to enrich the victors? All this talk of principle and righteousness, it's hog shit, boy. Men fight for gold, glory and God, and not necessarily in that order.'

'You're wrong,' Ilbert growled. 'A true knight fights for honour. For his liege. For a cause greater than himself.'

'Honour.' Eustace spat the word like bile. 'And what good is your precious honour now, FitzDane? Will it put food in your belly? Buy you a fine horse and a stout castle? Warm your bed on a chill night? Will it keep a friend by your side?' His smile widened as Ilbert flinched, the memory of Guillaume's betrayal striking deep. 'Oh, I am sorry your lordling companion no longer fights with you. I did try and warn you of the fickleness of loyalty, when last we spoke. But something tells me you already learned that lesson, the day you stabbed Earl William in the back.'

'Have a care, monk,' Ilbert snarled through clenched teeth. 'Your holy orders and your ships won't save you a cracked skull if you push me too far.'

Even as the words left his mouth, he felt a hollow sickness opening in his gut. As much as he longed to refute Eustace's accusations, to hurl them back in the man's rotting teeth, he could not. Not in truth.

William Marshal had raised him up and made him everything he was. Ilbert had repaid that loyalty with betrayal. Even at the time, swept along in the fervour of rebellion and promise of advancement, some part of him had quailed at the dishonour, the inescapable taint of having proved himself false. His bridges were well and truly burned, and the only path left was forward, into the teeth of the coming storm, come what may.

He met Eustace's gaze squarely. 'I have chosen my course. Placed my faith with the true king of England. That is all that matters now.'

'Matters to you, perhaps,' Eustace replied blithely. 'Me, I'll put my faith in steel and strong arms. And in the constancy of Blanche of Castile's coffers. I leave you to your scruples, FitzDane. Let's hope they stop an English arrow as well as a coat of fine French mail.'

With that parting shot, he bowed, turned and sauntered away, black robe billowing. Ilbert watched him go, fingernails biting into his palm.

Damn his black heart and the poison that dripped from his tongue. What did a base churl like Eustace know of loyalty, of fealty unto death? Naught but a mercenary brute, a man of no country, content to peddle his sword to any master for the right price.

But even as his anger burned hot and acrid, Ilbert couldn't entirely dismiss the monk's words. He had broken faith in the most fundamental way. Was his current course truly in service to Prince Louis, or a desperate attempt to outrun the consequences of his betrayal?

Across the harbour, the last of the horses had been wrangled aboard. The ships strained at their moorings, sails unfurled. So much power, so much deadly intent, poised like an arrow on the string. All of it bound for England's shores, to set a torch to the kingdom.

Let it burn. Let the fires of rebellion scour away the rot, forge a new order from the ashes.

Ilbert tilted his face to the salt spray whistling in off the quay. Somewhere, lost beneath the frenetic noise of the docks, the cries of circling gulls sounded a plaintive note.

A death dirge, perhaps. For all of them.

42

The dock at Sandwich was packed with men but Estienne could still hear the creak of ships' timbers, the flap of banners whipped taut by the stiff breeze. He stood amid the hushed throng, surveying the mighty fleet assembled before him. Eighteen large galleys and twenty smaller craft bobbed at anchor, straining against their mooring lines like eager hounds. Their decks swarmed with sailors hauling on rigging, men-at-arms checking their weapons, archers flexing bows. The air hummed with barely leashed tension, the knowledge that soon, they would sail to meet the enemy. To decide the fate of England upon the sea that surrounded her.

Estienne's gaze fell on the great lords who would lead this armada into battle. There was Philip d'Albini, his gambeson rich with thread-of-gold embroidery, four fusils proudly emblazoned on the breast. Beside him, Richard of Chilham stood grim-faced, wind tossing his sable locks. And at the head of the noble gathering, Hubert of Burgh himself, the grizzled justiciar looking as though he were hewn of granite.

A flash of crimson caught Estienne's eye, and he turned to see a small figure standing apart from the warlike throng. Young King Henry, barely ten summers old, surrounded by a ring of men-at-arms. Above the boy, the royal standard snapped in the breeze, the three lions passant guardant snarling protectively.

Estienne drew in a deep breath, tasting brine on the back of his tongue. Somewhere nearby, the solemn intonations of bishops rose above the clamour, the lilt of Latin carrying on the wind. They moved like crows among the gathered warriors, touching brows, anointing blades, murmuring blessings. Last rites for those about to hazard their souls to defend their king and country.

'I absolve those who are about to die for the liberation of England,' one intoned as he passed, his withered hand sketching the sign of the cross.

Estienne suppressed a shiver, fingers tightening on the hilt of his sword. The phantom taste of blood rose at the back of his throat, memories of battles already fought, and he swallowed them down like bile. It would not do to linger. All he could do was look ahead, and face what was coming with as much grit as he had in the past.

The babble of voices fell to a reverent hush as William Marshal spurred his destrier through the ranks. The warhorse's hooves clopped against the salt-stained wood of the quay, each step a bold challenge. At the head of the assembled host, Earl William drew rein, his mail glinting beneath his surcoat.

'Men of England,' he growled, voice carrying on the wind. 'Hear me now, before you embark on this final venture. God granted you the first victory over the French on land. Through faith and courage, we drove them from Lincoln, showed them the folly of setting their sights on England's great cities.'

A rumble of fierce approval ran through the gathered warriors, and Estienne felt the words shiver down his spine, the hairs at his nape prickling in response, as William raised a hand for silence.

'Yet still they come. The Lion of France is not so easily cowed. He believes God's favour has deserted us. That the land we bled for is his to claim. I say to you, our task is not done. Our work is yet unfinished. We cannot rest until the last French cur is scoured from England's shores.'

'God's will!' someone shouted from the ranks. 'God's will!'

The cry was taken up by a thousand others, rising to a thunderous crescendo. Estienne found his own voice joining them, the words torn from his throat.

'You have the might of heaven at your backs,' Marshal roared above the din. 'Today, we sail to meet the enemy in England's name. Your true king commands you. Obey him, and let the Almighty's grace steer your swords. Great reward awaits the faithful, untold glories in this life and the next. To your ships, men of England. Claim the victory that is your birthright. Send the French to the bottom of the sea, for God, for England!'

Marshal raised his sword high, the blade a bolt of lightning against the iron sky. The roar that answered him rose to a fever pitch, the stamp of feet and clash of steel drowning the seabirds' shrieking cries.

The host surged forward as one, striding to their vessels on feet winged by faith and fervour. Estienne was swept along in their midst, a fierce smile on his face as he made to follow the tide of men pouring onto the ships, but a voice broke through the noise, stopping him in his tracks.

'Estienne!'

He turned to see his lord still ahorse, watching him. Estienne picked his way to the Marshal's side.

'My lord?' The words came out louder than he'd intended, his throat choked by a sudden dread. Was Marshal about to forbid him from sailing? Deny him this chance for glory after all he'd done?

William looked down, eyes searching Estienne's face. 'You've served me true, lad. As loyally and bravely as any squire could. You've spilled your blood for me, risked your life for England time and again. By God, you've earned this a dozen times over.'

He swung down from the saddle, struggling more than he ever had in previous months and years. When he faced Estienne, there was something perilously close to pride in the set of that stern face.

'Kneel.'

Estienne obeyed, the worn wood of the quay hard against his knee. He bowed his head as Marshal's shadow fell over him. Then his master's blade touched Estienne's shoulder.

'I name thee Ser Estienne Wace. For valour, for fealty, for service to crown and kingdom. Bear this burden well. Rise as a knight and be counted among our brotherhood.'

Estienne stood and the world seemed suddenly unsteady.

'My lord...' His voice was scarcely more than a whisper. He couldn't find the words to express his gratitude or the fierce, singing pride that swelled his breast near to bursting.

Marshal took something from the saddle of his destrier, and Estienne recognised it immediately. The last time he had seen it, the weapon had been hanging from the belt of his mentor. Earl William pressed it into Estienne's palm.

'A hammer for the new-forged knight,' he said simply. 'Straight from Goffrey's hand. Let it serve you as well, as I know your sword arm will serve England.'

Estienne hefted the hammer, testing its weight, feeling as though a fragment of the old Templar's strength was now passed into his keeping.

'I'll wield it in your name, my lord. In England's name. The French will rue the day they thought to challenge us.'

'Aye, that they will. Their reckoning is at hand.' William jerked his chin toward the waiting ships. 'Go now. Whatever glory there is to be had this day, you've damn well earned your share. God be with you.'

Estienne offered a final bow, and without another word he was turning to stride toward the ships. Jogging up the gangplank onto Hubert of Burgh's vessel, he saw the crew swarming across the deck, coiling ropes, trimming sailcloth, each man absorbed in his own small but vital task.

'Ser Estienne.' Hubert stood at the prow, a grin on his bullish face.

'Lord Hubert.' Estienne moved alongside him. 'I almost feared I'd missed the tide.'

'Aye, it would have been a shame if you'd missed this.' He eyed Estienne shrewdly. 'Knighted at last, eh? And not a moment too soon.'

'Earl William said it was long overdue.'

'And he's not wrong. Let's just hope you live long enough to accept your spurs.'

Estienne grinned. 'I'll do my best not to disappoint, my lord.'

'See that you don't.' Hubert grinned back, but there was a new respect behind it now, as though they were closer to equals. His gaze cut away abruptly, voice rising above the waves slapping the hull. 'All right, you dogs, haul in those hawsers. Let's get this galley moving.'

Estienne glanced up to see the great sail unfurling, dropping open with a thunderous snap of wind-starched canvas. The ship shuddered, an eager hound straining against the leash, then began to surge forward, gathering speed.

All around them, the fleet was underway, banners straining above wind-filled sails. The cries of gulls and shouts of men faded to a distant drone as the ship broke from the shallows, cleaving out into open water. To the east, he could just make out the tiny sails of the French fleet crawling up from the horizon, and his heart hammered in time to the slap of the sail.

In that instant, none of his old victories seemed to matter. Only now would he find out what kind of knight he was. Only now would he learn if he was worthy of the rank he fought so long and hard to win.

43

The wind howled in Estienne's face. He blinked away tears, gaze fixed on the vast French fleet as it ploughed through the cobalt waves, sails billowing, straining against the lines like the wings of great seabirds, eager for conquest. Their course was set northward, toward the Isle of Thanet, gateway to the Thames and the rich prize that lay beyond – London. The beating heart of England herself.

His heart slammed against his ribs at the thought. After all the battles and blood, the kingdom's fate would be decided here, upon the heaving sea. Let the French fleet round the Isle of Thanet to reach the mouth of the river and it would be as good as offering the crown to Prince Louis himself. He would be resupplied, reinforced, and offered a chance to continue this costly war. It could not be permitted.

A shout went up and Estienne turned to see Hubert's galley was pulling away from the English ships, oars digging deep to drive them in a wide arc. They passed along the rear of the French fleet, close enough that Estienne could make out the jeering faces of the sailors lining the decks. Taunts in mangled dialects drifted across the water, mocking laughter underscored by the fluttering of flags.

'My lord,' a sailor called to Hubert, voice high-pitched with urgency. 'We've overshot. The French will reach Thanet before us.'

Hubert stood at the prow, an immovable hulk of a man. 'Calm yourself. They're exactly where I want them. Make ready to come about!' he bellowed, cutting off any further protest. 'Sharp to larboard, lads. Time to steal the wind from their sails.'

Estienne held his breath, pulse quickening as the ship tilted beneath him, cutting a clean turn. The deck pitched as they came about, the rest of the English fleet following suit behind them. Wind snapped in the sails, the rigging creaking as they strained for speed, and realisation dawned...

The wind was at their backs now. The sun too, a bright ally against the French sailors' eyes.

'Row, you dogs,' Hubert roared above the clamour of wind and wave. 'Put your backs into it.'

The drum beat out a steady tempo, the pulse of urgency surging through the oarsmen as they heaved against the water. Yard by steady yard, they began to gain on the French fleet, the enemy ships wallowing low and heavy with their cargo of horses, men and malice.

Estienne scanned the English ships, mapping their attack. To the left, the rest of their fleet fanned out, longbows bristling from every deck. After giving the order for them to turn, Hubert's own ship now brought up the rear as the others drew ahead, angled for the French starboard flank.

'Hendry!' Hubert's bellow brought Estienne's attention snapping back to the deck. The knight was staring up at a man balanced precariously atop the mainmast, yellow square of fabric clenched in one fist. 'The signal. Now.'

The man braced himself as the ship bucked beneath him.

Then, with a snap of his arm, the flag unfurled, whipping out like a tongue of yellow flame against the grey sky.

A heartbeat of stillness before the hammer stroke. Then the English line erupted as archers loosed, a deadly hail arcing up and out, sickly pale against the clouds. Estienne squinted, watching sacks and clay pots hurtle down upon the French ships.

The first volley struck the waves, the ocean itself seeming to smoke and seethe in response. Great geysers of bubbling water frothed up along the hulls, casting veils of mist to cloak the enemy fleet. Then came the screaming, faint at first, snatched away by the wind, but rising to a hellish chorus as the quicklime billowed and found its marks. Men blundered along the decks, pawing at streaming eyes and scalded skin, choking on the sting of a thousand needles in their throats. Some fell writhing, hands clasped in piteous prayer, while others clawed their way up the rigging in a blind, animal panic.

On swept the English ships, driving into the carnage. Grappling hooks snagged on rails, iron biting deep, and lime pots smashed across French decks in glittering sprays. More screams now, agonised and desperate, the sound of men tormented by a horror they couldn't fight.

Estienne tasted bile, sharp and sour on his tongue as those haunting wails drifted across the water. But he set his jaw and looked at Hubert, face hard as stone. No mercy here. No quarter asked or given. Today, the sea would run red.

To the south, a lone English galley surged from the billowing smoke like a wolf among sheep. At its masthead flew the banners of Earl Warenne and Richard of Chilham, the azure chequy and the twin lions passant bold against the soot-stained sky. Estienne watched, heart in his throat, as the galley smashed into the flank of the French flagship with a crunch of timber. Grapnels snaked out, biting deep, and battle was joined.

Another ship knifed through the chaos, the red lion standard of Marshal stark atop its mast. Its archers were already at work, longbows thrumming as they rained death upon the smaller French craft floundering ahead of the flagship.

And then, driving hard through the cloud, came a third vessel flying the colours of Philip d'Albini, its captain bellowing orders. Hooks spun out to bite into the railing of a French cog, and the two ships crashed together with a shuddering impact that Estienne could feel in his bones.

All around, the heraldry flew above a roiling sea of smoke, a dozen noble sigils thrust proudly aloft by men who would live or die beneath their colours. There was no turning back now, no hesitation or quarter. The wolves of England had the French lions by the throat, and they would not let go.

At last Hubert's ship cruised close enough to grapple, and Estienne found himself wedged shoulder to shoulder with knights and men-at-arms, stripped of heavy mail, all gripping ropes in white-knuckled fists.

Estienne hefted his hook, the rough hemp biting into his palm. Sweat and salt spray mingled on his skin, his heart a wild drum in his chest as he waited for the French ship to loom from the acrid gloom. There, rising from the smoke like a wraith. Now... it had to be now...

He hurled his hook in the same instant the others did, a deadly hail of barbed iron arcing through the murk. From the French deck, archers loosed their shafts in a thrumming volley, and the man to Estienne's left took an arrow full in the face. He collapsed with a wet thud before he could cry out.

No time to think. Estienne had his steel in hand, the leather of the grip steadying him as the ships collided with a teeth-rattling crunch. He leapt, hitting the French deck with a roll and coming up swinging.

His first stroke slashed an archer across the neck, spraying crimson to the wooden boards. All around, English fighters thudded down, steel hissing from scabbards. A burly man-at-arms bulled into a knot of Frenchmen, mace rising and falling with the workmanlike brutality of a butcher at his block.

'For England!' The shout tore from Estienne's throat. 'For King Henry!'

Then there was no more time for words. Only the savagery of blades meeting flesh and the crunch of breaking bones. Every heartbeat was matched by a hack or a slash, all the long years of training, all those memories flaring to life in his muscles, instinct and reflex taking over as men died around him.

Blood slicked the boards, turning the footing treacherous. Still Estienne fought on, teeth bared in a snarl, locking blades with a Frenchman who spat curses from a lime-scarred face. Steel scraped, and Estienne drove his knee up into the man's groin. He folded, and Estienne hacked into his neck.

Blood spattered his cheek, but he was already turning, already seeking his next foe. They swarmed from every quarter, driven by hate and desperation, but Estienne gave himself to the deadly dance, the world narrowing to the reach of his blade and the hammering of his heart.

The fighting had descended into a madness of struggling bodies and flailing steel. There was no art to it now, no technique or finesse, only barbarity as men grappled and gouged, seeking any advantage in the press of slick, blood-drenched flesh. Estienne plunged on, staggering over the dead and dying. Each struggling breath seared his lungs, quicklime scouring his throat as he peered through the drifting banks of stinging fog.

A figure loomed from the mist, tall and broad-shouldered. Estienne raised his sword, a snarl rising to his lips... until his blood ran like ice in his veins. The face that stared back at him was one he had prayed to never see again, contorted now in shock and fury.

Ilbert FitzDane.

For an instant, Estienne was a boy again, quailing under those barbed taunts, cheeks burning with shame as he was beaten into the dirt to the sound of mocking laughter. But he was a scared boy no longer... and there was nothing he feared.

Ilbert's lips curled back from his teeth as he raised his own blade.

'Wace,' he hissed, the name a curse. 'God truly stands with me this day to deliver you so readily.'

Estienne said nothing, meeting Ilbert's first stroke with a clang of steel, the impact shivering up his arm. His old tormentor was advanced in both years and experience, but Estienne had the benefit of rage and retribution on his side. He would not bend.

Back and forth they crashed, blades ringing a deadly duet. Where once Estienne had been hopelessly outmatched, now he met his foe blow for blow, fending off the rage-fuelled assault with a tight economy of motion he had learned from the Marshal.

Steel flashed as Ilbert charged in with a roar, hammering at Estienne's guard, each impact jarring shoulder and wrist. Estienne gritted his teeth against the onslaught, his own blade lashing out with cold precision. A heartbeat's lapse, a fleeting opening as Ilbert drew back for a killing stroke. Estienne lunged to take advantage, but Ilbert was quick to close the gap with a ring of steel. They strained against the bind, faces inches apart, snarling at one another like beasts.

Quick as a viper, Ilbert twisted his blade, sliding free of the lock and whipping his steel up across Estienne's face. Blinding pain, as wet heat lashed his jaw. Estienne reeled back with a growl, hand shielding the wound that split him from chin to cheek.

He blinked blood from his eye, tasting copper on his tongue. Ilbert gazed back with a triumphal grin.

'Still the black sheep, eh Wace? No matter what you do, what glory you find, you'll never be more than the Marshal's pet mongrel. A fucking outcast.'

Something snapped in Estienne. With a wordless howl, he flew at Ilbert, blade whipping in a deadly blur. Steel hammered steel, the crash and clang deafening as Estienne battered Ilbert back across the ship. No technique to it now, no precision or grace, only a vicious onslaught fuelled by hate and old wounds.

Ilbert met him blow for blow, teeth bared in a snarl as they strained against each other. Estienne lashed out in a great cleaving arc and Ilbert twisted aside. The sword bit deep into the ship's gunwale and wedged fast. Estienne strained to pull it free, but Ilbert was already charging, blade hissing down in a beheading stroke.

Reflex took over. At the last instant, Estienne threw himself sideways, tumbling across the deck in a desperate roll. Ilbert's sword slashed where Estienne's neck had been a heartbeat before, as he found his feet once more.

No thought. Only the red rage, the relentless urge to kill. Surging forward, his hand dropped to his belt grasping the heavy weight that hung there.

Goffrey's hammer.

Tight in Estienne's fist, it felt like the old Templar's strength flowed into him like fire in the blood. He lunged, bringing the hammer down in a scything blow. Ilbert's eyes widened, mouth gaping to shout.

Too late.

With a sickening crunch, the hammer's head caved in Ilbert's skull, shattering bone and pulping the brain beneath. He staggered drunkenly, jaws working as if trying to form words that wouldn't come. Blood sheeted from the ruin of his skull as he tilted over the ship's rail and fell into the roiling sea with barely a splash.

Estienne stared at the churning waters as Ilbert's body sank into the depths. The man who had tormented him, made his life a misery for so long... gone.

Slowly, as if surfacing from the depths of a dream, Estienne became aware of the world once more. The roaring rush of blood in his ears subsided, and he realised with a start that the clash of steel and the screams of dying men had faded.

He looked from horizon to horizon. The battle was over. All around, English sailors and men-at-arms stood tall among the French dead, their faces wreathed in fierce, exultant grins as they brandished gore-drenched weapons at the scattering of survivors. And there, striding the deck like a bloodied colossus, was Hubert, his surcoat rent and stained.

'Secure the prisoners. I want every knight and noble-born French dog in chains.'

A shout rose above the clamour, high and jubilant. 'They've got him, lord. The Black Monk is taken.'

Hubert's head whipped around. 'Where?'

'The flagship. They have him at sword-point.'

Estienne followed as Hubert strode to the rail, barking for planks to be run out. They clanked down on the flagship's bloodied deck, the vast cog wallowing low in the water, holed and listing after being rammed.

Hubert strode the span, Estienne close behind, and there, driven to his knees, was Eustace the Monk. The pirate who had harried England's coasts and sworn his black heart to the French cause, now brought low amid a ring of English blades.

'Mercy,' the monk babbled, spittle slicking his chin. 'Mercy, I beg you. Ransom me, my lord Hubert. I'm good for ten thousand marks at least. It's yours. Every coin.'

Hubert loomed over the cowering figure. 'You've slain Englishmen without number. Sunk our ships, burned our ports. Did you show mercy then? Even once?'

Eustace's mouth worked soundlessly, like a fish gulping for air, and he clawed at the hem of Hubert's bloodied surcoat. 'Please, I'll pay anything. Swear any oath—'

'Enough.' Hubert turned from the gibbering monk, nodding to a burly knight with an axe on his shoulder. 'Crabbe. Do it.'

The big man grunted assent, as two men grasped Eustace and bent him over. Crabbe paused to run a thumb along the axe's edge, looking down the haft to make sure it was straight. Then, as casually as a cook beheading a chicken for the pot, he brought the blade whistling down.

Eustace's head smacked to the deck like a round of wet clay. The body toppled forward, arterial gouts painting the boards crimson. Up and down the decks, a great roar rose from the watching English. Cheering, feral and triumphant, underscored by the clash of sword pommels against shields.

Slowly, Estienne felt the last of his bloodlust ebb from trembling muscles. He suddenly felt light, as though he might drift away on the salt breeze. After so long, so many trials endured, could it really be over?

A heavy hand clapped his shoulder, and he turned to see Hubert at his side, face split into a rare grin. 'It's done, Ser Estienne. The final victory is ours.'

Ser Estienne. God, how strange it still felt to be addressed so. He who had started as little more than an orphan boy, taken in on the Marshal's charity. It was almost more than he could grasp.

'I... I can scarcely believe it,' he managed. 'Peace, after so long at war.'

'Aye, peace,' Hubert replied. 'With his supplies and reinforcements gone, Louis will likely slink back to France, and good bloody riddance to the whoreson. Now all we have to do is keep our king alive long enough to reach manhood.'

Estienne nodded slowly. King Henry had triumphed this day, but the hard work of knitting his fractured kingdom back together had only begun. Yet as he watched the captured French being loaded into the holds, he felt the first lightening of the weight that had pressed upon him for so long. Now he was a knight, ordained by his master and by God. He could perform his duty with honour, as he had always strived to do.

Estienne met Hubert's steely eye as an equal. 'I stand ready to serve.'

44

He shifted from foot to foot on the muddy bank as he peered across the wide sweep of the Thames. His jaw worked, and he felt the pull of stitches that sealed the wound on his cheek. Mist hung low over the water, teasing glimpses of the small island where Earl William and Hubert of Burgh had met with Prince Louis to discuss terms. To buy peace for their fledgling king.

A stir of wind and Estienne glimpsed a flash of crimson and gold through the fog – the royal standard snapping above a small boat that cleaved a path to the shore. He straightened, one hand tightening on the hilt of his sword. Bargain though they might, he knew well the French were not to be trusted.

The boat's prow slid up to the muddy bank, and William Marshal stepped out, Hubert just behind. Neither one looked to Estienne like men satisfied with their morning's work – William's mouth set, a grimness to the cast of his features. Hubert nodded to Estienne as he passed, swinging astride his destrier without a word.

'Is all well, my lord?' Estienne ventured as William reached him. He feared he knew the answer already.

'We've a treaty, for what it's worth. Bought and paid for. The French will have their pound of silver.'

And the English would be bled dry for it, Estienne thought, but he held his tongue, falling into step beside the earl as they made for their own mounts. There would be precious little celebration in the halls of Windsor Castle tonight, that much was plain.

They rode north in silence but for the jangle of harness and the occasional huff of a steed. With men-at-arms at their back, at least Estienne felt safe as they travelled, something he had not done for the longest time since the rebellion began.

Eventually they cantered beneath the castle's barbican, standards hanging limp in greeting. When they entered the bailey, Estienne blinked in surprise at the sight that awaited – a small party of men clustered about their horses, mud-spattered from hard travel. And at their head, a figure both familiar and unexpected.

Richard Marshal looked to Earl William, a smile breaking across his wind-chapped face. 'Father. It's good to see you well.'

A trace of a smile on Earl William's face, before he hooked a leg over his saddle. Estienne would have helped him dismount, but one of the castle grooms was already at his side to do the deed.

'Son. It is good to see you too.'

'I landed yesterday. When I learned you were here, negotiating with the French bastards, I had to come with all haste.'

The men embraced as Estienne climbed down from his destrier. He watched from a respectful distance as the pair were reunited. They spoke brief words before William excused himself to enter the keep, and Richard turned.

'Estienne.' Richard crossed the yard to clasp Estienne's arm in a warrior's greeting. 'Look at you, a man grown. And knighted, if what I hear is true.'

'By your father's hand. The greatest honour I could have asked for, and more than I deserved.'

Richard cuffed him fondly about the shoulder. 'Ever modest, my friend. You've earned those spurs a dozen times over. And a trophy from your latest conquest.' He gestured to the stitched wound on Estienne's cheek. 'Any knight should be proud to call you brother.'

The words kindled a warmth in Estienne's chest. 'You honour me.'

'The honour is mine. But tell me, now that you've your knighthood, what will you do? What grand adventures are you planning? To win tourneys by the dozen? Earn land and title on the field?'

It was a question Estienne had scarce considered. 'I suppose... that depends on your lord father. Where he sees fit to send me, I will go. As I always have.'

'You've more than earned the right to your own path, Estienne. Perhaps it's time you thought about what that might look like. A chance to see more of the world beyond William Marshal's reach.'

Estienne blinked, taken aback by the boldness of the suggestion. 'I don't... I mean, I never thought...'

Richard smiled, clapping him once more on the arm. 'Peace, my friend. We'll speak more on it later. For tonight, we'll feast and drink and make merry. God knows you've earned a bit of celebration after the time you've had.'

'Aye,' Estienne agreed, mustering a smile of his own. 'I look forward to it.'

And he did, with an eagerness that caught him quite off guard. Some small part of him wondered if it might be the first winds of change beginning to stir, the promise of a wider world unfurling just ahead of him...

* * *

'You can't be serious.' William set down his cup with a clunk, brows lowered into a thunderous line. 'We've only just pried French claws from England's throat, and you want to go traipsing off into Louis' backyard?'

Richard leaned forward. 'Louis' backyard, perhaps, but Mother's rightful legacy. Those lands are held in the Marshal name. They must be watched over. Protected.'

'And this is a matter that requires you specifically?' William shook his head, mouth pressed into a grim line. 'After everything, the perils we've lived through, you'd risk yourself so readily?'

'Risk myself?' Richard laughed, picking up his cup. 'Father, it's a visit to our family estates in Normandy, not an invasion. The war is over; the danger has passed us by. And even if it hasn't, Estienne would be there to guard my back. My shield and my strong right hand, as he's been before.'

William blew out a gusty sigh. 'You're set on this course? Both of you?'

Richard nodded. 'Our holdings need to be overseen by one of the family, and I will do it. With a sworn brother at my shoulder. Think of it as a well-earned respite. God knows Estienne's had little enough of that after all these years in your service.'

William looked at Estienne. 'And you, lad? You're of like mind in this?'

'I... If it is your will, my lord, I would gladly accompany Richard. But I would not defy your wishes in this. My place is at your side, as it has ever been.'

For a long, taut moment, William simply stared at him, stern features inscrutable. Then, slowly, he reached for his cup and drained the last of his wine in a single, long gulp.

'France. To keep my bull-headed son from courting trouble.' The barest hint of a smile crossed his face. 'Aye, lad. You've more than earned a bit of peace. If you've the will for it, then you've my blessing.'

Estienne felt a wild exultation surging in his gut. 'My lord, I... I would be honoured.'

'Then that's settled,' Richard declared, lifting his empty cup in salute. 'To Ser Estienne. And to the poor French bastards who'll have to put up with us.'

* * *

Dawn broke sullen and grey, the sky heavy with unshed rain. Estienne heard the distant clatter of tack and hoof, the low murmur of voices beneath his window. For a moment he simply lay there, staring at the familiar ceiling, head pounding in time to his pulse. A reminder of the night before, the laughter and slurred stories and endless toasts to victory and their king and peace and ventures new...

That thought propelled him upright, ignoring the thud of protest in his abused skull. France. He was bound for France today, riding at Richard's side.

The bailey was abustle by the time Estienne made his way down, wincing at the too-bright glare off puddled rain. Everywhere he turned, men and horses jostled, readying themselves for the off. Destriers stamped and snorted, eager for the road, as grooms buckled saddlebags and made one last check of arms and armour.

In the centre of it all was Richard. Bright-eyed and windblown, cloak snapping about his shoulders as he swung astride his mount. He caught sight of Estienne and grinned.

'Awake at last. I was beginning to think I'd have to rouse you with a song.'

'Thankfully, I saved you the bother.'

Richard looked affronted. 'There's still time yet.'

'As long as you're not planning to regale us all the way to the coast?' Estienne shot back as he hurried toward his own mount. 'I think I'd sooner be deaf.'

Richard's laughter echoed through the courtyard as Estienne vaulted into the saddle. Heavy footsteps approached, and Estienne turned to see William appear in the morning mist. As ever, his face gave little away, all stern lines and furrowed brow.

'My lord.' Estienne bowed his head, fist to his heart. 'I thank you for this... gift. For... for everything.'

'Enough.' William's gruff voice cut through his stammering. 'You've served me well, Estienne. There's naught more needs saying on that. Just watch over Richard. He's a headstrong fool at the best of times, and not half so invincible as he thinks he is.'

'I will,' Estienne promised. 'On my life, I'll see no harm comes to him.'

William nodded, once. Then he stepped to his son, sharing words that Estienne couldn't hear. As he watched them, Estienne felt his throat grow tight. All those years striving for William's regard, his approval... and now with it so nearly in his grasp, he was riding away.

A shout from the head of the column, and the jingle of harness. Richard offered Earl William one final nod and set off at a brisk trot. Estienne gathered his reins, heels finding his steed's flanks as he moved to catch up. Then they were passing beneath the barbican, hooves clattering on ancient stone as the road unfurled before them.

A new dawn. A new path.

And for the first time in his life, Estienne felt ready to see where it might lead.

PART SIX: A GOOD END

FRANCE, 1219 AD

45

They thundered through the forest, sending birds scattering from the canopy in startled flight. Estienne leaned low over his rounsey's neck, wind whipping at his face, tugging his cloak out behind him like a sail.

Ahead, Richard's white courser flashed between the trees, mane and tail streaming. Estienne grinned fiercely, urging his own mount on, determined not to be outdistanced while the hounds bayed their eager chorus, stirred by the scent of their prey.

God, but he loved this. The freedom of it, the simple thrill of the chase. After all the strife and blood, the endless horrors of battle, he had almost forgotten what peace felt like. What joy felt like.

A year now, he'd dwelt in Richard's company, hunting and feasting across the sprawl of Normandy. Tourneys and drinking, dicing and wenching – though Estienne was more sparing in his indulgence of such pastimes than his rowdy companion, Richard being the soul of excess. But beneath his friend's swaggering bravado beat a heart both kind and true. He had welcomed Estienne as more than mere liegeman or sword-brother, but kin. The bond between them, forged in the peril of Bouvines, had only deepened in this year of ease.

Estienne had known precious little of brotherhood in his life, but he thought perhaps this was what it meant to have a true brother. To share burdens and bloodshed, victories and losses. To draw strength from one another, steadfast against all foes.

He met Richard's bright gaze as their horses pounded neck and neck. His grin was answered with a wild whoop of laughter that rang out above the hungry chorus of the alaunts. Ahead, the forest thinned, and Estienne glimpsed a dark shape hurtling through the trees. Their quarry, flushed at last from the undergrowth.

Richard bellowed a huntsman's cry, the hounds taking up the call as they bounded in the prey's wake. Estienne slapped his reins against his rounsey's neck, anticipation thrilling through him. The boar darted across their path, a bristling mass of matted hair and yellowed tusks. It squealed as it shot into the open, hooves churning the soft earth as it fought to outpace the hounds.

'There!' Richard's shout carried clear on the wind as he hefted his spear high.

Estienne gripped his own spear tighter as he spurred his horse on, and the hounds harried the boar from all sides, darting in to snap at haunch and hamstring before dancing away from those wicked tusks.

Then the beast faltered, maddened by fear, exhausted from the chase.

Now. It had to be now.

Estienne angled his spear, sighting down the ash haft. To the left, Richard did the same. They moved in concert, horses surging as one, Estienne to one side, Richard the other, the boar caught between them.

It screeched, high and shrill, as Richard's spear punched through matted hide and into the meat of the shoulder. A heartbeat later, Estienne's lance found the beast's barrel chest, the steel head piercing its grey hide. The boar sprawled, legs thrashing. It screamed again, blood frothing from its jaws, the sound turning to a gurgling sigh as it sagged to the trampled earth in a growing pool of crimson, and went still.

Estienne reined in and leapt from the saddle. He approached the downed beast warily and wrenched his spear free as the hounds crowded close, worrying at the dead beast. He heard Richard bellowing for the handlers to restrain the alaunts before they could rend the prized carcass. Already the dogs were snarling, snapping at each other in their eagerness.

Richard swung down from the saddle, striding to Estienne's side. 'Well thrown. Though I still say mine struck truer.'

'In your dreams, Marshal.' Estienne replied with a grin. 'Your arm's going soft, from too much wenching and not enough spear-work.'

Richard raised an eyebrow in mock offence. 'Though soft I may be, at least I know how to please. More than can be said for you, Wace, clinging to chastity as you do. You'll not earn your spurs there, I fear.'

Estienne shook his head. 'There's more to knighthood than tupping barmaids and deflowering shepherd's daughters.'

Richard laughed as he hooked an arm around Estienne's shoulders and dragged him towards the fallen boar. It was an impressive specimen, the coarse fur matted nearly black with blood, the span of its shoulders level with a man's waist. The handlers swarmed forth to leash the slavering hounds, keeping them at bay while the carcass was heaved onto a makeshift litter.

'We'll eat well tonight, my friend,' Richard said.

'We eat well every night,' Estienne replied, patting a belly that was frighteningly close to paunch.

'True enough. Best we be careful, lest you end up a fat, old man. No one will ever want to share your bed then.'

Richard laughed, returning to his courser. Estienne followed, climbing into his own saddle, and they reined in behind the huntsmen, the bloodied boar swaying on its rough-hewn litter. The hounds followed, still yipping their excitement, tongues lolling.

The sun was sinking low over the fields by the time they came out of the forest. The breeze was chill against Estienne's sweat-damp skin, but he welcomed it, letting it blow the cobwebs from his mind. But as much as he welcomed that trouble-free air, he could not rid himself of the notion he was wasting time here.

'Perhaps we ought to turn our efforts to other things,' he mused as they crested a gentle rise, the rooftops of Orbec coming into view in the distance. 'Surely there are graver matters demanding our attention than chasing pigs through the forest?'

Richard shot him a sidelong glance. 'I can think of no graver concern than keeping you fed.'

'I'm serious, Richard. Are there not weighty affairs to which we must attend? This idyll cannot last forever.'

'And why not? What more serious matter could there be than hunting game through the fair forests of Normandy? I'll hear no talk of duties on a day like this.'

Estienne bit back a sigh. 'There must be more to our lives than sport and revelry. Responsibilities to shoulder.'

'Oh, I'll wager you'd like that. Looking forward to bearing the burdens of rank are you, Ser Estienne? Ready to claim some lands of your own? Be chained to a fat, screeching wife and a squalling babe in each arm?'

The image provoked a laugh from Estienne. 'God forbid. I'd sooner a hairshirt and a hermit's cell.'

Richard clutched at his breast theatrically. 'Alas, he scorns the charms of wedded bliss. The tragedy of it. Why, think of all the willing maids who'll pine for your surly company.'

'Better surly than overused. I hope you're saving some coin for all the bastards you've likely sired since we arrived.'

Richard shrugged, unrepentant. 'Let God sort them out, I say. There's little enough pleasure to be had in this life as it is. I'll not stint myself while I'm able.'

Estienne saw the town walls rising against the darkening sky. How many conquests had Richard made within those confines? Sometimes Estienne envied him that abandon, but something in him, some core of hard-forged discipline, would not allow him to set aside the vows he had sworn, even for a night's fleeting gratification. And as the months had passed in a whirl of hunting and carousing, Estienne had felt a restlessness growing. A need for something more than meaningless amusements. He craved a higher purpose, a chance to prove himself worthy of the spurs he had fought so hard to win. To take up the burdens of a true knight, and forge a legacy worthy of the man who had raised him.

The gates of Orbec yawned open to greet them. Estienne's stomach grumbled as the smell of warm bread drifted from a nearby inn. The sights and sounds of this peaceful town reminded him how he ought to take advantage of home comforts while he had them. There was no telling when strife might rear its head, and he would have to don the trappings of war once again. He was about to suggest to Richard they stop at the inn and take some ale when the shouts of a rider broke the pastoral peace.

A bay charger cantered toward them. Its rider reined up so sharply his steed skidded to a dusty halt. Richard stiffened, good humour replaced by sharp focus.

'My lord Richard.' The man's face was bleak above his sweat-darkened tunic. 'I bear urgent tidings from England. Earl William has taken ill.'

Estienne held his breath at the news, as Richard remained stone-faced. 'Ill? With what malady?'

'I know not the particulars, my lord. I was sent to tell you only that the earl has requested your presence. That you must return with all haste.'

Richard was silent for a moment, then he turned to one of his huntsmen. When he spoke, his voice was leached of all levity. 'We ride for Caen at first light. See that the men are made ready.'

The huntsman bowed his head. 'As you command.'

Richard turned to Estienne with uncharacteristic gloom. 'My friend, will you ride with me? Back to England?'

Estienne met that hard stare. 'Of course. I would be nowhere else.'

Richard offered the ghost of a smile. 'And there is no man I would rather have with me.'

Then he turned, heels digging into his courser's flanks as he set off towards the castle. Estienne spurred after him, the boar forgotten in their wake.

46

Estienne rode through the gates of Caversham Manor, bright sky belying the grim purpose for which they had come. Beside him, Richard sat rigid in the saddle, jaw clenched tight, as if he could hold his grief at bay through sheer force of will.

The grounds were wrapped in a sepulchral hush. Even the birds were silent, as if they too sensed the pall of sorrow that hung over the estate like a fog. As they drew up their horses before the manor house, the great oaken door swung open. Guillaume stepped out, his face haggard. Behind him, Countess Isabel emerged, her head held high despite the redness rimming her eyes. Estienne slid from the saddle, bowing low as Richard dismounted beside him.

'Brother,' Guillaume said.

Richard clasped his arm, pulling him into a fierce embrace. They clung to each other for a long moment, as if each was the only thing holding the other upright. When they parted, Guillaume turned to Estienne.

'Wace.' He inclined his head, the gesture stiff but not discourteous. 'I am glad you have come.'

Estienne bowed. 'I am here to serve my lord, in whatever way I can.'

Guillaume nodded, then turned to usher Richard inside, one hand resting on his brother's shoulder. Countess Isabel lingered, her focus on Estienne. He saw the weight of her sorrow, the grief she couldn't quite mask.

He bowed to her, fist clenched to his heart. 'My lady, if there is anything I can do...'

'Thank you, Estienne,' she replied, her voice steady despite the telltale waver beneath the words. Then she swept after her sons, the door thudding closed at her back.

Alone in the yard, Estienne stood for a long moment, the breeze whisking the leaves around his feet. He looked up at the manor house, oppressive in its stillness, and felt his unease coil tighter. Some premonition of doom brushing cold fingers across his nape. He shook it off, chiding himself for a superstitious fool. Drawing a steadying breath, he turned to lead the horses to the stable...

'Hello, Estienne.'

He turned at that voice, soft as a sigh. Eva stood behind him, wrapped in a dark cloak. Even in her sadness she looked...

'Eva,' he replied. 'I didn't see you.'

A ghost of a smile touched her lips, there and gone. 'You never were the most observant.'

He took in her face, one that had sharpened in his absence, girlish softness giving way to womanly grace.

'You look different,' he said, the words awkward, inadequate.

Her mouth turned up in a pale imitation of her old impish grin. 'Do I?'

'Yes. You've... grown.'

'That tends to happen.' She tilted her head, assessing him. 'You've changed too. And I don't just mean this.'

Her slender fingers reached out, tracing the thin scar that ran down to his jaw, the healed wound Ilbert had given him a year before. Estienne fought not to flinch at her touch, so gentle it was almost painful.

'Less lost and lonely, am I? Less like the little boy you knew?'

Her hand fell away. 'I wouldn't say that.'

There was understanding in her voice, as though she saw through everything, saw the boy still lurking beneath a man's visage. Before he could reply, the clatter of the door opening shattered the fragile moment. Estienne turned to see Richard walk slowly down the steps, ashen-faced.

Estienne reached out to steady his friend. Richard lifted his head, and his naked anguish hit like a fist to the gut.

'Estienne,' he whispered. 'Father... he's asked for you.'

It suddenly felt as though there were a band of iron encasing Estienne's ribs. He shot a glance at Eva, suddenly afraid to leave her, to face what waited beyond that door. She looked back with only gentle understanding.

As though marching to his end, Estienne entered the manor. At the bottom of the stairs stood Guillaume, who offered a reassuring nod as Estienne made his way past. On the landing, Countess Isabel, who nodded toward the open door at the end of the passage.

Estienne's heart thudded as he slipped into the dimness of the Marshal's bedchamber, the air thick with the smell of medicinal herbs and the sickly-sour tang of impending death. In the great curtained bed, William lay shrunken and wasted, propped up on pillows that threatened to swallow his once-mighty frame.

'My lord,' Estienne breathed.

Glassy eyes fluttered open, fever-bright in the gloom. 'Estienne?' The voice was a thin rasp, a bare shadow of the ironclad bass that had once commanded armies.

'I'm here.' Estienne crossed to the bed, sinking to his knees beside it. Up close, William looked even frailer, skin stretched parchment-thin over the bones of his face.

'You came,' William murmured. A trembling hand groped across the coverlet, and Estienne caught it. 'Good lad.'

Tears welled, but somehow Estienne held them at bay. 'Of course, my lord. Where else would I be?'

The spectre of a smile touched the corners of William's mouth. 'Proud of you, Estienne. Proud of the knight you've become. The man.'

Estienne bowed his head, pressing his brow to their clasped hands, shoulders shaking with the effort to hold back the sobs that wanted to tear free.

'Everything I am... you made me.'

'No,' William whispered. 'You made yourself. I just helped you see... see what was always there. You're a Marshal in all but blood, lad. Don't ever doubt it.'

A small, broken sound escaped Estienne, halfway between laugh and sob. 'I never dared hope...'

'Hush now.' William's fingers tightened around his with a shadow of their former strength. 'I go to God knowing... knowing I leave a proud legacy behind in my sons. In you.'

He sagged back into the pillows, eyes drifting closed. Estienne held his breath, fearing the worst, but the laboured rise and fall of William's chest told him the end had not yet come. Leaning forward, he brushed a gentle hand over the fever-damp brow, the skin beneath his fingers delicate as a bird's wing.

'Rest now, my lord,' he murmured. 'You have earned it.'

William made a small, wordless sound, and for a long moment Estienne knelt there, willing his own strength into that battered frame. Then, with a shaky breath, he pressed a kiss to the knuckles of the hand that had taught him everything and rose to his feet.

He slipped from the chamber silent as a ghost, not looking back for fear that he would break completely. In the passageway outside, he leaned against the wall, fists clenched at his sides. The grief rose up like a black tide, threatening to drag him under, but he pushed it back with ruthless determination.

Now was not the time for selfish sorrow. This hurt belonged to the Marshals, to the trueborn sons, the faithful wife, the daughters. He was an interloper here, a cuckoo in the nest. No matter what William had said in his final moments, Estienne knew his place.

He made his way from the manor like a man in a dream, nodding his respects to the countess once more, passing Guillaume and Richard and Eva as they made their way to their father's chamber. Finally outside, Estienne stood alone in the yard, letting the sun warm the cold in his heart.

Bowing his head, he let the tears come at last.

47

The clop of hooves echoed dully against the packed earth as Estienne rode behind the funeral procession. Ahead, the lead-lined coffin rested atop an ornate hearse, draped in cloth emblazoned with the red lion rampant of Marshal. It seemed the only point of colour amidst a sea of mourners garbed in dark hues.

Westminster Abbey receded behind them as they made their solemn way through London's narrow streets toward the Temple Church. To either side, the city's smallfolk lined the route in respectful silence. Estienne saw old men doff their caps, women bow their heads, even children standing wide-eyed and solemn. Marshal had been a monumental figure, a legend made flesh. Now he was gone, confined within a casket, and the reality of it almost stole the breath from Estienne's chest.

Behind the funeral carriage, the Marshal family rode in tight formation. The sons – Guillaume, Richard, Gilbert, Walter and young Ansel – sat tall in their saddles. The daughters followed, Matilda, Sybil, Isabeau, Joan and Eva, their faces obscured by dark veils. And in their midst, Countess Isabel. Estienne could barely stand to look at her. The once indomitable woman seemed to have aged a decade in recent days. When they had carried Marshal's coffin into Westminster for the lying in state, she had nearly collapsed, so profound was her sorrow. Now she clung to the pommel of her jennet's saddle as if it alone kept her upright, her proud head bowed, shoulders shaking with silent sobs.

Estienne quelled his own grief. He could not let it master him now. Not here, where thousands looked on. He owed it to the Marshal's memory to clad himself in iron. His lord had raised him to be strong. To endure. No matter the cost to his own bleeding heart, Estienne would honour him with dignity.

As they plodded toward their destination, Estienne took note of the great and the good riding in Marshal's wake. It seemed as if every knight and lord in England had turned out to pay their respects. There was Hubert of Burgh, his craggy face set like granite. John of Earley rode close behind. The Earls of Salisbury, Arundel, Albemarle and Warenne were in attendance, their bright surcoats lending colour to the sombre procession.

But it was the white mantles of the Knights Templar that stood out starkly against the crowd. When word had reached the Temple that Marshal lay dying, Aimery Saint-Maur had ridden out to Caversham with all haste, determined to fulfil an old promise. Estienne still remembered the sight of him standing over Marshal's bed, intoning the vows that would see him join the ranks of that holy order, even as he departed this earthly realm.

That Aimery himself had passed away mere days after completing the rites was a fact that set a chill down Estienne's spine. As if Marshal's death had snuffed out some vital spark in Aimery. In a way, Estienne was grimly glad that the Grand Master had followed his friend so soon after. Aimery and William had been bound by ties that ran deep – and Estienne could only hope he might share such a bond of brotherhood one day.

And so it had been Templars, along with William's closest

companions, who held vigil over his body as it lay in state. Estienne himself had stood for long hours, taking his turn with so
many others, but now it was time for the last rites. To say a final
farewell to the man who had been more than mere master. The
man who had forged Estienne into who he was.

Ahead loomed the Temple Church, its pale stone stark against
the capital's brooding skyline. Estienne's heart clenched at the
sight of the building where the Marshal would be laid to his final
rest. He willed away the tears as they rode to where the crowd had
been cleared and the funeral carriage could be drawn to a halt.

On the steps leading up to the great oaken doors, a small figure
waited. Draped in ermine-trimmed crimson, a golden circlet
resting on his brow, he looked both older than his years and
impossibly young. King Henry. The boy who would be the
Marshal's final liege.

At some unspoken signal, the entire procession drew rein. As
one, the knights and earls and barons swung down from their
saddles, feet thudding against the flagstones. Estienne dismounted
with them, feeling a curious sense of detachment. As if this were
all happening to someone else, and he merely observed from a
distance.

He watched as the Templars approached the hearse, their
movements solemn and precise. With infinite care, they lifted the
Marshal's coffin, the lead within weighing heavy on their mailed
shoulders, but they bore the weight with pride, heads high
beneath their helms as they carried their newest brother towards
his final rest.

Estienne took his place along the path, joining the ranks of
knights and solemn-faced lords. As the Templars passed, he saw
King Henry bow his head, a gesture of respect so profound it sent a
fresh wash of grief crashing over him. That this child, who had
never known the Marshal beyond being a trusted regent, felt the

immensity of his loss. That as the most powerful figure in all England he would still bow his head in respect.

And then the coffin was passing Estienne, so close he could have reached out to touch the drapery, the vibrant lion rampant. His hand ached with the urge, but he kept it at his side, and as the coffin filled his vision, Estienne finally let his rigid control slip, just a fraction.

'Goodbye, my lord,' he whispered.

The Templars marched onward, the Marshal's mortal shell borne between them. And Estienne could only watch through a veil of stubborn tears, as every step took William further beyond his reach.

As the procession passed into the Temple, Estienne slowly lifted his head. There, directly across from him, stood Eva, her slim form draped in black, the gossamer veil doing little to obscure her anguish. But even swathed in mourning, hair hidden beneath a barbet, she was breathtaking. Achingly lovely despite the sorrow etched into every line of her.

As if pulled by an invisible thread, her gaze locked with his. Eyes, once so vital and dancing with mischief, now dulled by grief. And yet when they fixed on Estienne, something flickered in their depths.

He felt that look pierce him clean through, as swift and deadly as any knife. It seared through to lodge behind his ribs, and with that single, stolen glance, one truth crashed over him with staggering force...

He would want no other.

Not the ladies of Normandy who had vied coquettishly for his favour as he rode at Richard's side. Not the maids of Orbec with their bold smiles. Not a single woman he had known could hold a candle to the fierce, beautiful woman who stood a world away from him, yet who lived eternally in his soul.

Eva.

It had always been Eva. And it always would be.

But to have this realisation, this epiphany, here? Now? With her heart raw with loss? Estienne could have wept for the cruel irony of it. To finally understand the shape and depth of his feelings, even as he knew he must quash them.

Shame tightened his throat and he looked away. Estienne set his jaw, as Eva drifted back towards her family. To her mother, hunched and diminished. To her brothers, shoulder to shoulder as pillars against the tide of their sorrow.

They followed the procession to within the confines of the Temple Church, those closest to the Marshal granted the honour of witnessing him interred to his final rest.

For Estienne Wace, no such privilege. Despite his friendship with Richard, despite the Marshal himself proclaiming Estienne as beloved as his own trueborn sons, he would stand apart as they grieved. That he was so close on this final day would have to be enough.

48

The great hall of Pembroke echoed with the low murmur of conversation, punctuated by the occasional burst of laughter and the clink of tankards. The feast had ended but the men lingered, nursing their drinks and trading stories of battles past and glories earned.

Estienne sat among them, a cup of wine warming his hands, but he found little comfort in the familiar trappings of camaraderie. Though the long table still groaned beneath the weight of picked-over trenchers and the air hung heavy with the scent of roasted meat, it all felt hollow somehow, a pale imitation of the gatherings he remembered without the master of the house. Without the towering presence of Earl William at the head of the table, his voice booming out over the din. The very stones of the hall seemed to mourn his absence. Estienne could feel it, the sense that something crucial was missing, a lynchpin that had held them all together.

Countess Isabel had not joined them tonight, nor any night since their return from London. Her grief was a palpable thing, a shroud that hung over the castle and all its inhabitants. Estienne could not fault her for it. He felt the Marshal's loss like a wound that would not heal cleanly. He could only imagine the depth of her sorrow, having loved the man for so many years, borne his children, stood steadfast at his side through trials unending.

Guillaume and Richard did their best to fill the void, to bring some semblance of normalcy to the household with these nightly revels. They laughed and japed, toasted their father's memory with raised cups, but Estienne could see the shadow behind their eyes, the grief that lurked beneath their mantle of good cheer.

At the table, Goffrey held court with two Templar knights, their white tunics standing out starkly against the sea of sombre hues. Estienne recognised them from the Marshal's funeral procession – they had been among the chosen few to stand vigil over his bier as he lay in state.

'...and then he says to the bastard, calm as you please, "I'll pay you double if you come into my service instead".' Goffrey slapped the table, guffawing at his own tale. 'God damn me if the dumb sod didn't take him up on the offer.'

The Templars joined in his laughter, raising their cups in salute to the late Marshal's audacity. Richard, seated across from them, leaned forward with a grin.

'So, brothers of the cross, now that your duty to my lord father is discharged, what grand adventures are you off to next?'

The elder of the knights, Hoston, a grey-haired man with a scar bisecting his brow, seemed to sober for a moment. 'We sail for Damietta at week's end. The Holy Father's crusade in Egypt founders and our brothers have need of every sword and strong arm.'

'Aye, I'd heard tell of that,' Richard said, a pensive note stealing into his voice. 'A holy cause, to be sure, but a dangerous one.' He glanced at Estienne, a sly glint in his eye. 'I don't suppose you'd have a taste for such a venture, would you, Wace? You're on the hunt for some righteous quest to throw yourself at.'

The other men chuckled, Goffrey aiming a good-natured elbow at Estienne's ribs, but Estienne hardly registered the barb. His place had been here, at the Marshal's side, bound by oaths of loyalty. But now, set adrift by sorrow and loss, he couldn't help but wonder what path awaited him. The walls of the hall seemed to press in, the air growing thick and stifling.

Mumbling some vague excuse, he pushed away from the table, desperate for the cool night air, the space to breathe. He left the hall, making his way down the stairs of the keep and wandered across the castle grounds, letting his feet carry him over flagstone and sod until the sounds of the feast were little more than a distant rumble. No matter how he tried to push it down, grief lingered, a cold spot in his chest that no warmth could touch. He had thought himself familiar with loss, but this aching emptiness was something new, the pain of a son mourning his sire, though no blood bound Estienne to the Marshals.

He crossed the inner bailey, stopping at the chapel, dark and silent in the night air. For so long, his purpose had been clear – to serve the Marshal, to uphold his oaths, to prove himself worthy of the trust placed in him. Now, with William gone, his future stretched before him like a looming chasm, dark and depthless.

A flicker of movement caught his eye, and he turned to see a slight figure walking toward the north tower. Even at this distance, he knew her.

Eva.

His breath caught at the sight of her, the moonlight gilding her raven hair with silver, the graceful line of her neck. It struck him anew how much she had changed since they were children – the frolicsome mischief of youth replaced with a woman's composed elegance.

But it was not only years that separated them now. Her father had promised her to Gwilym of Braose, a young lordling destined for life as a Marcher Lord. A man who could offer Eva the security and status she deserved. What could Estienne give her by comparison? He might wear the spurs of knighthood, might wield a sword in service to a king, but he was still baseborn – an orphan raised by the Marshal's charity. He had no lands to his name, no title. Any affection between them could never be more than a wistful dream.

'Do you plan to spend the whole night brooding in the dark like some lovelorn minstrel?'

Richard's voice cut through Estienne's thoughts. He turned to see his friend grinning at him, two tankards gripped in his brawny fists.

'I was not brooding,' Estienne replied. 'Just... thinking.'

'Ah yes, *thinking*.' Richard sidled up to him, looking across the bailey to where Eva's form was silhouetted in the moonlight.

Estienne's face flushed hot, and he turned away. 'I wasn't—'

'Oh, spare me the denials. I see the way you look at her when you think no one is watching – like a shipwrecked sailor sighting land.' He sighed, offering one of the tankards. 'Why do you torment yourself, Estienne? Why not speak your mind, before it's too late?'

'What would you have me say?' Estienne took the drink but did not raise it to his lips. 'That I... care for her? I have no right. I'm naught but a landless knight.'

'Horseshit.' Richard spat. 'You think blood is all that matters? That the circumstances of your birth outweigh the strength of your heart, the courage of your deeds? You are more than the equal of any man. My lord father saw that. Why can't you?'

'Your father gave me more than I ever hoped for, Richard. More than I deserved. But his charity cannot erase the truth of what I am.'

'You're a knight, Estienne. In every way that matters.' Richard's voice softened. 'Were it up to me, I'd call you brother in truth, not just in bond. And if Eva feels for you as I suspect, then the match would be a good one. Better than the one my father made for her.'

A wild, reckless hope rose in Estienne, dashed suddenly by the reality of it. 'But her betrothal is decided. It could not be broken now. Not unless Guillaume decided on it.'

Richard laughed. 'And you see that as an obstacle? For all his airs, my brother knows where his loyalties lie. And you've more than earned them.' He glanced back to where Eva walked alone. 'The only thing standing in your way is you, Wace. Don't let her slip away. Not without a fight.'

Estienne had never run from a fight. He wouldn't start now.

Giving Richard back his tankard, he crossed the bailey, heart hammering. Eva glanced up at his approach, her face a mask of serenity.

'My lady.' His tongue was suddenly clumsy in his mouth. 'Forgive the intrusion. I saw you walking, and thought... perhaps you would appreciate... but I can leave you to your solitude, if you prefer.'

'No, stay.' A subtle smile touched her lips. 'I would welcome the company. I find myself in a contemplative mood tonight.'

Estienne fell into step beside her, hands clasped behind his back to hide their trembling. 'Remembering happier times?'

'Something like that.' Eva glanced up at the keep, its weathered stones pale in the moonlight. 'It's strange, how much smaller it all seems now. As a child, I thought Pembroke the grandest castle in the world. A kingdom unto itself.'

'We had the run of it, didn't we?' Estienne smiled at the memory. 'You and your maids, always dashing about, raising a ruckus in the halls.'

'While you tried your best to stay out of trouble.' Eva arched a teasing brow. 'A futile endeavour, as I recall. You must have some good memories of this place. Despite my best efforts to torment you.'

Estienne considered the question, sifting through the years, separating the chaff from the wheat. 'There were challenges, to be sure. It wasn't easy, being a fosterling amongst highborn children. Some never let me forget that I was an outsider.'

Eva nodded in sympathy. 'Ilbert was a brute.'

'Worse. But hardship is the whetstone that sharpens us, or so your father said.' Estienne shrugged. 'We all faced our trials, I suppose.'

'And now we all have new roles to take on. New duties to shoulder.' There was a distant quality to Eva's voice, as if she spoke from far away.

'You mean your marriage to Braose.' Estienne cursed himself for being unable to keep the bitterness from his tone.

'It is a good match. Gwilym is... from a powerful family.' She let out a humourless laugh. 'Listen to me. Young Eva would have raged at the very thought of such a marriage. She would have schemed and fought and cajoled until she got her way.'

'And what does Eva the woman want?'

She looked up at him then, her eyes piercing. 'To do my duty. As I must.'

'The Eva I knew would never let duty stand in the way of what she wanted.'

'Oh, she's still in here somewhere. Too stubborn to stay buried for long. Is that truly all you see when you look at me, Estienne? The headstrong girl you once knew?'

It would be so easy to give voice to the feelings swelling in his chest, to let the words pour out in a torrent. To fall to his knees before her and swear that she was the most beautiful creature he had ever beheld. But he held his tongue, the words sticking in his throat like fishbones.

'I see you, Eva. Just as you are. Just as you've always been.' She was standing so close now, the warmth of her body bleeding through the scant space between them, the scent of her hair making him dizzy. 'And what do you see, when you look at me?'

Eva stood silently for a moment, as they drank one another in. Then, slowly, she leaned into him. One slender hand came up to cup his cheek, and then her lips were brushing his. It was barely a kiss, the most fleeting of touches, but it seared him to his core. He made a soft, involuntary noise, his hands coming up to grip her waist, to pull her closer, but she was already slipping away, out of his grasp.

She stepped back, her lips parted as if she would speak, but then she turned, gathering her skirts, and fled across the bailey, back toward the keep. Estienne could only stare after her, his heart pounding, lips still tingling with the memory of her kiss.

He knew he should quash the wild, reckless hope. Knew that the obstacles between them were as vast as the sea. But in that moment, with the ghost of her touch still teasing his skin, he let himself believe that anything was possible. That there was a future for them, if only he had the courage to seize it.

49

Countess Isabel sat at the small writing desk in her chamber, quill poised over a half-written letter. The guttering candle cast the parchment a sickly yellow, the ink glistening in the wan light. Beyond the narrow window, the sky hung heavy and grey, as if the heavens themselves mourned the passing of her husband.

Her hand trembled, a single drop of ink spattering the page as she willed the tears not to fall. Not now. Not when there was so much yet to be done.

With a shaking breath, she opened her eyes and dipped her quill once more. The words came haltingly, each stroke an effort. To Guala, the papal legate, and to Hubert of Burgh, the kingdom's justiciar. Missives that she prayed would secure her hold on the lands and titles granted her husband on the day of their marriage. Properties in England and Hibernia that must be signed over to her with all haste, lest the wolves come circling in the wake of her husband's death.

A grim smile touched her lips, devoid of mirth. Let them come. She would not cower like a hearth-mouse while men sought to strip away all her family had built. Her sons were grown, strong and capable. Guillaume would have Pembroke, as was his birthright. The rest she would hold in an ironclad grip that would not be broken.

But it was not enough to shore up their English holdings. Even now, Isabel knew there were hungry eyes upon her Norman lands. A menace she must confront directly, a journey to France imminent.

Signing her name to the letters with a decisive flourish, she sanded the ink and sat back. There was more writing to be done, arrangements to make for her journey across the Channel, to treat with King Philip himself if she must. She would retain those holdings too, come what may.

A sudden knock at the door startled her. She glanced around the chamber, taking in the detritus of the last few days – discarded clothes, a tray of untouched food, the bed still rumpled from when she'd risen at dawn. A far cry from her usual fastidious neatness.

'Come,' she called, hastily straightening her kirtle.

The door creaked open to reveal Isabel's maid, Branwen, bearing a small oak casket. The woman bobbed a curtsy. 'My lady. I've brought the last of Earl William's... that is, I thought you might want to...'

Isabel forced a brittle smile. 'Thank you, Branwen. Just set it there, on the table.'

The maid did as bidden and laid the casket onto the scarred oak. With another quick bob, she retreated, leaving Isabel alone once more.

For a long moment, she simply stared at the thing, innocuous as it was. William's personal effects. The last earthly remnants of the man she had loved for most of her life. Did she have the strength to rifle through them like a barrow-thief picking over grave goods?

Unbidden, a memory rose. William, younger then, eyes crinkling in the sunlight as he laughed at something she'd said. The warm strength of his fingers twined with hers. For thirty years, he had been her rock, her guiding star. How could she face a world without him in it?

Angrily, Isabel blinked away the tears that threatened to fall. This would not do. William was gone, and no amount of weeping would bring him back.

Before she could think better of it, she reached forward and flipped open the latch. The hinges gave a soft creak as the lid lifted, and Isabel found herself staring down at the last worldly possessions of her husband.

His rings first caught her eye, winking dully in the candlelight. The great signet most prominent among them, the Marshal's lion rampant etched boldly into the gold. How many missives had he sealed with that proud device?

Beside it, the silver crucifix he'd worn against his heart every day of their marriage. He'd kissed it each night before bed, a ritual as ingrained as breathing. She'd always suspected it was his talisman, a rod of holy reassurance to ward off the spectre of death that dogged the heels of every knight.

Throat tight, Isabel reached to lift the cross from its resting place. As she did, her fingers brushed something else – small, hard and uneven. She frowned, dipping into the casket's depths, and drew out a key – small and iron, just large enough to fit into a palm.

For a moment, she stared at the unexpected find, trying to place the lock it might fit. Then, with a start, memory supplied the answer. William's bureau. The small drawer that had always been locked, for as long as she'd known him. A drawer she'd never dared to pry into, assuming it held the sorts of secrets a man kept from even his wife.

Slowly, Isabel curled her fingers around the key, its edges biting into her palm. Part of her recoiled at the thought of intruding upon those secrets now. To disturb that inner sanctum felt like a betrayal, a trespass upon William's unspoken trust. And yet... he was gone now. Had he kept any secrets from her, surely she had a right to know them.

She rose, moving to the bureau. The key turned stiffly in the lock and Isabel wrestled the drawer open, wood groaning like an arthritic joint. She hesitated, fingers resting on the lip of the drawer. *Trespasser*, a small voice seemed to hiss. *Faithless sneak*. She pushed the recriminations aside. If not her, then who had the right?

Isabel slid the drawer fully open. A sheaf of papers greeted her, neatly stacked and tied with a black ribbon. Several folded parchments, their seals broken, lay to one side. A small leather pouch, drawstring pulled tight. And there, atop it all...

A letter, just as unremarkable as its fellows but for one detail – its wax seal was impressed with no noble signet. No device of a lord's house or a knight's arms marked it, only a roughly circular stamp, the kind only a common man might own. Frowning, Isabel plucked the letter from its resting place, bringing it closer to the candlelight.

The parchment was weathered, its edges dog-eared. Unfolding it, Isabel squinted at the tight, spidery hand that crawled across the page, each word looking like an ink-black insect until a single name seemed to leap from the page.

Estienne.

Isabel sank into the chair, still staring at the letter clutched in her hand. Estienne. The quiet, grey-eyed boy who'd arrived at Pembroke with nothing but this parchment.

She read on. And with every word, that long ago day, when a lad from Anjou appeared at their gates, began to take on a vastly different cast...

Earl William,

You will not know me, nor I you, though we once served the same king. My name is Sandre Closier, and I was a routier in the company led by Mercadier, in the retinue of our late and beloved King Richard. Though we never met in person, I know you were close to His Grace, and he was often heard to speak highly of you as a loyal companion and peerless knight.

The boy who brings you this letter is named Estienne. He will tell you that he is my nephew and that I have sent him to be fostered as a squire in your household. In truth, Estienne is no blood of mine, though I have raised him as my own these thirteen years past. The story of how he came into my care is not one I have shared before, but now, as I face my final days, I can keep silent no longer.

That story begins in the year of our Lord, 1199...

INTERLUDE: THE DEATH OF MERCADIER

FRANCE, 1199 AD

50

The road had been an unforgiving one, and Sandre sagged in his saddle, every bone aching from two days spent ahorse. Beside him, Renier whistled a jaunty tune, seemingly oblivious to the weight of their errand.

'Not far now,' Renier said. 'We'll have the Lion's heart in hand and be off before the sun is at its peak.'

Sandre grunted a noncommittal sound. In truth, he wished this task had fallen to any other man. The thought of ferrying a dead king's heart across the breadth of France sat ill in his belly, like a meal gone rotten. And with every mile that passed beneath his horse's hooves, the guilt of his late return to Marion gnawed a little deeper.

Two years he'd been gone. Two years of blood and battle, sleeping rough and eating shit. All in service to a king who now lay cold on a church slab. A fine repayment for loyalty, to come home stinking of death, naught but a sack of silver to show for it. And a small one at that.

The road crested a rise, and Limousin came into view. The abbey stood stark against the rooftops like a misshapen toad, its walls dark with creeping ivy. Even from this distance, the air hung heavy with a sepulchral gloom, as though the very stones were steeped in decades of sorrow.

'Cheery sort of place, isn't it?' Renier smirked. 'What do you wager the food's like?'

'Is that all you ever think of?' Sandre growled. 'That is a house of God. Show some respect for a change.'

Renier grinned and faked a bow. 'As my lord commands.'

Sandre shot him a baleful look but held his tongue. He had known Renier for many years but still did not trust him. He was as likely to cut your purse as guard your back, but he was handy with a blade, and in their line of work that counted for more than trust.

They picked their way down the hillside, mud sucking at their horses' hooves. The abbey rose up to overshadow them, blotting out the sunlight. Empty windows yawned, and Sandre had the uncanny sense of being watched from their mysterious depths.

He shook off the unease. Too much time seeing foes in every shadow. There were no enemies here. Only servants of God.

The gates lay open as they approached, just wide enough to admit them. Beyond lay a muddy courtyard, empty save for a few skeletal trees and a well choked with scum. At the far side, a heavy wooden door stood shut against the world. The whole place seemed to hold its breath.

Renier leaned across his pommel, voice pitched low. 'If I didn't know better, I'd say the place was abandoned.'

Sandre frowned. 'Let's just get this over with.'

He swung down from his horse, boots squelching in the muck. A stable boy detached himself from the shadows, somehow invisible until that moment. He took their reins without a word and led the horses toward a nearby trough.

Drawing a steadying breath, Sandre strode to the door and raised a fist to knock. Before he could connect, it swung inward, hinges wailing. He exchanged a glance with Renier and stepped across the threshold.

Inside, the air was thick with the stink of mould and tallow. A few guttering candles cast a dim light, teasing the edges of dusty reliquaries and smoke-darkened tapestries, but it was the figure standing at the centre of the chamber that drew Sandre's eye and held it.

A woman, swathed in black, wimple covering her head, face lit by the flame of the taper in her hand.

'You are the men Mercadier sent.' It was not a question, but Sandre nodded anyway. 'I am the abbess. I have what you seek.'

She turned without another word, clearly expecting them to follow. Sandre fell into step behind her, Renier a shadow at his shoulder. They wound through narrow passageways, footsteps echoing off the flagstones. Deeper they went, the air growing thick and stale, until Sandre felt he might choke on it.

At last they came to a low arch, and the abbess ducked through. Sandre followed, stooping below the lintel, and found himself in a stone chamber that could only be the crypt. The dancing light of the abbess's taper threw grotesque shadows, and Sandre had the sudden sensation of being watched by generations of mouldering dead.

'Your king's heart lies there.' The abbess gestured to a lead casket lying on a plain stone altar. 'Awaiting its final journey.'

Both men looked at the box, then at one another, unsure of which should take up this hallowed object. Before they could decide, the abbess stepped in their path.

'But before you take it, there is something else you must see.'

With a whisper of robes, she glided to a shadowed alcove. In the flickering light, Sandre saw a body laid out upon a slab, wrapped in hemp and covered in fresh flowers that did little to disguise the stench of decay. The corpse was still recognisable as a woman, hands folded across a sunken chest.

'Who is she?' Sandre asked, voice echoing eerily in the close confines.

'She came to us near a fortnight ago,' the abbess replied. 'Heavy with child and fever-mad. Raved of serving at the pleasure of a king. Your king.'

Sandre stared at the dead woman. 'One of Richard's mistresses?'

'So she claimed, and according to local rumour, a claim that is true. She birthed the babe and promptly breathed her last, may God grant her soul ease.'

Renier glared. 'A royal bastard?'

The abbess inclined her head. 'Just so. And you, Mercadier's men, are the first to know of it.'

A rustling in the shadows heralded the arrival of another nun, this one cradling a swaddled bundle in her arms. Sandre felt the hairs on his nape prickle as a thin wail rose, quickly muffled. Richard's child. The bastard get of a dead king.

The nun held the babe out and Sandre found himself reaching to take it. The child was so light, scarcely more than a loaf of bread in his callused hands. He peeled back the swaddling, breath catching at the glimpse of a wrinkled, ruddy face.

'Ugly little fucker,' Renier said, leaning close. 'Looks like a shrivelled beet.'

Sandre barely heard him. This tiny scrap of humanity, this fatherless waif... could it truly be Richard's? And if so, what in God's name were they to do with it?

As if reading his thoughts, Renier said, 'Mercadier needs to know of this. He'll want the bastard.'

'No.' The word issued from Sandre's lips before he could think. 'Mercadier can't learn of it.'

Renier rounded on him, brows lowered. 'Have you taken leave of your senses? This child is—'

'I know what this child is.' Sandre clutched the infant closer. 'But it's... it's done no wrong. If Mercadier finds out then you know what he might do. It doesn't deserve—'

'It's not about right or wrong.' Renier's mouth twisted into a sneer. 'It's about keeping our skins. Mercadier will want to know of this child. Perhaps even use it to his favour in his meetings with the new king. Bastard or not, it could be a threat to John's rule. If Mercadier finds out we knew of it and didn't tell him—'

'A threat? It's a babe in arms. An innocent. You know what Mercadier will do. You've seen it.'

'Aye, I've seen it,' Renier growled. 'We both saw it, just the other day. And if it's between me getting flayed and this fucking little bastard... I am going to ride for Mercadier. See what he wants done with the whelp. If you know what's good for you, then you'll ride with me.'

'No.' That one word had a finality all its own.

Silence, as Renier considered that defiant reply. Then a shake of his head. 'You're a fool, Closier. It will be your end. But you'll not take me down with you.'

'Renier, listen—'

But he was already turning for the stairs, his footsteps receding into the dark. Sandre stood frozen. The weight of the babe in his arms was suddenly a millstone, dragging him down into unknown depths. But he knew, with startling clarity, that he could not abandon it to Mercadier's mercy.

He looked to the abbess. 'Please, you heard him. You must keep this child safe. Give it sanctuary—'

'The babe cannot stay here,' she replied with distinctly unchristian indifference. 'Not without risk to everyone who dwells within these walls. It must be claimed by its father's kin. As is proper.'

'Proper?' Sandre barked. 'You think any of that brood would welcome a bastard into their midst? King John would as soon dash its head against a wall himself.'

The abbess folded her hands. 'Nevertheless. I'll not be party to any of it.'

And with that, she swept from the crypt, leaving Sandre alone with a newborn child and his own galloping dread.

Marion. He had to get to Marion. She would know what to do. How to make this right.

Sandre took the stairs two at a time, child clutched to his chest. He burst into the courtyard, startling a pair of nuns who scattered like sparrows. His horse waited, standing placid in the gathering gloom. Quick strides carried him across the muck, and he swung astride, babe cradled in the crook of one arm. He dug in his spurs, reining through the abbey gates and out onto the open road.

His mind raced, a desperate prayer on his lips. Let him reach Marion soon. Let them find some way out of this ungodly tangle. But with each stride of the horse, each wail of the child, Sandre felt the weight of his choice settle more heavily across his shoulders.

He could only pray it would not crush them... all three of them.

51

The night closed in like a cloak, draping the countryside in darkness. An autumn wind knifed through the trees, rattling the bare branches like bones, and Sandre hunched deeper into his cloak, trying to ward off the chill.

His horse's hooves thudded against the hard-packed earth, a relentless drumbeat, but he dared not slow the gruelling pace. Not with his precious cargo pressed close against his chest.

Sandre looked down at the bundle of rough-spun cloth, so innocuous in the gathering dark. Impossible that it should contain something so dangerous. A newborn babe, scarcely more than a week old... the bastard son of his dead king.

God's wounds, what had possessed him to take the child? He should have left it there, in the abbey. Let the holy sisters decide its fate, and forget this whole sordid affair. But something in him, some long-buried flicker of decency, had compelled him to spirit the babe away. Now, with every stride of his horse, Sandre bore his prize closer to home. Closer to Marion.

The thought of his wife sent a wave of dread crashing over him.

How would he explain this insanity? How could he burden her with the terrible knowledge of this child's heritage?

In the distance, a faint light winked – their farmhouse, rising from the darkened fields. Sanctuary.

Sandre shifted the babe in his arms, feeling the warm weight of it. Such a small, fragile burden, and yet this would change everything. Would unmake the life he had hoped for when all the wars were over.

As he drew rein before the weathered door, Sandre looked down at the babe once more, seeing not a child but a harbinger of doom swaddled in rags. He took a deep breath of frigid air, steeling himself for what was to come, then slid from the saddle. Then, with the babe clutched tight to his breast, he reached for the door.

It flew open before Sandre's fingers could touch the wood, and he found himself staring into Marion's eyes. For a moment, her face was a mask of pure disbelief. Then came a succession of emotions – relief, confusion, and then, most terrible of all, a fury that ignited like tinder to flame.

'What in God's name...?' Marion focused on the squirming bundle in his arms.

'Marion, wait, I can expl—'

'Explain?' Her voice rose to a screech. 'You slither back after two years gone, a squalling whore's get in your arms, and you think you can explain?'

'It's not what you think, I swear it on my life.' Sandre held out a placating hand. 'Please, just let me—'

'You have whored your way across France while I withered here, waiting like a good, loyal wife.' She advanced on him, tears cutting clean tracks across her cheeks. 'Tell me, did she have yellow hair and pink teats like a sow? Did you bury your cock so deep between her legs it hit daylight on the other side?'

'No! Marion, it was never like that. Not one single time. Please, you have to believe—'

'I have to believe?' Her laughter held no mirth. 'I have to drink your sweet lies like poison? I have to clasp this mewling bastard to my breast and coo and coddle as if it were born of my own womb? You are a rogue and philanderer, Sandre Closier, come crawling home with your tramp's offspring held out like some vile offering, expecting me to—'

'It's the king's bastard!' Sandre yelled. It had the required effect and Marion fell suddenly silent. 'The babe's not mine. It's Richard's seed, and King John's men will surely slit its throat if they learn of it.'

The anger bled away from Marion's face like wine from a shattered cup, leaving her pale as bone. 'The... the king's child? Richard's son?'

'I couldn't leave it, Marion. Couldn't abandon it. Mercadier would have ordered it dead, or worse, taken it to the eager arms of King John to gain his favour. You know what he's capable of. I had to protect it.'

Marion looked down at the child still squalling in the circle of her husband's arms.

'You've brought death upon us,' she said softly. 'Treason to our very doorstep. You've fed us to the dogs on a whim.'

'Not a whim. A child's life. An innocent soul.' Gingerly, so gingerly, he offered her the struggling bundle. 'Please, it's just a babe. It didn't ask for this. It doesn't deserve to die for the sin of its birth. Just hold him, Marion. Please. He needs you. Needs us.'

Sandre gently eased the squalling babe into her arms.

'There has to be someone else,' she breathed. 'Anyone else. A church orphanage, a—'

'And how long do you think he would last? A fortnight? A month? Long enough for tongues to wag, for people to grow curious? Long enough for Mercadier's blades to find their mark? I've seen what he's capable of, Marion. The atrocities committed at his word. Babes ripped from their mother's arms, dashed against walls. Children gutted like pigs, left to rot in the sun.'

'Enough.' She glared at Sandre over the top of the child's downy head. 'You've made your point.'

Slowly, as if helpless to prevent it, she regarded the child as it gurgled softly. Marion's face remained stony, but Sandre saw a flicker in her eyes, a softening of her heart perhaps?

'We prayed for a child of our own. All those years, those bitter disappointments... What if this is God's answer?'

'God's answer?' Her brow furrowed and Sandre silently cursed his stupid tongue. 'A bastard dumped on our doorstep like a sack of corn, death and treason stalking his heels? You think this as a blessing?'

'Why not? Why shouldn't we see it as such? A child, hale and whole, filled with life's promise. Is such a gift to be spurned lightly?'

Marion stared, brows furrowed, but beneath the anger, the fear, Sandre thought he saw a yearning, a need that she dared not voice. 'You ask too much. We could never keep it secret. Never hide a child away in this small place and expect none to suspect.'

'Then we don't hide.' Sandre took a step closer, near enough to feel the warmth of the hearth within his house, the warmth of his wife and the precious burden she held. 'Let it be known that I have a sister somewhere, that she quickened but died in birth. With her husband already dead, I brought the child home to raise as our own. Let him be ours, Marion. No one need know the secret of his birth. He can be safe with us. The answer to all those years of prayer.'

Marion's face was a mask of indecision. Long moments passed, broken only by the soft mewls of the child. Then, slowly, she took a deep, shuddering breath.

'A blessing,' she whispered. 'You truly believe that?'

'I do, my love. I must. Else I'd have left him there, a lamb to the slaughter, and damned myself forever. This child... he belongs to us now. I feel it in my bones.'

Marion was silent for a long time. Then, in a voice scarcely louder than the wind's whisper, she breathed, 'Then he will be ours.'

'Good,' Sandre said, quelling a sigh of relief. 'Can we... go inside now? It's freezing out here.'

* * *

Days passed as if in a haze. Dawn bled into dusk, the rhythms of their simple life expanding to encompass this new, precious addition and Sandre threw himself into preparation, determined to make their home a haven fit for the child.

He laboured from sunup to sundown, hewing timber for a crib, busying his hands so his mind couldn't wander down the dark path of dread. The rasp of his plane, the steady whack of his hammer, these were the sounds that filled his days as he tried not to feel the weight of the secret they now kept.

And everywhere, threaded through even the most mundane of moments, was the child. His cries woke them in the grey light of pre-dawn, demanding to be fed, changed, held. His gurgles and coos becoming one with the welcome sounds of the farm going about its business.

Marion took to it as though the child were her own, hands gentle as she swaddled and rocked and crooned lullabies. Sandre would catch her sometimes, in unguarded moments, gazing down at the child with an expression of such raw tenderness it made his heart ache. He knew she was still afraid, but that fear was tempered now by something fiercer. A protective love that defied reason and threat alike.

Still, the babe was yet unnamed. It seemed an impossible task, to choose a name for a king's son when he was to be raised as a commoner. Sandre would find himself watching the child as he slept between them in their bed, trying out name after name in the privacy of his head. None ever seemed to fit, to encompass the enormity of the child's heritage. In time, Sandre knew they would choose. They would find some solid, honest name to gift the boy, to root him firmly in this new life they were building. He had to believe that, just as he had to believe they could keep him safe, keep him secret. The alternative was too terrible to contemplate.

A sennight after Sandre's fateful return he found himself putting the finishing touches on the crib. The fire crackled merrily in the hearth, holding the evening's chill at bay, and Marion sat in her chair, the babe nestled in the crook of her arm as she hummed a half-remembered tune.

Straightening from his work, Sandre stepped back to admire the results. Sturdy oak, pegged together with all the skill he possessed. A crib to withstand all the kicks and squirmings of a growing babe.

'There,' he said quietly. 'Fit for a king, eh?'

Marion glanced up at him, a wry twist to her lips. 'Or perhaps even good enough for the son of a farmer.'

Rising from her chair, she crossed to where it stood and lined it with the softest lambswool and scraps of linen. Then she lay the sleeping child in his new bed, tucking the blankets close around his tiny form.

For a long moment, they simply stood together, looking down at this miracle that had been thrust upon them. The babe's features were untroubled. He looked so pure, so innocent. Sandre felt Marion's fingers twine with his, her palm warm against his own. He squeezed gently, as something tight eased in his chest. Perhaps, just perhaps, they could do this. Could be a family, and build some honest life around this child that fate had delivered unto them...

The knock at the door almost stopped Sandre's heart.

He stiffened, head snapping around to stare at the pitted wood, mind reeling. No one ever came to their door after nightfall. Not in all the years they'd called this place home.

'Sandre,' Marion breathed, her fingers tightening convulsively around his.

He swallowed against the sudden dryness in his mouth, feet rooted to the floor. The knock came again, sharper. Insistent.

'Open up, Closier. I know you're in there.' A voice, low and gruff. Familiar as Sandre's own.

Renier. God blind them, it was Renier.

Sandre found himself moving, crossing the small space to the door. His hand, when he lifted it to the latch, was shaking so violently he could scarcely grip the iron. The door swung inward, and Renier shouldered his way into the room. In the hushed stillness, his nasal breath rasped like fingernails on stone, the sound setting Sandre's teeth on edge.

'What do you want?' Sandre whispered.

'Bit of a rude welcome, eh?' Renier's scarred face twisted into a parody of a smile. 'After I've come all this way to see you. Have you any idea how difficult this place is to—'

'Why are you here, Renier?' Sandre was astonished at the steadiness of his own voice. Inside, he quaked like a sapling in a storm. 'I thought our business was concluded at the abbey.'

Renier's head turned toward the crib with unerring precision. 'Was it now? From where I'm standing, it looks like you've quite the piece of unfinished business swaddled up over there.'

Marion made a choked sound, a sob bitten back, but Sandre silenced her with a sharp jerk of his head. He widened his stance, planting himself squarely between Renier and his son.

'You overstep,' he said coldly. 'I'll ask you again: why are you here?'

The cold light in Renier's eyes sharpened. 'Don't play the fool with me, Closier. You know full well why I'm here. Mercadier sent me to finish what we should have done at the abbey.'

Sandre clenched his jaw, refusing to let his fear show. 'I don't have the first notion what you're on about. There's naught here but me and mine.'

Renier's laugh was a short, ugly sound. 'You always were a shit liar, Closier. But no matter.' His hand vanished beneath his cloak, to emerge a heartbeat later gleaming with a short stub of bared steel. 'I'd rather cut to the chase.'

He started forward and Sandre threw himself into his path. 'Renier, stop. Please. It's just a child, an innocent—'

'Orders are orders, Closier.' In the depths of Renier's eyes there was nothing but winter. 'You of all men should know that. No royal bastards can be left to muddy the succession. King John's decree, and Mercadier's will.'

Sandre groped behind him, finding the crib, putting it at his back. 'You can't. Renier, he's just a child, barely a month old. Defenceless. Harmless.'

'For now. But we both know babes grow to men, and a man with a king's blood in his veins...' He slid forward another step, dagger held low and ready. 'Best to make this swift. No one else need get hurt.'

'Please.' Sandre could hear the naked desperation in his voice. 'I'm begging you. Spare him.'

For a moment, Sandre thought he glimpsed a flicker of doubt in that cold expression. A glimmer of humanity, of mercy, surfacing from some long-buried place. Then it was gone, Renier's face hardening into a mask of brutal resolve.

'No. Now step aside, Closier... or I'll cut right through you.'

'Renier.' Sandre's voice cracked. 'Brother, please...'

That feral grin twisted into a snarl and Renier lunged.

A whistle cleft the air.

A meaty thud punctuated by a crunch of bone.

A hammer blow, taking Renier full across the back of his skull.

The force of the impact sent the mercenary staggering, knees buckling beneath him. Blood sheeted black down his scalp as the dagger tumbled from his grasp. An animal moan tore from his throat, one groping hand pawing feebly at the ruined mess of his head.

Marion stood, bloodied hammer still in her hand – the one Sandre had used with such precise care to craft the baby's bed. Now it had been used to stove in Renier's head with equal efficiency.

Blood pulsed from the mercenary's scarred eye, and made a red track down his cheek. 'Sandre... do I have something in my eye?'

He stumbled, feet scraping across the floorboards.

'Sit down,' Sandre heard himself say, from what seemed a thousand miles away.

Renier's eyes rolled aimlessly. Sandre reached out, taking Renier by the arm and guiding him to a chair. The mercenary sat down heavily, gazing about the room as though he had no idea why he was there.

'Is there... is there anything to drink?'

His words were barely audible. Then Renier gave a final, shuddering gasp, and slumped to the floor.

The hammer thudded against the floorboards as it slipped from Marion's fingers. She stood motionless, face blank with the enormity of what she had done.

From the crib, the panicked wails of the babe rose to a feverish pitch.

Sandre stared at Renier's corpse, sprawled on his hearth. A man he had counted as a friend. Comrade. Now dead by his wife's hand.

He looked up to meet Marion's eyes, and in that shared gaze was a sudden, inescapable understanding. If there was any hope of survival, any chance of keeping their newfound child safe, drastic measures would have to be taken.

'Shit,' Sandre said.

52

Sandre picked his way through the grimy streets of Poitiers, feet squelching in the muck. Overhead, soot-stained buildings leaned drunkenly, their upper stories almost touching, shutting out the sullen sky. The stink of piss and shit hung heavy, and more than once Sandre had to step over the hunched form of some poor sot sleeping in his own vomit.

He pulled his cloak tighter, trying to ward off the chill. Not for the first time, he questioned the wisdom of this venture. Leaving Marion and their new babe, despite the danger that hung over them... but he had no choice. Mercadier would not stop hunting them. Would not rest until the boy was dead.

No, if there was to be any hope for his family, he had to see this through. Brandin was his only option. The mercenary captain had been Mercadier's fiercest rival for years, the two of them at each other's throats like a pair of rabid dogs. If anyone would relish a chance to put the bastard in the ground, it was Brandin.

Sandre sidestepped a pile of steaming horseshit and cast about for the inn he sought. The Suckling Pig, they called it. An unimaginative name for an unimaginative establishment, but it was where

Brandin could be found, or so Sandre had been told. He only prayed his information was good – too much rode on this desperate gambit for it to be otherwise.

There. Sandre caught sight of the inn's weathered sign, creaking in the fitful breeze. A crudely painted sow with a litter of piglets at her teats. Charming. With a last glance over his shoulder, hand resting on the hilt of his blade, Sandre stepped through the low doorway and into the smoky dimness.

The tavern's fetid warmth enveloped him like a wet wool cloak, the stink of sweat and sour ale enough to choke on. Candles guttered in their sconces, more smoke than light, as he shouldered his way through the press of unwashed bodies. Whores circulated among the drinkers, their kirtles cut low to display their wares. They cozened and simpered, draping themselves across the laps of leering men, but their eyes were hard, scouring the crowds for the heaviest purse.

In one corner, a troupe of minstrels sawed away at their fiddles, the music screeching and discordant. Sandre didn't spare them a second glance. This had to be swift.

He scanned the crowd, picking over the dregs and drunkards. One hulking brute caught his eye – a great, bearded slab of a man with a tavern wench bouncing on his knee.

'You there,' Sandre said, sidling closer. 'I'm looking for a man named Brandin. You know him?'

The thug looked up, porcine eyes narrowing in that brutal face. After a moment, he jerked his chin towards a shadowed corner.

'Might be you'll find him over there. But you'd be a brave man to interrupt him when he's holding court.'

Sandre followed the man's nod. There, sequestered behind a rough-hewn table, a group of men huddled over their tankards. They kept their heads low, their voices a furtive mutter lost to the din. At the centre sat a hawk-faced man. As if sensing Sandre's regard, he looked up, striking him with a dark stare.

Regardless of the warning glare, Sandre approached the table. The men fell silent, hands creeping to hilts, but Brandin waved them back with a languid flick of his wrist. Up close, the mercenary had the look of a bird of prey – a beak of a nose, eyes like a falcon hunting game.

'Something I can help you with, friend?' The words were mild, but there was still menace there.

Sandre offered a gesture just shy of a bow. 'I'm looking for Brandin. I'm told I might find him here.'

'You've found him. Though I don't know you from Adam.'

'Sandre. Sandre Closier.'

The name meant nothing to Brandin from the lack of recognition on that hawkish face. But still he leaned back in his chair, head cocked like a carrion bird eyeing a fresh corpse.

'And what reason would you have to interrupt my afternoon, Sandre Closier?'

Sandre took a steadying breath. 'I was a routier. In the company of Mercadier.'

Brandin frowned, his men shifting nervously. The screech of chair legs against the rush-strewn floor echoed as more than one made to rise.

Sandre spread his hands, a placating gesture. 'I come in peace. I seek no quarrel with you, only an accord.'

'An accord?' Brandin's lip curled into a sneer. 'With one of Mercadier's dogs? You've a queer notion of diplomacy, Closier.'

'*Former* dog,' Sandre said sharply. 'And one with no love left for his master.'

'Is that so? Fallen out of favour, have we? Sent you to the kennels with your tail between your legs?'

'I have my reasons for turning on him. Good ones. Reasons I
suspect a man like you would understand all too well.'

Brandin studied him for a taut moment before he gestured to
the empty chair across from him. 'Sit. Let's hear these reasons of
yours.'

Sandre did as bidden, the other men giving way with sullen
glares. 'Mercadier owes me. Coin, for service rendered. But the
bastard won't pay out. Thinks he can cheat me of the debt.'

A lie, bald-faced and paper-thin, but what choice did he have?
If Brandin knew of the babe, of Richard's bastard, he would want
the child for himself; a potent weapon to wield. Sandre would not
trade one threat for another. Better the mercenary think him moti-
vated by something as simple as greed.

'A matter of money, is it?' Brandin huffed a laugh, humourless
and cold. 'Somehow I think there's more to this tale than you're
telling. But no matter. The question is, what would you have of
me? And more importantly... what's in it for my trouble?'

'I want Mercadier dead. He has slighted me, and I will not
tolerate the insult. He is destined for an early grave, and I'm willing
to help put him there. I reckon that makes us friends.'

Brandin leaned back in his chair, the shadow of a smile playing
on his lips. 'Well now, that does make us friends. Depending on
just how far you're willing to go to make it happen.'

'I'll do what I have to,' Sandre growled.

Brandin was silent for a long moment, fingers steepled beneath
his chin, until he flashed his teeth in a smile. 'I admire your
commitment, Closier. Takes stones, to come in here and proposi-
tion a man like me.' He leaned forward, voice dropping to a
conspiratorial whisper. 'As it happens, you're in luck. I've had my
eye on Mercadier for a while now. Man's a tick on my arse, always
has been. And now he's in Bordeaux, sniffing around the Duchess

Eleanor of Aquitaine, trying to weasel his way into her good graces.'

Sandre frowned. 'What's he want with her?'

'What any lowborn whoreson wants – contracts, coin, favour. Only I'll see him in the ground before I let that happen.'

Sandre's heart kicked against his ribs. This was more than he could have hoped for, but he kept his face carefully blank. 'And you'd let me in on this merry little scheme, would you? Out of the goodness of your heart?'

'Goodness has nothing to do with it. You want Mercadier dead, and so do I. Like you said, it makes us friends. So here's the deal. You ride to Bordeaux along with some of my men. You find Mercadier, and you help send that bastard to hell where he belongs. In return, I'll make sure you're well compensated. Enough coin to cover whatever that shit-eating turd owes you.'

For a moment, Sandre saw Marion in his mind's eye, her gentle smile, the way she held their swaddled child close. He'd been a soldier for far too many years. The things he'd done, the orders he'd followed... they haunted him. Now he had a chance to wipe his slate clean. To cut the strings that bound him to Mercadier and all his cruelties.

'When do we leave?'

53

Sunlight lanced off the Garonne, the river's placid surface a stark contrast to the roiling in Sandre's gut. He pulled his hood lower, the rough weave scratching his brow, and huddled deeper into the shadow of the eaves. All around him, the market heaved with life – hawkers crying their wares, a cacophony of haggling, a riot of colour and noise assaulting the senses.

Usually, Sandre adored such places – the vigour of it, the sounds and smells. Today, the jostle and din only set his teeth on edge.

Somewhere in that teeming throng were the men Brandin had sent with him, five killers seeded through the crowd like caltrops. Sandre ran his tongue across dry lips, trying to pick out their faces. The swarthy Basque with the scar splitting his cheek. The slack-jawed Burgundian in the stained leathers. Brandin's men were vague silhouettes in his memory, blurred beneath a rising tide of dread. He had to be confident they would show themselves when the time came. And if they didn't...

A cold slither down his spine. No. He couldn't think like that.

Couldn't let the wings of panic beat at him now. He was committed. There was no way out of this but to see it through...

A sudden murmur among the crowd, like a flock startling at a predator's passing. Sandre's head whipped up, heart leaping against his ribs.

Mercadier. Striding through the market like a wolf among sheep. The big mercenary walked with the easy swagger of a man who knew he struck fear. Folk scurried from his path, smiles stretched taut, dread rolling off them in greasy waves. Mercadier paid them no mind as he dipped one meaty hand into a fruit stall. The costermonger opened his mouth, half in protest, then snapped it shut so hard his teeth clicked. He offered a clumsy bow, pressing a clenched fist to his heart as Mercadier bit deeply into an apple, juices dripping into his beard. No coin changed hands. None needed to.

Sandre's focus narrowed to the grin on Mercadier's face as he chewed. He had to move. Had to strike before his rage waned and left his killing edge blunted.

Slipping from the shelter of the eaves, Sandre wove through the crowd, one hand clenched white-knuckled on the knife beneath his cloak. Sweat slicked his palm, the hilt growing slippery in his grasp as he slunk through the market's busy confines. His cloak felt suddenly oppressive in the afternoon heat, the weight of the hidden blade an anvil at his hip.

Where were Brandin's men? He probed the crowd, seeking any sign, any flicker of aid. Nothing. Just the teeming multitudes, lost in the petty intricacies of their small lives. Blind, all of them, to the enormity of what was about to happen in their midst.

Ten paces now. Five. The reek of Mercadier reached Sandre's nostrils: horse and sweat. The mercenary still hadn't seen him, still browsing the stalls with that arrogance, so sure in his own legend he expected the world itself to bend to his whim.

Sandre's heart was a wild, panicked bird in the cage of his ribs, threatening to burst free. There was no one else. No one coming to his aid, to share the burden of this act. Only him. Him and the cold steel clutched in his fist.

He stepped into Mercadier's path. His tongue clove to the roof of his mouth, blood a roaring tide in his ears. Mercadier took one last bite of his apple before his shark's eyes landed on Sandre. Something flickered behind them – a glint of recognition.

'Sandre?' The name was a rumble. 'What are you doing in—'

The rest was lost in a choked grunt as comprehension dawned. Mercadier saw the knife in Sandre's white-knuckled grip. His eyes widened, lips peeling back from his teeth...

Too late.

Sandre lunged, quick and vicious, and buried the blade to the hilt in Mercadier's belly. It punched through his leather jerkin, parting flesh like butter, piercing guts. Hot blood jetted over Sandre's fist, startlingly red against his pale skin.

For an instant they stood frozen. Sandre stared at his hand, at the foreign sight of his knife sprouting from Mercadier's gut. Mercadier stared at Sandre, shock and disbelief writ stark on those brutal features.

Then the screaming began.

Mercadier swayed, one trembling hand pawing at his belly. His fingers came away glistening crimson.

'Sandre, wait—'

The plea died as Sandre wrenched the knife free in a gout of blood. He lunged again, snarling. This time the blade caught Mercadier in the ribs, parting leather and flesh with sickening ease. Blood pattered Sandre's face, and he was barely aware of his own voice, torn raw with animal rage as he struck again and again.

Mercadier staggered back, crashing into a stall. Pots shattered as he flailed, eyes rolling wildly in his head, mouth agape.

Sandre stood back, breath held, knife hanging slack at his side. His mind was a roaring abyss where thought and reason should be. Dimly, he became aware of the warm wetness painting his face, his hands. The cloying stink of copper in his nose and throat.

A hand clamped on his shoulder, wrenching him back to himself. He blinked, sound and sensation crashing back in a dizzying rush. Screams clawed the air. The market seethed, bodies churning, feet pounding as folk fled in blind panic.

'Sandre!' The voice was a bark in his ear. 'We have to go, now!'

Sandre staggered like a drunk, numb fingers still locked around the wet hilt, unwilling or unable to let go. The hand on his shoulder tightened, hauling him bodily away from the corpse he had made.

'Move, curse you.'

The other mercenaries, Brandin's hounds, were already fleeing. Sandre's legs moved after them, and he let himself be pulled along, a vague ringing in his skull. A glance behind to see Mercadier's body sprawled in a lake of pooling red. Those wide shark's eyes stared sightlessly at the blue sky as if searching for a reprieve that would never come.

Sandre tore his gaze away, fixing it on the road ahead. Out of the square they raced, out of the city itself. Leaving Bordeaux and murder most wretched in his wake...

* * *

His farmhouse, hunched by that gentle river. A sight he thought he might never see again. He had walked through two dawns to get here. Now, his legs were weak beneath him, exhaustion a grey fog wreathing his body.

He stumbled on the porch, caught himself on the doorframe.

The rough wood dug splinters into his palms, grounding him in the reality of this moment. He was here. Home.

The door swung open at his touch. Marion stood silhouetted against the ruddy light of the hearth fire, their child a swaddled bundle tucked into the crook of her arm.

'Is it done?' Her voice was soft but tense.

Sandre could only nod. Marion's eyes searched his, dark wells brimming with unasked questions. Fear. Relief. A tenderness he scarcely deserved.

'What now?' she whispered.

Sandre swayed on his feet. The familiar smells of the house engulfed him – woodsmoke, rabbit stew, the milky sweetness of the baby. All of it suddenly too much to bear, pressing in like a hand around his throat.

Marion took a step forward, one hand outstretched. 'Sandre?'

He wrenched himself from his stupor. His hands shook as he fumbled inside his jerkin, fingers catching on the lining. With shaky hands, he drew out the pouch and upended it over the table.

Silver poured forth in a glittering torrent. It clattered against the rough-hewn boards, spilling across the stained wood – more coin than either of them had ever seen.

Marion's breath caught. The babe mewled, stirring against her breast, and she hushed it with an absent murmur.

'Now we leave this place.' Sandre replied. 'We take this chance we've been given and we start again. Somewhere new. Somewhere safe.'

Marion stared down at the riches scattered before them. 'Where will we go?'

'It doesn't matter.' Sandre reached out, closing his fingers around her wrist. 'Anywhere we please. So long as we're together. You, me, and the boy.'

He looked down at the child, so tiny, so fragile. The most

precious jewel of all, bought with the death of a king and the blood of a killer.

Marion nodded, before handing Sandre their son. 'Then I'd best pack some belongings.'

Sandre cradled the boy to his chest, one weathered palm cupping that fragile head. The babe nestled into him, so innocent and unaware.

'Have you thought about a name yet?'

Marion looked up from her packing, an unruly hank of hair escaping her kerchief. 'I was thinking Estienne. After my uncle. He died defending King Louis at Mont Cadmus. He was a good man. Loyal to the end. I'd like to think our boy could grow to be like him.'

Sandre looked down at the child in his arms. 'Estienne. Aye, that's a fine name.'

Marion turned back to the task at hand, their meagre possessions vanishing into saddlebags and sacks – a handful of clothes, a few pots, the Good Book Marion's mother had pressed into her hands the day they wed under a bower of wildflowers.

'I'm ready,' Marion said finally, brushing her hands down the front of her kirtle.

Sandre nodded and turned to the door, Estienne still clutched tight to his heart. Outside, the night lay soft and welcoming, a sickle moon above. Their horses stamped in the yard, eager for the road.

With one last glance at the home that had sheltered them, at the life they were leaving behind, Sandre stepped across the threshold into the cool embrace of the dark...

PART SIX (CONT.): A GOOD END

WALES – 1219 AD

54

And so, in great secrecy, we spirited the child away. Chose his family name as Wace, after the poet admired so much by King Richard, his natural sire. To name him for both an old warrior and a poet seemed to offer some balance to it. We raised him as our own, and I believe we did well by him, but now with Marion gone these past two years, and me in the twilight of my days, he deserves the opportunity I could never grant him. A chance to forge his own path, guided by a man of peerless honour.

That is why I have sent him to you, William. Because I can think of no one I would rather entrust with the keeping of Richard's son. In your household, he may thrive, grow strong and worthy, a credit to the father he will never meet.

The boy knows nothing of this. In his mind, he is just a humble commoner. I thought it best to keep him ignorant, until such time as you deem him ready for the truth. Let it be your judgement that decides if, or when, he learns of his bloodline.

I beg you, Earl William, by the love you bore his father, do not turn him away. Take him as your shield bearer, your squire,

and let him grow to be a knight who would make Richard proud.
I know I leave him in the worthiest of hands.
    Your servant,
    Sandre Closier

Isabel stared at the letter clutched in her trembling hands, the enormity of the words crashing over her like a wave of icy water. It couldn't be true. It had to be some cruel jape, too wicked to countenance.

But there it was, spelled out in stark ink on weathered parchment. Estienne Wace, the boy they had taken in as charity, was Richard Lionheart's bastard son. The product of some illicit tryst, spirited away in secrecy. Now hidden among her household like a cuckoo in the nest.

She read the words again, willing them to change, to form some less ruinous truth. But they remained stubbornly fixed, each one a knife twisting between her ribs.

King Richard's son. A potential claimant to the throne.

Isabel barely smothered the hysterical laugh bubbling up in her throat. To think, all these years they had sheltered him, clothed and fed him, raised him up as if he were one of their own, and all the while he carried this regal blood, this thrice-damned legacy that could doom them all. The solemn boy, so intense and eager to please. The man he'd become, steadfast and loyal, everything a knight should be. But beneath it all, he bore a bloodline that, if known, could see him hunted down like a dog. And her family, her children, could be caught in the teeth of that same pursuit, torn to shreds for the crime of harbouring a bastard rebel.

There was no way of telling what kind of king the boy Henry would make – wise as his regent, William, or cruel as his father, John? No way to tell, not yet. And if the truth of this were discovered, retribution might be swift, now or in the future.

Estienne might bring the houses of Clare and Marshal crashing down were there to be contestation for the throne. He might be used by the very barons he had just fought alongside, the country set aflame once more, and it would be her own sons and daughters caught up in such calamity.

A sudden fury ignited in Isabel. Sandre Closier. The whoreson mercenary who had started this whole terrible affair. Curse him for a rogue and a fool, for laying this serpent's egg at their door.

Well, she would not have it. Would not let this insanity poison her family. Estienne would have to go, before this spark could catch and grow into a wildfire that might consume them all. The danger was too great, the risk too high. She would cut out this canker, no matter the cost. No matter how much it pained her to do it.

The letter crumpled in her fist as she rose. Every step felt like a knife in her side, but she did not slow. Could not slow. Their survival depended on swift decisiveness. No matter how much it tore at her to contemplate, Estienne could not remain among them.

With shaking hands, Isabel placed the letter back in the drawer and turned the key in the lock of the bureau, hearing the hollow clunk as the tumblers fell into place. Such a small thing to safeguard so deadly a secret, but it would have to serve until she could decide what was to be done with the accursed missive. Then she slipped the key into the pocket of her kirtle, the metal burning cold even through the fabric. A reminder of the doom that lurked, waiting to strike. But she would not let it. Not while breath remained in her body.

With determined strides, she left her chambers, the letter's poison still churning in her gut as she descended from the keep. She had to find her sons before sentiment could stay her hand from what must be done.

Distant voices reached her – Richard and Guillaume, in the hall. A lance of grief pierced her as she approached them. What would William say, if he could see her now? See the choice she had made, the doom she must rain down upon the head of the very boy he'd taken in as his own?

She shoved the thought away. There was no time for echoes from the past. She had to be strong, had to be the unyielding steel that held her family together. Even if it meant breaking her own heart in the process.

Isabel followed the murmur of conversation to the doors of the great hall. There, she paused on the threshold, drinking in the scene before her. Richard and Guillaume, hunched over a chess-board, their faces a study in concentration. A pitcher of wine sat close to hand, along with a platter of bread and cheese, as if they'd settled in to make an afternoon of it.

'I swear, Guillaume, I know you are cheating. I just can't work out how...'

Guillaume answered with a laugh. 'As if I need to cheat to best your pitiful defences, brother. A page could do it blindfolded.'

Richard scowled, reaching to take a gulp of wine. 'I'll show you pitiful. See if you're still crowing when I sweep that board clean.'

Isabel took a steadying breath then stepped into the hall, the heels of her shoes ringing on the flagstones. Her sons glanced toward her, their humour draining as they marked her grim visage.

'Mother?' Guillaume half rose from his chair, brow furrowed. 'Is all well?'

'Sit.' The word came harsher than she'd intended, the tone of a countess, not a mother.

Slowly, Guillaume lowered himself back down, unease written starkly on those handsome features so like his father's. At his side, Richard remained still.

'Estienne must be sent away.'

The words fell like a stone into the sudden silence.

Richard's eyes widened. 'Away? But... why? He's done nothing to warrant—'

'I'll not discuss my reasons.' Isabel cut across him, tone brooking no argument. 'All you need know is that it must be done, and done swiftly.'

'Mother, surely there must be some mistake,' Guillaume said. 'Estienne is one of us. He's earned his place, proven his loyalty a hundred times over. To cast him out now, with no explanation...'

Isabel met his protestation with a sharp shake of her head. 'My word is final, Guillaume. Estienne cannot remain at Pembroke, nor be offered shelter at any estate of the Marshal family. He must go. As far from us as can be managed.'

Richard surged to his feet. 'If this is your command, Mother, so be it. But I'll not cast him out like a dog. I can take him back to our holdings in France, away from England. There, at least, he will not—'

'No. He cannot be tied to us, in any way.' She saw her sons' confusion, the rising tide of protest. But what could she tell them? That the man they loved as a brother was a danger to them all? No. They must never know the deadly truth carried in Estienne's blood, lest they ignore it. Lest their love for him overcome their sense of self-preservation. 'He must be sent away. I'll hear no more debate on it.'

Guillaume shook his head. 'This is madness, Mother. After all he's done, all he's sacrificed for our family... You would repay that loyalty with exile? It is pure cruelty.'

'You forget yourself, Guillaume. I am still countess here. Still your mother and liege. You will obey me in this, no matter how it may gall you.'

'But why?' Richard burst out, slamming a hand down upon the

table, chess pieces toppling. 'At least give us a reason. He deserves that much, surely. After everything.'

'He deserves to live.' The words were soft, barely more than a whisper, but they silenced her sons as effectively as a shout. 'You must trust that I only do what is right. What is necessary. I would not ask it of you otherwise.'

'Mother.' Guillaume's voice wavered, thick with emotion. 'Please. Do not ask this of us.'

'I have decided. Estienne must go. Must be cut free, no matter how much we might wish it otherwise. There is no other way.'

'Then let me do it,' Richard whispered. 'Let me be the one to tell him. I'm his friend. His brother. If... if it must be done, best it come from me.'

'So be it,' she replied. 'You will tell him he must leave Pembroke. Must forswear all ties to our family. And that he must do it now, before the sun sets this day, and be gone on the morrow.'

Gathering her skirts, Isabel turned sharply on her heel and left the hall. Let her sons think her heartless, think her cold and cruel. Let them rail against the seeming injustice of it. As long as they obeyed, as long as Estienne was sent far beyond the reach of the Marshals, she would endure their resentment.

She did not slow her steps until she reached her chambers once more. Only there, with the heavy oak door closed did she let some of the rigid tension bleed from her. Isabel leaned back against the door, knees threatening to buckle. What had she done? Exiled the very boy her husband had vowed to protect? Ripped away the only family he had left?

Her eyes fell on the bureau, on the locked drawer that held the letter. Before she could stop herself, she strode to it, unlocked it, and wrenched open the drawer. The letter sat there, crumpled and accusatory. With shaking hands, she snatched it up and held it over the guttering candle on her writing desk, the flame licking at one corner. It would be so easy to let it catch, to consign this poisonous secret to the fire. To pretend it had never been.

But even as the parchment began to smoulder, curling inward in a caress of heat, she could not do it. Could not destroy this last vestige of truth, of Estienne's heritage, no matter how ruinous.

Isabel pulled the letter back, placing it gently back in the drawer. But even as she locked it away once more, slipping the key around her neck on a chain, the first prickings of remorse began to surface beneath the steel of her resolve. She had done what was necessary. What was right, to protect her family, her children. Her king. And yet... Estienne was blameless in this. As much a pawn as anyone, moved about the board by the whims of fate and the follies of long-dead men.

But perhaps there was a way to lessen the blow. To offer some balm to the grievous wound she had been forced to deal. Estienne could not remain tied to their family. Could not claim any bond, not without risking discovery and ruin. But there was one last gift she could give him.

A reminder of the house that had fostered him. The legacy that had forged him...

55

Estienne's hands trembled as he folded his spare tunic into the saddlebag. So few possessions to show for his years of loyal service. A handful of clothes, a dagger, his boots. Paltry offerings to whatever life awaited him beyond Pembroke's walls.

He brushed a thumb over the leather-wrapped hilt of his sword where it lay atop the pile, the metal cold and unyielding. Beside it, Goffrey's hammer seemed to mock him with its stolid weight. Reminders of the man he could have been. The knight he had bled to become. Now reduced to no more than a vagabond. A landless exile.

Domnall shifted uncomfortably where he stood in the stable doorway, watching as Estienne continued his cheerless task. The stable hand had been the only one to wish him well in his leaving, the rest of the castle's denizens nowhere to be seen. As if they feared whatever sin Estienne carried might taint them too.

'Got the tack fixed up proper,' Domnall said, breaking the uncomfortable silence. 'Horse is ready when you are. Lord Richard said you were to have the best palfrey in the stable.'

Estienne managed a nod, not trusting himself to speak around the stone lodged in his throat. He was not ready to abandon this place, but what choice remained? When Richard had come to him to deliver the news of his expulsion, Estienne had searched those familiar features for some hint of jest. Some sign that this was all an ill-conceived prank. But there had been only grim certainty writ on his friend's face.

The words had fallen like hammer on anvil. Banished. Exiled. Cast out. Estienne had pleaded for an explanation, some scrap of reason to cling to in this surging tide of confusion, but Richard had none to give.

'It's Mother's will,' he'd said, voice cracking on the words. 'You're to leave Pembroke, Estienne. To cut all ties. I'm sorry. God above, I'm so sorry.'

And what could Estienne do but bow his head and accept? Whatever Countess Isabel's reasons, he had no choice but to honour them.

Estienne cinched the saddlebag closed, the ties biting into his fingers. He hoisted it over one shoulder, its paltry weight a millstone, nonetheless.

'Guess this is farewell then,' Domnall said.

'Aye.' Estienne clapped him on the shoulder. 'Thank you for the help, Domnall. I won't forget it.'

The words sounded hollow, but they were all he could muster. He slung his saddlebag over the palfrey's rump and drew a steadying breath of the stable's hay-sweet air. Tried not to think about how he would never again breathe it. And as he stood in that final moment, he felt one regret lance through him keener than all the rest.

Eva.

He had not seen her since Richard delivered the cruel edict. Could not bring himself to inflict more grief upon her. In the deepest recesses of his heart, Estienne knew the shape of his regard for her. Knew it for the impossible thing it was, a dream he could never hope to make true. She was promised to another. To a grand fate as Lady of the Marches. What could Estienne have ever offered her in comparison? To even speak his heart would be the gravest presumption. An insult to her and to the betrothal her father had sealed.

No, better he slip away unseen. Let her remember him fondly, if she remembered him at all.

Estienne guided his mount from the dimness of the stable into the pale light of early morn. The bailey was still shrouded in morning mist, and he felt some relief that it would conceal him as he left.

'Ho there, lad.'

Estienne glanced up to see a familiar face, and a welcome one. 'Goffrey. What are you doing here?'

'Saying my farewells. And to perhaps bend your ear, one last time.'

Estienne frowned. 'Are all your lessons not done?'

'This is not a lesson. Walk with me a moment.'

Bemused, Estienne handed the palfrey's reins to Domnall and followed the old knight. They fell into step with one another as they walked across the bailey, all the way to the north tower, taking the steps up to the parapet, where the river was visible just beyond the mist.

'I'll not mince words, Estienne,' Goffrey said. 'What's been done to you is not right. You deserve better than being tossed out like a pail of pig slop. I don't pretend to know the Countess Isabel's reasons, but I know your quality, lad. Known it since the day you arrived at Laigen, all skin and bones and burning to prove yourself.'

'And I'm grateful for all you taught me,' Estienne said. 'I'd not be half the man I am without it.'

Goffrey waved off the praise. 'You've got a fire in you, lad. One that was always going to burn bright, with or without my meddling. It's that fire makes me think you might be suited for the path I'm about to set before you. If you've the stones to walk it.'

Estienne met Goffrey's stern gaze. 'What path is that?'

'The one that leads across the sea. To Outremer.' Goffrey tipped his head toward the harbour. 'I spoke with Brother Hoston. He's got a need for swords in the fight at Damietta.'

Estienne's heart quickened. 'They'd have me?'

'Have you and thank God for it.' Goffrey clasped his shoulder. 'It'll be no summer feast, mind. You'd be wading hip deep in blood and shit. But there's honour in it. Purpose. A chance to forge glory in God's name. Hoston leaves on the morning tide. If you choose to sail with him... just be at the docks afore he goes.'

Estienne nodded slowly. 'I will think on it. And Goffrey... my thanks. For this and for all else.'

'No need for thanks between brothers.' Goffrey enfolded him in a swift, hard embrace. 'No matter how far you roam, Estienne, know you'll always have a place in this old bastard's heart. Wherever your road takes you.'

With a last clap on the shoulder, Goffrey made his way from the bastion, leaving Estienne alone at the parapet. He stood in the swirling mist, the weight of choice settling like a mantle upon his shoulders.

Perhaps this was the path meant for him. The road he was born to walk. Not a knight adrift, but a soldier of God. It would be a hard choice to make, in so short a time...

But perhaps there was no choice at all.

56

The dock thrummed with activity, sailors swarming the ship as they hauled on lines, trimmed sails, stowed barrels and bales with the efficiency of men long accustomed to the labour. Above them, herring gulls wheeled and cried, their chorus nearly drowned by the slap of waves and the snap of wind-taut canvas.

Estienne stood apart from the bustle, watching from the jetty. The weight of his meagre pack pulled at his shoulder – a handful of clothes, his hammer and sword. The sum total of his life.

He shielded his eyes against the glare off the water, to better see the men standing on deck. Hoston watched proceedings with a judgemental eye. Alongside the Templars, Estienne hoped he might find a place, a brotherhood. It was a slim hope, but it was all he had left. All the Countess Isabel had deigned to leave him.

Estienne set his jaw, shouldering his pack. He had no time for self-pity, nor room for doubt. Whatever awaited him in Outremer, he would face it. Drawing a steadying breath of the salt-tanged air, he made to step towards the ship.

'Were you going to leave without saying goodbye?'

The words froze Estienne where he stood. He turned, seeing

Eva an arm's length away, the wind whipping strands of black hair across her face. In her arms she clutched a bundle – rough sackcloth bound with twine. Estienne's heart lurched at the sight of her, his tongue suddenly a useless weight.

'Eva, I...' He trailed off, unable to finish.

'You what?' She stepped closer. 'Thought it best to slink away like a thief in the night? No word, no farewell, just gone as if you'd never been?'

Estienne flinched at the fire in her voice, the hurt beneath it. 'I'm sorry. I didn't... I thought it would be easier this way.'

'Easier? For who?'

'For both of us.' The words felt cumbersome, but he lumbered on. 'There are things that cannot be, Eva. No matter how much we might...' He couldn't finish, the ache in his chest too painful.

'Things that cannot be? And who decides that? You?'

Estienne spread his hands helplessly. 'You are pledged to another. Bound by your father's word. There is nothing I can do to change that.'

'And if I wasn't?' She took another step, so close now he could feel the whisper of her breath. 'If I were free to choose, would you have me then?'

Estienne closed his eyes against the sudden sting. A vision rose behind his lids, taunting in its clarity. Eva in his arms. Her carefree laughter. The love with which she spoke his name. And with a sigh, he shattered the image, grinding it to dust beneath the heel of cold reality.

'It doesn't matter. Even if you weren't promised, I am still not worthy of you. I never was. It was a childish dream, nothing more.'

For a moment Eva simply stared at him.

'I was a fool,' she bit out finally. 'To ever think you more than what you are. A coward, too craven to take what is his.'

The words struck like knives, each one burying to the hilt. But Estienne held his ground, knowing he deserved every wound.

Eva thrust the bundled cloth at him. 'Here. A parting gift from my mother. To remind you of who you are, though I wonder if you've ever truly known.'

Estienne clutched the package to his chest. Questions burned his tongue – why would Isabel offer him anything, when she'd been the architect of this exile? – but Eva was already turning away.

'Eva, wait...' He stretched out a beseeching hand, but she slipped through his grasp like the morning mist.

Estienne could only watch as she marched toward Pembroke, never once looking back. The bundle in his arms was a dead weight, sackcloth rough against his palm. Harsh. Accusing. It was no less than he deserved.

In a daze, he turned to make his way along the jetty and up the gangplank, the rhythm of his feet on the wood discordant. The thud of his measly pack against his hip seemed to mock him with every step, a reminder of all he had lost. All he was leaving behind.

Hoston greeted him as he gained the deck. If the Templar noted his distress, he gave no sign, merely offered a terse nod.

'Good that you've joined us, Wace. Stow your kit in the aftcastle. We make sail with the tide.'

Estienne mumbled some vague reply, the words lost to the wind. He made his way into the small cabin. The ceiling hung low enough to brush the crown of his head, the walls seeming to press in on all sides, but it was blessedly dim, cool and shadowed.

He dumped his belongings onto the narrow bunk, the bundled cloth landing atop them with a muffled thump. For a long moment he simply stared at it. Isabel's last gift to him. A final cruelty? Or something else?

Slowly, he reached for the package and fumbled with the

knotted twine. It came loose with a snap, the cloth falling away to reveal what lay within...

A surcoat, black as a raven's wing.

Estienne drew it free with trembling hands, the linen whispering as he held it aloft. The garment was finely made, the fabric dense and sturdy, but it was the device blazoned on the chest that snatched the breath from his lungs.

His fingers traced the badge almost reverently. A shield, bisected with green and gold. But where the lion rampant should have been crimson, this one was black. Stark. Unforgiving. To remind him of who he was...

No longer the black sheep. Now the black lion.

And he would have to be. In the trials ahead, on the far shores and blood-soaked sands that awaited him, he would need every scrap of strength he possessed. He would need to be fierce.

For this crusade would yield no mercy.

And neither would he.

ACKNOWLEDGEMENTS

First and foremost, I should thank Caroline Ridding and all the lovely folks at Boldwood Books for making this novel happen and giving it such care and attention. Caroline stepped in when I was just about to give up on the whole idea, so I guess it's all her fault if it goes wrong. Also, thanks to author M J Porter for the introduction – it's not what you know...

This was a new period for me to write in, so obviously research had to be done. Along the way, the works of Thomas Asbridge, Christopher Gravett, Dan Jones, Sean McGlynn and Mark Morris have all come in very handy. A special shout-out must go to Catherine Hanley, and her editor at Osprey, Kate Moore, for sending me a pre-release copy of her awesome book *1217: The Battles That Saved England*. It was invaluable to the writing of this novel, and I highly recommend it to anyone interested in reading more about the period (and thanks to Myke Cole for hooking us up).

And obviously thanks to you, the reader, for joining me at the start of this journey. I hope there will be many more adventures for Estienne Wace, and I'd love it if you could join us for the ride.

Best,

Richard Cullen

ABOUT THE AUTHOR

Richard Cullen is a writer of historical adventure and epic fantasy. His historical adventure series *Chronicles of the Black Lion* is set in thirteenth-century England.

Sign up to Richard Cullen's mailing list for news, competitions and updates on future books.

Follow Richard on social media here:

x.com/rich4ord

instagram.com/thewordhog

ALSO BY RICHARD CULLEN

The Chronicles of the Black Lion Series

Rebellion

The Wolf of Kings Series

Oath Bound

Shield Breaker

Winter Warrior

War of the Archons (as R S Ford)

A Demon in Silver

Hangman's Gate

Spear of Malice

The Age of Uprising (as R S Ford)

Engines of Empire

Engines of Chaos

Engines of War

WARRIOR CHRONICLES

WELCOME TO THE CLAN ✕

THE HOME OF
BESTSELLING HISTORICAL
ADVENTURE FICTION!

WARNING:
MAY CONTAIN VIKINGS!

SIGN UP TO OUR
NEWSLETTER

BIT.LY/WARRIORCHRONICLES

Boldwood

Boldwood Books is an award-winning fiction
publishing company seeking out the best
stories from around the world.

Find out more at www.boldwoodbooks.com

Join our reader community for brilliant books,
competitions and offers!

Follow us
@BoldwoodBooks
@TheBoldBookClub

**Sign up to our weekly
deals newsletter**

https://bit.ly/BoldwoodBNewsletter

Made in United States
North Haven, CT
20 October 2024

59171082R00215